Praise for *Ready or Not*

"Bastone delivers on this truly heartwarming, funny, and real story. Come for the dog bar, stay for the special slow-burn romcom."

—Abby Jimenez, *New York Times* bestselling author

"A wholehearted meditation on all kinds of love, this novel is pure joy."

—Annabel Monaghan, nationally bestselling author of *Same Time Next Summer*

"*Ready or Not* is the very definition of the perfect slow burn, friends-to-lovers romance. Cara Bastone's voice is wholly unique and sparkles with effervescence and joy. I savored every page."

—KJ Dell'Antonia, *New York Times* bestselling author of *The Chicken Sisters*

"With loads of humor, lovable characters, and a first kiss that will leave you flushed and breathless, *Ready or Not* is a delightfully romantic story that celebrates modern love and the excitement of the unexpected. Readers will adore Cara Bastone's joyful, swoony novel!"

—Amy Poeppel, author of *The Sweet Spot*

"An absolute treasure of a book! Cara Bastone gives readers a gift, and pays humanity a compliment, with this warmly witty, profoundly tender story of a love that makes the world bigger and better. *Ready or Not* introduces indelible characters who navigate their entanglements with abundant, heart-bursting kindness. The result is one of the most emotionally satisfying romances I've read in years."

—Joanna Lowell, author of *Artfully Yours*

BY CARA BASTONE

When We First Met

Just a Heartbeat Away

Can't Help Falling

Flirting with Forever

Ready or Not

AUDIBLE ORIGINAL NOVELLAS

Call Me Maybe

Sweet Talk

Seat Mate

Love at First Psych

Ready or Not

Ready or Not

A Novel

Cara Bastone

THE DIAL PRESS
NEW YORK

Ready or Not is a work of fiction. Names, characters, places, and incidents are the products of the author's imagination or are used fictitiously. Any resemblance to actual events, locales, or persons, living or dead, is entirely coincidental.

A Dial Press Trade Paperback Original

Published in the United States by The Dial Press, an imprint of Random House, a division of Penguin Random House LLC, New York.

Library of Congress Cataloging-in-Publication Data
Names: Bastone, Cara, author.
Title: Ready or not: a novel / Cara Bastone.
Description: New York: The Dial Press, [2024]
Identifiers: LCCN 2023018887 (print) | LCCN 2023018888 (ebook) |
ISBN 9780593595718 (trade paperback; acid-free paper) |
ISBN 9780593595725 (ebook)
Subjects: LCSH: Unplanned pregnancy—Fiction. |
LCGFT: Romance fiction. | Novels.
Classification: LCC PS3602.A84956 R43 2024 (print) |
LCC PS3602.A84956 (ebook) | DDC 813/.6—dc23/eng/20230509
LC record available at https://lccn.loc.gov/2023018887
LC ebook record available at https://lccn.loc.gov/2023018888

Printed in the United States of America on acid-free paper

randomhousebooks.com

2 4 6 8 9 7 5 3 1

Book design by Jennifer Daddio

For Jordan and Lauren.

Pregnancy would have been a lot more confusing without you.

Ready or Not

One

I didn't start this day thinking I'd be handing over a Dixie cup of my own urine to a woman in lavender scrubs.

"What's the verdict?" I ask about seven seconds after the nurse dips the stick into the cup on the other side of the exam room.

She is one of those ageless people whose fluffy gray-brown hair could have been that of an unfortunate thirty-five-year-old or a banging hot fifty-five-year-old. Her face gives away nothing as she looks up at me.

"The doctor will be in to discuss your results, Ms. Hatch."

AKA, *I'm not gonna be the one to tell you there's an egg in your biscuit.*

"Call me Eve and, look, you can just tell me. I'm sure you can read the stick as well as the doctor can. I know I'm pregnant anyways. I took three tests on my own. I did the research." (On the train on the way over here.) "I know that false positives really only happen for women who were just recently pregnant or taking certain fertility meds. There's no way I'm *not* pregnant."

I'm telling her. I'm telling myself. I'm telling the universe, because the facts are grounding me. I'm trying to be realistic here. I refuse to be secretly hoping for either outcome.

The nurse's face shows zero signs of life. Maybe that's the secret to her ageless success. If one never, ever moves one's face, one can look forty in one's seventies. I make a mental note to start having fewer emotions. Probably a super achievable goal right at the beginning of an unplanned pregnancy, right?

"The doctor will discuss it with you. Now, I just need some basic info from you." She has me hop on a scale and then takes my blood pressure. I'm shocked when I don't blow up the machine like a desktop plugged in during a lightning storm. She confirms my family history. And then the fun questions begin.

"Are you sexually active?" she asks the computer screen.

"You know, the term 'sexually active' has always been so weird to me. It doesn't make sense. If I had gone on one run in the last three months and that was it, no one would classify me as being *physically* active."

The nurse gives me that blank look as her hands twitch over the keyboard. Obviously, she is waiting for me to answer the damn question.

"But you schtup one bartender . . ." Apparently, I can't resist.

Her blank look evolves into a slow blink.

"Anyways," I continue through a small cough.

"Miss . . ." the nurse prompts.

"Right. Yes. I had sex about four weeks ago. If that answers your question."

Her fingers type-type-type away, sealing my fate into the computer. I am now, officially, an irresponsible sex-haver. Add it to my permanent record.

My eyebrows rise as the nurse continues typing. Thirty seconds pass. Another fifteen. I don't think *had sex once four weeks ago* should possibly take that long to input. What is she, writing a novel over there? A diary entry? Updating her blog?

Finally, she looks up. "Date of last period?"

"I don't know. I'm really irregular and I don't keep much track. Maybe September?"

More novel writing. This woman is obsessed with typing. Her grandfather invented the typewriter. In her family, it's a rite of passage to learn how to type six thousand words a minute.

She looks up from the computer. I brace for more questions that all seem like they *could* contain the word *vagina* but for some reason never do.

"Honey," the nurse says. "Are you all right?"

I blink at her. That was not the type of question that I expected her to ask me. I hate it significantly more than all the others.

"I'm on my lunch break," I say to her, as if that explains absolutely anything about my well-being. *Stay in your lane, blank-faced nurse. Let's get this over with.*

Apparently, though, it answers her question. She nods briskly and turns back to the computer screen. "I need to ask a few more questions before the doctor comes in."

"Okay."

"Are you in a monogamous relationship?"

"Can't we just talk about my feelings again?"

She slants me a look.

I clear my throat. "No. I'm not. It was a random encounter."

"Do you have sex with men?"

"I have had sex with men. I'm not currently sleeping with anyone."

She types, clicks, scrolls, and types and clicks again. Apparently, I answered two questions in one.

"Do you have sex with women?"

"Nope."

"Do you have vaginal sex?"

"Yes."

"Oral sex?"

"Yes and yes." I answer that way because that question can be construed in two ways. I promptly realize I've revealed too much when the corner of her mouth lifts for a brief second before she clicks, types, and scrolls.

"Anal sex?"

"Haven't had the honor."

More clicking. More scrolling. She turns to me. Her hands are folded. I don't take it as a good sign.

"We recommend a full panel of STI testing for our patients who are not in monogamous relationships."

"Okay." Because what else can I really say? "But I really need to be back at work soon. Can I make a second appointment for that?"

"Yes," the nurse answers briskly. "They'll schedule you in for later this week, as it's important to get it done as soon as possible."

"Great."

What a silly word *great* is. I only said it so she'd know I'm not trying to avoid my STI testing. I should have just said *fine* and moved on with my life.

She asks about fifteen more invasive questions and then stands up to go get the doctor. I watch the clock tick-tock. I made a New Year's resolution this year that I won't aimlessly scroll on my phone when I'm waiting for something. I've never wanted to break my rule more than I do right now, but it's already October and even though I'd love to drown in a round of Technicolor point-and-shoot I'm only a month and a half away from being the only person on the face of the earth who has ever held to their New Year's resolution for an entire year. This little speed bump shall not be my undoing. Because that's all an unplanned pregnancy really is, right? A speed bump? A tiny little momentary blip that barely affects your regularly scheduled programming? Someone please confirm that for me.

My parents dealt with an unplanned pregnancy at the whopping age of fifty-two.

The results? Moi.

I spent my childhood having other kids ask me why my mom had gray hair and watching my parents' necks get red in church while people whispered over raised eyebrows about the fact that after three *appropriately* spaced older brothers, I, two decades later, must have been an accident.

Maybe accidents are genetic? I got my mom's pointy nose, my dad's bony feet, and both of their proclivity towards apparently irresponsible sex. How embarrassing.

They passed away when I was in college, but even if they were still around, this isn't exactly the kind of thing I'd ask them for advice about.

My thumbs twitch, begging me to open my phone and let me match dancing fruit to other dancing fruit. But nay! A massively unexpected life change will not break me.

The uneaten peanut butter sandwich in my bag just might, though. The seconds of my lunch break are splintering away as I wait for my doctor. At this rate, I will definitely not have time to eat lunch before I get back to work. And it's not like I can eat at my desk, or even right before I head back into the building. Micah, the junior accountant at Wildlife Fund of America, where I work, sits kitty-corner from me and is deathly allergic to peanuts. I stow a toothbrush in my bag to keep the peanut-related homicide to a minimum. But I won't have time for that at this point. My sandwich could kill him with one puff of my breath and it would be all this tardy gyno's fault.

There's a brisk knock, not enough time for me to answer, and the OB-GYN strides into the office. My former doctor apparently moved practices since the last time I was here, so this is a meet-and-greet as well as the moment I find out I'm officially pregnant.

You know, just to make things easier.

The doctor is a statuesque bottle blonde who looks like a female version of a Ken doll. No, I don't mean Barbie. This woman is ripped.

Nurse Blank follows in after her. The welcome brigade. Exactly the two people I would have chosen to tell me that my life will never be the same.

The doctor says what I was expecting to hear, but the words wobble upon entry to the atmosphere. I respond somehow. I'm lying on my back with no pants on and the OB-GYN, who I've decided must be named Bridget, rolls a condom onto an enormous wand, slathers it up with frankly an absurd amount of lube, and my eyes squeeze tight while she does her internal exam.

There's a picture on a screen that looks like nothing to me. The doctor pulls the wand away from me, and the only noise in the room is the snap of her gloves as she tosses them in the trash.

"Nurse," the doctor says. "Where's the testing tray?"

"She's coming back in later in the week for her testing."

The doctor lowers her voice and says something I can't hear. My feet are still on the stirrups and the nurse leans around me and taps my big toe with her finger. "You can get dressed, honey." She pulls a curtain around me and they're on the other side.

"She needs to get back to work. She'll be in later this week," I hear her say firmly.

Nurse Blank may not be my cup of tea, but I'm obliged to see that she's not cowed in the least by Dr. Bridget Muscles.

Then my pants are back on, and I'm work-ready and standing in front of the receptionist, who schedules me in for Friday.

"Oh, good," I tell her. "I was so worried I wouldn't have something to look forward to all week."

Unlike Nurse Blank, she actually gives me a big, radiant smile and a hearty laugh. "Well, we aim to please here at Lower East Side Partners in Obstetrics and Gynecology."

The fact that she says the entire name makes me laugh too. I wave goodbye and totter out to the street, pulling my phone out, scrolling to my best friend Willa's name . . . but I'm not ready for that yet. So I automatically scroll to her mother, Corinne, a lifelong reflex for when things get hard. But no. Corinne's been gone for over a year now and I slide my phone back into my pocket. One breakdown at a time, please.

I can't call anyone, but food? Sure. Let's fix at least one problem, shall we? I pick up a falafel sandwich from a halal cart outside my office building. It'll stink up the office but it's better than sending Micah to the ER.

Maybe it's the power of (absolute, ironclad) suggestion but I'm suddenly feeling really freaking pregnant. Not like there's-a-golden-little-angel-sleeping-peacefully-in-my-sacred-womb sort of pregnant. But like, sore boobs, gonna be sick, already bloated, can't-believe-I-just-took-a-pregnancy-test sort of pregnant.

"Hey, Eve," Christina the receptionist says as I come off the elevator onto our floor. She looks up from solitaire or the GapBody website or whatever memo she's sending everyone about the out-of-control fridge space issue.

"How was your night?" I stop at her desk. I like Christina. She's funny and a little loud. We consider it egregious that she is expected to be here half an hour before the office workers so that she can get the enormous vat of subpar coffee percolating.

"Meh," she says, fully looking up at me for the first time since I came in. The makeup around her eyes looks shellacked on with a paint scraper. Her red hair is braided to the side instead of blown out to perfection. Unusual for her. "Ryan and I got into it again."

Ryan is Christina's live-in girlfriend who'd seemed like a reasonably good partner at last year's holiday party when I'd met her. She'd laughed at Christina's jokes and refilled a bunch of people's drinks from the open bar. Lately they've been having trouble and it makes me nervous. I'm single, have been for years, and pretty much fine with it, but I can't help but panic whenever I hear about couples considering breaking up. It awakens the conservative, midwestern upbringing in me. I have to viciously swallow back all the knee-jerk *but you're so good togethers* and *but it's almost Christmas, who wants to be alone at Christmas?*es and *don't you know that people are supposed to mate for life no matter whats* that bubble up without my permission.

"Oh no," I say. "I'm sorry. Are you okay?"

She scrunches up her face. "Merp."

"I'm gonna take that as a . . . yes?" I guess.

"It's a yes-ish."

"Was it the same argument as before?"

Christina sighs and plunks her chin on her palm. "Yah. She wants to get married, like tomorrow. I want . . . time. She's ten years older than I am and we have different levels of urgency and blah blah blah." Christina's slightly pink eyes slick up to mine and she sighs again.

"I hope you don't include the *blah blah blah*s when you're talking about this with Ryan," I say dryly.

She laughs, spots the big clock on the wall, and groans. "How is it only noon? Hey, wanna grab lunch?"

I pause. "Can't today, I already took mine. Had an appointment."

"Oh, that's too bad. We're gonna take Marla out to celebrate. She's pregnant with number four."

"*Wow.*" My hands slip off the strap of my messenger bag and hang listlessly at my sides.

Christina wags four fingers at me and then makes her pinky dance. "She says it was a surprise. And that she's pretty sure it happened after those happy hour drinks in August? Apparently she and Topher got a bit . . . creative when they got home." She waggles her eyebrows and makes her pinky dance again, this time an absurdly suggestive little move that I'm frankly shocked that anyone could perform with just a single pinky.

"Wow," I say again, hollowly. Just then, two interns from the Events department come bustling in and I take the opportunity to head down the hallway. I swing through the side door that leads to the sad little admin annex where me and three co-workers try not to die from lack of sunlight forty hours a week.

Almost as long as I can remember I've wanted to work in conservation. Growing up, of course I had the requisite Nick Lachey poster on my wall. But I also had polar bears. Red pandas. Aerial shots of the shrinking Amazon. I begged my parents to take me to the Gulf so that I could scrub the oil off seabirds with a toothbrush. (They signed me up to volunteer at the local animal shelter instead.)

Girls with big dreams and honest hearts always get into the most renowned conservation and climate study programs, don't they?

Nope. Most of us gratefully attend a state school and work a part-time job so that we finally have just enough money to . . .

Move to New York, hoping to work at the Wildlife Fund of America to make a difference! Which is exactly what I'm doing now . . .

. . . as an administrative catch-all, plugging holes in every single department.

Ever since I heard about WFA, I've dreamed of becoming

one of their esteemed policy analysts. I imagined myself crafting programs to protect endangered species, planning missions to shrinking habitats, wearing a low-cut dress and schmoozing billionaires into caring about marine iguanas. (Just joking about that last one—sort of.)

But alas. I was too desperate to finally get out of Michigan, so I didn't stay to complete the necessary graduate degree there. But once I got to New York, I never felt like I had the extra funds or time to enroll in a program. So here I am. The only directly dream-related thing I do at work these days is something I don't even get paid for. Each month I voluntarily pore over each funded project's research notes and budget and synthesize it all into an org-wide newsletter so that all of us understand what everyone else is actually doing around here. If it weren't for me, the Galapagos Penguin team wouldn't even know the Pacific Salmon team existed.

And then I get back to my regularly scheduled programming.

Next on the docket for me today? Ordering toner cartridges and helping Barbara update her operating system.

The annex door slams shut behind me ominously and I hear my own words to Christina in my head. *Had an appointment.*

A lunchtime appointment.

At my freaking OB-GYN. Because two little lines decided to make some random night a few weeks ago the most important night of my life.

And here I am talking about creative sex and surprise pregnancy with my co-worker. Without letting on that I personally really overachieved at both.

I can't think about how happy Marla apparently is to be on number four. Because at the moment, the concept of pregnancy exists only within the two square inches of my traitorous uterus. It is nothing more than a mere condition. There is nothing beyond that. The future can't exist for me right now. Not yet.

When I sit at my desk and unwrap my sandwich, Micah stares at me through big hazel eyes. "No secret, shameful peanut butter today?"

"What can I say?" I tell him through a mouthful. "I live for surprises."

1st Trimester: How to Master the Art of Stealth Panicking

Two

"**But your periods** are irregular." This is Willa's first response to my news. Her eyes are completely bewildered. "And you said you used a condom."

"Yes," I reply stiltedly. "All of that is true."

Willa stares at me.

This is Willa, who did a three-minute victory dance when I got the job at WFA (back when we thought that being dream-adjacent was as good as being dream-fulfilled). Willa who laughs way too loud on the train and frightens passersby with aggressive compliments on their style choices. She does not react quietly to the world. But here she is, staring at me. Not a peep coming from her direction.

I didn't assume this conversation was going to be a walk in the park. I know how badly Willa wants to be pregnant. How badly her husband, Isamu, wants to be a dad. How many times they've been disappointed in the last two years. I knew this wasn't going to be easy for her.

But Willa and I have dealt with not-easy a lot. When my parents died, one after the other in my freshman year of college, and Willa transferred back home to be with me. When, after college, we both put Westbrook, Michigan, in our rearview mirrors and moved to the Big Apple with nothing but each other. When I wanted to move out of our old apartment a few years ago and live on my own. She'd been devastated but we'd gotten through it together. When she told me that she and Isamu were engaged and I—to both of our complete surprises—burst into loud, snotty tears in a restaurant, convinced I was going to lose her to the clockwork cogs of marriage⟶children⟶Midwest move⟶mortgage⟶ Fourth of July barbecues and phone calls only on our birthdays. And then, hardest of all, when her mother, Corinne, passed away last year. That had been the most not-easy thing of all. Until this, it seems.

I'm just starting to consider waving my hand in front of her face when she finally moves, squeezing both hands between her knees. "You don't even want kids."

I rear back from her in surprise. "When did I say that?"

She doesn't answer. She just turns her face away from me in a way that suggests she doesn't want to be looked at. It's wrong and off. Willa always wants to be looked at. She's movie-star beautiful and loves every second of it. It's a bad day for her if she hasn't stopped at least some traffic.

"Hey there, party people." The apartment's front door clanks open and in walks Willa's brother Shep. He's two years older than we are and currently living in Willa's guest bedroom. He just split with his girlfriend of a decade and promptly moved out. He insists that he's been looking for a place of his own. But Willa suspects that she's been making it too comfortable for him to have much motivation to leave her place. Shep has always been like a cat lounging in a patch of sunlight on a busy sidewalk; as long as it's warm, he doesn't care about the ambiance. He'd rather overstay his welcome at his sister's house than take on the wretched task of apartment hunting in New York.

I stare at Shep's back instead of at Willa because everything is weird and I don't know where to look. He kicks his shoes in the general direction of the shoe basket and dumps his gym bag next to the umbrella stand. His T-shirt has two dark patches of sweat that arc out from his shoulder blades like the beginnings of wings. Even after all these years of friendship, it's still weird to me to see Shep work out.

Back home in Westbrook, he was a clumsy, sweet nerd who played so many videogames in his basement that his skin was almost translucent. He moved to New York for undergrad, grew into his limbs, and finally met some other computer geniuses. Nowadays he's well into a freelance coding career that I'll never understand and takes breaks from work to play pickup basketball at the Y down the street from Willa's.

He bangs his elbow on the doorframe as he turns and snags his sock on a loose nail in Willa's hardwood floor. "Ow. Damn."

He's a dork and everyone loves him. "How's everybody doing? Willa, let's just order in tonight. I was thinking sushi. Eve, you want in? We can get some vegetarian rolls for you, of course."

He flops into an armchair, his knees knocked out to either side, his head lolling as he clicks through his phone to get to whatever app he's gonna order dinner from. When no one answers him, he glances up in confusion and then looks back and forth between me and Willa, finally sensing the vibe.

"Uh . . . what's going on?"

I glance at Willa and if my face looks anything like hers, we belong in a Van Gogh painting. Blurry, devastated versions of ourselves.

"Um," I start, trying to think of something to say.

"Eve's pregnant," Willa says.

"*Willa!*" I'm instantly strobe-lighting between shock and dismay. I'm a hundred degrees. Covered in sweat from head to toe. My hair's gone white. I know it has.

"What?" Shep's phone belly-flops to the carpet. "Are you serious?"

I can't read the expression on his face and honestly I don't try very hard. I'm still staring at Willa's rigid profile, her bottom lip between her teeth, her eyes shiny. She's about eight inches taller than I am, but now, she looks so tiny.

"Yeah." My voice is like a heavy chair dragged over tile.

He's staring into nothing for a moment, his hands in his hair, and then there's a rush of movement, the clean smell of fresh sweat, and Shep is standing directly in front of me. I tear my eyes from Willa and blink up at him. Shep takes me by the shoulders and stands me up, his arms wrapping around me in a hug that is deeply familiar to me. He's always hugged like this. Hard. No finesse. Shep's hugs end in stepped-on toes and armpits to the face.

"Wow," Shep says. "Wowpregnantwow."

He shifts his arms, squeezes me hard again, and then tips me back to see my face.

"This is big." But the look on his face says that he means it in a good way. His eyes are bright and happy for me, if not a little worried. But it would be weird if he weren't a little worried. His eyes search my face and then drop all the way down to my toes. "How're you feeling? Do you need anything? You should sit," he reprimands me, as if he hadn't been the one to drag me up to my feet in the first place. He deposits me back onto the couch and then sits on the coffee table in front of me, his oversized knees knocking into mine.

I let out a big breath, the tears in my voice but not in my eyes anymore. I can't look at Willa. "I have no idea how I'm feeling. I only found out this morning. Confirmed it with an OB on my lunch break."

"Wow." One of his hands scratches at the back of his blondish head and his eyes glance at Willa, who has gone silent again since blurting out my life-changing news. He soldiers on. "Do you know how far along you are?"

"Six weeks," I say quietly. "Which is weird because it only, ah, happened four weeks ago. But they mark it from the date of—"

"Your last period. Not from conception," Willa cuts me off. "So you're really only two weeks pregnant when they say four weeks and so on. Most people don't know that."

Her voice trails off at the end. She's still not looking at me. I'm still not looking at her.

"Have you told . . ." Shep starts.

Don't say the father, don't say the father, I internally beg him.

"Anybody?" he finishes.

"Just you two so far. My brothers . . ." I trail off with a shrug and Shep nods, instantly understanding. I have three brothers. Dustin, the eldest, is twenty-eight years older than I am and sometimes feels more like an uncle than a brother. He enlisted at eighteen, ten years before I was even born. I saw him maybe twice a year until I was fifteen. At which point he'd retired from army life and came home for what was pretty much the most awkward summer of my life. He lived in our basement in Westbrook and watched TV all day. He met a woman towards the end of the summer, moved in with her, married her, and had three kids in three years. They were married about ten years when they got a divorce. Last time I saw him, he told me all about his new therapist and apologized for never being around when I was a kid. These days he posts deeply liberal political messages on his Facebook and reserves his Instagram for pics of his kids.

My other two brothers, the twins, have very little in common with me and even less in common with each other. We're all scattered about the country and see one another once a year at Christmas, when we Prodigal Son (and daughter) our ways back to our childhood home, which Dustin currently occupies.

My brothers are good people, but not exactly who I call in a pinch. I didn't even do that with my parents when they were still alive. They loved and supported me, but they never really knew what to do with me. Unexpected daughter in their second act and all.

No, the person I tell stuff to, any and all stuff, is currently studying the carpet instead of me.

I clear my throat. "I actually almost called your mom this afternoon when I left the doctor's office. Had my phone out and everything."

"Muscle memory," Shep guesses. "Happens to me too, still."

Willa makes a small noise and moves her hand to her forehead so we can't see her eyes. I don't know if it's because of my news or because we're talking about Corinne.

"I'm . . . gonna go," I decide.

"No, Eve," Shep says, reaching forwards to sandwich my small, cold hand between his two large, warm ones. "Stay. Don't go." He glances at his sister. "Let us feed you dinner. We don't have to talk about it if you don't want to."

"No." I search for an excuse that doesn't sound like a pregnancy symptom. *I'm tired. I don't feel well. Sushi sounds fucking disgusting right now.* Pregnant, pregnant, pregnant. "I have some work to get done."

Willa glances at me. She knows I'm lying.

I stride to the door and quickly bundle up, wishing I hadn't worn so many layers today. I can't help but feel like I'm making a big show of leaving, just hoping that Willa will quit doing an impression of a marble statue and stop me.

Nobody stops me. But Shep does follow me to the door and gives me one more Shep hug, this time accidentally knocking his chin against the top of my head. I hear his teeth clack closed and it's so Shep it makes me smile. Which makes those bright, sharp tears needle at the corner of my eyes again. I have to get out of here.

I lean around Shep. "Willa, I'll call you tomorrow, okay?"

She nods. "Great."

That's what I said to Nurse Blank today. *Great. Everything's great. Nothing is wrong. This is exactly how I would have planned for all of this to turn out. Great. Great. Great.*

Okay, so the thing that Willa said about me not even wanting kids isn't, like, *wrong* wrong.

Does anyone actually believe an almost thirty-year-old woman when she says she's never really given the kids issue a lot of thought? Well, I hope they would, because that's actually the case for me.

I've given it a ton of *adjacent* thought, because it was the topic du jour for about a million jours in a row with Willa.

But for myself?

I think there are some people who are born to have children. On the playground, they were the kids wrapping rocks in blankets and turning them into baby dolls. Heck, I used to babysit for a little girl who would pretend to breastfeed her teddy bears.

Corinne, Willa's mom? *Born* to have kids. A mother so natural she even mothered kids who weren't hers—i.e., me.

Then there are the people who have kids because that's just what you do after a certain age. An example of this second category would have been my parents. The certain age being early twenties after being married to their high school sweetheart for just over a year. Cue my oldest brother. Then, because kids are supposed to have siblings, apparently, came the twins. Every box checked. Then waaaaaaaaaaay down the pipeline, there was I. The check without a box.

And then there are some people who *might* start to think about having a family when they meet someone they'd like to start a family with.

I'm sure there are more than three categories of child-havers, but for the sake of argument, let's say I'm in the third category. And let's say that I've never exactly dated anyone who knocked ye olde socks off.

I've had exactly two serious boyfriends and they were both named Derek. Derek One lasted for two and a half years and he was extremely into spelunking (lots of trips upstate with his caving club while I stayed back in Brooklyn with Willa eating tacos and watching free concerts in Prospect Park). We were twenty-five when we broke up, just around the time that everyone starts hinting about marriage. Though the breakup was initially heart-wrenching, by the end of the conversation, we were actually both relieved; we knew it wasn't the right fit. I left his house that night with a goodbye kiss and about ten thousand pounds off my back.

Derek Two was a bit more of a landslide. We met on Tinder, had very much very interesting sex for about four months. And then considerably less, considerably less interesting sex for about ten more months. And then an operatic (honestly, kind of fun) breakup. In the weeks after it was over, I had that feeling you get when you eat too much processed sugar at once. But when he was out of my system, there was no residue.

So yeah. Not a lot of daydreaming about bassinets and Derek (pick a Derek) tossing a toddler into the air.

All of this is to say that in the day after I tell Willa, most of my ire over her reaction starts to just sort of smoke away. Because, yeah. She and I have never, and I mean never, talked about *me* having a kid.

It's five o'clock on the dot the next day, the minute I'm clocking out from work, when she calls me. I know the timing is on purpose. She wanted to catch me the very first moment that she could.

"Let me just start by saying I'm the worst," she says after I answer the phone.

"Let *me* just start by stopping you right there."

"Oh, thank God."

We both laugh the kind of cathartic, bursting laughs that are primarily characterized by relief, but there's still a sense of hesitation, tension crackling on the line.

"I know I didn't react well," she says. "But . . . it was a shock for me."

"Well . . . it's been a shock for me too?" For the first time it occurs to me that last night she'd made the entire situation completely about her. Sure, it was a genuine reaction and people need time to have their genuine reactions—

"Of course! Of course. I just think I need a little time to, ah, get used to the idea. You know, process it all."

The idea.

She needs time to get used to the *idea* of me being pregnant? Meanwhile, I'm getting used to actually being pregnant.

"Okay," I say, unsure if I want to push back or if I want to move on. Maybe both? Willa and I don't really fight. We problem solve. But something about this conversation is irritating me.

"You kind of sprang it on me," she says.

And there it is. The reason why I'm so irritated. Because she's waiting for me to *apologize* to her. For sitting her down and telling her. What was I supposed to do? Mangle a *Newsweek* and send her one serial killer letter at a time? I AM PREGNANT.

I'm completely unsure what to say. How can I tell her she's being an arse when I know exactly how hurt she is? "Well, next time I'll make sure to bring chocolate. And wine. And twenty bucks in ones. Every minute that passes, I'll give you another dollar. It'll help ease the blow."

I joke to break the tension and it's as close to an apology as she's getting this afternoon. She laughs and I can't help it: twenty years of friendship have me smiling at the phone too.

"So . . ." she says. "The guy . . ."

Ah, yes. The guy. Mr. Overzealous Sperm.

"What are you gonna tell him?" she asks.

"I was thinking sometime after my STI panel comes back. That way I can jam all the awkward into one convo if I also have to tell him—oh, wait. Did you say *when* am I gonna tell him or *what*?"

"I said *what*."

"As in . . ."

"As in . . . I was thinking . . . that you might not even need to tell him at all if you're not going to . . ."

"Keep it?"

"Keep it," she confirms.

There's a whole lot of words we're not saying right now. Willa usually says all the words. She is such a loudmouth word-sayer and I feel so confused as to why she hasn't shouted *Are you getting an abortion* into my earpiece.

". . . I don't think I'm going to do that," I say eventually.

"Keep it?" she asks.

"No. Not tell him."

"Wait, so . . . you're saying that you're going to tell him that you're not keeping it?"

"NO! I mean that I am not *not* keeping it? . . . No abortion for me." There. I've said it. I'm the one who said it. I thought it might feel like a curse word. Something you're definitely not supposed to say in front of your impressionable egg+sperm but . . . being the one to have said it out loud oddly makes me feel like the grown-up in this conversation.

"Do you . . . mean that you're not considering one at all? Or that you're waiting until you see the guy again to consider all your options?"

"I mean that . . . I . . . don't want to get one."

"Okay . . ." she says. "Okay, WOW! Eve!" I think she's happy with a dash of sad. Or maybe the other way around. I can't quite tell. She's both. I think I'm both too. I love her. I need to puke.

"Well, first things first," she says, and I can practically hear her dusting her hands of the awkwardness of the last few minutes. She's gotten her answer and now she's moving into fix-it mode. She's finally sounding like the friend who bought my first bra for me because I was too embarrassed to hand it to the cute checkout boy.

"First things first?" I prompt her.

"Yes, first on the list is telling Loverboy."

"Ah, I see we're using his baptismal name now."

"We'll take this one step at a time, okay?" she says. "I gotta run, though."

One step at a time. We've gotten the particulars out of the way, but there's still so much we haven't said.

"Sure."

"Love you, Evie."

How easily the words trip off her tongue reminds me of Corinne.

"Love you too."

Two weeks later, I'm at home when my phone rings.

"Hello?"

"Ms. Hatch?"

Ah, the dead, dulcet tones of Nurse Blank. I'd know thee anywhere. "That's me."

"I'm calling from the Lower East Side Partners in Obstetrics and Gynecology—"

"Ah, yes. The old L-E-S-P-I-O-A-G."

Occasional "honeys" aside, I'm not sure Nurse Blank is ready to take our friendship to the next level.

"I just wanted to let you know that I'm looking at the results of your STI and blood panel here and you're negative for all." I'm silent. "All clear," she adds.

"That's . . . that's great." And there's that word again. The one that won't die.

We hang up and I text Willa: *I got the STI results back from the OB. All's quiet on the western front.*

The three dots appear, then disappear.

Just to be clear, I text again. *My vagina is the western front in this scenario. I'm STI free.*

Finally, Willa ding-dings me. *Sorry! I was jogging. But great news about your vagina.*

When she married Isamu, they moved into an apartment in South Slope, close enough to Prospect Park that she runs the bike path every morning. Twice on Saturdays. I don't bother asking her which lap she's on. I'm jealous. I had to quit my indoor soccer league because Dr. Bridget Muscles said I'm allowed to jog and do yoga and Pilates but contact sports are off the menu. So far, it's been the worst part of pregnancy. Besides, well, the pregnancy part.

And now there is nothing in the way between me and the world where I tell this guy I'm pregnant. Nothing. No excuses.

I text again. *I guess I'll tell him tonight.*

Ding ding. *Tonight?*

What's wrong with tonight?

She texts back quickly. *It's just, I don't know, not something you tell someone on a Saturday night, I guess.*

I kind of see her point, but still: *Sure, but I don't have a choice. All I really know about him is which shift he works at the bar. If I don't track him down tonight, I'm just gonna have to do it next week.*

I keep forgetting he's a bartender, she texts.

I laugh. *How do you keep forgetting that? It's literally the only thing we know about him!*

Right. Tonight, she answers. *Meet you out front of Good Boy at nine?*

I feel a swell of relief and gratitude. Of *course* she is coming with me. Willa wouldn't let me do something like this on my own.

Perfect! I text.

It's perfect for me that my best friend is coming with me to tell a rando he's the person who got me pregnant? Sure. And now I've got, oh, six hours to sweatily perseverate over progenerating before said excursion? Yup, absolute perfection.

I work on the WFA newsletter for a few hours, but a particularly depressing bit of data about Amur leopard habitat gets me all misty, so I pivot to cleaning my clean kitchen. Something to know about me is that I hold myself in perpetual audition for a feature in *Better Homes and Gardens* magazine. I've got to be the only renter in New York City who has paid to install her own tiled backsplash. My furniture is painstakingly curated, my corners scrupulously dusted, I've got vases for different types of flowers, for God's sake.

After I've scrubbed the inside of my vegetable drawers, I decide to reorganize my spice rack for the ninetieth time in my life. It bothers me when the jars are half full, so I take the train to a bulk spice shop in the city and re-up on cumin, chili powder, and cinnamon. My C shelf is going to look amazing. It better because my nose is pregnant-ized and I nearly expire from the scent of the spice shop. By the time I'm home and the spice shelf looks perfect, it's six o'clock and I decide it's time to start getting ready.

Ho-hum, just a night on the town with Willa. Nothing too special. La di da di la la la. I tell myself this on repeat until I realize that I'm actually singing this to myself and the tune is anxious and high-pitched. Not a good sign.

If my oven weren't bunned, I'd have a beer.

Instead, I blow-dry my very straight, dark brown hair, add some eyeliner that always makes my eyes look a little bluer than they are, and rewatch an episode of *The Great British Bake Off* while I decidedly don't deliberate over what to wear.

That's because I've already spent valuable work hours pre-deliberating this exact issue. I'm wearing a black high-necked tank top tucked into high-waisted, wide-legged jeans that I'm *almost* too short for. I'll pull on my little bomber jacket before I go, and it's the coolest I could possibly look.

And that's how I want to look, right? Cool?

At eight I decide I'll walk to the bar. I'm tired (because I'm always tired now) but time on the claustrophobic train sounds miserable.

I live in the Midwood neighborhood of Brooklyn, south of the park, and Willa lives on the west side of it. The bar where he works, Good Boy, is on the southwest corner in a neighborhood called Windsor Terrace or Kensington, depending on who you ask.

I'm speedwalking down Parkside Avenue when I get a phone call from Isamu. I bet he came home to find Willa gone and now she's not answering her phone. I get so many phone calls from Isamu about this issue that I should just change his contact info from *Isamu* to *Where's Willa?* "Hey, Isamu."

"Eve." His voice sounds funny. Isamu plays trumpet for a million different bands and is one of those people who is always tapping out a rhythm on the edge of his dinner plate. But right now, he sounds weirdly sedate.

"What's up? Is everything okay?"

"Um. Everything's fine. But, uh, we got some . . . bad news today and she—she was wondering if maybe you guys could do your . . . errand next weekend?"

I stop walking and I must pause too long because Isamu cuts back in.

"Eve? You all right?"

"What kind of bad news? Is she okay?"

Isamu sighs. "She'll be all right. It's just . . . she got her period. We thought this time . . . I think she's been hoping that maybe because you . . . that she would . . . that you could do this together."

I'm still standing in the middle of the sidewalk, the sky dark as a hat over my eyes and all the buildings looming orange in the streetlamps. On my right side, the tangled, shadowed park stands sinisterly between me and Willa.

"Oh, gosh. Okay," I say. She was hoping that because I'd found out I was pregnant, this would be the month that she'd find out *she* was pregnant and then she could finally forgive me for being pregnant. It makes such dreadful sense. "I'm sorry, Isamu."

"She really wants to go with you," Isamu insists. "She just wants to go next week."

"Next week. Cool. No problem. Tell her I understand and that next week is great."

"Oh. Okay!" Isamu brightens considerably. "Great!"

"Have her call me when she wants to chat." The words make my mouth taste like I've licked carpet. Isamu doesn't pass messages between me and Willa. There's never been a reason for him to.

"Will do." He pauses. "Love you, Evie."

I wilt a little bit. It would be so easy to put this awful feeling directly onto Isamu's shoulders. But none of this is his fault. He's not just a good husband to Willa, he's been my good friend for years. "Love you too."

We hang up and I keep walking towards the bar. Maybe, if I'd still been at home, about to take a cab to Good Boy, then I would follow Willa's directions and save this whole thing for next week. But I've walked halfway, I'm dressed to the nines, and there's nothing for me at my house right now. Even the spices are topped off.

I walk the rest of the way to the bar. I can tell him without her.

I can and I will. I arrive and take a deep breath out on the sidewalk, staring at the bar. It's tucked between a laundromat and a sandwich shop, the façade redone in a red wooden siding that I think is supposed to make it look like a doghouse. I reach for the door handle that's shaped like a dog's paw.

"Eve!" a voice calls from behind me. "Eve, wait up!"

Three

Shep jogs across the street to me, waving his arms like I might not see him there, glowing like a firefly on the other end of the sidewalk. He keeps jogging, even though I've clearly stopped walking. His giraffe legs eat up two sidewalk squares at a time.

"Glad. I. Caught. You," he pants, bending to put his hands on his knees. He sticks his tongue out and says *haaaaaaaaa*, trying to get some of that extra carbon dioxide out of his system. A sheen of sweat shines on his brow and makes his blond hair an even darker gold than it usually is.

"Shep," I say in surprise. "Did you run here?"

"No cabs," he pants. "Train too slow."

"Your cardio is abysmal."

Still bent over, he scowls up at me in a friendly way. "I run across two neighborhoods for you and this is what you say to me?" He folds over farther. "Hee hoo. Hee hee hoo hoo."

"Are you doing Lamaze breathing?"

"Seems apropos?" He stands up, pressing his long fingers into a cramp at his side.

I groan and roll my head to one side. "Pregnancy jokes? Really?"

His eyes grow serious. "Willa was guessing that you weren't going to wait. For next weekend. So I came instead."

He holds his arms out and I go straight into his chest, burying my forehead against his bony sternum.

"I'm sorry she didn't come," he says.

I feel ridiculously grateful that he said *didn't come* instead of *couldn't come.* His arms are just as tight as usual.

She didn't come. But she knows me well enough to know that I was going to go anyways. I can almost, *almost* not be mad at her.

"You ready for this?" I ask him, tilting my head up and stepping back a foot.

His arms fall to his sides. "Yes," he says resolutely. "What's our plan?"

"Well, he's the bartender on Saturday nights so I think we just go sit at the bar. I'll ask to talk to him alone when he can get a break, and hopefully, he'll be friendly."

"And I sit at the bar and just be my charming self and then I'll walk you home."

The thing I love about Shep is that he's actually telling *himself* this, not me.

"Sure," I say.

He nods and reaches for the door handle. "Ready?"

"Yes," I say, trying to re-create the surety of his tone.

He swings open the door, we step inside, and a Chihuahua bum-rushes us.

"Close the door! Close the door!" a woman yells, sprinting towards us.

Shep promptly tips his humongous foot in front of the Chihuahua's chest and shuts the door. The woman drops to her knees, picks up her dog, and looks up at Shep with her lip between her teeth. "Thanks."

His cheeks get pink looking down at a woman on her knees in front of him and he clears his throat. "You're welcome."

She flips her long, auburn hair back and slowly stands up. "I'm Melanie."

Oh no. Hell no. My buffer is not tumbling face-first into a meet-cute when I'm supposed to be telling someone I'm pregnant with their zygote. "Hi, Melanie," I say, baring my teeth in a chimpanzee smile. "I'm Eve."

Melanie gets the picture and skedaddles.

"You're a little scary," Shep tells me happily as he trails along after me. There're no seats at the bar so my plan is immediately shot to hell. But then, seating promptly becomes the less important issue because there's no man behind the bar either. An unfamiliar woman pulls a pint.

I'm immediately and irrevocably stymied. I'm the one who planned an outfit for a week and walked for an hour to get here. The only thing he had to do tonight was be here. He's already failed me miserably.

"Let's sit in that booth," Shep suggests gently, obviously spotting the problem at hand. "I'm kind of hungry anyways."

He guides me to a corner booth in the back. We sit and his eyes scan around the bar. "Eve," he says slowly. "What the heck is this place?"

I know exactly to what he's referring. "It's a dog bar. People are allowed to bring their dogs. You didn't notice your new girlfriend's Chihuahua?"

"A dog bar," he muses, ignoring the girlfriend comment and looking around at the little dogs tucked into purses and backpacks. The big dogs sleeping under barstools. The medium-sized dogs sniffing one another's butts and desperately trying to place themselves in this big, scary world. "Huh. Cool idea."

I'd thought so too, the first and only other time I'd ever been here. "Oh, thank God," I say, my eyes catching on familiar fur. "That's his dog. He must be here somewhere."

A one-eyed mutt of indiscriminate shape and size bullies his way through a crowd of human legs and beelines straight for the assortment of water bowls that line the back wall. He drinks primly, his curly tail poised perfectly atop his back like a donut.

"What's his name?" Shep asks.

"Bones," I reply, and consider calling for the dog. But I'm already worried enough that his owner won't remember me. I don't think I could handle getting snubbed by a dog tonight as well.

"No," Shep laughs. "I meant the guy, not the dog."

"Oh." I laugh too and it feels good.

"Hi there, y'all want food menus tonight? Or just drinks?" Another pretty waitress. Do they only hire lookers in this joint?

"Just a ginger beer for me, please," I say.

"Fries?" Shep orders, one eye on me, and I'm grateful he's astute enough to know that I'm not interested in him perusing a menu for twenty minutes while I sweat my candied apples off and try not to think about what I have to do in a second.

"Sure."

"And whatever IPA you have on tap. The stankier the better."

The order makes the waitress laugh with surprise, her expression melting from busy service worker to potentially interested girl.

"Jeez, Shep," I gripe when she leaves.

His light brown eyes catch the dim bar lighting. "What?"

"You've already had two women making googoo eyes at you and we haven't even been here ten minutes."

His mouth opens and closes. Opens and closes.

The waitress is back with his stanky beer in record time. "Here you go."

"Miss?" I catch her eye. "Do you know if Ethan is working tonight?"

She looks at me like I just asked her if she knew the ABCs. "Ethan works every night."

My eyes find the chick behind the bar and then flick back to the waitress. "Is he here right now?"

"He's in the back."

"Okay. Would you mind telling him that . . . a friend is here to see him?"

"Sure thing. Let me just get the order in for those fries." She smiles hugely at Shep and walks off, her tray under her arm.

"Why didn't you tell her your name?" he asks, taking a sip out of his beer. "Oh. She forgot your drink." He catches the waitress's eye and signals to the empty place in front of me. The waitress mimes smacking herself on the forehead.

"Because if she tells him Eve is here to see him and he doesn't remember my name, that would be the ultimate humiliation."

Shep's eyes are immediately back on me, softening, warming, going desert gold. "Eve, who could forget you?"

"Thanks, Shep," I say dutifully, because he's known me forever, and he has to say stuff like that.

"Seriously." His big foot nudges mine under the table. "There's nobody else like you. You're a dynamo." He snaps his fingers. "You're like a living, breathing Powerpuff Girl."

That makes me laugh and think of elementary school afternoons in Shep and Willa's basement, the two of us forcing him to be the third Powerpuff Girl.

But then the waitress is back, sliding my drink and fries to me and looking Shep up and down. I catch her eye and she gives me a nod, pointing towards the back of the bar and then heading there herself. There she goes. *Wait! Come back!* I want to shout.

"So," Shep says, tucking into his fries. "You were last

here . . . six weeks ago?" He squints into the past, as if he's trying to remember what he was up to whilst I was off getting unintentionally inseminated. "I must have just moved in at Willa's."

Something crosses his face. "That wasn't—Was that the weekend you, me, and Willa went out?"

I grimace. "Yep. It's a long story." It's not.

Me and Willa took Shep out to cheer him up after his breakup with Heather. It was the first night in years it was just the three of us. No others, significant or otherwise. So we got properly drunk and silly. When they were exhausted, Shep and Willa grabbed a cab back to her house, but I was still revved up from the reunification of our trio and not ready to go home yet. I sent my cab packing and popped into this bar. I let the bartender flirt me all the way back to his place. There. That's the whole story. But I can't imagine telling Shep any of it.

Shep absorbs my gentle rejection. After a long moment, he tilts his head and sort of squints at me. "So, do you often, uh, pick up guys in bars?"

I turn to stare at him, and pink washes over his cheekbones. "Sorry, sorry, that sounded so judgy," he murmurs, his hands coming up in a sign of surrender. "It's not my business. I guess I'm just curious."

Ah. I can understand Shep's curiosity. He'd been in a relationship with Heather for literally a decade. I'm not sure if he's ever slept with anyone else, to be honest. For him, sex-in-the-wild must seem like a fairy tale in some ways.

"I'm pretty sure *he* picked *me* up. His game was far superior to mine that night."

"Do you *have* game?"

I laugh at the playful insult, but when I look up at Shep, his big, brown eyes are brimming with sincerity, curiosity, intrigue. I narrow my eyes at him and the blush on his cheeks deepens.

"I've been known to have a little game."

He eats his fries for a while, a thoughtful expression on his face. "So, how'd he do it?"

My eyes are scanning the bar. I don't see the waitress, Bones, or Ethan.

"What?"

"You said he picked you up. How'd he do it?"

I turn to concentrate on Shep because he's big and safe and familiar. "Oh. I was sitting alone at the bar. And Ethan came over to me and leaned down and said, 'So, you gonna hit on me or what?' "

Shep's eyebrows rise and I can't tell if he thinks the line is funny or absurd.

"It worked." I shrug. "We chatted for a couple hours and then went back to his place."

Shep says something but I'm not listening anymore because Ethan walks out from a back hallway, our waitress at his side.

Holy *God*, I forgot how beautiful he is.

Ethan is built like a geometry problem. Shapes on shapes on shapes. He's tall, with round shoulders, a broad, flat chest, muscular butt. Tonight, he's wearing a button-down and a pair of slacks. His burnished, coppery hair is set off by the dim bar lighting, shining like a garnet.

One look at Ethan and my armadilloed heart suddenly stretches and unfurls. I realize I'm not breathing, just watching him, and I nearly choke on all the air I suck in at once. This is apparently what chemistry feels like. From ten yards away.

I'm retroactively impressed with myself that I managed to bag a babe like that. How did I handle touching him without hyperventilating? I must have just risen to the occasion like an athlete at the Olympics. That night, the world expected great things from me. And boy did I deliver. So did he, if I recall correctly.

The waitress is pointing to our booth.

I wait, a tightness in my throat like I've swallowed too much food at once, as he looks in my direction. There's a half second of nothing on his face, in which I have to come to terms with the fact that he picks up girls at this bar so often that he legit doesn't remember me, Powerpuff Girl or not. But then—thank you, Jesus Christ, Superstar—his face lights up in recognition.

He starts moving through the people at the bar, his dog next to him. They both just sort of push through crowds, the destination much more important than the journey.

When he's close enough that I can finally see the robin's egg of his irises, he jams his hands in his pockets. "Eve."

Somebody's cut the puppet strings because I almost collapse into a pile on the floor when he remembers my name. "Hi," I say, scooting out from the bench and standing up.

His hands stay in his pockets a split second too long and our hug is of the pat-pat variety. Not everybody knows how to hug short people, especially not short people they've banged against a closet door. I don't hold it against him.

"Oh," he says over my head, and steps to the side with his hand out for Shep. "Hi. I'm Ethan Rise."

"Shep Balder," Shep says, his fist too full of fries to shake hands with Ethan. His solution is to shove all the fries into his mouth at once, wipe his hand on a handful of napkins, and then shake Ethan's hand. "I'll go . . . over there."

Shep disappears and I have the urge to call him back, make him sit between me and Ethan.

"He's one of my oldest friends . . ." I explain to Ethan as I slide back into the booth. He takes Shep's seat and leans his elbows on the table.

Something brushes my leg and I jump, wondering if Ethan is already trying to put the moves on me again. But then a furry brown head pops up at my thigh and Bones does his one-eyed scowl at me. Even though his lack of one eye always makes Bones look a little teed-off, I can tell from the wobble of his head that his tail is wagging under the table. I pat the bench next to me and Bones jumps up.

"Hi," I say solemnly to Bones, giving his ears a scratch.

"It's, uh, good to see you again," Ethan says after a second. "You didn't leave me your number."

"Right."

Honestly, it hadn't even occurred to me. I'd left while Ethan was asleep, Bones seeing me off at the door. "Sorry about that," I say, meaning it both casually and sincerely. "I . . . don't do . . . that . . . very often."

"Me either," he says, letting out a breath.

"So. Rise, huh? That's an unusual last name." Involuntarily my brain conjures a pesky little hyphen that it inserts between his last name and mine. Hatch-Rise. I hate that I've even had the thought.

The thing is, when a man like Ethan fertilizes your egg, it's a nearly impossible task to completely ignore the question of whether or not you might just end up together. In my darkest hours over the last few weeks, I've wondered to myself if a surprise pregnancy could just possibly be the meet-cute to end all meet-cutes? Haven't I seen that movie before? Aren't they secretly soulmates and their pheromones recognized it before their hearts did? His sperm, determined to one day wife her, clawed its way through the condom to tie her to him for all eternity?

Ugh. The cloying stench of the will-they-won't-they perfume is so overpowering I nearly ralph all over the booth.

"I think it's English?" he says, scratching at his neatly shaved cheek. "Or British, I mean?" He's still talking about last names while I quietly wither away in a romcom hell of my own miserable making. "Are you all right?"

I take a deep breath and sip my ginger beer. "I'm fine?"

Honestly, at this point, his guess is as good as mine.

"I think Clarice likes your friend." His eyes are focused across the bar.

I look over my shoulder to see Shep, red-faced and nervously laughing at something the waitress is saying to him.

"Something tells me she'd eat him alive."

Ethan's studying me when I turn back to look at him. His eyes zipping from me and then back to Shep. I can practically hear the words he's thinking. *Are they really just friends?*

"You been playing soccer?" he asks instead. That's right. We both like soccer. We talked about it that night.

I blink at him for a minute. He had legitimately paid attention. It wasn't attention solely for the hope of getting me against the wall of his bedroom. How refreshing.

"A little," I respond. *I had to quit my favorite league because you knocked me up, but . . .*

A silent second passes. I know that I'm making this awkward.

People can tell when you have something to say and aren't saying it. I came here tonight and asked to see him. Which means it's a fair assumption on his part that I want to connect again. Meanwhile, I'm fiddling with his dog's ears and barely even looking at him.

His hands spread out, palms flat on the tabletop. His light eyes take in my nervous fingers on Bones's ears, the scant inch of ginger beer gone from my sweating glass, my eyes I'm certain are open a little too wide.

"Are you *sure* you're okay?" he asks.

All the jokes have left the building along with Elvis, my brain, and my plan. Bones's presence at my side goes from comforting to nonsensical. Why are there so many dogs in this bar?

I wish I'd never learned Ethan's last name. I hate that it's a verb, just like mine. That's *my* thing. I hate that he's so achingly handsome I want to hide my face. I hate that I *do* hide my face, but just for a moment.

I wish Willa were here.

When I drop my hands in a pile on my lap, he looks genuinely alarmed at my behavior. *Great, Eve, freak him out before you change his life forever.*

Great. Great. Great.

"Ethan," I whisper, reaching across the table, deeply relieved when he puts his warm, rough hand in mine. "Turns out I'm pregnant. And it's yours."

Four

"Come with me."

He's suddenly standing beside the booth, his hands in his pockets like a Boy Scout, his eyes on Bones, not on me.

Bones and I stare up at him. "You mean me?" I point at myself between the eyes. "Or him?" I point between Bones's . . . eye.

"Her," he corrects. "But I meant you. Well, both of you, I guess."

"Bones is a her?" I turn and survey the scruffy li'l pile of wagging fur. "Huh."

"Bones, come," he says, tap-tapping his leg. "Eve . . ." His eyes flick to me and then over his shoulder for half a second. "Eve, can we please just go . . ."

Bones is paws and dead weight as she pads her way over my lap and leaps down to stand next to her owner, all faithful wags and trusting eyes.

Oh, what I wouldn't give to be Bones right now. To have a handsome man say *Come with me* and to know what he really means is *Trust me to make everything all right.*

But I'm not a dog, I'm a pregnant human and I know no such thing. To me, in this very moment, *Come with me* sounds much more like *Can we please not do this in public.*

Which. Fair.

I'm up and following him back to the hallway from whence he came and then we're behind a heavy wooden door and the friendly din from the bar goes from Technicolor high-def to softened pastels in the background.

"Okay," he says, standing just a touch too close to me. "Okay. Can you just . . . Would you mind just sitting?"

He waves his hand behind me and somehow summons a leather couch up from the ether. I sit and suddenly he's too far away, standing on the complete other side of the room.

"This is . . . a weird thing to ask but could you just . . . please . . . could you just not look at me for a minute," he asks quietly. He's already halfway turned away from me, his hands in his pockets again.

I blink. Then I clamp my hands over my eyes and, honestly, the dark solitude is kinda nice.

I can hear him on the other side of the room, breathing hard. His pacing footsteps say *Oh, shit, oh, shit, oh, shit.* Or perhaps they say *Preg, nant, preg, nant, preg, nant.*

An untold amount of time passes, likely less than thirty seconds, before he speaks.

"Okay," he says again.

"Can I look?"

"Yeah. Thanks. Sorry."

I jolt a little because when I take my hands away from my eyes, he's actually right in front of me, crouching down on the balls of his feet and clamping the back of his neck in the Vulcan death grip. Or something.

"How . . . are you doing over there?" I ask.

He's been staring in the general direction of my face, but as soon as I ask my question, he drops his head down and he balances himself against the floor with two fingers on one hand. An upside-down peace sign. Fingers white at the pressure points. One finger for him, one for me, straining like our lives depend on it, trying like heck to keep everything balanced.

"I . . . am probably going to say some really dumb shit by

accident . . ." he says after a long moment. "I . . . don't know what to say . . . and . . . I've never been a fast . . . please, just, don't make any decisions based on what I do in the next . . . little while . . . okay? I can't . . . I won't . . . be good at . . ."

"Ethan," I cut in. "This isn't a test."

"Okay," he says.

And then he's quiet for two of the longest minutes of my life.

Finally, I crack. "Your legs will fall asleep if you stay like that."

He jolts when I speak and he's instantly on his feet. "Right. Yeah."

He sits carefully next to me on the leather couch, and Bones, who's been minding her own business on a dog bed in the corner, plods over and jumps up beside him, her head on his thigh.

"So," he says, clearing his throat and finally finding my eyes. "You're pregnant."

I can't help it. I burst out laughing. "Yes."

He laughs a little too, but it's the nervous kind. The *what-the-fuck* kind.

He puts all ten fingers in the air and one by one he's folding them down. "That means you're . . ."

"Eight weeks along," I supply.

He glances at me and then frowns at his half-folded fingers. I quickly explain about those extra two weeks, an uneasy feeling starting to march like ants down the back of my neck.

"You can google it," I hear myself say.

All those folded and unfolded fingers are carefully stowed away, once again, in his pockets. "No, no," he says quietly. "I believe you."

He believes me. I take a breath and it seems endless; I didn't know I had that much real estate to fill in there.

"How long have you known?" he asks.

"A couple weeks. I wanted to wait until the STI panel came back—negative, by the way—before I contacted you."

He nods, like that makes sense, but then he just keeps nodding and nodding, and it's clear that nothing makes sense. He's bent forwards over Bones, who—God bless her—is snoozing right through this little mess. We're a rerun of a familiar program to her. *Humans do talk talk and make big deal out of life.*

He's propping his forehead up on one palm, his elbow digging into his knee. I watch as a surreptitious thumb sweeps something shiny away from one eye.

He clears his throat and sits back up. "Okay. And, ah, how are you feeling? You're healthy?" He glances down at my bomber jacket. "Everything is healthy?"

I play a quick, personal thumb war and then immediately realize why he's been sending his hands to their rooms this whole time. Because hands are ridiculous and in the way and there's never anything to do with them. His—I check—are in his pockets again. Mine, I decide to make go fish-limp on my lap.

"Um. Everything is healthy so far. It's obviously very early. They don't even give you the pamphlets and stuff until you're eight weeks along, because things go screwy so often in those first few weeks."

He blinks at me. "But . . . nothing has . . . gone screwy?"

Now that we've both said the word *screwy,* I can see that it is an absurd word and no one should say it, ever. I could not have chosen a more ludicrous euphemism for *got pregnant, still pregnant* if I'd tried.

"No. No. Like I said. Everything is healthy."

"And you're feeling all right?"

I answer that question—the second time he asks it—in

the most benign way possible. "I have normal first-trimester symptoms."

He glances at me and then glances away, roughly scrubbing a hand at the back of his head and then dropping it down into Bones's fur. He's far more gentle with her than he is with himself.

There's a two-toned knock at the door and then it opens. I jolt. It's the door that we came through initially, but since we've been in here, it has become the door that keeps out the world. That's the door that separates the land where time moves from the land where time doesn't. The laws of doors don't apply when someone is pregnant in here. It's the betrayal of a lifetime, me and that door.

A youngish man with light brown skin and curly black hair peeks his head around the corner. "Hey, Ethan, do you mind if I alter the specials? We're out of—"

His eyes have just bounced from the empty desk at one end of the room to the two people perched on the couch where he clearly wasn't expecting to see them.

"Oh. Sorry." The man is backpedaling, his eyes on the floor.

"No, no, Charles, it's fine." Ethan stands, dislodging Bones, and strides over to the door. They converse about ingredients and Bones picks her way on stick legs across the couch to me, her new pillow in Ethan's absence. Her head is light and warm and there, *finally*, something to do with my hands.

Ethan closes the door and turns back to me. "Sorry about that." He surveys the distance between us. How will he ever return to his seat? He's all the way over there.

"Is this your office?" I ask. And that's the thing about moments like these. Your world shrinks down completely. There's been nothing but Ethan and occasionally Bones for the last fifteen minutes. I haven't even really looked at the desk by the far wall, the lamp with a stained-glass shade, the tiny window that looks out onto things it's too dark to see.

"Yeah."

What kind of bartender gets a personal office? "Are you the manager? Owner?"

"Yes," he says. "And I fill in at the bar when there are gaps in the schedule for one reason or another."

I pet Bones and chew on this piece of information. Ethan the Bartender is not, in fact, Ethan the Bartender. He's Ethan the Business Owner and Bar Moonlighter. I know absolutely nothing about this man.

The door flings open again. "Ethan, I've got Rudy from Plainview Distributing on the—oh crap, my bad. I'll find you later." A short woman with a newsies cap on has entered and exited all in one breath.

Not that I really had any other choice, but I suddenly feel very bad about showing up at someone's place of work to completely change their life.

"Maybe we should . . ." I start and stop and start again. "Should we make a plan to meet up soon? It's a lot to take in and there's no reason to . . . push it."

I'm the Monopoly Man. I've just gifted Ethan with a one-night-only get-out-of-jail-free card and his soul is resurrecting before my very eyes. "Yes. Yes, good idea. Let's—let me get your number, yeah? When are you free usually? I work nights, obviously, but I'm pretty free during the days."

He's unlocked his phone and handed it over to me.

"I work days," I say. "And sleep at night. Old school."

He laughs, shaky and loosened now that he knows I'm leaving. "Right. Right. Well, I'm off Tuesdays. I could meet you after work?"

"Sure. Yes. Okay."

He dips at the knee, catches my eye, and stands up straight, dragging my eye line up to his height. "Yes?"

"Yes."

I hand his phone back to him and he looks down at the contact information I've just poked into his phone. "Hatch," he says. I wonder if an unwelcome hyphen is surfacing in his brain the way it did in mine. He taps my name with his thumb and for some reason I wince. Then my phone is vibrating in my bomber jacket and I nod at him. *Call received, contact info retrieved.* I'm double thumbs-upping him and this is why Bones is necessary. My thumbs can't be trusted when I'm not petting the dog.

"Tuesday," I say. "I'll call you."

I give Bones one last pat on the head, then step around Ethan to the door. I feel him walking behind me and that makes me move a little funny as I step into the dim hallway. I take a sharp turn towards the bar area and my foot catches on something large and intractable.

In a millisecond I'm suddenly down, one knee jammed into Shep's lap, who has apparently decided to sit on the floor outside Ethan's office.

"Oof," Shep says, folding forwards over the spot my knee is currently trying to lever into two pieces. "Sorry."

My elbow is sharply complaining, in the air at an odd angle, and I look up to see Ethan gripping it, clearly having lunged forwards to keep me from falling. I've hurt Shep, and Ethan's hurt me. Hands from below and hands from above help me come to a stand again.

Everybody had better stop touching me or I'm going to start spin-kicking well-meaning men. My face must telegraph my inner monologue because once I'm on my feet all four hands retreat back to their own personal bubbles. Shep scrambles up from the floor.

"Sorry, sorry. Didn't mean to get in the way. I just wanted to make sure . . ." His eyes are searching my face and then Ethan's face. He doesn't finish that thought. Instead he tips up onto his toes for a moment. "Everybody all right?"

"Yeah. Sorry, what'd you say your name was again?" Ethan asks, and I don't have to look to confirm that he's glancing between Shep and me again.

"Shep. Balder." Now Shep's the one glancing between the two of us. "I know this is a . . . moment. I'm happy to leave if—"

"No!" I say, and I've suddenly got the hem of Shep's T-shirt pinched between two fingers so tightly my bones kiss. "I was just about to head out."

"Do you need a cab?" Ethan asks me.

The answer is yes. "No, that's all right," I hear myself say. "We'll walk."

Ethan blinks, looks like he has more to say, but our waitress is suddenly there, leaning into our group with one hand on Shep's shoulder. "Ethan, sorry, we're struggling with that special, could you . . ."

"Yes. Definitely. Be right there."

He turns to me and it's all over his face. We're standing in a dog bar and how, *how,* do you casually say goodbye to the woman you've progenerated with?

I cut him a break. "Tuesday," I say, and my hand does a friendly little wave.

He looks so relieved I could cry. I'm making this so easy for him. I'm dipping it in honey, putting it on a spoon, making airplane noises for him.

"I'll text you on Monday," he says, because of course he has to say something. "To make a plan."

"Great."

Shep is lingering fifteen feet away, pretending to find the wallpaper very interesting. Ethan's eyes are on my face.

"Can I—should we—can I give you a quick hug?" he asks.

"Oh." And just like that, he's finally, finally gifted *me* with relief. "Yes. Please."

The hug is gentle and warm and I'm instantly brought back to that night. Not because I'm suddenly incapacitated with lust, but because on that night, there were moments where he was genuinely sweet, just like this. Both arms around me and *with me.* But it's a quick hug, and he steps back right away.

I don't offer him any more parting words, but he doesn't seem to need them. We walk side by side to the bar and he peels off to go doctor this apparently AP-level drink special. I head towards the front door and leave it to Shep to ward off any Chihuahuas attempting a run at freedom.

The night air is just chilled enough to show me all the places I've been sweating. There are more than I thought there'd be.

"We're not really walking, are we?" Shep asks me, and I give him a look so droll he laughs.

"No, but let me save face, let's get one over there." I point towards the park, far enough away that if Ethan happens to look out the window of the bar, he won't see me getting into the cab I didn't want him to hail for me.

"You all right?" Shep asks, his elbow giving my shoulder a friendly little tap.

"What is it about our culture that made me assume he wouldn't want to hug me?"

"Huh?"

"I was shocked he wanted to hug me. At the end there."

"Oh. You didn't want him to?"

I look up at Shep and there's an orange spray of light kissing at his head as we pass a streetlamp. "I really *wanted* him to hug me. And obviously I'm not disgusting to him, ya know, see the whole knocked-up thing. But I was just . . . so shocked that he wanted to hug me."

"Ah. So . . . he didn't take it well?"

I sigh. "He didn't take it *badly.* Then again, does anyone take sudden, life-changing news well?"

Shep is quiet as we make it to a corner and the cars sleepily propel themselves out of the stupor of the red light. "You know—" he says after a moment. "You know this isn't bad news, right?" He's watching my face; I'm watching the red hand across the street that's telling me to stop in my tracks. "I mean, it can be bad news if that's what it feels like to you. But you . . . you aren't the bearer of bad news just because you're pregnant."

Says the only person who's been truly happy for me so far. Including myself.

"Shep—" I say with a slice of my chin through the air. I'm walking the second the light changes and he kicks into gear to keep up with me. How to explain that sometimes being nice hurts? How to explain that every time he's sweet to me, I can't help but think about how not-sweet Willa was?

"Eve! Eve, wait!" I stop in the crosswalk and turn to see Ethan sprinting towards me. He's a square, natural runner, like the bulls in Pamplona tearing pajama pants off clotheslines. "Wait," he says one more time as he gets all the way to me.

A grubby penny of a car gives a polite toot of its horn as it idles, waiting for us to move out of the crosswalk. As soon as the three of us turn and look at it, it lays on the horn full stop, its front windshield reflecting us back to ourselves like mirrored sunglasses.

Ethan and Shep move in the direction we'd been walking, but I go back to the curb I had just crossed from.

They both turn, see I'm not at their sides, and blink around for me. There's too many cars sliding between us and they both look comically stymied. Twenty feet: no way through. I feel oddly powerful standing here by myself, for just a minute.

As soon as the light changes Ethan is back by my side. After a quick, silent *Come over there or stay over here* pointing session, Shep stays on the far side of the street.

"What's up?" I ask Ethan.

"There's something I didn't say back there. I . . . don't know why I didn't . . ."

"Oh. Well. Go ahead now, if you want." I can't help it. There's a small part of me that waits for him to take my hands and tell me he's happy.

He's breathing hard. He's looking at me with an intensity that makes me wonder if I'm even the one he's seeing right now. His head tips up towards the sky and then back down to me. "I—*God*—I have a girlfriend."

Someone's pulled the drain on my internal bathtub and all the water gets sucked away. Rubber duckies spin idly until there's nothing left but cold, wet tile.

"You. Have. A girlfriend."

"Oh. No, no . . . We weren't together, um, back then . . . when you and I . . . I didn't cheat. She'd left me and I thought for sure she really meant it that time. But she came back. A few weeks ago. And . . . I love her so much and I . . ."

He's tipping his head back again, and now I know who he was seeing when he was looking at me: the woman he'd really like to be running towards on the street. The one he loves so much that his eyes are as sparkly as engagement rings. One lone diamond matures under the blue of his iris and then slips over his cheek.

"Oh, God. I'm so sorry," I whisper. Because I am. Because this is . . . this is . . . I don't even know what this is. It's the sound of a thousand doors closing when I hadn't even known they were open in the first place. I feel silly and unlucky.

"Don't be sorry," he says gently. "I don't deserve . . ."

"Wait. Yeah. Why am I sorry?" I ask, and it's not a rhetorical question. "You were there too. *I* didn't know about the love-her-so-much thing."

He hangs his head and his obvious adoration of this woman is a lead blanket over both our shoulders. "I just needed to tell you . . . I couldn't go another two days without telling you that I can't . . . I'm not gonna be able to . . ."

"Acknowledge the pregnancy?" I fill in for him with remarkable aplomb. Seriously, I've found my calling. People should start hiring me to deliver the bitterest medicine with the least emotion. I'm gifted. It can't hurt if it's simply the truth, right?

"What? No! That's not what I meant. I just meant that . . . the way we were that night . . . the flirting . . . the . . . other stuff. I . . . can't be that for you. I can't . . . pick up where we left off."

"Right. Yes," I say awkwardly. "I wasn't assuming . . ." Apparently, I sort of was, but I'll run naked over the Brooklyn Bridge before I let him in on that little secret. Who dreams of happy endings? Clearly losers.

"I didn't think you were!" he hurries in, eagerly game for helping me save face. "I just wanted to be . . . fair to everyone. By being as clear as possible."

I nod and wish he were hate-able. "Thanks," I say. And it seems as ridiculous as saying *Sorry* just moments earlier.

I can no longer pretend I'm not tired all the way down to my white blood cells and so weepy I'm about to burst like an overripe peach. "Ethan . . . thank you for telling me, but . . . can we just pick this up on Tuesday?"

"Yes. Of course."

For him, Tuesday is an elixir and for me it's a poison. Who the hell wants to think about Tuesday when Saturday night was just about all they could take? Ethan, apparently, who's grabbed on with both hands.

He tilts his body towards Shep, so I do too. And there's my friend standing with one foot in a cab, its arms opening around him like I'd like to do.

"Have a good night," Ethan says to my back, and I toss a wave over my shoulder and cross the street to Shep.

"I figured the cab was out of the bag," Shep whispers to me as I come level with him.

He holds the door; I slide past him and the cab is stale cigarettes and bologna sandwich. I roll the window down and breathe into the night. He must've already told the cabdriver my cross streets because we're zooming down Parkside Avenue without another word.

The park is blue and black curlicues out my window, and I bet the air is deliciously crisp between those trees. Maybe there's a witch in there and she's got the spell that will set all this right again.

When we pull up to my apartment, Shep pays the driver and scoots out my still-open door. He pats the top of the cab like it was a good horse and then he leads the way to my door.

I have a classic New York stoop. The kind that midwesterners move here to pay rent for. Red-brown concrete forms wide, substantial steps that end in banisters as thick as the armrests on a recliner chair.

He sits down on those steps and that sounds just about right, so I do too.

"He has a girlfriend," I say tonelessly, my eyes on Shep's feet, which are two inches too long to be confined to one step.

"I heard," he says quietly. And then, when I don't respond, "Your head must be spinning."

"How do other people deal with shocking new information?" I ask him, tracing the zigzag of my shoelaces with one finger.

"Oh, they make big scenes and ruin weddings and throw whipped-cream pies. Or they don't make a peep and they get into their bathtubs and cry their eyes out and believe that all of it was their fault and they were born doomed."

"I think . . ." I say. "I think I'd like to be smack-dab in the middle of those two reactions. A little of column A, a little of column B."

"Ah . . . so you'd like to *eat* the pie in the bathtub."

"Exactly." I snap my fingers and point at him. "He has a *girlfriend*," I groan, and scrunch myself down into a discarded ball of paper. I'm the draft that you mess up irrevocably and have no choice but to toss in the trash can.

"Hey," Shep says. "Question: can someone be 'smack-dab' in anything else but the middle?"

I laugh, against my will, and look up at him, my temple resting against my knees. "How do I seem right now? Like I'm taking this all right?"

"Honestly?" he says quietly. "You seem hurt."

I turn my forehead back down to my knees and the tears gather and drop, gather and drop, a slow-motion spill.

Shep pats my back like he did the cab and it's saying the same thing: *Good job, good job, you're doing exactly what you're supposed to be doing right now.*

And I just snap.

The crying is wretched, ugly, and requires a safety harness. Shep is the perfect fit. My forehead is in his shoulder and then my arms are around his ribs. Our butts are parallel but our tops are twisted towards each other. If he's surprised by the sudden armful of crying friend, he doesn't let on, and the pat-pats turn to round circles the size of a pancake.

"I didn't want to . . ." I'm snorting into Shep's shirt. Only the pillow on my bed in the dark of my midnight bedroom has gotten this sort of undignified treatment. Shep and my pillow: the only two things on this earth that know how I really feel.

"You didn't want to what?"

"I didn't want to tell him that I have to pee *all the time*."

"Oh," Shep says, and I can't be bothered to care whether or not he understands where I'm going with this.

"The first trimester is all weird, personal aches and hunger vomiting and fatigue so deep it's like being pressed to the bottom of the ocean. Having to pee all the time . . . it's, like, the most benign pregnancy symptom ever, and he asked how I'm doing, how I'm feeling, and that's the first thing that came to mind, but I didn't want to tell him. Because I don't *know* him."

"Ohhh." He finally gets it. "Eve, that's okay. You don't have to tell him anything you don't want to."

"But if I don't tell him . . ." *Then I have to go through this alone.*

And there it is. The words are Godzilla big and they've been floating above me for weeks. Now they're falling down around me. Boom. Boom. Boom.

My body tightly shakes.

"And I wanted to *keep talking*," I say, disengaging from the hug and putting my forehead back on my knees. "There are so many things he and I needed to talk about. But I *couldn't* keep talking. Literally. Because I walked all the way to that bar and I'm pregnant and I needed to lie down. So I told him we should talk later . . . and he seemed so *relieved*."

A group of scream-flirting high schoolers chase one another past us on the sidewalk. They get briefly quiet as they witness me crying and hunched over on the stoop, Shep with one hand on my back. *Did you see her? I bet he's breaking up with her.* I don't blame them for thinking it.

After they're gone, the word *relieved* is still ringing in the space between Shep and me.

"What're you thinking up there?" I ask him, because he's got his deep-thoughts eyebrows going, his bottom lip caught between white teeth.

"I'm thinking about my mom . . . at the end. You remember my aunt Carol? Carol is really . . . well, she's a piece of work. And my mom always, *always* spent time with her on Sunday afternoons. But it was always terrible and she'd come home in a bad mood. But towards the end, my mom was too sick to do it. Her body just wouldn't let her go there. At first, she felt terribly guilty, like she was failing somehow. But then, eventually she realized that . . . sometimes . . ." Shep says slowly. "Sometimes our bodies take charge of us. My mom's body just knew that she didn't need to be prioritizing Carol in the last few months of her life. It helped her let go of that crappy relationship. And for you . . . your brain wanted to keep talking to Ethan tonight, to get everything hammered into place, but your body knew that it wasn't the time. You got tired and had to leave. Maybe that's your body taking care of you."

Shep and I sit in silence for another few minutes until he stands up in front of me and holds two hands out. "Bedtime," he says firmly.

I take both of his hands and let him gently haul me to my feet.

He waits while I unlock the door and when I get upstairs and peek out onto the street, he's still standing on my stoop. I click on the light by the window; he sees it, then turns and walks in the direction of the nearest subway station.

I'd like to say I do more than shuck off my shoes, pants, and bomber jacket and shimmy my way under the covers, but you know when you have a 103-degree fever and you're thirsty but mustering the energy to lift a glass to your lips is inconceivable? Those are the fatigue levels we're talking about right now.

I'm in my bed, itchy with exhaustion, and my mind does a few frantic circles of the night I've just had. Willa somewhere, crying over a period she desperately didn't want. Ethan asking me to cover my eyes. Bones, oblivious, ever-present. *I have a girlfriend. I love her so much.* Tuesday, Tuesday, fucking Tuesday. And finally, my mind rests on Shep's words to me on the stoop.

Don't worry, Eve, your body is taking care of you.

It's a novel idea. Because if it's not just *me* taking care of my body. If listening to my body means that *it's* taking care of me too, then . . . maybe, just maybe . . . I'm not completely alone.

Five

Can we just not talk about pregnancy for a little bit? Great. Thanks.

How about work?

Yeah. I'm all about work these days. Just joking. I haven't been all about work since about a month after I got hired. Here's the thing about working in admin at a do-gooder non-profit. You are not the rock star. You order lunch for the rock stars. All the policy analysts and research fellows and liaisons to the this or that, they need constant care. Behind every man is a strong woman blah blah puke. Well, behind every non-profit's earnest tears-in-the-eyes mission statement is an administrative team keeping the organization's belt from falling around its ankles.

Exhibit A: It's Monday afternoon and the admin team is standing in front of our boss's desk. Xaria is intensely badass. She's the only original remaining member of WFA from when it officially became an NGO in the seventies. She was the cleaning lady who moved up to facilities manager and up and up the admin ladder until now, where she's the highest you can possibly go without being an executive: the head of finance and administration.

She wears exclusively animal print and even in her seventies has hair so shiny and dark it's like coffee spilling in slow motion. She scares the absolute shit out of the program staff.

She is the admin team's last resort. If the rest of us are dart guns, Xaria is a bazooka.

"It's Monday afternoon," she says. *Battle stations,* she means.

Micah, Bevi, and I ready ourselves for dispatch.

"Bevi, today I'd like for you to organize the outstanding vendor invoices."

The three of us freeze. That's normally Micah's job.

"Micah, show Bevi the folder with the invoices and teach her our filing system. When you're done with that, make rounds and collect the overdue expense reports."

Micah and I exchange glances. Collecting the overdue expense reports on a gloomy Monday afternoon is my job. Poor sap. He's going to spend the next hour reteaching half-listening policy analysts how to press command-P while they frantically answer emails and pretend that their work is more essential to the org than ours is.

But I can't worry about Micah's fate right now because if Bevi has Micah's job and Micah has mine, then . . .

"And Eve, I'd like you to stay behind."

Oh, boy.

Micah and Bevi head back out into the annex, casting worried glances back at me. I mean, I know I'm not winning any Nobel Environmental Prizes anytime soon, but I don't think I'm so useless as to get sacked on this random Monday.

I shift on my feet and try not to preemptively panic. "Everything all right?" I can't help but ask.

Xaria drums her perfect manicure (jet-black nails, two gigantic silver rings, neither on her ring finger) on the desk and then taps a stack of papers, drawing my eyes to it. I squint. I can't be sure, but something about them looks familiar. Is that . . .

"You've been doing this newsletter for how long now?" she asks.

Something about the fact that she's printed and collated the entire backlog of my e-newsletter tells me she already knows the answer to this question. It's something I started doing when I realized that no one ever knows a thing about anyone else's projects around here. I send the email out about once a month, just to update everyone about the state of each project we're running. I gulp. "About two years?"

She nods. "I'm a fan."

"Oh! Oh, that's great. Yeah. Thanks."

She leans back and crosses her arms in a thoughtful way. "It's not in your job description."

"Right . . . Well, I work on it on my lunch hour, or at home. Or—" I gulp again. "Or if all of my other work is already finished and I have a spare minute." I think I've accidentally just admitted that I occasionally get paid to sit around. And also that I'm willing to do unpaid work on my own time. Can I have a do-over, please?

But Xaria just nods placidly. "You must care a lot about the org if you're doing this on your downtime."

"Of course!" I rush to say, because re: my job: I really freaking need one. "Yes, I really do!" (Do I actually? IDK.)

"It's interesting to see WFA through your eyes. You clearly want to help the org run smoothly."

I blink. I mean, sure. When things are humming along smoothly, my days are a lot less hectic around here. But I mostly write the newsletter because I'm a fangirl for conservation work. And without that pesky graduate degree, it's the only way I can get a taste of what the policy analysts are actually doing up there.

"And frankly," she continues. "Having a clear layout of

each program's progress and efficiency has been extremely illuminating to me."

She pulls out another sheaf of papers. These ones are filled with numbers and dollar signs. And red highlighter.

I didn't even know they made red highlighters until I met Xaria.

"We use the expense reports to understand how our budget is spent on a micro level," she says, putting on a pair of cat-eye readers. "But it can be harder, on a macro level, to get a clear picture—" She cuts off and eyes me. "Take a seat."

When I first got pregnant I had this precious little hope that I might be the one woman who could keep wearing heels to the office and my morning sickness wouldn't be that bad and a bluebird would perch atop my shoulder and tell me how awesome I am at every turn.

But alas, my feet are basically pulsing potatoes filled with too much blood.

Needless to say, I take a seat so fast that the chair tips onto two legs before it settles.

Xaria is still eyeing me. I think she senses my raging nerves because she smiles. "You're not in trouble, Eve. I'm thanking you. I think you might be extremely helpful in managing a bit of our budget crisis."

I know, I know. Shocker! Environmental nonprofit in the midst of a dire financial hemorrhage. Still, I glance down at Xaria's papers; that's a *lot* more red than I thought there might be.

"When you're working on your newsletter, just try to keep these numbers in mind." She slides the highlighted financials over to me. "Jot down some notes on what fits where . . . moneywise."

She wants me to weigh each program's efficiency and results against their existing budget. AKA, she wants me to decide which program to axe.

Oh, lord. I picture a face-off between the Bowhead Whale team and the Javan Rhino team. The fate of the conservation for each animal resting squarely on my shoulders.

Sure, Eve. That sounds like something you can totally handle right now.

"I'm really not sure I'm the right person for this job," I say quietly.

She claps her hands once, like I've already agreed. "Well, give it a shot for the next couple months. We'll see what you come up with."

I'm dismissed and as I'm passing through the door, Xaria calls to me again. "And go see if you can't rescue Micah. I'm sure they're eating him for breakfast up there."

Tuesday I wake up and all I can think about is plain cake donuts. And the fact that it is *the* Tuesday. By the time three PM rolls around I'm dozy and grumpy and hungry and nauseated. I want a sleeping bag in the sun next to an ice-cold stream with water so clear and crisp it hurts. On Tuesdays I generally do an inventory of all—count 'em—seven supply closets so that I can put orders in for anything that's running low. But those seven supply closets are on three different floors and even the idea of standing up to get on the elevator makes me want to cry.

Three thirty hits and I still haven't done my inventory. Four o'clock.

"Are you all right, honey?" Bevi asks from behind me where she's watering the plants with a watering can the size of a medium-sized dog. She's got biceps like a shotputter.

"Yes!" I say immediately, jumping to my feet. I scurry out of the annex and resolve to do my job double time: (1) because I don't want my co-workers to suspect anything is off about me, and (2) because once when I confessed to Bevi that I felt a little under the weather, the next day she brought me some homemade beet juice and made me drink it in front of her. I had the runs for a day and a half.

Five o'clock hits and it's time to go sit with Ethan in Prospect Park and *talk* like we said we would. Which means I have to come face-to-face with the fact that all I've done is fantasize about donuts and I haven't prepared for this conversation at all.

"Hi," I say from ten feet away, waving one mitten at him.

"Hi!" He jumps up from our pre-decided-upon bench, looking absolutely gorgeous in a wool coat. Even in the blue dusk, his hair is the burnished orange of an heirloom copper pot passed down as a wedding present. I collapse onto the bench, gazing at the little lake on the south end of the park that does a great job of pretending it doesn't have six inches of litter lining the bottom.

"Wow," I say. "That's a lot of geese." Because it is. There must be at least sixty geese I can see without even turning my head.

"Yeah. I thought they'd all be down in Florida by now. Or wherever they go." He kicks a rock.

"Probably Florida," I agree.

"So . . ." he says when it becomes clear that neither of us has anything else to say about geese or Florida. "How are you feeling?"

I wince a little. But he doesn't know this is a sensitive topic. For any pregnant woman, probably, but especially one who doesn't know you well enough to tell the truth. "I'm okay," I halfway lie. He patiently waits for more, his hands in the pockets of his coat and his knees tipped towards me. "A little nauseous," I add.

He nods, like that's the answer he'd been looking for, and then sits back to watch the lake.

"How are *you* feeling?" I ask after a long pause.

"Um." He clears his throat. "Scared."

My stomach cramps down.

"And . . . and something else," he continues. "But I can't quite . . . identify it."

Well, *something else* is certainly no *happy*, but I guess I'll take it.

I groan and cover my face. "This would be so much easier if one of us were just blindingly happy."

When I look up, he's studying me, his lips sucked into his mouth. "So . . . you're not happy, then?"

The idea of simply saying *No* makes me feel like a total piece of shit, so instead I go with "Not . . . quite . . . yet."

He reels back an inch and I watch as his eyes stop seeing me and start seeing his inner thoughts. He's a mile a minute in there and I don't know why.

"Ethan?" I ask, and he drops his face into his hands and leans forwards and breathes deeply. "Are you okay?"

"You said 'not yet.' Which . . . which means that you're thinking there will be a *later*."

I blink at him. "Um. Yeah? What do you . . . Oh." The penny drops. "You're asking me if I'm planning on keeping it?"

His hands slide forwards off his face, poised for praying, as he tips his head and looks at me. "Are you?" he asks quietly.

Obviously, I figured he'd ask, because this is information he deserves to be privy to. But even so, this is one of those questions that is so raw, so tender, so life-changing, that there is no preparing for it.

When I speak, my voice is cheese-grater nervous. "I am

going to keep . . ." I trail off and the two words that would finish that sentence float up, unsaid, between us. *The baby.* "Being pregnant," I finish lamely.

"Okay," he says, taking a deep breath and then pushing it out all at once. "Okay." His hands run over his face, all the way up, over his hair, and then grip his knees. "Okay. Thank you for telling me."

He opens his mouth, a question on his face, but thinks better of it and turns back to the geese instead. He tries one more time with the same result.

"I know this is overwhelming, but . . ." I say, laying one hand on his shoulder for just a half second. "Maybe we can figure it out as we go?"

He pauses and something occurs to me.

"Unless," I start slowly. "Unless you're thinking you already know that you don't want to be involved."

"That's not what I want," he says immediately. He's up like a shot and walking so fast towards the lake I actually think he might step right off the bank and in. But he doesn't. He stops abruptly, watching the geese with his hands in his pockets and when he walks back towards me, something about the set of his shoulders makes tears sting in my eyes.

He sits back down on the bench, but this time on the opposite side of me as before. It's vaguely disorienting.

"My sisters have all been pregnant."

"Oh." I blink at him. "How many do you have?"

He smiles but it's momentary and a little sad. Nothing like the rocket-fuel, pointy-toothed, crescent-moon grin that got us into this mess in the first place. "Four."

"Wow."

"I'm just saying," he says, and kicks another rock. This time it goes unexpectedly far and startles a goose. "Oh. Whoops."

I can't help but laugh. He's embarrassed that he's agitated an innocent creature. He jolts as I chuckle, and now *he's* the unsettled innocent creature.

"I just . . . I know, from my sisters, how . . . intimate pregnancy can be. And I . . . I'll let you take the lead on the when and where of my involvement."

"Ah. Okay," I say. But what I mean is who wants to *take the lead,* ever? Right now, sitting on this bench, dreaming of donuts and a ten-year vacation and a pair of fleece jammies, I've never wanted to be in charge less.

I imagine what he's imagining. Doctor's appointments, surely. Now, not only do I have to get my ass to these appointments, open my legs, let Nurse Blank poke around and take pictures . . . *Now* I also have to figure out beforehand whether or not to invite Ethan? I know he's trying to be thoughtful, but all I actually want is for one of us to know exactly what to do next and to take us there at top speed.

But my single *Okay* seems to be the same fairy dust as *Tuesday* once was for us. He's sitting there looking immensely relieved that I've agreed to his arrangement. I'm the brains and he's the muscle. All he has to do is whatever I tell him. It's such crap I want to cry.

I need to change the subject before I actually do cry. I clear my throat. "So, how'd your girlfriend take it?"

He freezes in place and only his eyes slide over to look at me.

"Oh." I realize all at once. "You haven't told her yet."

"I . . ." he tries, and his voice flames out like a faulty match. "I didn't know what to tell her." His eyes move again. "But now I do."

Ah. Of course. The highlights: I won't be terminating the pregnancy and he's my minion now.

I understand the desire to have all the information when

you drop a bomb like this on the girlfriend you love so much it makes you cry on the street, but still, it strikes me as slightly *off* that he didn't tell her yet. It's been almost three full days since he found out. They must have been three terribly hard days for him. Keeping it as a stiff little secret seems . . . almost as incriminating as the secret itself.

"Ah. Well, good luck." I look at my hands in my mittens. Why don't they make giant mittens that can cover you from the part of your hair to the tips of your toes? "Let me know if . . ."

I trail off and don't finish the sentence.

. . . if you need me?

. . . if it doesn't go well?

. . . if she leaves you?

. . . if there's anything I can do?

I'm exhausted.

"Eve . . ." Ethan starts, and suddenly, he's facing me. Full on. Everything I want to know is right there in his eyes. He's open and handing it to me in fistfuls. "Look, just to be clear—"

A sudden, unexpected pressure on my arm has me jerking around. And there, right there, is a man sitting in the spot where Ethan first sat at the beginning of this conversation. And he's just wedged about six fully loaded grocery bags onto the bench between us, crowding my space and smooshing me to one side. I glance to either side of us and see empty benches fanning out in a long, neat row. It's a chilly November dinnertime, all of New York is inside breaking bread, there's an entire park full of empty benches, and this rando chooses ours.

"Unbelievable," Ethan mutters.

"I need a donut," I mutter to myself.

Ethan stands up and offers me a hand. It's a light touch between us and my mitten slips. I haul my own weight up. Ethan brings his hand up to his hair and muss-muss-smooths it. He glances at the man who has just pinched open a loaf of bread.

There's a blur of gray-brown movement, a sudden onslaught of bleating honks, and I laugh in horror as dozens of geese come rushing us on their waxy, flapping paddlers.

"Oh, shit." Ethan's pinching me by the elbow and we're scrambling and barely make it out alive. The bench-stealer is the king of the geese.

Both of us are stunned, watching the churning, honking mess from a safe distance. Finally Ethan breaks the silence. "Should we . . . ? Should we walk around the lake instead? It's kind of chilly for sitting anyhow."

"I . . . I should probably go home and rest." I say it like it's doctor's orders and not my potato-feet's orders.

"Oh. Right. Of course." He looks like he hates himself for suggesting a stroll.

"So I'll call you—or text you—soon, okay?"

He nods and I nod. His hands come out of their pockets. "Can I?" he asks.

And this right here is quickly becoming my favorite thing about Ethan. The goodbye hug. No, it's more than that. It's the *Can-I?* hug.

"Yes."

I can't feel his warmth through our winter wear, but that's okay. He smells like wool and cool air on warm-blooded breather. I'd like to ice-skate next to that scent.

We walk out of the park side by side and silent. When we get to the cobblestone sidewalk that lines the exterior of the park, it's clear we're going to walk in opposite directions. We wave and turn our backs.

"Hey, Eve?" he calls, and I turn back to him. "I know I said . . . but can I . . . would it be all right if I texted or called you too?"

His *Can-I's* are balm for so much that is stinging and raw in my gut. I love his *Can-I's*.

"Not for anything specific," he clarifies when I don't immediately respond. "Like I said, you're in charge, so . . . I'm asking in general, if it's okay for me to check in with you."

"Yes," I say firmly. And I mean that *yes* in every way possible.

Six

Enough is enough. I'm standing on Willa's welcome mat, staring at the outside of her apartment door. It's Saturday night, a week after Shep escorted me to Good Boy, and I haven't seen Willa since any of that happened. Normally I would have laid the entire story at her feet the morning after, but knowing what she was going through, I opted for space instead. She didn't ask and I didn't offer. I have no idea where we stand, and I have no idea what to do about it. So that brings us to here: welcome mat. I'm frozen, too nervous to knock. I've never once hesitated to burst into Willa's home, but I don't think I can take more awkward, nowhere-to-look treatment. *Okay, pull it together, Hatch.* I raise my arm and before I can think much more about it, I knock knock knock.

Willa throws open the door in nothing but Spanx and a sports bra. "Does this bra give me uni-boob?" she asks, and just like that, my nervousness evaporates. The week of silence immediately seems . . . less consequential in the face of all this normalcy.

An hour later, I'm on Willa's couch and she's got two thumbs punishing the arch of my foot for ever having been born. I gurgle my appreciation into one of her throw pillows. It's torture, delicious and necessary. At this point I'd endure anything if it means my feet deflate.

Twenty minutes after I arrived there'd been another knock on her door, and she'd bounded over to collect a mysterious, greasy paper bag from a delivery man who looked like he was going to faint at the sight of her Spanx.

"Ta-da!" she'd said, and shoved a bag of the most perfect almond brown plain cake donuts I'd ever seen in my life at me. *How did she . . . ?*

That's her unique skill. Fixing me right up good.

I give her the rundown on Ethan and she gasps in all the right places. I tell her the story in linear order, so she doesn't find out he has a girlfriend until she's standing there on the sidewalk either. I tell it like the great story that it is and I almost, almost don't feel like that crumpled-up ball of paper at the end.

"Well," she says, hauling herself up from the couch to pour herself something green from the fridge, "honestly, it's probably better this way? I mean, what were the odds you were gonna end up in a functional relationship with this guy? Probably pretty low. Not because there's anything wrong with either of you, but it's hard to find something functional with anyone. Even when you're looking hard and dating and vetting them and shit. Yeah, I think this girlfriend, whoever she is, probably saved you from, like, an eventual nasty breakup from the guy who got you pregnant."

It's a horrible thing to say and it immediately makes me feel better. "That's a fantastic point."

She wags the acid-green liquid at me in offering and I stick my tongue out, gagging.

"You need fluids," she says. "Pick your poison."

"Oh . . . ice water, please."

"Okay," she says with an authoritative clap of her hands after she hands me the ice water. "It's time to run the numbers."

I put my hands over my eyes and play dead on her couch.

"Eve, we *have* to do this. You need to know the financials of having a kid."

She parks next to me with her laptop and pulls up a spreadsheet with a shocking number of tabs. Words like *diapers* slap me across the face. But it's the tabs labeled *Hospital, Daycare,* and, of course, *Emergency Fund* that really make my eyes water. By the time we run the numbers, the numbers are running me.

Willa is wearing librarian glasses and aggressively showing a calculator who's boss.

I'm torn between being ecstatically relieved that my sweet friend is taking charge for me and terrified of what she's about to tell me about my finances.

"What's the damage?" I finally get up the courage to ask.

She surveys me over the glasses. "You're tired."

"*That's* your answer? Oh, God, it must be bleak."

"No," she says slowly, folding her glasses up and putting her laptop aside. "It's . . . incomplete. There are things I haven't accounted for . . . Let me work on this and I'll send it to you when I'm done?"

"Willa, it's okay. You don't need to panic about my finances for me. That should be *my* responsibility."

She looks down at her hands for a long moment. Her eyes are filled with something when she looks back up at me. "Eve . . . I couldn't . . . I can't . . . But I *can* do *this* for you. Let me. Please."

I think of Shep showing up at Good Boy. All the awkward conversations and moments with Willa since I told her I was pregnant. The week of silence since she got her period. Yeah, there are a lot of things we can't do for each other right now. Can I let her do this for me? In place of everything else?

"Okay," I whisper.

Her front door jangles and clangs as someone gets their

key stuck in the lock, jimmies it free, and then tries again. It swings open all at once, smacking the adjacent wall, and bounces back on Shep, who fights his way inside.

He looks up, sees me melted into the couch like a chocolate bar somebody sat on, and gives me a surprised smile.

"Hey!"

"Wait a second," I say with a frown. "Don't I know you from somewhere?"

He instantly frowns back at me, stroking an imaginary beard. "Yeah, you look awfully familiar."

"Oh, I know," I say with a snap of my fingers. "You're the guy whose shirt I snotted all over last weekend."

"Aha!" He points at me. "That's *right.* I thought I recognized that schnoz."

Willa rearranges a pillow under my feet. "You snotted on his shirt?"

She looks back and forth between us.

The joke dissolves and the actual memory sets in. The catatonic cab ride and tears on my front stoop.

"Yeah," I tell Willa. "I had a rather *poignant* moment of self-doubt."

She squeezes my feet again and looks blankly at Shep. "You had told me that it all went well."

Her blank-angry looks are scarier than her angry-angry looks, but Shep is an expert at evading her. He flops down into the armchair across from us. I expect him to say something like *I didn't want to tell her business.* But instead, he leans his head on one hand, his knees knocked out to the sides, and looks me straight in the eye as he talks to her. "It *did* go well."

"Shep," I say with an incredulous laugh, my chin dropping down an inch. "Come on."

"No!" he insists, sitting up straight. "I really think it did."

Willa glares at him. "The guy has a *girlfriend,* Shep. And

he didn't tell Eve until the very end. And now I hear she had a poignant moment of self-doubt? How does that translate into 'went well'?"

He's indignant. "You should've seen her, Willa. She marched in there, so brave I—it was really something. And then he wasn't behind the bar and even so she persevered. And she was patient and really kind to him, and even though he freaked out a little, he was kind too, right, Eve? They *hugged* at the end. And he told the truth about having a girlfriend. He could have just not said anything and that would have been far worse in the long run. And then, when the truth was hard to hear, she cried instead of pretending she was all right. In my book, that means it went well. She did great. She did better than great."

I blink at this description. A moment in my life through Shep's eyes. "I . . . guess he's right if you think about it," I say to Willa. "The facts are the facts. At some point I was going to have to tell a man with a girlfriend that I'm pregnant because of him. And all things considered, the outcome of that could have been far worse than what happened last weekend. I hadn't really . . . thought of it like that." I say the last in Shep's direction and I don't have to look at him to know that he's beaming.

Willa's about to say more when the front door gets smoothly unlocked and Isamu quietly pads in, sliding his shoes neatly into their parking spot in Willa's shoe basket and giving everyone a wave. Isamu is half Japanese and half white. He spent part of his childhood in Japan with his dad and half his childhood in Poughkeepsie with his mom. These days he's been wearing charming-ugly glasses with huge wire frames and his shiny hair in a shag he has to constantly shake out of his eyes. Something about his personality makes him utterly un-micromanageable, which is why Willa fell so freaking hard for him.

He's the one person in the world she completely relaxes around. "Hi. *Hi!*" he says when he realizes I'm there too. "Are you staying for dinner? I brought Thai food home."

He proudly holds up a paper bag, the smell wafts over, and I must go green because Willa is on her feet like a warrior, one finger slicing towards her husband. "Put that in the hallway! You'll make her ralph!"

Isamu disposes of the food like he's just been informed there's a bomb in need of disarming in there. He even double-locks the door when he comes back inside.

"Sorry," he says, eyes wide.

"No, no." I wave my hand. "Actually, I should go anyhow."

"What?"

"Stay!" Willa and Shep intone at the same time.

It's only eight-fifteen, but by the time I get home it'll likely be about eight-forty-five. Showered-lotioned-tucked-in-by-nine-fifteen sounds like just the cure for this past week.

"I'm tired," I say to the Balder siblings, and their protests die on their tongues.

Isamu is suddenly bright as a full moon, toeing back into his shoes. "Hey, I'm borrowing a friend's car right now so that I can move some equipment tomorrow. I can give you a ride home!"

He's clearly thrilled to redeem himself from the accidental Thai food mishap, and there is absolutely no point in not taking the ride when he's smiling at me like that.

I get a hug and a hair-fix from Willa, a hug and a squashed toe from Shep, and then I'm buttoned into my coat, a mitten pushed onto either hand by either sibling, and I'm toddling after Isamu down to the car.

"Sometimes they're so alike it's freaky," I say as we buckle our seatbelts.

"Who? Oh, Willa and Shep? Yeah, I know."

"Are you sick of him living with you yet?"

"Um?" Isamu scrunches up half his face, accidentally making eye contact with me, and we both burst out laughing.

"So, that's a yes."

"It's not a yes," Isamu says, pulling up cleanly to a red light, his knee jumping impatiently. Isamu's always been an interesting set of contradictions. He's anxious and full of snap-snap energy, but also somehow smooth. He knows how to harness all that energy, I guess. Maybe it's being a lifetime jazz musician, but he always shows up in the exact right moments.

"But it's not a no."

He sighs. "I'm sure you and Willa have been through this already, but the whole actively-trying-to-get-pregnant thing is stressful enough without knowing a family member is in the next room with noise-canceling headphones on."

"Oh. *Yikes.*" I shudder jokingly, and Isamu laughs. But on the inside, I'm wilting. No, Willa and I have not talked about that. It's an intensely private thing, but we almost always talk about intensely private things with each other. I hadn't thought about how having Shep there might make their conception-sex endeavors more awkward.

When they first started trying a couple of years ago, Willa kept me horribly abreast of the situation. We charted *everything* together. I knew more about Willa's cervical mucus than I knew about my own. But as time went on and she just kept *not* being pregnant, she let me in less and less. It's her body and her life, so I let her set the pace on what she told me. But now I'm wondering if she just turned off the faucet of information completely. Now I don't even know how she feels about her brother hogging up her guest bedroom.

Tears pinch and I turn my head to look out the window so

that Isamu can't see. Do pregnancies just naturally disrupt your friendships and that's that?

I can't help but wonder . . . if Willa were the one who was pregnant . . . would everything be changing? Is this because I'm *pregnant*? Or is this because *I'm* pregnant?

Seven

"Isn't this early to be showing this much?" I pull my sweater tight over my belly and peer down at it.

"That's constipation. Not the baby." Nurse Blank's bedside manner: 12/12. "You haven't had a bowel movement in"—she consults her chart—"seventy-two hours. Prune juice will help. Take your pants off and put this on. The doctor will be in in a moment."

This twelve-week appointment is the big one, according to my pregnancy book. Everyone stops tiptoeing around because it's far less likely to lose a pregnancy after week twelve.

I've spoken to Ethan twice in the last three weeks. Both times over the phone. The first time went something like this:

"Hello?"

(Silence.)

"Ethan? Are you there?"

"Yes, Yes, sorry. I'm here." (Wind whistling on his end of the line.)

"Are you in the arctic tundra? Why is it so windy?"

"Sorry. I'm just on a walk. A long one."

"Well, you sound cold."

"I've been out since this morning."

"This *morning*? It's four PM!"

"Yeah. Well. I told Eleni."

(Silence on my end, now. A wash of unexpected relief and gratitude. He's done something, a big something, to show me

I'm not in this alone. My heart swells with whatever the opposite of despair is.) "How did it go?"

"Well, I've been on a walk since nine in the morning, that should tell you something."

"That well, huh?"

"She . . . she can't even look at me right now."

". . . I'm sorry."

"Please don't be. This is all my—" (All his *fault,* I presume. My previous relief and gratitude withers by at least sixty percent. For a moment there I'd felt like comrades. Now I remember that my whoopsy-daisy = his mistake of a lifetime.)

"Well, thanks for . . ." (Telling her? What was he going to do, bring it to the grave?) "Telling me that you told her."

"Sure. Yes. Of course. Um. How are you feeling?"

(Frustrated at the moment, and I'm not exactly sure why.) "Good! Fine. Tired a lot. Still pretty queasy. But such is life for a pregnant person."

"Okay. Well. I'm glad it's going . . . according to plan." (This almost makes me burst out into maniacal laughter, but I restrain myself.) "Call me if . . . well, anytime, actually. You can call me anytime."

". . . Okay. Thanks." (Sweet of him to say that, really. But still, I can't help but note that this likely means he's probably not going to be calling *me*.)

Anyways, the second phone call was just this very morning. I'd dutifully informed him about my twelve-week appointment today and neither of us could tell whether or not I was inviting him. He'd wished me luck and I'd hung up.

And now he's probably pants-off in bed with the love of his life and I'm pants-off under a paper blanket once again trying to figure out what to do with my hands.

Dr. Bridget Muscles comes in and she's got Princess Leia buns in her long blond hair today. She pokes and prods and asks me all the same questions that Nurse Blank has already asked. She shows me a black-and-white screen with my insides pulsing and living there for everyone to see.

"Hi," I say to the screen. Because I still can't make out a dang thing, but it seems rude not to say anything.

Everything looks good to her so she asks me to come back in four weeks and then it's just me and the nurse again. She slides out a cloth curtain to let me change in privacy and I can hear her out there on her keyboard, writing another novel.

"Nurse?" I say.

"Do you need a hand?" she asks automatically.

"No! No. I just . . ." I'm talking to the curtain, which I realize now is covered in a pink pattern that looks disturbingly like puddles of blood. I immediately feel that this is a Rorschach test I've almost certainly failed. "I'm just wondering if it's . . . atypical that I'm here alone."

There's a brief pause. And then, "No. Many women do this alone."

"*This* meaning the exams or—" I skate open the curtain and look at her back. "Motherhood?"

"Both," she says briskly, turning to me. She's got a stack of pamphlets in her hand.

I don't take the pamphlets, and she lowers her hand.

She sighs. "Some women don't *have* partners to join them here. Some women have partners but prefer to do the exams without an audience. Some partners work during the day and can't make it to all or any of the appointments. We see everything here."

Now that she's given me more than a one-word answer, I'm willing to take her pamphlets. I look down at the first one I see and laugh with a shake of my head.

"What?" she asks.

"These are always such *crap*. The woman is always smiling and looking out a brightly lit window with one hand on her perfect bump. If these were accurate, she'd be yakking her guts out in a trash can on East 54th Street hoping her co-workers don't see her on their lunch break and think she's hungover."

Her lips twitch and I mentally high-five myself. A slight lip twitch on Nurse Blank is like making an average person pee their pants with laughter.

"Pregnancy is different for everyone," she says.

"Have you . . . ?" I ask her. There's something about her, *something* that tells me she's definitely been through this firsthand.

"Yes."

"And were you gazing peacefully out a window or publicly yakking in a trash can?"

"I was a peach," she tells me with a straight face.

I burst out laughing. "Fair enough."

She turns and starts digging in a drawer. "No. I was tender and sore and everything made me cry. The grocery list made me cry. The sound of my dog's nails on the kitchen tile made me cry. Just remember, when you're pregnant, nothing is real. Everything is seen through the funhouse mirror of pregnancy. Try not to make any big decisions. Heavy machinery, et cetera. Everything you're feeling is a pregnancy symptom. Don't take it too seriously. These'll help with the nausea." She puts a handful of bright red lollipops into my hand atop the pamphlets. "And it should be letting up soon."

I look at the perfect, round candies, handed to me by someone who doesn't like to show she cares, and maybe it's the echoing ghost of a dog's toenails but I'm feeling the sting of tears in my eyes.

"Week twelve," she says after a moment, "is also when a lot of women start to tell their outer circle about the pregnancy . . .

if you need something to tell your co-workers about the public yakking."

"Co-workers?" I say, unwrapping the cellophane off one of the lollipops. "I haven't even told my family yet."

She points one finger at me. "Prune juice. Or else that"—the pointing finger moves down to my belly—"is not gonna be a secret you're gonna be able to hide for much longer."

My twelve-week appointment was a lunch break appointment, so I head back to the office with yet another silver-gray ultrasound tucked neatly into my messenger bag. It's right next to the other two I've been given in previous appointments. They're obsessed with these things at Lower East Side Partners in Obstetrics and Gynecology. The woman at the desk hands them over every time I leave like it's the best part of her day. Every time I don't squeal and coo over the blurry, shadowy image, she clearly dies a little inside. I'm definitely failing her.

Speaking of people I'm failing, I have a meeting with Xaria.

She's clickity-clacking an email at an alarming pace when I knock on her door. She immediately gives me her complete and utter attention and I immediately wish I were a pebble on a beach far, far away from here.

"So," she says, waving me into the chair across from her desk. "How's our project going?"

How does one tell their boss they've literally just *not* done what was asked of them?

"To be honest . . ." I clear my throat. Honesty is terrible. Who invented it? They should be the one who has to break this news to Xaria. "I haven't made any headway."

She gives one brisk nod. "Can I ask why?"

"Um. Well . . ." Because I don't want to be responsible for

putting valuable projects on the chopping block? Because I don't want to undercut the work of people whose jobs I'd kill to have? Because I don't want to take the one thing I truly enjoy about my job and turn it into a misery? "It's a . . . big task to take on."

To my surprise, she nods again. "You're right." *I am?* "Maybe what I asked of you was unfair. Unpaid work . . . not my style. I like to take care of my team, and I didn't think about how this would impact your workload."

I can think of nothing to say, so I go ahead and don't say anything.

The silence extends. And then . . .

"Eve," Xaria asks me, her chin resting on one perfectly manicured hand. "What do you like about your job?"

I like having one.

"I . . ." I search desperately for a version of the truth that won't get me fired. "I like the people I work with." Which is true. Partially. I like Micah and Bevi and Christina. And I fear Xaria. In a sort of wholesome way. "And I like knowing that I'm . . . helping."

"Helping. Okay. Well, how would you like to start helping me in an official capacity?"

I gape. "As . . . your assistant?"

She laughs. "No, no. Instead of continuing on as an administrative assistant, I was thinking of taking you on as a financial assistant. It would be a lateral move, same pay and vacation, et cetera. But it would put you on the financial team. And then projects like this would align more with your job description."

I pause. She pauses.

"There's a lot more room to move up on the financial team," she prods.

Which is true. My stomach's gone sour.

I say the first thing that comes to mind. "Oh, wow . . . um . . . thank you. But . . . I'm really very happy where I am, Xaria."

She frowns. "Why don't you give it some thought?"

I nod, because I know I should. "Okay. I will."

She dismisses me with a discerning eye and a tip of her chin.

My mind spinning, I plop down into my desk chair and wait for my afternoon siege of fatigue and nausea to hit me. It doesn't but I pop a lollipop anyhow. It's cherry-flavored perfection.

I've been clicking around in spreadsheets for an hour when my phone da-dings twice in a row. I have two texts. One from Ethan that reads: *How did the appointment go?* And one from Shep that reads: *Puked in any trash cans today?*

I laugh. But I know who I have to respond to first. *Healthy on all counts,* I text back to Ethan. Our texts to each other are just so . . . dutiful. *I go back in four weeks.* I chew my lip for a moment and then add, *Thanks for checking in.*

Then I text Shep back. *Surprisingly no, but the night is young.*

Da-ding. *How come we say that the beginning of the night is young but we don't say that the end of the night is old?*

I laugh again. *Why do we say that we have to get our ducks in a row when we want to get something organized?* I text back. *What's so important about lining up ducks?*

Da-ding. *Yeah, yeah, you're right! And what are we lining them up to do? Oh, God . . . it's not for execution, is it?* He sends a gif of a little girl crying facedown on the floor.

I'm laughing more. *That got dark so fast. Thanks for cheering me up.*

Da-ding. I look down for my next text from Shep but it's actually Ethan. He's thumbs-upped my doctor's appointment update.

Shep texts. *Why did you need cheering up?*

Solo doctor's appointment, cold exam table, no pants, stirrups etc. Straight into a meeting with my boss.

That's so weird! he texts, *I had a no-pants/stirrups appointment today too.* He sends a gif of a stripper dancing in assless chaps.

I can't hide the smile.

The rest of the afternoon goes more quickly than expected. When five o'clock hits I'm pleasantly . . . well, not surprised, because even on my best days at work I'm still watching the clock like a hawk . . . but let's say *pleased.* Everyone else makes road-runner dust swirls as they jet out of work, but I stay behind and finish up an email. I hit the bathroom and am just walking out of the building at five-twenty-eight when I get a text.

I look down and see it's from Shep. I can't help but smile. *What time do you get off work?*

Just got out, I text back.

"Eve!" I look up and twenty feet away, there Shep is, one arm drawing an upside-down U over his head. And then he's jogging towards me.

"What are you doing here?" I ask, shocked.

"I wanted to surprise you, but when five o'clock passed, I realized I should have asked before I came and *ooomph.*"

The revolving door of my office is starting to turn and though there are a whole building's worth of other orgs that are housed here, I have the horrid suspicion that it is definitely gonna be a group of my co-workers coming out right now, about to see me with a man.

And normally, I wouldn't care. But I'm pregnant. And

Nurse Blank's voice is echoing in my head: pretty soon they're gonna *know* I'm pregnant. And if they see me now, standing with this random, tall, wide-shouldered man who shouts my name and surprises me after work, they might think that this man, this one right here, whose mouth I'm covering with my palm and dragging to one side like a rag doll, is the father. My brain glitches.

I'm tugging Shep around the corner of the building and into the dumpy copy shop next door.

"What the—what?" Shep mutters as soon as my hand slips and his mouth is free.

I'm craning my neck, looking over my shoulder and pressing him back and sure enough, a cluster of my co-workers are just rounding the corner, headed towards the train.

There's a half-open door next to us and I push Shep into it. He stumbles, I stumble. We catch each other by the elbows and the door slams behind us. We're in pitch dark. I smell paper and printer ink and . . .

"Why do you smell like wheat bread and the forest?" I ask him.

"Why are we breaking and entering in a copy shop storeroom?" he counters.

"I . . . didn't want my co-workers to see me with you," I tell him after a brief pause.

There's a not-so-brief pause and then, "Uh . . . why?"

"I just . . . didn't want to turn you into a baby daddy, you know?"

Which is ridiculous. Because Shep and I have never even kissed. We've held hands exactly once. It was in the weeks directly preceding his mother's death. He'd just gotten back from visiting her and he'd asked me to meet him for a walk. I've never seen him like that before or since. We sat on a bench in Central Park (halfway between our houses at that point) and he held one of my hands in both of his and pressed it to his forehead. It was a hot, sticky summer and I only let go of his hand to buy him an ice cream cone from a man pushing a cart with a bell. He finished the ice cream cone with one hand, the other gripping my fingers for dear life. "I'm not ready," he'd told me over and over.

Some sort of Liam Neeson–style instinct kicks in for me now: *Must protect Shep.*

"Oh . . . um . . . okay?" There's the slightest downturn in the corner of his mouth, a blush rushing to his cheeks.

"I—" I search for a way to explain. "I just didn't want to put that on you, you know? If people start thinking that you're the . . . Look, you're the only blissfully uncomplicated relationship in my life right now and I . . ."

There's a pause. "Sure," he says easily. "I get that. I'm sorry. I didn't think . . ."

"No. That's okay. It's really a nice surprise that you came."

There's another longer-than-expected silence. "I made bread today. That's why I smell like wheat bread. You should've seen Willa when she walked in mid-mambo. I cleaned everything up, obviously, but mostly because she threatened to drop-kick me if I didn't. So I thought I should probably give her some space. I think your co-workers are probably gone now."

"Oh. Right." I let us out of the storeroom and the guy working there doesn't even look up from his magazine.

We exit into the sharply chilly nighttime.

"Man . . . the temperature dropped out of nowhere, didn't it? I guess it's officially Christmastime," I say. After weeks of high forties and sun, today was twenties and gray. I pull my wool coat a little tighter, wishing I'd worn more layers today.

"Well, actually that's sorta why I came . . . I wondered if

you wanted to go Christmas shopping—without actually shopping—but if the weather is too—"

"Yes!" I squeak in delight. "I do!" I know exactly what he's talking about. After Thanksgiving there are outdoor holiday markets set up in some of the major parks in New York. They're charming and twinkly and filled with rows of booths. Yummy food and glittery jewelry and handmade toys and artisanal vinegars and you name it. It's the kind of thing you'd see in a movie where the characters get all their Christmas shopping done at once. In reality it's so expensive you can feel your wallet bleeding the second you step foot on the grounds, but it's always fun to wander through and see the sights.

Shep and I take the train together and he doesn't comment when I walk us to the second-closest train station in order to avoid any run-ins with my co-workers. We come aboveground at Union Square. Cinnamon mixes with the scents of kebobs and peppermint. To my surprise it actually smells good. The first booth we come across contains highly realistic-looking puppets. I'm leaning forwards to inspect them when one of them stands up and is actually a living, breathing man.

"Holy mother of God!" Shep shouts, stepping between me and the puppet salesman from hell.

"Can I help you?" the man asks blandly.

We scuttle sideways and find ourselves safely ensconced in a booth selling paper cartons of noodles. He must see my sudden, furious hankering because he laughs and hands over cash and then plops a carton of noodles into my hand.

They are salty, carby nirvana, each noodle as wide as my pinky finger and a foot and a half long.

"You should see your face right now," Shep says, tucking his lips into his mouth to keep a laugh inside.

"The mouthfeel on these things," I say. "You've gotta try them."

He borrows my fork and we stroll and eat noodles and look at all the shiny, pretty things we can't afford.

We pass a booth with hand-embroidered throw pillows. If Willa were here, she'd be talking her way into at least a forty percent discount right this very second.

"Hey, Shep?"

"Mm-hmm?" He lifts noodles high above his head and lowers them down into his open mouth; he must have a big mouth, because now you see 'em, now you don't.

"You ever think about moving out of Willa's?"

"Huh? Oh. No." He doesn't even have to think about the answer, it's just right there at the surface. He throws the empty noodle carton into a trash can. "Hey, do you like that hat? I like that hat."

Then there's a knitted pink monstrosity being mashed over my hair and eyes. My world is hot pink with bits of the twinkling night peeking through the weave. Two warm fingers inch the hat up from my eyes and Shep is revealed one bit at a time.

"So, you *like* living there?" I prod him.

I'm momentarily disoriented because he leans into me. He's bending down, so it's a direct hit of my nose and that soft triangle of skin between his collarbones, at the base of his throat. He's saying something to the woman behind me, his arm extending, and then he's straightening back up and leading me away from the booth. "Look, they have apple pie over there. You want some?"

"Wait a second." I lift a hand to my temple. "Did you just buy me this hat?"

"It's cold." He shrugs. "Apple pie?"

Three minutes later I'm on a park bench with a slice of

steaming apple pie on my lap, a hat on my head, and a very warm Shep sandwiched in beside me. The rest of the marketgoers are in a steady stream in front of us, arm in arm and pointing at all the things for sale. A mother walks by with a crying child holding either hand; they're wearing matching fur hats so large that both Shep and I laugh. Christmas music tin-cans over the loudspeaker. "Do you think we can make it?" a teenage boy asks as he stumbles after a very pretty girl his age. "The movie doesn't start for twenty minutes," she says to him in an exasperated tone, tugging him along. He looks so happy he could die.

I know how he feels. A thought occurs to me and I turn to Shep. "Shep."

"Yeah?" He puts a fork in my hand and nudges the pie plate to remind me it's there.

"Am I being *managed* right now?"

He pauses. "It's cold," he says again. "You're being *warmed up* right now."

His shoulder is, indeed, so warm and so *there* that I give in to the whole concept and lean my weight against him. I take a bite of apple pie—heaven—and then offer him a bite. I expect him to take the fork like he did with the noodles but instead he lets me feed it to him. My heart kicks and I feel a flush of nerves and I remember what Nurse Blank told me about the pregnancy funhouse. Everything's a symptom.

"Do you like where *you* live?" he asks after a long, quiet moment.

I realize that he's picking up our conversation about Willa's place. He'd evaded it so cleanly before that I figured he wasn't going to talk about it.

"I love my apartment. It's . . . the exact place I want to go home to."

He uses the edge of his shoe to scrub the dirt off a cobblestone, his eyes distant. He leans towards me and opens his mouth and I blink for a moment before I realize he's asking for another bite of pie. I feed him and he chews. "I haven't felt that way about a place I've lived since my mom died." He looks up at me. "Since we packed up her house, I mean."

His mother's house, his and Willa's house growing up, was the homiest home I've ever been in. Mismatched stained-glass windows, the warmest quilts on every bed, popcorn on demand, and a clawfoot tub she'd fill to the brim with bubble bath if you asked. "It was the best house on the planet," I confirm for him.

He nods. "I think I'll never feel that way about a home again."

"You didn't feel that way about your apartment with Heather?"

He shakes his head. "No. Neither of us cared very much about . . . I don't know. You know?"

I think about that apartment, I was only invited over a handful of times in all the years he lived there. But it was shockingly . . . college? Souvenir cups in the cabinets and IKEA furniture that'd seen better days. I never saw their bedroom.

"But Willa's place is nice."

"Yes." He nods dutifully.

I knock our shoulders together. "But it doesn't feel like home?"

He gets a line between his eyebrows. "Every place except my childhood home has just been a place I sleep at for a while. I don't need much, so it always works out fine. But . . ." He's scraping the cobblestone again. "I guess I haven't thought much about leaving Willa's because I haven't thought much about *staying* at Willa's either. I'm just there."

I Rolodex through Shep's living situations over the years

and realize that he went from his mother's house to the dorms to a horrible spot filled to the brim with nihilistic postgrads to his place with Heather to living with Willa.

"Have you ever wanted to live alone?"

He glances at me and then away. "I wouldn't even know where to start." I so rarely see Shep embarrassed, but he's telling the truth right now even though he wishes it weren't the truth.

"Well, I'd help with that. If you ever wanted. I'm an expert live-er alone-er."

He smiles at my phrasing. "Yeah. Yeah, maybe I'll take you up on that."

I'm feeling a little zip just thinking about it. "I would seriously help with *everything*. I know this great email list for rental apartments. And we could figure out what style you'd want your furniture to be. I could do it for cheap, I swear! There's so much good stuff in secondhand shops in the city. You don't want to get everything at once, though, you know. Little by little is the key or else you end up with a bunch of stuff that's only *sort of* perfect instead of *exactly* perfect. And I'd want your place to be *exactly* perfect. Any thoughts on what neighborhood you'd want to be in?"

His smile has been growing bigger and bigger the more and more animated I become, but when I ask that last question he freezes. You never really think of a smile as a moving, breathing thing until someone freezes in the middle of one.

He searches my eyes and then clears his throat, looking away. "I'm liking Brooklyn."

He lived on the Upper West Side as a student and then his and Heather's apartment was in Harlem. His tenure at Willa's has been his only time on our side of the East River.

"Oh, *good*," I say, immediately swamped with relief. "I barely got to see you when you lived in Manhattan."

It's true. Pretty much the minute he and Heather broke up I started getting to see Shep seven hundred times more than usual.

He's animating again. He leans forwards and scrubs a hand over the top of his head. Like he's trying to erase a thought. But then he sits back up, asks for another bite of pie, and the moment has passed.

"So," he says, his eyes jumping from face to face as they pass in the crowd, his long legs stretched out in front of him. "I think we've seen it. Home?"

"Home," I agree.

We weave through the market and down into the subway. We're on the train platform and a man in a top hat and platform heels is singing a tear-jerkingly gorgeous version of "White Christmas."

"I'm duh-reamin' of a whiiiiiiiiiite Christmas." I'm watching him from a distance, my hands warming in my pockets, when panic dumps itself onto me, an upturned can of red paint. "Shep! My bag. I don't have my bag." I'm patting my coat and turning in a circle like it'll just appear if I wish hard enough. "I must have left it on—"

He grins and thumbs the strap of my messenger bag up off his chest like people do with old-timey suspenders. "I've gotcha."

"Oh, my *God.*" I sag against a nearby pole and he pinches the collar of my coat and tugs me towards him.

"Don't lean on that."

I've got my elbows pressed against his rib cage and my chin tipped up towards him. "I can't believe I forgot my bag. I *never* do stuff like that. That could have been so bad."

"I've gotcha," he repeats. "So. What about that?"

He nods towards the man singing his heart out.

"That busker?"

"What he's singing about."

He's on to the next song. "Bells will be ringin' the glad, glad news . . ."

"Please Come Home for Christmas." I name the tune out loud and straighten up from my stoop against him.

"I know you haven't told your brothers yet . . ." he says gently. "But you've never skipped a Christmas before, have you?"

I shake my head. "I'm gonna go home. I have to. It's the only time of year we ever see one another since Mom and Dad died. If I break tradition . . . well . . . that's not an option. I'm just not sure if I tell them before I get there or . . ." I trail off and watch the caroler. But then I notice something. "Did you realize he's not wearing any pants?"

Shep squints and leans forwards and his mouth drops open. "That is some extremely impressive leg hair."

"He must be cold."

Shep's eyes slide over to mine. "I don't think so."

We're laughing as the train streams into the station, bringing that musty scent with it. Shep runs a five-dollar bill over to the man's open guitar case and we get on the train. It's not overly crowded but there aren't any open seats, and Shep looks around in consternation.

"I'm okay," I tell him.

We ride companionably, both holding the same pole and swaying with the zoom and screech of the train. At Canal Street a crowd of people get on the train, and unfortunately one of them has some truly righteous B.O.

Pregnancy nose is a very, very real thing in my world these days. I take a step towards the train doors, my only thought being of escape, but they're already closing. I turn back to Shep in despair. We're on the Q train and this is the longest wait between two stops, Canal Street to DeKalb. You cross the East

River over the Manhattan Bridge, which is normally a delight. But tonight I might very well spend that time puking among strangers. The scent makes the noodles and apple pie barrel-roll each other down a hill.

Shep, seeing my desperation, opens the top of my bag. "Do you have anything good-smelling in here?" he asks in a panicked whisper. "Something to stick your nose into? Lotion or a muffin or something? Or maybe—"

He cuts off because I quickly maneuver the messenger bag away from his chest and unzip his puffy coat.

I have no thoughts in my head other than *B.O. bad.* I've got one hand on the pole to steady me, but the rest of me is in the circle of Shep, my nose pressed against his sternum and his jacket mostly closing around me, blocking out the B.O. And blocking *in* Shep's scent. Wheat bread and forest floor and . . . bar soap as white as snow.

He smells vaguely familiar. We grew up together but I'm not sure I could have picked out this scent before today.

"Well, that's one option," he says on a short laugh, looking down at me unexpectedly inside his coat.

"It's better than man-smell."

He frowns. "*I* have man-smell."

"You have *good* man-smell." I take a hearty sniff. "Seriously, you could charge."

"Okay. Pay up."

I shoo his words away with one hand. "Check's in the mail."

The train brakes and one of his hands presses my shoulder blade for just a moment. I hold my breath and peek out from his coat. There's the Brooklyn Bridge, geometric, graceful perfection outlined in orange lights, stark against the sapphire sky behind it. The East River is an inky black ribbon dotted with ferries and ocean liners in the distance. The Statue of Liberty waves hello from Liberty Island, no bigger than my thumbnail.

I think of other things that size, small enough to fit in the palm of a hand. My hand. Silver grays and shadows, hiding in the bag firm over Shep's back. I've been thinking of the ultrasounds as photos of something that would prefer to stay hidden, under the covers, thank you very much. Who wants a photo of their insides? But I picture myself as I am now at this very moment, surrounded by Shep's coat, one eye peeking out to get a glimpse of the city's night lights. Maybe there are things that need to be hidden for now but wouldn't mind a peek at the world.

2nd Trimester: Tips on How to Satisfy Your Man (-Sized Cravings for French Toast)

Eight

Finally this all-staff meeting ends and I hang around in my chair for a bit to watch my co-workers systematically demolish the cheese-and-fruit plate I put together for them. I know I won't get any sort of actual thank-you, so I'll have to be satisfied simply through my powers of observation. Hopefully that Tillamook cheddar fueled up one of the policy analysts enough to make them charge forth and save the spider monkeys! Do I sound purely happy and not at all jealous? Great.

My phone buzzes, sliding across the conference table, and I see that it's Shep calling me.

I decide to leave the cheese plate dangerously unchaperoned and grab my phone. I head out of the conference room and out into the stairwell, the door slamming closed behind me. "Hello? To what do I owe this afternoon phone call? Is this a butt dial? Do I have the honor of speaking with Shep's fantastic ass right now?"

"Do you really think it's fantastic?" he asks. "I always thought it was just average."

"You're twisted backward to look at it right now, aren't you?"

"No! Yes. Is it fantastic?"

"It's quite nice."

"Man, thanks. I should randomly call you in the middle of the workweek more often."

"Yes," I say, making my feet dance one way on the stairs and then the other. "Why are you calling me?"

"Ah." He pauses. "I wasn't sure who else to ask and Google got . . . weird very fast."

" 'Kay. Well, I've got about five minutes, so talk fast."

"Willa sent me out for tampons."

"Oh." Oh no. Tampons mean another month of disappointment for her. And if my hyperprepared friend got caught unawares without any tampons in the house, then she might have truly thought that this time was the real deal. "Where's Isamu?"

"He's at a gig. Willa says she's okay. But I think she wanted me out of the house."

"Okay . . . so the matter at hand is tampons."

"Yes. I can't mess it up. It's my one job. I fully intend to buy the *crap* out of these tampons."

"That's the spirit. Now, did she give you any directives?"

He reads off a long list of tampons of many different flow levels and brands as well as pads and panty liners. He's out of breath by the end.

"Okay," I tell him. "So, the good news is that I'm fairly certain she's completely fucking with you. I know for a fact she thinks pads are like wearing a diaper. And if she's joking, then she's not utterly devastated."

"So . . . I shouldn't get everything on the list?"

"No. Definitely get everything on the list. She's expecting you to fail. Let's wow her."

"Yes, yes. I'm in. Okay. I wish you were here to slap me across the face or make me drink a pitcher of raw eggs or something."

"You need that much psyching up just to go into a drugstore for feminine hygiene products?" I muse.

"I've never done it before!"

"What? You were with Heather for like a decade. You never bought her tampons?"

"No way. She was super private about all that stuff. And it wasn't a decade. It was only seven years."

"Eight," I correct him.

"No. Seven. The last year we lived together we weren't together."

My eyes squeeze closed and then pop back open. "Wait. Really?"

"Really. I . . . thought you knew. Willa knew."

"She mentioned that you weren't doing great, but . . . How does that work exactly? Living together but not together?"

"Quite amicably, actually. I moved into our guest room."

So, Shep has *actually* been single for about a *year* and three months. Not just three months. For some reason I can't make that piece of information fit with all my other pieces of Shep information. I put a square peg in a round hole. Doesn't work. Try again. Still no.

"Why?" I ask, flabbergasted. If there's one thing this city is not lacking in, it's crash pads. Even now, he's crashing at Willa's. Why wouldn't he have done that right after they broke up?

"It's . . . kind of a long story actually."

When people say that, they actually mean that it's a regular-length story that they don't want to tell you right now. "Okay. Well, someday I'd like to hear it. But for now, tampons?"

"For now, tampons. Which should definitely be the name of someone's biography. Very catchy."

I laugh. "Yes. Whenever Mr. Tampax gets around to finally penning his memoir."

We're both laughing but then Shep stops laughing. "Oh, boy."

"Are you standing in the feminine hygiene aisle right now? Eyes dilating in fear?"

"You really know everything."

"Here. I have an idea."

I don't think twice, just tap the little button and there's Shep's face popping up on my screen. He's got earbuds in and a baseball cap on. I rarely, if ever, see him in a baseball cap.

"Oh, hi!" he says, delighted to be video chatting with me.

"Did you jog there? You look . . . sweaty." What he actually looks is warm and disheveled and, honestly, kinda handsome with his hair all curling out from the sides of the cap and high color in his cheeks, but there's no need to go into detail.

"Sure did. And you look . . . not sweaty."

I lean forwards and study myself in the tiny thumbnail. I'm wearing heavier-than-normal eye makeup and my hair in a frizzy-ish braid. I slept reasonably well last night, but even so, the pregnancy has certainly had an impact. "Hopefully this look is waifish. I think that's the best I can achieve at this point."

Shep frowns at me. "Are you looking at the same image I'm looking at? You look as pretty as always. Here, would it make you feel more attractive in comparison if I held the camera like this?"

He moves the phone down so that he's all double chins and nostrils. He rolls his top lip back and gives me a simpering smile. "How's this?" he asks.

"Perfection. You have a true eye for angles. You should be a wedding photographer."

"Yes, if I ever quit my job as a . . ." he prompts, waggling his eyebrows as he waits for me to fill in the blanks.

"Coder?"

"Oh, boy. Sure. Close enough."

"Well, what's *my* job, then?"

"You're a . . . you know . . ."

I raise my eyebrows.

"You're the lady who gets it done!" he ultimately decides. "Okay, let's get back to the matter at hand." He points the camera to the rows and rows of boxes, and together we find everything. He's checking out ten minutes later and for some reason, we're still video chatting. He even introduces me to the checkout lady, Vicky, and she and I have a good laugh at Willa's joke on Shep. We keep chatting on his walk back to Willa's and it's only then, when he's about to get on the elevator in her lobby, that he frowns. "Hold on . . . didn't you say you only had five minutes of time to give me? I'm not complaining, but—"

"Oh. Crap." I check the time. "Gosh, I'm such a . . . *Shoot!*"

"What? What's wrong? What'd you miss?"

"I talked right through my lunch break. Ugh."

"Are you not allowed to eat at your desk?"

"No, I am." I stand up and brush myself off because it's time to get back to said desk. Unfed. "But I brought a peanut butter sandwich today and—"

"Micah's allergic," Shep cuts in. "Dang. That's a pickle."

"Don't say pickles to me right now. I'm starving. Hey, how did you know that Micah's allergic to peanuts? And how did you know my co-worker's name, for that matter?"

He squishes up one side of his face and gives me a look. "I listen when you talk, Eve."

I ignore the little flip in my stomach. "Except when I talk about what my *actual* job is, huh?"

"Yeah," he says with a shake of his head. "What's wrong with us? We've been friends forever. Why don't we care about the other one's job?"

I lean in and whisper, "Maybe because we don't care about our *own* jobs?"

"Ah. Yes," he whispers back. "Unfortunately, I think you're right."

"Okay, I really have to go."

"Thanks for the help with the tampons! Bye!" He signs off and I'm left standing in the now incriminatingly silent stairwell. I walk down the three steps to get to the door and every clack of my flats is a disapproving tut. I've just been scream-laughing on a social call in a common area at work. Straight through my lunch hour. How very unlike me.

I make it back to my desk in time.

"*You* sounded like you were having a good time in that stairwell," Bevi calls, giving me a sly look over her hand of cards. She and Xaria are sitting in Xaria's office continuing their weekly lunch hour gin tournament. It's been neck and neck for roughly four years. I think they're almost up to thirty thousand points apiece. Both Bevi and Xaria lean to one side to see me through Xaria's open door.

"Oh, just . . . on the phone with my brother," I lie easily, automatically. My hand wants very much to touch my lower belly right now, so instead I rifle through my desk drawer for something I don't need. Hello, Miss Stapler, yes, help me keep up the ruse. *Ca-chonk.* I staple two innocent sheets of scratch paper together.

Brothers are not good gossip, so they both sit back up and continue their game. I glance at Micah, who is looking in confusion at the scratch paper. But he doesn't say anything.

"Eve Hatch?" a man's voice says, and I jolt out of my reverie. He's standing in the doorway of our annex and wearing an unlatched bike helmet and a reflector vest. He's got a delivery in his hands.

"Oh. Me!" I jump up and accept the paper bag from him, digging a few bucks out of my pocket for a tip. I poke into the bag before I'm even back to my seat. A savory smell that I'd recognize anywhere wafts out. It's a tempeh Reuben from my favorite vegetarian sandwich joint. I sit down at my desk and pull the cardboard container out of the bag and just stare at it for a second. There's a receipt stapled to the top of it. I don't even have to look to know whose name will be on it.

"Everything all right over there?" Micah asks, a line of worry between his eyes.

I have no idea how to answer him. I flip open the box and laugh when I see it. He's ordered me an extra pickle.

I'm almost sixteen weeks along and I haven't puked in public in weeks. It feels jinxy to even bring it up, but as someone who apparently measures time in distance between cookie-tossing sessions, I feel it bears mentioning. Christmas is days away, and so is my trip home, but I've got more nerve-racking things to think about because Ethan actually called *me* and asked to meet.

I'm currently swallowed up in a booth with backs so high I could stand on the seat and not see over the top. Houseplants the size of folding chairs hang from the ceiling and creep over the tops of the booths. It would be dim in here if not for the multicolored twinkle lights that candy-stripe the pillars holding the ceiling up. The restaurant is an old Brooklyn standard. They've had the same menu since 1974 and they think brunch is for losers. Breakfast turns to lunch at eleven o'clock on the dot and if you miss it, well, they have no pity.

Ethan is fifteen minutes late and eleven o'clock is marching inexorably towards me. If he makes me miss out on their strawberry French toast (with a double side of hashbrowns and a fried egg, because . . . reasons), I legit might not be able to be nice.

I have to order without him. I lean out of the booth to get the waiter's attention. "Hey, Argy?"

"Can I put in a breakfast order?"

A person in the booth behind me has just leaned out of his booth and we're doing the exact same vague I-have-a-question-for-the-waitstaff finger-point in the air. We turn our heads to look at each other.

Ethan bursts out laughing. "Hi! How long have you been here?"

This is only my fourth time seeing Ethan in person. The second and third time . . . well, they were tense and had only the briefest moments of *this* Ethan, the one who is laughing with all his white, sharp teeth and pretty eyes. But the night we first met, he led with this version of himself, all that open charisma. I didn't stand a chance at resisting that guy.

"About twenty minutes?" I guess.

"Me too. We must have just missed each other on the way in." He stands up, still chuckling, and does some fancy gesticulating with his hands to indicate to our waiter that he's combining booths with me. He brings a backpack and a cup of coffee from his table and sits down across from me.

I reflexively look under the table.

"Whatcha lookin' for?" he asks.

"Checking for Bones."

"Ah." He smiles again. "Sadly, she is not welcome in most establishments in Brooklyn."

"What an oversight."

"I agree. That's why I started Good Boy. I lived in New Orleans for a couple of years after college, and there are tons of bars and restaurants that are dog friendly. I realized that New York didn't have much of an equivalent. So, yeah . . ." He's trailing off. "That's that on that." Throat clear. It dawns on me: Ethan's first instinct at seeing me is happiness, until the reality of our situation sets in. Like that night Shep and I showed up at Good Boy. He was genuinely excited to see me . . . until we talked about the pregnancy. Or just now, finding me around the side of the booth? Insta-grin. But now he's remembering why we're here and I watch the curtains close. He's gone wooden again. "So. How are you feeling?"

I groan and cover my eyes and sink dramatically down into my seat.

"What? What?" he asks, leaning forwards across the table.

"I'm fine. Two thumbs up. Nothing to worry about. I just liked hearing about you for a change. Tell me more about New Orleans. Or Good Boy."

The waiter clears his throat and I scramble up from my sag. He's in his late fifties, has a mustache (that, honestly, probably legally requires a hairnet) and a bored expression that I know for a fact he's putting on for Ethan. When it's just me and Argy he's animated and affectionate.

"The usual?" he asks me.

"Yes, please!" I chirp. "But also a double side of hashies and a fried egg."

He raises an eyebrow at me.

"I'm hungry today," I tell him with my eyebrow raised right back.

He shrugs and moves on to Ethan's order.

"Thanks, Argy!" I call to his retreating back. He tootles his fingers over his shoulder and I know that he's telling me the jury is still out on Ethan.

"The usual?" Ethan muses. "My whole life I wanted to have a usual."

"You've gotta be like a jackhammer," I insist, punching the palm of my hand. "Come back every week and order the exact same thing. For years I said the words 'strawberry French toast, *my usual*,' to Argy before he finally took pity on me."

"You've been coming here every week for years?" He's aghast. In a city of restaurants, I've chosen to habituate.

"I've fallen off a bit in the last few years. But yeah, when

Willa and I first moved here—have I told you about Willa? She's my best friend. She's Shep's little sister."

"Shep is the guy . . . who came with you to Good Boy?"

"Yeah. Anyways, when Willa and I first moved here we thought New York was gonna be the way it is in the movies. You know, where you have a bartender who knows your name and when you leave for work in the morning there are little girls double-Dutching on their way to school. That kind of thing."

"But then you got here, watched a drunk guy pee on the subway tracks, and realized you weren't in Kansas anymore?"

I laugh. "Uh, pretty much exactly right. We were overwhelmed. We thought having a regular breakfast joint was a good place to start feeling at home."

"Did it work?" Ethan looks up and smiles at Argy, who is just setting down a glass of fresh-squeezed orange juice on the table for me. Argy does not smile back.

As soon as he leaves I push my glass across the table. "Quick! Drink this!"

Ethan blinks at me. "Why?"

"Because I forgot to cancel my juice order but if I don't drink it, Argy will know something is up. He's already on my trail because I brought a man here. Seriously, if you want to make it through breakfast alive, polish off the juice."

"That is . . . definitely the most interesting threat I've ever gotten. Why can't *you* drink the juice?"

"Heartburn."

He picks up the juice glass and eyes it for a moment. "So . . . you don't want Argy to know you're . . ."

"I haven't told my family yet. So it feels weird to tell . . . waiters."

"Is your family local?"

"No." I shake my head. "I've got a brother in Austin and

two brothers in Michigan a few hours apart from each other. That's where we're from originally."

He clears his throat. "And your parents . . . ?"

"They died when I was in college. They had me late in life, so they were older. But, yeah. It's just me and my brothers now."

He nods, remembers the mission he's been tasked with, and takes the juice down in three big swallows.

"So . . . heartburn? Is that . . . new for you? Or something you always . . ." Ethan asks, carefully setting the glass back on my side of the table.

"It's the newest treat that pregnancy has in store for me."

"Ah. I see."

I've said the P word.

He looks around at the houseplants and then at his fingernails. He checks the buttons on his button-down (still perfect) and rebuttons one just for something to do.

I drum my fingers and take matters into my own hands. "Ethan, was there a specific reason you wanted to meet today? Not that it's not nice to see you. I just wondered . . ."

When he called to invite me somewhere, anywhere, I took it as a sign of decisiveness. You don't invite someone out to breakfast just to mumble good luck on their next prenatal appointment. Do you?

The only thing is I had no idea which direction this decisiveness might be leading us. Option A: Good luck without me and farewell.

Option B: I'm all in, I've always wanted to be a father.

"Yes, actually." He suddenly looks a little ill. "Two reasons. I didn't want to . . . over the phone. Um."

"Ethan, please, cut the suspense."

He takes a deep breath and nods. His palms spread flat across the table. When he looks up at me, I know that it's because he's forcing himself. "Look, I . . . I *hate* to do this . . . but Eleni thinks . . . ah, *we* think that it's probably best for me to know . . ." He blows out another breath. "Would you mind telling me a little bit about your sexual history . . . around the time that you got pregnant?"

Aha. So, this is actually an option C breakfast. The good old-fashioned are-you-lying breakfast.

"You are the only person I've slept with in the last year. But I'd be happy to have a DNA test performed once the baby is born." The answer is ready-made, Styrofoam-perfect and plucked straight from a *what-the-fuck-do-I-do* message board about two days after I found out I was pregnant.

I assumed I was going to have to say it at some point. I just didn't realize it was going to make me tear up.

It's a misty, stinging cry. The raw emotion of it in direct contradiction to how unaffected my voice just was.

"Oh. God." Ethan sees the tears. He hands me a napkin, scrapes his hands over his hair and just stares at me. His eyes go bloodshot and then, *look,* there go all the tears that *I* wanted to cry. He's a leaky faucet. One two-three four five-six-seven, look at them sliding over his cheeks.

I hand the napkin back to him and he turns towards the back of the booth, scrubs the tears away and blows his nose.

"I'm so, so sorry, Eve," he says after he takes a big gulp of water, staring at the table. "If it were just up to me . . . But Eleni's devastated. And I'm trying so hard to figure out what's fair. For her. For you." His head goes into his hands. "God, part of me still can't believe this is happening."

His girlfriend is somewhere right now—probably his bed—absolutely convincing herself that I'm a floozy. She's probably got her fingers crossed that there are a handful of different dudes whose DNA could be currently canoodling with mine. She's probably hoping for, at the very least, an ambiguous answer she can cling to. Things would just be so much easier for them if I were a good-natured harlot.

But I'm not. And if he's still in the can't-believe-this-is-happening phase, then maybe he needs a little slap of reality.

"Ethan, we used a condom and still got pregnant. It is what it is." I turn and start digging in my bag. "And condoms notwithstanding, this is our situation." I pull out the most recent ultrasound and slide it facedown across the table to him, like a backdoor deal between two mobsters. "Until we get a DNA test—if that's what you want—I can't offer you anything more than my word that it's yours. But in case you're interested, that's the most recent scan."

He does a quick, involuntary drum of his fingers and stares at the shiny white back of the scan. Maybe putting it facedown was a touch too dramatic.

"Here you go," Argy says, and I almost scream when I realize that Ethan and I are not the only two people in the world.

Public. We're in public.

He slides our plates across the table to us.

"Thanks, Argy."

He gives me a quick smile and then skedaddles.

I reach for my fork, glance up at Ethan, and freeze.

He's holding the ultrasound and looking down at it with his lips tucked into his mouth, his eyes unblinking.

I missed it! The moment he first looked at the ultrasound. I was too busy salivating over French toast and I totally missed the moment.

"Oh, boy," he says and covers his eyes with one hand.

"Is that 'Oh, boy, this ultrasound is so meaningful to me'? Or 'Oh, boy, I must be a monster because this ultrasound actually means almost nothing to me'?"

I'm strategically, methodically demolishing my French toast, chewing aggressively and eyeing Ethan. I must look ridiculous because when he looks up he laughs in a startled sort of way.

"Does *anyone* feel the second way when they look at an ultrasound?" he asks, reaching for his fork and knife.

I raise one hand. "Me. I have to confess, all I see are a bunch of blobs."

"Huh." He looks at it again.

"You really get all squishy inside when you look at that? Maybe I really am a monster inside."

"I'm not *squishy*, exactly." He squints. "Probably because it doesn't exactly look like a person yet. But yeah, I guess this is . . ." He hunts for the right word. "Context. And context is important, you know. It's not just nausea and heartburn. It's . . . also a blob."

"I get that." I push my empty French toast plate away and start in on the hash browns. "I get a lot more context on the daily than you do. It is, after all, happening inside my body."

His eyes drop down to where the table covers me from him and I realize what's happening. After a brief battle of wills, I convince myself to set my fork and knife down. I scoot back as far as I can in the booth and sit straight up. His eyes widen and—maybe? hopefully?—brighten.

"You're showing."

"Just a skosh."

"Oh, boy." He's covering his eyes again.

"Okay, so," I say, casting about for a subject change. "Reason one for meeting up was to determine paternity." He winces and I smile. Prodding him is a little fun. "What's reason two?"

"Right, right." He blinks and then finishes yanking something out of his bag. "This is for you."

He hands me a wrapped gift. "Sorry that it's not . . . nicer. The wrapping, I mean. I should have asked them to do it at the store." It's wrapped in brown paper, like he's cut up a grocery bag, but it's neat and he is clearly discerning about how much tape he uses. I like this infinitely more than a fancily wrapped present with shiny paper and a useless bow.

"Should I open it?" I ask.

"Sure. It's nothing special."

I'm normally a present ripper, but he went to such care to line up the edges of the paper bag that I peel instead of tearing. And inside . . . is a shoebox. I flip it open and there are two of the most perfect slippers I've ever seen in my life.

"The woman at the store said that pregnant women sometimes need extra arch support, even in slippers . . . so they're like gel liners or something? And if they're not the right size I bought three pairs so we could size up or down. I'll obviously return the ones that don't fit. And don't worry, that's not real fur. I know you're a vegetarian. But if your place is anything like mine the floors are like ice in the morning." He just keeps talking, probably because I haven't said anything.

"I don't have any slippers," I say hoarsely. "Until now, of course." I take one of the slippers out and rub the fake fur against my cheek.

He sags back against the booth in relief. "Oh, good."

"I love them. Thank you."

"I know footwear can be kind of a . . . nothing gift."

"No. A nothing gift is actually nothing. Which, unfortunately, is exactly what I got you." I grimace in chagrin.

"Well," he says with a shrug, nodding towards my belly. "You *are* gestating my kid, so I think we're even."

I honk a laugh because that statement is the strangest kind of funny. It's a stinging, bright-hot relief. Like when you put freezing hands under hot tap water. It helps and hurts at the same time.

My *kid,* he said.

We hold each other's eyes even when the smiles melt away.

Hear that sound? That's the earth-deep groan of tectonic plates shifting, so low and far away you barely know you're hearing it until your water glass trembles.

As unsteady as the ground is between Ethan and me, there's an upside to it all. Nothing has been settled. Everything can always change in a second. And nine months is made up of an awful lot of seconds.

Nine

"Oh, Eve, please don't be swayed by slippers," Willa says from where she's scrubbing the counter in her kitchen. "It's nice that he thought to get you a gift on the one holiday of the year when literally everyone gets literally everyone a gift, but still it's just a pair of slippers. The bar is so low it's just in the basement for men, isn't it?"

Isamu and I are laughing and rolling our eyes at Willa's tirade. She's started rage-washing dishes and calling to us over the faucet.

"Eve can be swayed by that if she wants to be swayed by that!" Isamu insists. "Sure, they're just slippers, but he went to a store and told a salesperson that Eve was pregnant and then got her an appropriate gift. That's not nothing!"

"If I see some video proof that he told the salesperson that Eve was pregnant with *his* baby and he wanted to select a gift to show his commitment to co-parenting and the salesperson recommended those slippers, *then* I'll give him the points. Otherwise it's bupkis in my book."

I was going to put the slippers on, but instead I find myself fitting them back into the shoebox. "Do you hate Ethan just because he has a girlfriend?"

"I don't hate him! I'm sure he's really great. But, yes," she finishes up. "It bugs me that he has a girlfriend." She tosses the sponge in the sink, rinses her hands, and comes to sit next to me on the floor. "I just want you to have someone who is absolutely nuts about you and wants to raise a kid with you and is proud to be the father of your kid. This guy hit the *jackpot* and he's throwing it all away on some other chick."

Isamu makes eye contact with her and she sighs and turns to me. "Let me see these slippers."

I nudge the box over to her and she picks them up one at a time, inspecting them.

"Quality stitch work," she concedes. "And the gel liners are nice. Try them on."

Pleased with her approval, I model them with a walk from one side of the room to the other.

"Very nice," she says with a nod.

"Very nice," Shep parrots, coming out of his room. "Are we just admiring Eve in general or is there something specific? And how come nobody told me Eve was here?"

"I don't knock on the door of that masturbation den," Willa says with a curled lip.

"I'm sorry," he says, flopping onto the couch. "Would you rather it was a sex den? I thought you told me no visitors."

I stop walking, momentarily stymied by the idea of Shep being the proprietor of a sex den.

"Slippers," Isamu says, talking over the Balders. "We were admiring Eve's slippers."

Shep leans up, peeps the slippers, and gives me a robust nod. "Yes, those are very nice."

"They were a gift from Ethan," Willa says with a completely straight face and even tone. How does she still manage to inject a sneer?

"Oh." Shep flops back onto the couch. "You met up with him again?"

"Yeah. We've been texting here and there and he asked to meet up so we could talk in person."

"What'd you talk about?" Shep asks.

"Something else," I say, waving my hands in the air. "Sorry, I meant can *we* talk about something else?"

I haven't mentioned to Willa that Ethan brought up my sexual history. But I *just* got her to admit she doesn't hate him, so I don't want to undo progress.

"So, Michigan tomorrow, huh?" Willa asks, throwing me a bone.

"Yeah. I fly in the afternoon."

"Want me to come?" she asks casually. Her eyes darken menacingly. "I'll make sure your brothers take the news well."

I laugh. I love when Willa's on my team. "Better stay here. I don't think we can threaten my family into being happy for me."

Isamu gets out his mandolin—his newest musical experiment—and starts fiddling around with it. We all listen and chat and Willa decides we're allowed to eat dinner strewn around her living room.

Afterward, the conversation slides easily from Isamu's next gig to Willa's New Year's resolution (a six-minute mile and the side splits) to whether or not Shep should get a bird (no, according to the two owners of the apartment).

I start yawning.

"Hey," Shep says with a tap to the back of my hand. "Before you head home, I have something to show you. C'mere."

I follow him to his room. He's standing in the doorframe, his hands in the pockets of his sweats, grinning hugely at me.

"Welcome," he says.

"Why, thank you."

He goes in and sits at his desk, waking up his laptop. "Hold on, I have to get it set up real quick. Make yourself at home."

This room is very much a guest room. It's painted a lavender purple with framed black-and-white photos of wheat on one wall. The bed is white on white and neatly made. Only a half-drunk water glass on the nightstand proves that someone lives in here.

I haven't been in a Shep bedroom since we were in high school. Once when he was out of town, I was sleeping over with Willa and she woke up with the stomach flu at around midnight, so Corinne set me up in Shep's bed for the night. I vividly remember that room. Navy blue walls, a green patchwork quilt on his bed, and a gigantic poster of *Baywatch* babe Carmen Electra on the inside of his closet door.

He does a double take over his shoulder. "What are you smiling about?"

"Your *Baywatch* poster."

He throws his head back and laughs. "Lotta fond memories of that poster."

"Do you still have that green quilt?"

He looks up at me in surprise. "The one from my bed? Yeah, actually. It's boxed up with most of my stuff. There wasn't enough space here for me to really unpack, so most of it's in storage for now." His eyes slice over to me for just a moment. "When were you in my room in high school?" He reaches up with his socked toes and gently nudges my thigh until I park myself on the edge of his bed. His big foot settles next to my hip.

"Are you joking? You know how much time I spent at your house in high school. It was only natural that I'd make my way into your room every once in a while."

He squints. "I feel like I'd remember."

"Willa and I would go in and snoop around when you were out. And I slept in your bed once."

His foot slips to the floor. "You slept in my bed."

"Yup."

"In high school."

"Yes."

"Where the hell was I?"

The look on his face makes me burst out laughing. "I forget. It was during the summer, so probably computer camp?"

"Fucking computer camp," he gripes, spinning back around in his chair and clicking around on his laptop again.

Grinning at his back, I bounce on the edge of his bed. It's excessively squishy but that's how I like a mattress to be. And those pillows look like they might be made of—yup—memory foam magic. Firm pillows and a squishy mattress. Killer combo. I'm lying on my side now, watching Shep's profile while he clicks and types. He looks so serious when he's working. It's rare to catch him in a mood like this.

The glow from his lamp is amberish and clear, like I'm looking at him through a glass of beer. I think of Shep asking the waitress for a stanky IPA and I chuckle. I think I'm immune to some of Shep's charms because I grew up with them. It's a little hard to find a man mysterious when you know the exact pose that Carmen Electra used to strike in his closet.

I'm warm and is it just me or is this bed getting softer? Somewhere in my brain, I hear a click and realize that the light has gone from amber to blue. There are footsteps and then a door softly closing. But then I'm gone.

I wake up in the lonely-blue quiet of two AM. Shep's scent is so strong that I think for a disorienting second that I might roll over and see him. But no, that's just because I'm lying under the covers in his bed. The lights are out and I'm still in my clothes from the day. I wiggle out from the covers and quickly pad across his bedroom and out into the hallway. I use the bathroom and then gulp water straight from the faucet. When I emerge back into the living room, I see it. A gigantic foot hanging off the end of the couch. I follow the linear line from the toes to the ankle to the knee and there's Shep, not fitting on the couch. The afghan is like a tea towel over his waist. He takes these never-ending breaths. In for an eternity and then out for even longer. His blood must be rich with oxygen, lazily backstroking to all of his edges.

I put a hand on his shoulder. It's very firm and warm under his T-shirt, so I backpedal and touch him with less of my hand. "Shep," I whisper. "Shep."

He blinks awake, looks at me without seeing me, and closes his eyes again.

I try once more. "Shep. *Shep*."

This time one eye opens and holds. "Eve?"

"You should go get in bed. I'm gonna head home."

"Huh?" He puts two arms up over his head and now the couch looks comically small. He makes his hands into fists and then into starfish. "Wait. No. I wanted to show you something!"

He sits up and his hair is both flat and spiky. He tosses the afghan away and I see he's wearing just a plain white T-shirt and red plaid boxers. Half dressed, messy hair and sleepy eyes, his arms and legs look ridiculously long. I'm used to daytime Shep. Nighttime Shep looks fever-warm and like he'd taste like toothpaste.

"C'mere." For the second time that night I follow Shep to his bedroom. This time he holds the desk chair out for me and when I sit down he spins it towards his laptop.

His computer is closed so he leans over me to open it up and click into a program. He's got one hand on the back of the chair and one on the mouse pad in front of me so it's almost, almost like he's hugging me from behind. Almost. He yawns in my ear and makes the *HHHah* sound.

For just a flash, I picture spinning the chair again, so that I would be facing him. His red boxers in front of me and his arms on either side of me. He's a clumsy hugger, but is Shep clumsy in bed?

I mentally slap myself away from that thought.

"Here." He retracts his arms and comes to his knees next to the chair. We're the same height like this. "Press play."

He's smiling, his teeth turquoise in the light from his computer. There's a screen with a triangle play button in the center of it. I press play.

"Is this . . . is this *me*?" I ask Shep.

"Yeah," he says, a little shyly. "It's you as a Powerpuff Girl. Well. Powerpuff Woman, I suppose."

"Me as a *pregnant* Powerpuff Woman," I correct him, because he's glossed over the best part. Me, agile and kick-ass and pregnant all at the same time. Is this how he sees me? "You made this?"

"Yeah."

"I didn't know you could do something like this!"

"Computer camp, remember?" He gives me a little smile. "I've been fooling around with digital painting for a long time, but I only got interested in animation a year or so ago. Anyways. Merry Christmas."

I watch the animation twice more, my body humming with delight, and then I swivel the chair and maybe because we're, for once, the exact same height, our hug just notches perfectly together. My arms around his neck, his around my ribs. His chin hooking over my shoulder. I've accidentally got a gentle fistful of his hair and I feel my shirt slide against my skin where he grips me.

"Shep," I say, one hundred percent unclear on where this sentence might end, just knowing I've got to start it. "Shep, I—"

There's a small but unmistakable *tap* where my middle is pressing against his middle.

I freeze. He freezes.

"Was that . . . ?" he starts.

"Did you feel that?" I ask, scrambling back from him. "*Did you feel that?*" I've got tears in my eyes and shaking fingers as I take the hem of my T-shirt and peel it back. Both of us look down at my semi-rounded belly, a silvery crescent moon between us.

"I felt it," he whispers. And then, like it's the most natural thing in the world, his palm is flat against my belly. He's fresh-bread hot and firm in his touch. His hand slides half an inch to one side and half an inch to the other.

"Thank you," I whisper down to my belly. "*Thank you.*"

Thank you for kicking in the first place and thank you for kicking when I was flat up against someone who loves me. Thank you for letting someone else remember this moment, treasure it with a hand against my body.

"That was a *kick*, Shep," I whisper to him, emotion clogging my throat.

"I thought so," he whispers back, a huge grin on his face. "That was the coolest thing I've ever experienced."

He puts his other hand on my belly too. They do that half-inch slide again. He's still kneeling in front of me, my knees pressed onto either side of his ribs.

"Is this okay?" he asks, looking up at me.

"Yes." I nod. "No one else has actually touched it yet . . . so this is kinda fun."

He presses with the pads of his fingers, as gently as if he's testing the yolk of a cracked egg. "It's so firm," he whispers. His head cocks to one side. "And not quite round."

"Yeah, I know," I whisper back. "The OB-GYN says it's normal. Everybody has a little bit of a different shape. And that it'll all change as things progress."

"Hi," Shep says, and I realize he's not addressing me. "Please kick again. Unless you're too tired, and then I'll just be happy with what I got."

I laugh and it hurts. That's been happening to me a lot lately. When something is good and painful all at once. No one else has talked to the bump yet.

He shifts a little on his knees.

"Let's sit over there," I say, and point to the bed. "And we can keep waiting." I don't know how these things work, obviously, and have no reason to believe there will be any more kicks immediately. But right now I have the warm hands of someone who loves me, and ending it is inconceivable. I'd very much like me and my kicking bump to be treasured. Even if just by a friend, and even if just for a moment.

He's up off his knees and holding a hand out to me, hoisting me up, and then I'm both knees on the bed, scooting to one side and he's sliding next to me. I recline on pillows and he's on his side, facing me, eye level with my shoulder. His hand slides over my belly again and that's when I have to come to terms with just how big that hand is.

There's a deep shadow between each knuckle that I want to press my fingertips into. He's got veins and wide, clean fingernails and I swear his wrist is the size of my ankle. I have this weird sensation like up is down and I'm falling towards the ceiling, but it's okay, because Shep's hand, right there, is catching me.

"Oh!" he says, lifting his head, his eyes big. "Was that one?"

I chuckle and shake my head. "Just a gurgle, I think. My stomach is in there too, you know."

"Ah. Right."

I think I might feel a kick but I'm not sure and we both say "Ooh!" and turn to stare at each other, wide-eyed. My hand joins his on my belly and our fingertips are touching, our noses six inches away from each other.

Have I mentioned that Shep has a really good face? Kind

of a big nose and a soft mouth. He's got those friendly eyes where the top eyelid folds down and creates an angle just so. His eyelashes disappear at the ends and everything just looks so soft. Sleepy even when he's not sleepy. He's got a face that's constantly inviting you to lie in a hammock and find shapes in the clouds. I've never seen it from quite this close up before, though.

His exhale whispers against my cheeks and I look up at his eyes. Whoops. I guess I've been looking pretty intently at the bottom half of his face. I lean back and he leans back but his hand stays on my belly.

"Are you tired?" he asks, and there's a bit of gravel I don't normally hear.

"Not really," I admit. "Should I get go—"

"We could watch a movie," he suggests. "Until you get sleepy."

And then he's rolling away from me and I'm lying on his bed with my shirt pulled up and I stare at his ceiling and all I can think about are his hands. On me. And that up-is-down feeling is back, only he's not there to catch me and oh, *God* I have to go. Right now. Before everything—

"How about *Spirited Away*?" he asks, putting his laptop on my knees and clicking around.

An old favorite. I first watched it in his basement with Willa sandwiched between Shep and me on their couch, a bowl of popcorn filled and filled and filled by their mom.

He gets the movie started and I reach up to fix my shirt but his hand is back, hot and firm and comfortable, waiting for more kicks. "This is seriously so cool," he says.

It *is* so cool. And terrifying. And I don't even know which part I'm talking about. I'm tired and the movie is familiar and pretty and I'm warm and nervous and comfortable and freaked out all at once.

I wake up at dawn lying on my side. Shep is on his stomach, facing away from me, but one of his hands is still underneath my shirt. I get a half-second flash of a different universe. One where I'm allowed to put my face in that corner right there, the one that his neck makes against his shoulder. The universe where he's sleepy and warm and putting his hands all the way inside my shirt. Where our clothes could all just slip a few inches in one direction or another and then I could be on top of him and I could make those big, slow breaths of his come quickquickquick.

He's so relaxed and loose and I'm momentarily seized with longing to see him tight and frantic.

I shift so that he's not touching me anymore and I let my blood cool, sitting in the light blue of dawn. I let myself go all the way cold. And then I carefully climb out of his bed, and I go home.

Ten

I deserve my own action movie.

Later that afternoon, I fly across country and then basically somersault into my brother's house from the cab, purse perfectly angled over my belly. I fling myself from shadow to shadow, blowing kisses to random family members on my way up to hide in the room where I'll be staying, making vague excuses about freshening up. They obviously all think I'm being super weird, but at least I haven't blown my little secret yet. Well, my big little secret.

The belly.

It's a thing now.

I've read that some women just sorta pop overnight. And I didn't really believe it. How could it be true? Pregnancy is a gradual thing, little by little, blah blah blah.

Why do I ever think I know anything? I clearly know nothing, ever.

Because I woke up this morning, slid out from under Shep's arm, tiptoed out of his room, and caught sight of my belly in Willa's hallway mirror. First it was The Kick and then it was The Bump. There is no longer any denying it. This is not constipation. I'm full-on preggers. Public preggers.

I get to my brother's dinner table ten minutes before anyone else and scoot myself so fully in that someone would have to be underneath to see the belly.

There. I've done it.

My one goal was to make it to the dinner table where I could tell all three of my brothers at once.

"Eve! What an honor for you to finally join us." That's my brother Dal, one of the twins. He slides into the chair next to mine and sneaks a bite of roast chicken. "What, are you hiding a boy up in your room or something?"

"You didn't even come help with dinner?" Mal, the other half of the twin equation, glowers at me as he slides in at the head of the table.

The twins are actually named Malcolm and Dalton but Dal had such a hip-swinging, free-wheeling confidence as a toddler that he quickly became Dallas the Cowboy to all who knew and loved him. People love to make twins rhyme so what could Mal be called other than Malice? Malice and Dallas. The names were almost too perfect for their personalities. Mal's Achilles' heel is that he shared a womb with Dal. I wouldn't dare call Mal anything but Mal. He'd slice me in two with his dagger eyes. His wife, Jenny, is sweet as pie but does anything he says. Their daughter, Rosie, is eight now and still attached to her mother's hip.

"Mal, you didn't help with dinner, either," Dustin, my oldest brother, says as he comes in through the sliding glass door that leads to the back deck. He must have been shoveling snow. He's old enough to be my dad, but Dustin's never quite given off Dad vibes, even when he became one. His salt-and-pepper hair curls out from under a Tigers cap and he's got a tie-dye shirt under his Carhartt work jacket. Barely tied Converse, bubble gum in his mouth. These are couch surfer vibes. Except for the lines on his face, he looks exactly the way he did when I was a teenager and he was getting back on his feet after leaving the military. Sitting here, hiding my belly under the table, watching my ageless older brother wash his hands and spit out his bubble gum, I really do feel like a teenage kid with a secret.

He comes and gives me a kiss on the top of my head and then plunks down across from me, not seeming to care in the least that Mal has taken the chair at the head of the table even though this is Dustin's house. "Looks delicious, Jenny," Dustin says.

We all chime in our appreciation as Mal's wife brings one last dish in from the kitchen and she and Rosie find their seats.

Dal is single and Dustin's kids are with their mom tonight. Which means the gang's all here.

This is it.

"So," I say to the group, and everyone turns to me at the same time, so in sync it's like a horror movie. "Well. So. I'm pregnant."

"Ha!" It's one deafening exclamation from Dustin and I can't tell if it's joy or shock. Maybe both? "No shit?"

"None," I say with a nervous shrug.

"Are you keeping it?" Dallas asks me, his eyes wide.

"Of course she's *keeping* it," Mal snaps at him. A thought occurs to him and he turns to me in horror. "Wait, you *are* keeping it, aren't you?"

I wish I had a big stinky fish to slap the judgment off his face. "I'm keeping it."

He sinks back in relief.

"But not for religious reasons."

He scowls at me.

"Congrats, Eve," Jenny says, and Rosie gives me a big smile. Dustin and Dal push out from the table and give me a double hug, their arms overlapping me. Dal sits back down and Dustin gives me two more gentle squeezes and then resumes his seat, his eyes glossy with tears.

"Pregnant," he muses. "So . . ." He rolls his hand in the air to indicate that more information is necessary.

"Well . . ." I rack my brain for the right thing to say. I thought I'd feel instant relief once I got over the hard part, but my heart has started racing and won't stop. "I'm sixteen weeks and everything is healthy."

"Great, great." Then he pauses and I pause too. "And . . ." he prompts me.

"Um?" I'm not sure what he's getting at.

"And where did the sperm come from?"

"Oh, my *God*, Dustin! Why did you have to ask it like that?" Mal splutters. Dal laughs. Jenny hides her smile behind a biscuit.

"Oh, fine then." Dustin raises both hands in the air. "If we're being *proper.* Eve, who knocked you up?"

I'm pinching the bridge of my nose and laughing. "A friend," I eventually go with. I laugh again, for no reason, and this time it sounds funny, like it's been squeezed through too small an opening. "A good person. We're not together."

My brothers glance at me and then at one another and then at me and then at one another. "Is it—?" Dal starts, blinking hard.

Dustin jumps in. "What's the guy's name?"

"Ethan. Ethan Rise."

"Ethan." Dustin tries the name out. "Cool. Okay. Hey, do you need money? I have some."

My throat constricts. Both at his easy generosity and at the reminder that it will obviously be my financial responsibility to care for a whole other human. "Willa's helping me figure out all the budget stuff. I . . . I think I'm fine?"

"Oh, Willa's on it? That's great," Dustin says with a wave of his hand. "She'd never let you crash and burn. Hey, Izzy will wanna know this guy Ethan's star sign." Izzy is his middle daughter.

"She's into astrology?"

"Big-time. She'll do a whole chart for you. I don't know. It's kind of cool. You acquire a whole new set of interests when you have kids. Whatever they're into, you kind of have to get into yourself, otherwise you have nothing to talk about with them. Anyways, you'll find that out the hard way in about five to ten years. Do you know the sex of the baby?"

And then I shock us all by absolutely disintegrating into tears.

"*This* is why I've been avoiding telling you," I remember all at once.

"What?"

"Why?"

My brothers' eyes are the size of fruit pies as they watch me self-destruct.

"I knew," I say with a little sob. "That once I told you guys, you'd ask stuff about the *baby*. Nobody asks about the *baby*. It's just been a . . . pregnancy. Now it's a *baby* too."

"Well, you'd hope so," Dustin says, and something in his tone makes me burst out laughing. But I'm back to tears moments later.

"Oh, God. A baby. The tiny onesies and a crib somewhere in my microscopic apartment and the diaper rash cream and . . . And one day that baby is a person who is an astrology expert and I'll have to share their interests and I'm not ready!" I'll admit that at this point I'm wailing. What's the use of denying it? I'm a total and complete mess and I probably should have woken up Shep before I left this morning, right? It's weird that I didn't, right? It made it super one-night-standish and if I'd woken him up, he would have smiled at me and calmed me down and maybe I wouldn't still be feeling the mark of his hands on my belly right this very second.

I have my palms over my face but then there's a little touch on my arm and Rosie is handing me her napkin. I wipe tears away and lay one hand on the top of her soft curls. "Thank you, sweet girl." I lean down and pull her into a hug. "Sorry I didn't give you a proper hello."

"That's okay," she says sagely. "You're having a baby." Like this turn of events all makes perfect sense to her. She trots back to her chair and I wheeze into the napkin.

"Come on, Eve. You're all right," Dustin says. "You gotta know that this is how everyone feels at some point or another when they're about to have a kid."

I peek out from behind the napkin. "Really?"

He nods boisterously. "If you're not at least fifty percent *Oh, shit,* then you're probably not thinking about it hard enough. I mean, it's a human, Eve. A whole human! You're entitled to freak out about that."

Most of this pregnancy has been one day and then the next but suddenly the next eighteen years are rushing at me all at once. Every load of laundry, every Christmas present purchased, every birthday party planned, every spring vacation to nowhere because I won't be able to afford it. "Oh, what the hell am I gonna *do?*"

My brothers look at one another and Dal shrugs, like *Don't ask me, I'm not a father.* Mal looks suitably stymied. Dustin sighs.

"You'll do what the rest of us do," he finally says. "And just make it work *today.* That's the whole trick with kids. You just do what works today. Today is not so scary, right?"

"Everything is scary."

"Good point, good point," Dustin concedes, stroking his rather scant facial hair. "For now, just eat some dinner."

I take his advice and miraculously, my family finds other things to talk about for the next half hour, though I can feel them sneaking glances at me between bites.

After quickly cleaning up the kitchen, I build a fire in the little hearth in the living room and take a nap on the floor in front of it.

I wake up to two feet right next to my eyes.

"So. You don't really know the guy, huh?" Dallas asks. The fire pops and a black-and-orange coal lands next to my feet. Dallas immediately stomps it out.

I blink fully awake and sit up. "Not really. No."

"He's not one of your Dereks?"

I laugh and stick my tongue out at him.

"How'd you meet him?" Dallas asks. "Some app?"

I shake my head. "I was only on the Tinder circuit for a minute."

"You haven't really been dating? Besides this . . . whatever this was?"

"No. Not for a long time."

"Why?" He finally takes a seat next to me.

"Mmmm. Well, things ended with Derek Two. And then Corinne died and . . . I wanted to be available for Willa, so I just didn't really date. And then I slept with this guy, Ethan. And yeah, you're up to date."

Dallas is quiet for a long time. "And you don't want to . . . be with him?"

I shake my head. "He's actually with somebody right now. He didn't cheat, but yeah, she's an on-again, off-again and I guess now they're on."

"Oof. Shit. That's . . . Damn. Women really get the short end of the stick, don't they?"

"What do you mean?"

"I mean that he's got his girlfriend and his pretty much normal life and meanwhile you're—" He cuts his eyes towards the bump. "Multiplying."

I laugh and pinch his arm. "It's not *spawn*."

We're quiet for a while. Until he asks, "What're you going to do about your apartment?"

"Hm?"

"Your apartment. How are you going to reconfigure it?"

Dal is an interior architect for a corporate design firm down in Austin and has an incredible eye for aesthetic. We both suffer from the same affliction. A single, posed sunflower in a jar next to our beds. Bowls of fruit on the dining room table that we have to eventually give to the neighbors so it won't go bad. Coat closets stacked embarrassingly tight with cleaning utensils and supplies. We buy certain books because we know how good they'll look on the shelf. Save for weeks for that particular toaster, you know, the one that'll make the backsplash really pop. Leave it to my design-minded brother to address my apartment.

"Ugh. I don't know. I . . . get hives when I think about redoing my perfect apartment."

He's already up and grabbing scratch paper and a pencil. He's only been to my apartment twice but he draws an almost perfect floor plan from memory. We spend the next half an hour imagining my furniture in various arrangements.

Mal comes in and looks over our shoulders and laughs. "Ha. Yeah, right."

"What's your problem?" Dal asks, studying the floor plan.

"You think that's all the space you need for a kid?" Mal points at the kid corner that Dal and I have just demarcated. "Multiply that by seven."

"By seven? That's the whole apartment!"

He taps his nose and smirks. "What's the rent on that apartment anyhow?"

"None of your business," I grumble. "A million dollars a month."

He flops onto the couch. "I'm just saying, you could probably get a two- or three-bedroom *house* in Westbrook for the amount you're paying on that glorified closet."

"I live in Brooklyn. I'm not uprooting."

"I mean . . . honestly, why delay the inevitable? You know you're going to end up back here. Dustin and the kids are here. Jenny and I are just a few hours away."

"And I love you all," I say slowly. "But I live in Brooklyn."

His brow comes down. "You can't raise a kid alone just to prove a point."

Whap. A pillow smacks Mal soundly in the face from across the room. Dustin stands in the doorway to the living room dusting his hands off. "She can do whatever she wants. Everybody lives differently. Don't act like you've got all your shit figured out."

He's been ex-military for almost as long as he was in the military, but every once in a while his I-mean-business voice comes out. It's alarming coming out of a man who looks like he enjoys piña coladas at two PM on a workday.

Mal, red-faced and angry, huffs out of the room. Dustin comes over and looks at my and Dal's floor plan. He grimaces. "Unfortunately, though, he's probably right. Babies don't necessarily take up much space, but kids do. If you're planning on staying there for a long time, things'll get tight without a second bedroom."

"I physically cannot think about a move right now. My budget can't handle it. I'll have to move way farther from my job to afford a second bedroom. And then I'll have to think about affording daycare and all that time out of the house and . . ." I lie backward and then switch to my side when that gets uncomfortable. "The thoughts won't think."

I can feel my brothers exchanging eye contact.

"Well," Dal says. "When you start to think about it, call me. I'll help talk you through it."

"Sorry. I was eavesdropping earlier. But I could drive out and wear my fatigues and scare the shit out of this guy for having the nerve to have a girlfriend who isn't you," Dustin offers.

I laugh. "We all have our unique skills," I say.

"And what are Mal's unique skills?" Dustin asks.

"Reddit," Dal and I say at the same time and crack ourselves up.

Told everybody, **I** text Willa from my childhood bed.

And?????? I get back about four seconds later.

They were . . . sweet? Well, Mal was . . . Mal, but Dustin and Dal were sweet.

Well, she texts, *we probably could have predicted that, right? Are you relieved they know?*

Dreading it was exhausting. So, yes. Merry Christmas, by the way.

Your Christmas present is under the tree. I had Dustin put it there the other day.

Yours is under your tree!

I saw. Love you. We're headed to Isamu's aunt's in a sec.

Love you too.

Next I try composing a text to Shep, but I exit out of it. I still can't shake this morning-after feeling.

Old friends occasionally fall asleep in each other's beds. While one of them puts their hands underneath the other one's clothes. That's totally normal, yup.

Oh, God . . . how can I just *text* Shep right now?

I text Ethan instead. *Merry Christmas! I told my brothers, by the way. They took it well.*

I toss my phone aside and wonder when exactly texting Ethan became easier than texting Shep.

My phone starts buzzing next to my head and I pick it up

and squeak. It's Shep who's calling me right now. Did he somehow psychically intuit that I was freaking out about texting him? Maybe I closed out the text to him and the hairs on his arm rose up and he set down his sandwich and reached for his phone? Is this where I find out that I can keep no secrets from Shep?

"Hello?" I sit back against my headboard and pull my knees up.

"Hi!" Gosh, he sounds good.

"Hey, Shep." Just to provide some perspective, I sound like I'm really trying to get my Minnie Mouse down.

"Willa just told me that you told your brothers, and I just . . . wanted to check in."

I ignore the fact that this gives me butterflies and I soldier on with the conversation. "It went all right. I mean, there was some definite eye-poppage. And Dustin said 'sperm,' so that was the worst moment of my life. But other than that . . ."

He laughs and then slows down a little. "You're really all right, though? You're not just saying that because we're halfway across the country and if it went poorly there's nothing we could do?"

"Thank you for assuming I'm capable of that kind of selfless subterfuge, but I assure you, if it had gone poorly, you would know. Everyone in a ten-state radius would know . . . I admit there was a lot of crying, but parts of it were actually way nicer than I thought they'd be."

"Good, good. I was worried thinking about you having to do all that on your own . . . Hey, Eve?"

"Mm-hmm?"

"Ah. Never mind. Sorry. Merry Christmas."

He pauses. I pause. I really, really want to know what it was he just never-minded but I don't want to set the precedent that we're not allowed secrets in this conversation because I really,

really would like to keep mine zipped into my mouth where they belong. "Are you going with Isamu and Willa to his aunt's house?"

"Nah. We'll celebrate the three of us tomorrow. But I think I'll just stay in tonight. Maybe watch a movie."

The specter of last night's movie-watching certainly rises up in front of my eyes, and I wonder if it's done the same for him. The lavender of his room surrounds me. I feel the push of his pillow against my back, the sensitized scrape of clothes against skin. His breath, his heat, adrenaline. And all we did was lie a foot apart and fall asleep watching a movie. It's the most PG non-sex sex scene of all time. But even so, I shift against my clothes and clear my throat. This is so not good.

"Are you sure you're gonna be all right in old Westbrook, Michigan?" he asks me.

"Yeah. I wish you were here with me, though." (WTF am I doing right now?) "I mean, I wish you and Willa were here. It's always better when you two are here." I feel like a cartoon dog in a Disney movie walking backward with a broom in my mouth, scrubbing out my footprints as I go. He must—and I mean must—sense something is off between us. "It's weird to be home without you guys." I can't tell him everything I'm thinking, but I can at least be this honest with him. "Especially this time of year."

"Peppermint ice cream at Klein's and then a stroll by the river," he reminisces. He and Willa and I have done that exact thing approximately seventy times.

"Watching the ice fishermen freeze their future children off."

"Making my mom shout at us when we aggressively shake the presents to guess what's inside."

I laugh, remembering that pet peeve of hers. "*You're gonna regret doing that if I ever buy you fine china!*" I imitate Corinne.

"And it would be, like, a package of wool socks."

"What can I say? She really hated having her socks shaken."

There's a pause where I think he laughs, but maybe he sighs. "I miss her, Eve."

"Me too."

"Hey, come back to Brooklyn already. We need you here."

My heart skips.

"I'll be home soon," I promise. "We'll see each other in the New Year!"

"A whole new year," he muses.

"A fresh start," I concur. And it makes my stomach flip.

Eleven

On Christmas morning I'm up before anyone else. I bundle up in boots and a coat and a scarf and mittens and a hat and when I step outside . . . it's really not that cold. I disrobe item by item as I make the ten-minute walk. All the extra winter wear is stuffed into my pockets by the time I step into the cemetery.

There's about four inches of melty snow still on the ground from when it last fell. Everything is in shades of black and white and gray except for a few sprays of red and pink where people have left flowers.

I've only been to Corinne's grave once, besides her funeral, and that was the last time I was here in Westbrook.

Her grave is simple and small and neat. The snow makes everything better.

I set the small key chain I brought on top of her marker stone and start talking.

"Corinne. I'm having a baby."

I tell her all about finding out I was pregnant. I tell her about Nurse Blank. The ultrasounds. The puking in trash cans. I tell her all the things I haven't figured out yet. I tell her about The Kick (leaving out the part where Shep put his hands under my shirt). And then . . . I just tell her everything I can think to tell her about Willa and Shep. Every detail I've absorbed or observed. I give her everything I can think to say about her kids. And then I just stand there quietly, relishing the cool air, the quiet, absolutely aching for Corinne.

I hear my own words said back to me. *Corinne, I'm having a baby.* I sounded . . . a tiny bit happy. And if I were, she'd be the only one who could get it out of me.

I hear crunchy footsteps in the snow and don't think much of it.

The steps get closer and closer, and then Dustin is standing beside me.

"Hey!" I say in surprise.

"I saw you from the entrance. I was headed over to visit Mom and Dad but thought I'd come here first."

"I was headed to them next."

He puts an arm around my shoulders, gives me a quick squeeze, and then lays pink tulips on Corinne's grave.

"You brought flowers for Corinne too?" I ask.

He shrugs. "It's Christmas. She was my friend, you know."

"Wait. Really? You and Corinne?"

He nods. "She was only two grades above me. We knew each other. I've been trying to visit her every so often."

I'm gaping at him. "I . . . have never really thought about that before. That you are pretty much the same age as Willa and Shep's *parent.* How come I never knew you were friends?"

Dustin gives me an uncharacteristically sheepish look. "I had a pretty big crush on her in high school. But I enlisted without asking her out. And then the next thing I heard she'd had Shep. And then Willa too."

"Did you reconnect when you retired and came back to Westbrook?"

That sheepish smile turns into a wistful one. "Ah. Yeah. Remember that summer I lived in the basement? I was sorta seeing her. A little bit. I thought she was just . . . Well, you knew her."

"She was the literal best." My brain is reeling from surprise, but it takes zero presence of mind to remember how incredible Corinne was.

"Yeah. She was the one who helped me find a therapist and . . . yeah, it didn't take long for the two of us to realize that I wasn't in any position to date. And she especially didn't want me around Willa and Shep in that state. So we called it quits."

"But you dated Courtney right after that," I recall, thinking about the timeline of Dustin's romance with his ex-wife.

He puts an arm around my shoulder. "Correction. I got Courtney pregnant right after that."

"What?" I throw his arm off and turn to him, hands on my hips.

"Yeah. Crazy, I know. I guess promiscuity runs in the family?" he says, palms up. "I never had the courage to tell Mom and Dad, though. Courtney and I just tied the knot right away and told everyone that Keeley was a month early." He bumps my shoulder with his. "I'm glad you told us the truth."

"I . . . know . . . nothing . . . about you," I decide.

He laughs and magics some fingers across his face. "And that's the way I like it."

"You and Corinne," I muse, turning back to her grave.

He reaches forwards and puts two fingers on the stone. "I couldn't believe it when I found out she was sick."

"I know."

"And then when it all happened so fast."

"I know."

"Are Willa and Shep all right?"

"Yes. No. They'll always struggle with not having her around. But she made them into really strong people." I think about them for a moment. "Strong in completely opposite ways."

"I'm glad you have them."

"God, me too."

He fiddles with the key chain I left for her and then sets it back down. I loop my arm through his. We walk like that, quietly, linked, our breaths misting in front of us.

Mom and Dad's headstones are side by side and tidy. They remind me of pillows on a perfectly made bed. The ten years since they were laid in the ground has not been time enough to soften the lettering or the sharp corners. Nearly a third of my life has passed since they've been gone, but their grave sites still look young compared to many of the wizened, mossy plots that dot the cemetery.

I unlink from Dustin and lay a small green wreath on each of their headstones, careful not to obscure their names.

What would they have said to me, had they been sitting at that dinner table last night? Would they have been Team Dustin or Team Mal? They certainly had firsthand experience with the shock and panic of an unexpected pregnancy . . . but they were married and had already reared three children.

I squat next to my mother's grave and lay a hand on her headstone, feeling her name underneath my palm. "I really screwed up your retirement plans, didn't I?"

At fifty-two, they'd probably just started dreaming of snowbirding to Florida in the winter. Or maybe getting a little cabin on Lake Michigan where they could play cribbage and watch the sunset. Instead they went back to the maternity ward and spent the next eighteen years diligently raising me.

I wept for days when we lost Mom to a heart attack my first year of college. And I'd barely pulled it together when Dad followed not three months later. It's hard to imagine ever healing from a wound like that, but standing up and pressing a palm to my belly, I realize that I'm a different person now. I was still a kid when they died. And now I'm getting ready to have a kid of my own.

"Thank you for . . ." I say to my parents, resting so well together. *For having me. Raising me. Deciding I was meant to be a part of your lives.* "Just, thank you."

I step back and watch the sky while Dustin lays his flowers and talks to them for a little while. Just when I'm starting to get a little chilly, he appears at my side and the two of us start the walk home.

"So, what's with the salamander?" he asks.

I blink at the non sequitur. "Oh, the key chain I left for Corinne? It's kind of an inside thing between me and her."

"Tell me," he says. And what a charming thing to say. In a world full of evasions, a simple *tell me* is refreshing.

I look up at him and against the bright white sky, he looks handsome.

"When I was little," I start. "Maybe seven or eight, there was this big hubbub a few counties over because some development company wanted to build a cookie-cutter housing development on undeveloped land. But it was this whole mess, because apparently there was this one special kind of salamander that only lives in that two square miles in the whole world."

"Whoa," Dustin says. "Didn't know we had salamanders in Michigan."

"Yeah. So the housing development would basically extinct the species. People were up in arms about it. Corinne wanted to go protest the development one weekend, but Willa and Shep didn't want to go. She turned to me and said, 'Wanna come?' and I did. We went together and she helped me make a big sign. We just kind of sat there, but there were a lot of other protesters and scientists to talk to. The next weekend I asked if she'd take me again, and she did. We went almost every weekend for maybe two or three months, and then finally the developers gave up, because someone had secured all this paperwork claiming the salamanders were a protected species and . . . yeah. The rest is history. It was my first taste of conservation work."

"I never knew that," Dustin says, watching his feet as we walk. "That Corinne was the one who got you interested in it. I guess . . . she was kind of the opposite of Mom and Dad for you, huh?"

I chuckle. "Yes. You could probably say that. Corinne was so full of energy and always . . . wanted me around. She thought Willa and Shep and I were hilarious and interesting. And then, yeah, when I wanted to stop going to church and started leaning far more into science and the environment, she understood. It was nice to be known."

I wipe at the tears that are drip-dropping off the end of my nose, and Dustin hands me a crumpled tissue from his pocket. "I just feel so relieved, having told her." I sigh. "Sometimes it's hard for me to get my thoughts straight about her because I spend so much time with Willa and Shep. And their feelings definitely take precedence."

It occurs to me then, walking arm in arm with Dustin, that he was the first person to talk to me about "the baby." And Corinne was the first person who *I* talked to about "the baby."

For a moment I can totally see them as a couple. Sometimes it's baffling how little a person can know.

He's quiet until we're almost all the way back to the house. And then he says, "You can do this, you know. The single mom thing. Corinne did. And you had all those years of watching her do it."

When Dustin inherited this house from our parents, he left my room the way it was. So Christmas night, I sit in my childhood bedroom at my childhood desk and I write in a notebook that sports Christina Aguilera in her "Dirrty" phase on the cover. I'd had to hide it underneath a drawer so my parents wouldn't find it (way too risqué for them), and to my delight, it was still there when I looked for it a few minutes ago.

My delight has pretty much ended there, however. Because my phone is glowing with undigestible information. I'm looking at Willa's budgeting spreadsheet that she had sent me a couple weeks ago but felt too scary to open until now. After all, it's Christmas and I might as well start practicing stressing about money, right? I take imaginary numbers and subtract them from my bank account. The numbers that are left are very small.

At least there *are* numbers left.

I can't help but think about how lucky I am. I have health insurance. And hand-me-downs from my brothers' kids. But the harsh reality is that once my parental leave is over, I will need to afford daycare. Which is a second rent. Thousands a month. My salary minus rent and living expenses and the cost of daycare equals *just* enough to keep me in diapers and canned goods.

We'll be living just for the joys of being alive, I guess.

Hope this kid doesn't want to go to college.

Or travel.

Or get presents on their birthday.

I groan and slap the notebook closed and rest my forehead on Christina's tasseled chaps. I say a silent prayer of thanks to my job. Enough money to live alone in New York City all these years. I'm the luckiest bitch on earth. Maybe I should take that finance assistant job and work my way up a ladder I don't want to be on. It'll be penance for spending my savings on throw pillows and decorative tiles all these years. Why don't I have three roommates and a mattress on the floor? Then maybe I could afford to actually raise my kid.

I imagine how Ethan is spending his Christmas night. What do couples do on nights like this? Ah! I know. I bet he's giving Eleni a heart-shaped necklace right this very second. She's in knee-high, green-and-red-striped socks, a thong, and a Santa hat. He can't believe his luck. A woman who is sex on two legs *and* understands the true meaning of Christmas? Jackpot.

Okay, that's probably not what's happening to him right now. But I doubt he's subtracting money from his life savings in a Christina Aguilera notebook. Has he thought about daycare? Or how much diapers cost? Or car seats?

It occurs to me that I'd be a lot less confused if he were just a total piece of shit. This whole good-guy-but-understandably-addled thing is absolutely exhausting. It would be so much simpler to just write him out of my future. Or to write him in, for that matter! I suppose I've given him the gift of time. Figuring it out as we go. But that just means I pick up the pencil to write him in and then drop it back down. Pick it up. Drop it. Pick it up. Drop it.

He says he thinks he wants to be involved. But these are just words. Meanwhile the bump is bumping along and you know what the opposite of "just words" is? A literal human child.

For the first time ever, Eleni's DNA test actually sounds like a bang-up plan. Paternity testing gets such a bad rap. It's for moms on daytime talk shows who may or may not be lying, right? Wrong! It's so your kid can eat fresh vegetables and have a qualified professional watch over them while Mom is at work, putting those fresh vegetables on the table. Is that too much to want?

I exit out of the glowing spreadsheet on my phone and go to my texts. I'm not sure what I'm about to text Ethan. Maybe something ghoulishly ominous. Is it possible to Ghost-of-Christmas-Future someone into paying child support?

But to my surprise, I see that underneath my last text to Ethan, there's actually a response from him that I didn't see at the time. He must have texted while I was on the phone with Shep and I didn't notice.

Merry Christmas to you too, the text reads. *When are you getting back to Brooklyn? Can I come see you? I have something to give you.*

Is it an extra 20,000 dollars a year? I type into the text box and then delete it. *New Year's Eve,* I text instead. *And yes, you can.*

Twelve

And now, here I am, a week later, in the freezing cold, waiting on my stoop in New York for the father of my unborn child. My toes are slowly turning into frozen baby carrots in my boots while I glance up and down the block, feeling like I swallowed a pineapple.

And there he is all of a sudden.

He's carrying a big, flat box under one arm and squinting up at house numbers.

"Ethan!" I call, and wave one arm over my head.

There's that familiar moment of genuine happiness when he sees me. Those first few seconds when he recognizes me and his whole demeanor bursts into a sunny *hi.*

He's at the bottom of my stoop, looking up at me. I've probably mentioned he's attractive, yeah? Well, he is. That shiny hair and one of those low browbones that bring to mind Tarzan and the kind of sex that makes one of your hiking boots get caught ten feet up in a nearby tree.

"Hi," I say. With any luck he thinks I'm normal. And not currently beating away thoughts of Tarzan sex.

"Happy New Year. Thanks for letting me come over."

"Sure thing. Want to come up?"

He bounds up the stairs and puts one arm out. He gives me the *Can-I?* eyes and I melt. Of course he can.

I get an absolutely fantastic New Year's hug and then I'm

leading him inside, up the wooden steps towards my second-floor unit.

"I love these old brownstones," he says, whisking one hand along the ornately carved banister, stopping for a moment to look at the tinny brown corners of the ancient mirror that lines one wall.

"I know. They each have their unique charms."

"How'd you find this place?"

We creak up the stairs and pause at my front door as I dig my keys out of my pocket. "The old-fashioned way."

"Craigslist?" he guesses with his head cocked to one side.

I laugh. "Bingo."

I let him in and hold my breath. New people don't see my setup very often and I'm vain enough to admit that I *live* for this moment. The one where a newcomer sets foot in my house and reevaluates all their own life choices because my apartment is just that awesome.

"Dang," he says as he toes off his shoes. "Nice place." He lifts up the flat box. "Okay, so . . . this is—"

"Hold on." I hang up my coat and stalk towards him. "That's all you're gonna say? 'Dang, nice place'?"

"Oh." He blinks down at me. "You wanted more?"

"Are you kidding?" I throw my arms out towards my living room. "My throw pillows pick up the accent colors in those prints—which are in handmade, antique frames by the way. Those flowers are *real*, which means I stopped by my flower guy on the way home from the airport. Look at my bookshelf! It's a work of art! Hold on. Hold on. I know what the problem is. You need the full effect. Here. Go over there. Stand there. No. Sit down. That way you can see into the kitchen area and down towards the bathroom and bedroom. You can see it all from there. And wait. Just wait. Do you like lemonade? Homemade raspberry lemonade?"

He looks dazed. "Um, sure?"

"Great." I go to the fridge and pull some out. "Admire this pitcher, please. It's an heirloom. Probably. I got it at a yard sale. And these glasses are *actually* an heirloom. They were my great-aunt's. Here. Here's your lemonade. Enjoy it, and while you're enjoying it, please appreciate the incredibly aesthetically pleasing and super relaxing aura of my home."

"Incredibly relaxing," he assures me as he sits on the edge of a wooden chair that's basically in a hallway in order to better appreciate the long, skinny view of my apartment. He takes a big gulp of lemonade, winces as he swallows it down. "Yum."

I eye him for a long moment. "You don't like raspberry lemonade, do you?"

His cheeks pink up. "Um. No. I don't."

My hands fall off my hips and I dance sideways to lower myself down into my favorite armchair (I had it reupholstered with a limited-edition Italian satin I scraped and saved for six months to afford, but I decide not to mention this tidbit to Ethan). "Any chance we can blame the last four minutes on me being very, very pregnant and thus a bit more loopy than usual?"

And then he says the exact right thing: "We can blame whatever you want on being pregnant."

I grin at him. He grins back. His phone buzzes in his pocket and his grin disintegrates. He pulls his phone out so fast I'm surprised his pocket doesn't rug-burn the skin off the back of his knuckles. "Sorry," he mutters to me. And then he type-type-types on his phone. He looks up at me. It buzzes. And then he's type-type-typing again. "Sorry," he says again, sliding his phone back into his pocket. "Eleni is . . . still getting used to this whole thing. The least I can do is make sure I'm available when she reaches out."

I decide not to touch that one with a fifty-foot poker.

He clears his throat. "So, uh, you have a flower guy?"

Yes, good idea, Ethan. That's actually a fantastic way to placate me right now. He's smarter than he looks. "Yup. Ted. He's an absolute gem. He calls me when he has extra blooms from someone else's arrangement, so I usually get these very unusual bouquets. They're cheap too. Sometimes they're amazing and sometimes they're duds, but I like that they're—"

"Unique? Yeah. I gathered that. That's the cool part about antique-y or heirloom stuff. It's usually pretty one-of-a-kind."

He stands up and walks over back towards the front door, where he'd leaned the box he'd brought over. "Um." He clears his throat. "Speaking of unique . . ."

He brings the box over to me and sets it at my feet. He looks miserable. Or mortified. Or both.

"Um. What is it?" I ask him because the thing he's doing with his face is not typically how you want someone to look right before you open a mysterious box they've just presented to you.

"My mom," he croaks, and then clears his throat again. "Is an artist and . . . yeah. After I told her about you, she painted this and wanted you to have it, but she wouldn't let me see it first and she does some pretty out-there stuff and—" He drags both hands down his face. "And so all I can do is preemptively apologize."

My fingers are now gripping the box so hard I'm shocked it doesn't puncture in ten tiny points. I immediately could not care less what this is a painting of. This could be a nude portrait of John Travolta and I would hang it on my living room wall. Because this painting is physical proof that the man standing right here in front of me told his family that he's going to have a baby with me.

DNA tests and solo doctors' visits immediately seem like teeny-tiny little ants next to the elephantine painting that's resting up against my knees.

"I guess I didn't realize you were going to tell them, um, yet." (Or at all.)

"Well." He rocks back onto his heels. "You told *your* family. It seemed only right."

Right? I file that word away for later inspection.

"So she told you not to look at the painting and you didn't?" I find this almost nauseatingly endearing. I've learned more about Ethan in the last minute and a half than I have in all the preceding months since I met him.

He shrugs and puts a hand up to the back of his neck. "She has kind of a sixth sense about these things. She always knows when I try to pull one over on her. Anyhow . . ."

He's grimacing at the box as I start to tear it open.

"How did your family take it?" I ask him.

His eyes flick up from my hands to my eyes. "Oh. Pretty well. They were surprised, because it's, you know, surprising. But they took it well."

"They don't think it's weird that you're having a baby with someone who isn't your girlfriend?" I don't know why I poke at that, but I do. I test to make sure it still hurts. And yup, doesn't feel great.

"Well, like I said, it's a surprise, but no. They know that Eleni and I weren't together when you and I . . . So, it's not like they're disappointed in me morally or something.—Oh, thank *God*, it's just a sunset."

I've pulled the painting out of the box, but the painted side is facing Ethan. He takes it out of my hands and faces it towards me.

"It's a sun*rise*," I correct him. Because I'm absolutely certain I'm correct. I take a long moment to just look at the painting. It's pointillism, acrylics, great color sense, and an interesting, blurryish point of view. "It's a sunrise right before you've had your first sip of coffee," I decide.

He nervously looks from the painting in his hands to me. "Do you like it? It's okay if you don't. Just stick it in a closet or something."

"I really like it." And I'm not placating him. I actually do. It's not my usual taste, but I was serious when I said that anything that came out of that box I was going to love. "Put it up over there, please. You can take that big print down."

I know I've said the right thing because as he's turning away I see that his eyes have lit up with relief and . . . pleasure, maybe? It seems like it might be sort of a rare experience for someone to respond positively to one of his mother's paintings.

My phone buzzes on the coffee table (bespoke, fifty bucks from a farmer's market in Virginia, had to buy an extra bus ticket to haul it up here), but Ethan thinks it's his phone and he dives into his pocket, nearly bobbling it in his scramble to answer Eleni at warp speed.

"Hello?" I say pointedly into my phone, one eyebrow raised at him. He quickly turns back to the painting and fiddles with the balance on the frame just a bit more.

"Happy New Year's, you pregnant floozy!" Willa shouts into my ear.

"Hi! Happy New Year's!"

"Buzz us up, we're downstairs." I had plans to see Willa and Isamu later today, but apparently they're early. My eyes flick to Ethan, currently standing with his shoes off in my living room.

"Oh."

"Wait, are you not home yet? I probably should have checked on the timing."

"I'm home." I gulp. "Ethan's here too."

"Oh. Well then you *definitely* have to buzz me up."

"Hold on." I cut her off because Ethan is waving his hands at me.

"I was just gonna leave," he tells me. "Don't worry about me."

"All right," I tell Willa. "Come on up."

He bends and starts quickly clearing up the box. I've never seen someone fold a cardboard box into neater squares. It's the size of a milk carton in about six flat seconds.

I buzz open my downstairs door. "That was Willa," I say.

"Your best friend." He hands over the remains of the box to me. "Does she . . . know?" He glances at my clearly pregnant belly. And then scrapes a hand over his head. "Of course she knows. Sorry. Does she know who *I* am? Should I introduce myself?"

"Yes and yes. She's intense but it's gonna be fine."

My front door sails open and there's Willa. She's in leather boots up to her knees and a trench coat that's open at the waist. Her beautiful blond hair is tumbling everywhere. She completely ignores me and lioness-pounces Ethan using only her eyes. If she were a single panel in a comic, the caption would read *Jury's Out, Bitch.*

"Uh. Hi?" That's Ethan, he's probably just seen some key scenes from his life play before his eyes. I step between them.

"Ethan, this is Willa Balder. Willa, this is Ethan Rise."

"It's nice to finally put a face to the name," she says, leaning down to unzip one boot and then the other.

"Willa, just go inside already." She's gently shoved aside and then—*WTF*—there's Shep. When Willa said "we" I automatically thought she meant Isamu.

I feel like one of those Technicolor soap bubbles floating on the breeze. And Shep is a toddler's pudgy finger. *Pop.*

My first time seeing Shep since he cuddled me in a lovely dark room and it's in front of Ethan. I'd love a chance to blink out of existence for a little while, please.

"Hey, hi." Shep says the first to Ethan and the second to me. "Happy New Year's, everybody. Ethan, it's good to see you again." Shep has kicked his shoes off and strides towards Ethan with his hand out. Which is a good thing because if he'd strode towards me with his hand out I might have jumped straight into it. I go back to my armchair before anyone has a chance to see the look on my face.

"You too, man."

When I finally look up, I'm alarmed at suddenly how tiny my living room looks. It's because there're three extra people here—oh, who am I trying to kid. It's because there's one person in particular and he had his hand up my shirt the last time I saw him.

"So . . . sorry we barged in," Willa says, not looking sorry in the least, her eyes on Ethan, testing his reaction.

"I thought you were coming over later?" I glance at Shep. "With Isamu?"

"Isamu got a last-minute gig, so I'm stuck with this loser."

"Is that raspberry lemonade?" Shep asks, spotting Ethan's mostly untouched glass across the room.

"Yup," I say.

"*Your* homemade raspberry lemonade?" he clarifies.

"The very same."

He could drown a canoe with the wake he leaves behind. He emerges back from the kitchen already halfway through his glass. "Oh. Sorry," he says, looking around. "Anybody else want some?"

"I already have some," Ethan says. And then he crosses the room and gets his glass and gulps some down.

His eyes are on Shep. Shep's eyes are on me. Mine are on Willa. Who, unfortunately, is my best chance at making this situation at all handle-able.

"We wanted to see if we could convince you to go out for a little bit. I know the plan was to hang at home, but if you're up for it we thought it would be fun to hit the town. We haven't done that in forever," Willa said.

Actually, the last time we did that, I went home with Ethan. The only person who puts that together is Shep, and I can feel his eyes on the side of my face. "Oh. Sure. I can't promise I'll stay out too late, but sounds fun."

"Come to Good Boy," Ethan says, and I blink at the now-empty glass in his hands. He looks around at us. "I have to work tonight, but I'll make sure you get a great table and even on the rowdier nights, it's never too crazy in there. It could be fun." He stands up and pulls his coat on, steps into one boot and then the other, bending to tie them. "If you want, I mean. Just an idea."

First he polishes off the lemonade and now he wants me around for New Year's?

I can see in Willa's eyes that she thinks it's the best idea anyone has ever had. A VIP table where she can freely judge Ethan from on high? He's willingly opened himself up for her scrutiny and she shan't be passing up the opportunity. It's all a girl like her could ever ask for. But before she can say a *hell yes*, I'm up and meeting Ethan on my doormat. "Hold, please," I say to the Balders.

I duck out into the hallway of my building, closing my door behind me so we can get a second of privacy. Ethan, looking thoroughly confused, frowns down at my bare feet on the hallway floor.

"Will Eleni be there?" I ask him. "Because I should probably meet her someday, but I think tonight might be a little soon for me. And on a big drunken holiday, I just think it might be a little chaotic and—"

He gently takes my shoulders and gives them a quick squeeze before he drops his hands away. "No. She won't be there. I wouldn't do that to either of you. I know . . ." He pauses. "I know I haven't made this easy for you, but I swear, Eve, I'm not trying to make it *harder.*"

I nod. Nod again. Then I push my door open and lean my head back into the living room, where Willa and Shep are engaged in some sort of whisper fight. They freeze and glance up at me guiltily. "We're going tonight," I tell them.

Willa breaks into a semi-evil grin.

Ethan ducks back in as well, says a quick see-you-later, and then he pounds down the stairs and is gone. I didn't get a *Can-I?* hug, but then again Willa probably would have scissor-kicked him if he'd tried.

I close the door, lock it, and sigh. "Instead of going to the bar," I ask them. "What if we all just fell asleep and woke up when the baby is about ten years old? That should be enough time."

"We're going to the bar," Willa says before producing her phone from her pocket. "Oh, this is Isamu. Let me take this. I'll be one sec." She heads into the bathroom and lightly shuts the door, and Shep and I are more or less alone.

"I guess I should go get ready, then."

I head into my bedroom. And I just know that Shep's followed me to the doorway. I can feel it.

"How do you do this?" he asks, and I turn to see him, one shoulder on the doorframe, peering around my room.

"Do what?"

"Make a room look like this?"

There's enough awe in his voice that I begin to feel the glow of pride. And the glow of something else. "Is that the proverbial you? Or me in particular?"

"Yes, both. Teach me your ways."

I go to my closet and start rifling through it, looking for something to wear tonight. "Well, you have to really *consider* it. Like, it can't just be something you decide to get done all in one weekend. You have to think about what style you want, how you want to feel when you're in the room, what colors you like. And then you choose things one by one. And slowly you get it right."

"Sounds impossible. What was wrong with that one?" He's watching as I take blouse after blouse out of my closet and then put them back in, fully nixed.

"The red one? Won't go over the belly, I don't think. I haven't done a ton of wardrobe updating yet."

"Ah. Shame. I like that shirt . . . I've been thinking about what you said. About moving out of Willa's."

"Really?" I stop my clothing perusal and turn to face him. "And?"

"I'm ready to start looking at options, I think. I think it'll make me happy to be somewhere, uh, on my own. Even if it's a ton of work to do that."

"Really! You should look at that email list I mentioned. A bunch of people I know have found their place through it." I scamper across to my little desk in the corner of my room and sit him down in front of my laptop.

"Wow. Okay. Yeah." Shep is bemused but he immediately leans forwards to start scrolling through listings. I head back over to my closet.

I really, actually, might not have anything to wear tonight. I've been able to get away with structured jackets and flowy blouses and big shapeless dresses so far, but I'm realizing that with all this newfound poppage I'm not sure I'll be able to button any pants.

I stop putting things back into my closet and start piling them on the bed instead.

"This one might actually work," Shep says, and I turn around to see him holding up a fuzzy sweater and squinting in my general direction.

"That's—no. Just no. I'm not going to the bar looking like Cookie Monster. And are you already done with the listings? Nothing piqued your interest?"

"You look good in blue!" he insists, then studies the sweater again, seeming to eventually agree about its Cookie Monster-ishness and tosses it back on the bed. "I did. I just emailed one to see about getting an application and a viewing time."

"What? You were only over there for like three minutes!"

He shrugs. "The apartment looked nice enough and it's close by. Works for me."

He goes to my closet and tugs on the hem of a gray dress.

"This one," he says,

I consider it. "Well, I guess a dress would solve the pants situation."

I pull it out and study it. I haven't worn it in a couple years but it's simple enough to not have gone out of fashion. In my current state, it'll be skintight.

"You're having a pants situation?" he asks, looking thoroughly amused as he pushes aside a pile of clothes to sit down on my bed.

My brain shorts out. I've been doing a decent job up to here of pretending like everything is coolcoolcool between me and Shep, but . . . now he's sitting on my bed and I've got skin-memory of exactly how warm his palms are.

"Ah. Pants. Yeah. None of mine fit."

"They make those expander bands, you know. They're like

an elastic band that goes around the top of your pants so that you can keep them unbuttoned but they still stay on."

"Right, but I haven't gotten around to all that. I've just been kind of . . . wearing my oversized stuff and—" I freeze, lower the dress out of my eye line, and turn to him. "Wait. How do you know about expander bands?"

He shrugs but it is not nonchalant. He starts messily folding the pile of clothes. "I dunno. Common knowledge."

I playfully slap his hands away from my poor clothes. "You call that folding?"

He blinks down at the sloppy stack of clothes he's just made. "What would you call it?"

"Piling."

Willa calls out, "Sorry that took so long!"

"In here!" I yell to her. "Just despairing over the fact that nothing will ever fit me again!"

She appears in the bedroom door and if she thinks it's weird that Shep is sitting on my bed, she doesn't say anything. Which must mean she *doesn't* think it's weird because Willa always says something. Why isn't she saying something? It *is* weird, right?

"Ooh. The gray is a good choice, I think. It should stretch, right?" She crosses the room and tests the fabric. "Shep, turn around."

And then she's reaching for the hem of my shirt and Shep barely turns around in time. He's obviously seen my bump before. Heck, he was on his knees in front of it a little over a week ago. But still, stripping my shirt off while he watches feels like an entirely different matter.

The stretchy pants go next and then Willa is bunching up the dress and lining up the neck hole like I'm four years old. Frankly, it's delightful to be manhandled.

Willa, take the wheel.

We struggle me into the dress and she straightens it where it narrows tightly at my knee. "Yeah," she says. "That's a yes from me. Shep?"

He turns back around and I busy myself with flattening a wrinkle at my hip. "Yes," he says with a slight cough.

"Mmmm," Willa says, turning me ninety degrees. "I don't know, actually. We've got some underwear lines back here."

"I never understand why women are so concerned with underwear lines," Shep says. "Underwear lines are great. They show you where the underwear are." He squints at my bottom half. "Or aren't."

"Thank you for that invaluable insight, Shep. Moving on!" Willa claps. She's the cruise director tonight. "We should power up. Is that Cuban place on the corner still around?"

"Yup."

She turns to Shep and they automatically shoulder-hunch down into rock-paper-scissors stance. The words *choose your fighter* dimly echo through my subconscious. The rounds are viper-fast and just as vicious. Ten seconds after they start Shep stands, two fists raised in the air, his head back, surely thanking God.

"I'm getting you a dirt sandwich," she tells him, stalking over to her coat and punching it on. "And for you I'll get the rice and beans platter," she calls to me. And then, in a shocking move, she strides over, bends down, and addresses my stomach in a perfectly normal voice. "And don't worry. For you, I'll get some plantains."

My hands automatically smooth over my bump. Damn these Balders, the only two to talk directly to the baby and making me go all squishy inside.

"Back in a few," Willa says, and she's gone.

I start trekking back and forth from the bed to the closet, resituating all my clothing.

Shep hands things to me, piece by piece, getting them ready on their hangers. "You really do look . . . nice," he says.

"Thanks." I still haven't looked right at him since I put the dress on. I can't be sure, but I think he might be doing enough looking for the both of us.

"But your legs might get cold," Shep says quietly.

I look down at the pair of legs that Shep is officially looking at. "I have tall socks and tall boots. And a long coat. I'll be all right."

He doesn't look convinced but he doesn't say more. I reach up to put the final hanger back in place and turn to the mirror on the inside of the door. "Why is it lumpy up here?" I ask as I try to smooth down the bunched-up fabric at my shoulder.

Shep turns to inspect the issue. "Oh. I think your bra strap . . ."

I lift the dress at the collar to try to untwist the bra strap that must have gotten candy-caned in Willa's vigorous dressing of me. Shep watches me one-handed fail for a patient ten seconds before he steps to my back, leans down, and smooths one finger down my bra strap, straightening it out. He sets the dress back into place.

He's painted a luminescent line over a bra strap and suddenly my shoulder is having a conversation with my entire body. Even my cheeks have gone pink. I watch him in the mirror and he's watching my shoulder and then, without moving away, he meets my eyes in the mirror.

There's a slow zoom-in, a sway, no more oxygen left in the entire world.

He's quiet for a long moment. And then, in a very low voice, he asks, "Did you tell him?"

My brain immediately transports me back to the lavender room, Shep's even breaths, the best movie ever playing in the background while his big hand makes subtle movements under my shirt. He can't possibly be asking if I told Ethan about that night, can he?

"Told him what?" I ask, wishing my voice could just play it cool.

"That the baby kicked."

"Oh." *Right.* "No, actually." I turn to him and I swear, *I swear,* I don't intend for these next words to mean more than one thing. "I haven't told anyone."

But the sentence lands hard between us and we're finally looking in each other's eyes, no mirror between us.

"Why?" he asks eventually, and I'm almost positive he means more than one thing just like I did.

"Because . . ." I'm searching for words like a beached goldfish gasping for water. *Because it's private. Because it's too new to talk about. Because it's a secret I don't want anyone to spoil. Because I want to protect it just a little longer.*

There's no answer I can give that doesn't sound blatantly like *Because I'm apparently horny for you and have no idea what the fuck to do about it.*

Willa slams back through the front door. "I'm back!" And I'm out of the bedroom in a flash. Leaving Shep, and the moment, behind.

Thirteen

It's a Friday night at ten PM and I am currently sweating with my arms over my head and dancing with a stranger.

It's the third weekend in a row that Willa and I have come to Good Boy.

On New Year's Eve, the three of us walked in post–Cuban food and were immediately treated to a view of a very droll-looking pit bull being vigorously humped by a collie. "This is my new favorite bar," Willa decided, and further events did not disappoint.

The music was good, the company was fantastic, and the drinks flowed (for free, courtesy of Ethan). He even made me a long string of virgin mojitos with his very own two hands. Halfway through the night, Willa turned our corner of the bar into a dance floor and it only took about ten seconds before at least five more people flocked towards her energy. By the end of the night, the entire bar was rocking.

I flopped into bed that night happy and sore and feeling more normal than I had since the ol' pregnancy test flipped my life upside down.

The next weekend, Willa had decided to replicate a great night.

"You can't," I'd insisted. "It'll pale in comparison."

But I'd been dead wrong. The second night out at Good Boy was even more fun than the first. Isamu joined us for the last half and if you've never seen Willa and Isamu on a dance floor together, well, honestly you're probably lucky because it's basically soft-core porn.

The third weekend, I didn't argue when Willa showed up at my house with a new dress for me and a big smile on her face. I texted Ethan to let him know the two of us were coming and got a thumbs-up in return.

So we're friends now? Or at the very least, people who can coexist peacefully. Which is exactly what you want from someone you're having a kid with . . . except for the part where his partner hates me and he hasn't said whether or not he actually wants to help with said kid's life.

I mentally slap myself away from wanting it all. That silly little impossibility where absolutely everything is right all at once.

Because, Eve, Eve, don't you know this by now? No one has it all.

But what I *do* currently have is an excellent dance partner. Most men take one look at the bump and either invisible me or sprint from me. This man simply offered me a hand and a smile and spun me around during an old Drake song we both clearly enjoy.

"Am I gonna get beat up?" he asks a few songs later.

"Huh?" I shout back over the music.

"By your boyfriend."

"Oh," I laugh reflexively. "He doesn't exist. No boyfriend."

"Then who's the guy behind the bar staring at us."

I glance over my shoulder just in time to see Ethan looking at me with what appears to be utter misery. I blink and the expression is gone. He's saying something to the bartender and sliding out from behind the bar. He disappears into the back hallway that leads to his office.

"The baby's father," I tell the man.

His eyes grow large. "Ah."

"I think I should go . . ." I point with my thumb in the direction that Ethan went.

"Yeah. Sure. Of course." He's all palms up and already bopping to the beat of the next song. "Good luck, mama."

I dawdle at the entrance to the hallway. It's clearly an employees-only zone and to boldly infiltrate seems like a girlfriend-y thing to do.

Luckily, Ethan is heading back out before I have to decide whether or not to head in.

"Oh. Hey," he says, hands in his pockets. "You looked like you were having a good time."

"The dance floor's fun tonight!"

He purses his lips, covering a smile. "You know that there *is* no dance floor . . . unless Willa's here."

I grin at him. "Yeah. She's good at that." I glance behind me and spot an open booth. "Wanna sit?"

"Yes. Sure." His eyes track around the bar and I wonder if Eleni *actually* knows I'm here.

When we get to the booth, silence descends. "So," he says, drumming his fingers. "Twentyish weeks, huh?"

"Almost twenty. Halfway there."

"Wow." He scrapes a hand over the back of his neck.

"Yeah. I have the big ultrasound on Wednesday morning at nine. They do all the 3D imaging and genetic testing and stuff."

He nods. I wonder if he's going to ask to come with me, but he stays quiet. His eyes go to my belly. "So, uh. Is the baby . . . moving and stuff?"

"Yeah! A lot, actually." It's been my little secret for a few weeks. But if Ethan is outright asking, I'm telling. "The kicks are getting stronger."

"Kicks?" His eyes press closed for a second. "It's been kicking?"

"Yup. Every so often."

He lifts a hand and lowers it. Lifts it again. "Do you think I could . . . ?"

"Oh, sure! Of course! Actually, if I drink something cold, I can sometimes get some butterfly kicks if you want to try that."

"Great. Yes." He's standing up and disappearing towards the bar. He seems . . . *stoked* right now.

He comes back a few minutes later with one of his virgin mojitos that is about ninety percent ice.

I laugh and he looks a little embarrassed. "You said cold," he mumbles.

"Come sit." I pat the bench beside me and he slides in. His hand is flat on the table in front of us and instead of both of us just awkwardly staring at it, I do the kind thing, the Willa thing, and take the wheel. His hand is heavy and tense in my hand and I press it firmly to one side of my belly. "I usually feel them around here."

He's stock-still, his eyes on his hand. My eyes are on his hand too. *Kick, kick,* I think. *He really seems like he needs this.*

The door to the bar opens and, bar owner that he is, he looks up to clock the new patrons. "Oh," he says. "I didn't know Shep was coming tonight."

I didn't know either and my eyes shoot to the door. There he is. In his puffy coat and gigantic winter hat.

The horny-for-Shep thing has not subsided like previously hoped. It . . . is gaining energy and I have absolutely no idea what to do about it. As evidenced by the fact that I would very much like to do bad things to that puffy coat. No one on earth has ever been aroused by a puffy coat before, yet here I am ready to sleep naked inside of it.

"Oh!" Ethan says. And then looks down at my belly. "Oh. *Wow.*"

"Yeah!" I agree, brought back to this current moment. The one where the baby we made together just kicked for Ethan. "Isn't it awesome?"

"*Yes.*" His eyes flicker to my very cold drink, which I have yet to take a sip of. And then to my belly, and then, once more, to Shep. "Yeah. Yeah, it is." His hand slides away.

Shep spots us and heads over, sliding off his big hat and unzipping from his coat. The collar of his plum purple button-down is turned under on one side, and his hair needs a trim. I'd like to spread him on toast and eat him in the bath, please. Thank you.

This is a nightmare.

He half trips over a passing long-haired dachshund who shoots him a withering look. He laughs and gives her a little bowing apology before he slides into the opposite side of our booth.

"Hi!" he says brightly, fluffing a hand through his hair and making it even more messy. "How's it going?"

He seems genuinely happy to see Ethan and I can't explain it, it just . . . deflates me a little.

I've been wondering if Shep is feeling at least a teaspoon of the horny-toast-bathtub thing that I'm feeling. If he is, it doesn't seem to go beyond that. Because if those horny feelings were at all tender, then how could he be so chummy with the man who got me pregnant?

Ethan, on the other hand, is always the tiniest bit stiff with Shep. "Not much, man. How are you?"

See, Shep? That's how it's done. Technically polite, prickly enough to soothe my ego.

I'm officially a mess, by the way.

"I'm good," Shep says, a happy expression on his face.

The three of us sit there in silence until Ethan sits up straight. "I'll, uh, I'll grab you a drink. IPA, right?"

"Oh, you don't have to—"

"I have to check something at the bar anyhow. I'll be right back. Eve, you good? You need anything?"

"No. I'm fine. Thanks, Ethan." He nods and stands up and leaves.

"So, how's it going here?" Shep asks, scanning the bar. His eyes snag on Willa on the dance floor. "Yikes."

"Yeah, she's been a little more . . . vigorous than usual."

Shep studies his sister for a moment, a line forming between his brows. When he turns back to me, the line is still kinda there when he says, "So, you and Ethan seem . . . good?"

His words surprise me, but so does his expression. Is it my imagination or does he seem *not* happy about that? Am I piecing everything to pieces? Am I likely raising my blood pressure right this very second? I take a deep breath.

"I guess so. It was encouraging that he told his family. I feel like that's a forwards movement? That maybe I'm in less of a holding pattern with him? I guess we're becoming better friends. It's been nice spending more time . . . But that's all. Come here." I wave him closer to me. "I can't look at this anymore."

He's confused but he leans across the table towards me. I hook a finger under his collar and it's a sunny-hot day at the beach under there. If I didn't already know he smelled like trees and fresh air and bread, I'd bet a million bucks he'd smell like sunscreen. I smooth his collar and then pat some of his wavy hair back into place. His eyes are cast down towards the table, patiently waiting for his grooming to be over.

"There. Much better."

He clears his throat and sits up straight. "Thanks."

"You know, Shep, you're a real head-turner." I've got my chin resting on one hand and I'm feeling a little sleepy and warm. Probably I'm drugged from the residual effects of putting my fingers inside his clothes. It's the only explanation for why I'm complimenting his looks right now.

"Come on," he says, his cheeks going pink as he slides his palms down his thighs.

"No. I'm serious. You've got this messy/handsome charm. You look like you're the kind of guy who could teach an uptight businesswoman how to sleep in on Sundays. Women love that kind of thing." I'm dead serious, but I'm also putting a liiiiiittle extra sauce on my assessment. It is very fun to watch the tips of his ears get that pink.

He's gaping at me.

"Actually," I continue, "now that I say it, why *aren't* you regularly rocking some uptight businesswoman's world? You're single now."

He clears his throat again. He's looking . . . nervous. I try to think of the last time I saw Shep nervous and come up empty. "Oh. I . . . I'm not really thinking about that these days."

I drag some of the condensation down my glass and onto the table. I draw a squiggle. "Still caught up on Heather?"

"Ah. No." His eyes are on my hand. "No, that's been over for a long time."

I look at him until his eyes finally lift to mine. "About a year and a half, huh?"

He nods.

"Can I ask . . . the whole breaking-up-but-still-living-together thing. How did that *work*? You really never fell back into old patterns?"

I'm pretty much asking if he and Heather kept sleeping together even though they were technically broken up. Sue me.

"No." He shakes his head. "Honestly . . . there wasn't much of an old pattern to fall back into anyhow. By the time I broke things off . . . let's just say that most of our romantic feelings had been gone for a really long time even before that."

"Oh. Wow."

He eyes me. "That's a surprise to you?"

I shrug. "You always seemed . . ." Happy with her? It's an automatic response, but now that I think about it, is it right? Shep pretty much always seems happy no matter what, but did he specifically seem happy with Heather? "Like it was working for you."

"It did. For a long time it was exactly what I needed." He switches the way he's sitting and slides his hand across the table to steal some of the condensation from my glass. He draws an arrow and it's pointing right at me. "I can't believe you called me messy/handsome." He modifies the arrow and then wipes it away. "I've been called messy before. But not handsome."

I purse my lips in disbelief. "Oh, give me a break."

"No, really. I think it's having that one for a sister." He juts his head towards the dance floor, where Willa is having a ball dancing by herself while about ten different guys watch her out of the corner of their eyes, salivating and daydreaming about her in the shower. Probably. "I suffer in comparison."

I raise an eyebrow. "Try having her for a best friend. At least you're a *boy*. For me and her, it's always been a direct comparison."

He gapes at me. "You can't be serious."

I shrug. "It's always been that way. Willa's the movie star and I'm . . . an extra?"

He bursts out laughing. "Tell me you're joking. You have to be joking. There's no way you actually think that."

I shrug again, laughing a little. "Okay, I'm exaggerating. But, I mean, just look at that." I gesture to the crowd of men dancing in Willa's vicinity, eyeing her up.

He studies the dance floor and then points at me. "Men are absolute buttheads and for the love of God, please don't let them dictate your self-worth."

I'm really laughing now. "Fair enough."

"It just kills me that you think that, you know. Because it's so far from reality. You and Willa just have completely *different* vibes. But the two of you . . ."

"What?"

"You know that you two were, like, the *only* thing that the guys in high school ever talked about."

I have no idea what to say to that. "The conversation must have really changed when I accidentally got that short, short haircut."

"You were cute!" he insists. And then pauses. "In a . . . gerbil sort of way."

We both burst out laughing and that's how Ethan finds us. He slides a beer in front of Shep and a little bowl of raspberries in front of me.

"Wow! Thank you!" I start in on them.

"What's so funny?" he asks, pausing for a moment and then sliding in to sit next to me.

"High school," I tell him.

"Ah." His eyes flick between me and Shep. "You went to high school together too?"

"Yeah," Shep says. "I was a grade older. Nerd." He points to himself. "Hot girl but didn't know it." He points to me. "What were you like in high school, Ethan?"

"Oh." He squints and thinks back. "I was . . . my sisters' chauffeur mostly. They were always going shopping and on dates and to the library, and I just tried to look after them all."

"Four sisters," I explain to Shep.

His eyes go wide. "Wow."

"I played lacrosse," Ethan lists. "I got decent grades, but

not great. And my junior year I got drunk in the woods with some buddies and tripped over a tree root and broke my leg. So I had to be on crutches for like three months."

"Ah," I say. "You were the drunk-injury-sloppy-mess kid. We had a couple of those at our school too."

"If you tell me their names, I might know them. We're a very tight-knit community," he says with a straight face.

Both Shep and I burst out laughing and Ethan seems a little bit surprised.

Willa appears at our table panting and fanning herself. "Man, it's fun out there," she says, reaching for my half-melted drink and downing it. She parks herself next to her brother.

Ethan is staring at my now-empty glass. "Should I make you another one?"

"No, thanks," I say with a yawn. "I actually think I wanna head home." I glance at Shep. "Oh, but you haven't finished your beer yet."

"I'm good. You go ahead." He makes a shooing motion with his hands.

I stand and Ethan makes way for me to slide out from the booth. Willa is standing now too and we're all just looking at Shep sitting there alone in the booth.

Ethan clears his throat and then scoots around me and sits back down. "I'll hang."

Shep looks as surprised as I feel, but then his face melts into a smile. "Great."

Willa is pinching me by the elbow and hauling me towards our coats. "All right, see you later!"

"Bye," Shep and Ethan say at the same time, giving identical waves.

I can't stop looking over my shoulder at them even as Willa is bundling me into my coat. "They're talking," I whisper to her.

"Well, it would be weird if they weren't, considering they're alone at a table together."

"What do you think they're talking about?"

"I don't know. What do men talk about? And more importantly, who cares? Ooh! A cab." She's bustled me out onto the sidewalk and is chasing down a cab. It brakes so fast it leaves two feet of black rubber on the street. We slide in and two blocks pass.

"Whatcha thinkin' 'bout?" Willa asks.

"Shep," I tell her honestly. "He . . . told me that he and Heather hadn't had romantic feelings for each other for a long time before they broke up, and it surprised me. But then, when I got to thinking about it, I couldn't actually remember if they seemed happy together or not. It's weird. It's like he and Heather are a blind spot in my memory." I grimace at her.

We pull up to a stoplight and I watch as a crowd of women cross the street in front of us. They're wearing wholly impractical clothes for January, but they look beautiful and glamorous and fun. Jewelry and hair and laughter. That could have been me and Willa a year ago. I can't help feeling like last year was a completely different life.

"Were they happy together?" I ask Willa.

"Shep and Heather? Um . . . yes and no. At the beginning, definitely. Shep has always had this . . . *thing* where he feels like everyone's sidekick. He never tries to be the main event. I think it's probably because of the way he was when we were growing up."

I furrow my brow. "What do you mean?"

"Oh, come on, you know. He was dorky and all about computer games. He had friends but got picked on a lot too. The only reason he wasn't completely annihilated in high school was probably because he was my older brother."

I just stare at her profile. Those swoops and valleys all adding up to visual perfection. "Wow. What's it *like* to have that kind of confidence, Willa?"

She laughs. "You're saying I'm wrong?"

"No. I'm just saying that most people don't say that shit out loud."

She laughs again. "It's you, Eve. I can say anything to you."

There's a distinct pause. I prod her along. "So . . . Shep's a sidekick."

"Yeah. Right. But when he got to New York for school, he, like pretty much everybody who moves here, saw an opportunity to reinvent himself. In the middle of that reinvention he met Heather and she was the first girl who was ever like, *You. You and no one else.* I think it kind of knocked him off his feet." She glances at me. "He'd never been liked like that before."

"Huh." I consider that. He certainly never dated anyone in high school. I knew he wasn't exactly a hot commodity back then. But I honestly never gave it too much thought. To me he was just Shep. Willa's big brother. The kid on the other side of the popcorn bowl. "But then what? They just stayed together too long?"

She nods. "I think so. Neither of them are very confrontational, so they just kept on going. I remember asking him if he was going to propose and he nearly aspirated his drink. Being with her forever seemed like an inevitability, but it wasn't something that he wanted to . . . encourage." Her legs are crossed and she bounces one of her feet, looking out the window as she talks. "He got really sad when Isamu and I got engaged. I think he saw how much I wanted to get married. How happy I was."

"Ugh." I tip my head back. "I hate thinking about Shep being sad. It's the worst."

"I know."

A thought occurs to me. "Do you—do you think he's happy now? These days?"

"I'm not sure," she says. "It's hard to tell with him. He's the sort of person who is happy if you're happy, you know?"

"Yeah." And I do know. I know exactly what she means.

Fourteen

"Is a crush a pregnancy symptom?" It's the first thing I ask Nurse Blank when I see her the following Wednesday for the big imaging appointment. We're in a different part of the clinic that I've never been to before. The room is filled with tubes and vials and equipment that looks like R2-D2's elderly uncle.

"I'm sorry?" she says, glancing up from her clipboard.

"I like your glasses, by the way." They're new, purple, and make her look kinda badass. "A crush. On someone . . . that I should *not* have a crush on. That could just be a pregnancy symptom? It'll go away once I'm not pregnant anymore?"

She blinks. The clipboard lowers. "Honey," she says, and my stomach drops because I do not think she's about to give me the answer I was hoping for.

"This thing is just really messing with my head," I cut in. "And I can't figure out . . ." How not to ruin my friendship with Shep.

"Pregnancy can certainly affect your libido," Nurse Blank offers. "It sends some women into . . . overdrive, shall we say? And pregnancy can also be an emotionally vulnerable time."

I absently stroke my imaginary beard. "Libido plus emotional vulnerability. That kind of sounds like a recipe for a crush to me."

There's a brisk knock-knock on the door and Nurse Blank goes to answer it, holding it open just a crack because I'm already in a robe. "Yes?"

"Ms. Hatch's husband is here for her. Can he join her?"

"I'm sorry, *what?*" I say, leaning around the nurse and making the paper underneath me crinkle. "Who? My husband? By all means send him back, I'd love to meet him."

Nurse Blank turns to me. "You weren't expecting anyone to join you?"

I start to shake my head and then freeze. "Hold on."

I lean over to where my clothes are folded up and extricate my cellphone. I have a stream of missed texts from Ethan.

Big appointment today, right?

Okay, I know this is something we definitely should have gone over before this exact moment but . . . is there any way it would be okay for me to join you today?

Obviously, it's okay if you say no.

I can see that these texts aren't being delivered because you're probably on the train. Okay, I think I'm just gonna come to the office. I'll be in the lobby.

I'm here. I hope this isn't weird. Seriously, it is totally okay to send me away. I just wanted to be here in case it was actually okay for me to attend the appointment with you.

"Oh," I mutter to myself, and then look up to see both the nurses looking at me expectantly. "Is it Ethan Rise in the waiting room right now?"

The second nurse consults her clipboard. "Yes."

"Um . . ." My brain goes seven hundred miles a minute. A series of memories pass through me at light speed. Ethan and me running from geese. Ethan drinking my orange juice for me. Ethan watching through his fingers while I opened his mom's painting. Lovely moments with a lovely person. These are moments I might describe for the baby one day. *The first time your dad and I ever saw you, we were sitting in a doctor's office watching you on a TV screen . . .* "Um, yes. It's okay for him to come back."

The second nurse disappears and closes the door. Nurse Blank looks at me sternly. "Is this the crush?"

Tears automatically cloud my vision and she becomes a blur with light green scrubs on. "No," I whisper miserably. Then there are more memories. These ones decidedly more inconvenient. "*I have a girlfriend.*" And him texting Eleni fifty times while he stood in my apartment. And then, the least convenient memory of all, Shep's lavender room, a kickity-kick, a warm hand under my shirt. I scrub the tears out of my eyes and I watch as she opens the door to the room and flips the little sign on the outside that tells other nurses not to disturb us and then she crosses over to me. She looks like she's considering taking my hand but decides against it.

"Honey, do you not want him to come back here? You can change your mind."

"No, I do. I think, secretly. Somewhere. I just . . . I stopped daydreaming about having someone with me back here a long time ago because he and I aren't together and that's fine—"

I cut myself off because I did not intend to confess quite that much. But her face doesn't change one iota.

"We'll have to pull your robe open to expose your belly, as you know, but he can stay on one side of the curtain, if that would help?"

"No. That's all right. He can stay with me."

She nods, opens the door, and there he is.

He's nervous energy personified. His lips sucked into his mouth, his eyes blown. He looks messier than I've ever seen him before. He's in mismatched athleisure. Joggers in black and a hoodie in green. His wool coat looks out of place tossed on top. His shoes are coming untied. He clearly made a last-minute decision and ran out of the house to make it on time.

"Hi," I say with a dorky little wave.

"Hi," he breathes, his eyes wide as he takes in all the machinery. "Can I?" he asks, pointing at the threshold of the door.

I melt. "Come in."

"Hello, I'm Ethan." He introduces himself to Nurse Blank. He's got his hands in his pockets and he's shuffling sideways towards me.

"I'm Nurse Louise." She introduces herself, and I almost burst out laughing. I guess it's probably time I stop internally referring to her as Nurse Blank.

He comes to stand next to my head and there are blood draws and pricks and questionnaires. Next is the imaging. This is what we've all been waiting for. The sonogram machines they use at a regular appointment create images that are almost unintelligible to everyone but the medical professionals. But this is the equipment they use to see every single nook and cranny of the baby. And we'll apparently leave with refrigerator-quality pics.

Nurse Louise opens the door for the tech to come in and she steps back. I think for a moment that she's going to leave, but then she doesn't.

The tech lubes up the little camera wand thingy and opens my robe. Ethan's eyes are on my belly and I resist the urge to cover myself. The last time he saw my bare stomach I looked very different. If we were alone, I'd demand that he say something. Instead, he just stares.

The wand gets pressed to my belly and I jump because it's cold. We all turn to the screen where the image is about to pop up.

"Wait," Nurse Louise says from behind us, to the tech. "She doesn't want to know the sex."

She asked me that a few appointments ago and I'm, frankly, ridiculously touched that she's remembered.

"Oh," the tech says. "Then don't look at the screen and let me check which position the baby is in, because there are times when it can be obvious from the imaging."

"Even this early?" I ask.

"Oh, yeah."

"You don't want to know the gender?" Ethan asks me.

"Sex," I correct him. "We won't know the gender until the baby knows its own gender. But no, I also don't want to know the biological sex of the baby either."

He blinks at me. "Okay . . ."

I can see I'm gonna have to explain this one. "The sex is not important to me, and I don't want preconceived notions of gender roles already interfering with the way I think about this person." I point to my belly. "Plus, I don't want the sex to be the thing that everyone focuses on when I inevitably start getting gifts and wind up with a bunch of blue stuff with trucks or pink stuff with ballerinas. I'd much rather wind up with a bunch of stuff that's more gender neutral."

"Do *you* want to know?" the tech asks Ethan. "Because if you look right now, I could show you."

His head half turns, but his eyes stay on me. "No. No, I'll wait to find out the gender too."

"Sex." Nurse Louise and I correct him at the same time. I legitimately love her.

"All clear," the tech says. "Take a peek."

We both turn and do identical intakes of breath. Because that, right there, is a perfect little hand. And foot.

"Look at that *foot*," I say.

"There's two of 'em," the tech says, doing a lot of clicky-clicky stuff on the keyboard and making the image freeze every few seconds. I guess she's taking lots of pictures. The whole thing takes about half an hour, because they really do look at every inch of the baby. For a while, the baby has its face turned away, towards my back, and they have me roll from side to side to get the baby to move.

"A drink of cold water?" Ethan suggests when the side-to-side thing doesn't work.

"Good idea," the tech says, and I swear I have literally never seen anyone look prouder of themself than Ethan looks in that very moment.

Nurse Louise gives me a glass, and I drink deeply. Sure enough, the baby squirms, turns. And . . .

"Face! Face! There's the face!" I shout.

"Look at the eyes!" Ethan whisper-shouts.

"The *nose.*"

The baby's mouth opens and it's a perfect oval. There's something extremely familiar about that posture.

"That's a yawn," Nurse Louise says.

"A *yawn.*" Ethan has two hands covering everything but his eyes. "Please tell me you got a picture of that," he tells the tech.

She smiles. I smile. I look back and Nurse Louise is almost smiling. Is there anything more charming than a new father demanding comprehensive photos of his child doing nothing but yawning?

After that, the fun part's over. There is more poking and prodding and question-asking. Everyone leaves and I put my clothes back on. Ethan and I are shuffled to a small office and Nurse Louise comes in with a set of pamphlets in each hand. She hands one set to Ethan and one set to me.

There's the usual suspects of pregnancy nutrition information, pregnancy exercise information, pregnancy mental state information. But there're also some new things as well. How to start preparing your home for a baby. What to have on hand in case the baby comes early. A checklist for everything you'll need to have prepared for the hospital stay.

I stare at the pamphlets, a little shell-shocked.

The tech knocks on the door and delivers us a little folder. "The images," she says with a big smile.

"Only one set?" Nurse Louise says with a frown.

"Oh." The tech looks back and forth between us. Most couples likely only require one set. "Sorry."

I flip open the file folder and Ethan and I look at each photo.

"Can I take this one?" he asks. It's a perfect still of the left hand. "And this one?"

Of course it's the yawn that he wants. I say yes to both and throw in one foot photo out of the goodness of my heart. Everything else is mine.

Then suddenly we're back on the sidewalk. I look up at Ethan and the winter sun is directly behind his head. I can't see his face. "Am I a total fool for not having considered the birth at *all*?"

He steps out of the sun. "No. I think you're probably taking this one thing at a time."

"But I . . . I just got used to the fact that there's a baby in there." I point to my stomach and then let my hand drop. It's one thing to have Dustin say "baby" at Christmastime. But these scans, these pamphlets, these are a finish line. "But now I have to get used to the idea that there's gonna be a baby out here." I gesture to the world. "What the fuck."

"Yeah. I know. What the fuck." He scrubs a hand over his hair. His ears look cold. He rushed out of the house without a hat.

"I'm gonna have to take care of this kid," I tell him. "Like, *all the time*. Twenty-four hours a day. For the rest of my life."

He opens his mouth and closes it. Looks distinctly uncomfortable. "Lunch?" he asks.

"Oh. Yes. Okay." I let him lead me to a fancy little brunch spot with a single peony in water on every table.

"Oh. Congrats," the bored waiter says when he sees the

ultrasound images laid out on the table between us. Ethan and I cannot tear our eyes away. "What'll you have?"

Ethan must see that I am not capable of the read-choose-speak progression that is required of ordering food at a restaurant and kindly orders one large stack of pancakes and one huevos rancheros.

"You can have either of them," he tells me. "Or both. Or all. Oh!" He flags the waiter back down and orders an extra side of hash browns and fruit salad.

"Eve," he asks eventually. "Are you all right?"

I'm still staring down at the images. Everything that seemed novel and thrilling when it was on the screen in the exam room now seems all too real when it's printed on paper. These photos feel almost like a legal document. Each photo is a hidden clause in a contract I signed months ago while half drunk and seconds away from orgasm. What a terrible time to make a life choice.

"I'm gonna have a baby," I say dimly.

"Yes," Ethan agrees quietly.

"And kickoff is in twenty weeks."

"Give or take."

"Is time suddenly moving, like, bullet-train fast for you too? Because for me . . . Okay. Okay. I'll get twelve weeks of maternity leave," I say. Which is generous in comparison to most jobs but now seems absolutely ludicrous. "What do I do at the end of the twelve weeks? I haven't even looked into daycares yet. Maybe I need one of those Rottweilers that feeds your baby butter sandwiches and dances to records while you're out doing errands."

"What?" He's alarmed.

"You never read that children's book? *Good Dog, Carl?*"

"Oh." He looks relieved I haven't actually descended into gibberish. "You're saying you're worried about childcare."

"And you're not?"

He takes a deep breath. "We'll figure it out. I work at night, you work during the day. Between the two of us we'll be able to—"

My chair makes a hyena screech as I scrape it back across the tile floor. I charge out through the restaurant. I'm on the sidewalk. No coat. Not even Shep's pink Christmas market hat to keep me company. The air is slicingly cold in my lungs. I take huge gulps of it and sag against the brick wall of the restaurant.

My coat is placed over my shoulders and my two hands are smooshed together and rubbed for warmth. "Eve?" he asks me, his eyes soft and worried.

"You can't just *slide that into conversation*!" I half shout. My voice is shaking. I've got adrenaline tingling in my hands and feet. "You have to actually *tell* me!"

"What?"

It feels incredibly good to yell at Ethan.

"I'm over here, mincing words and trying not to scare you away. Meanwhile, I'm panic breathing in the shower because I am about to have a baby *by myself*. And you have the audacity to sprinkle in 'we'll figure it out.' Who is *we*, Ethan? You can't just casually mention that *we'll* figure it out and that you'll be willing to take care of the baby during the day when I'm back at work when you haven't even told me if you're going to be around *at all*! Mentioning is not telling! Jesus Christ, I need some clarity already."

"I'm sorry," he says. "I'm so sorry." I'm folded into a hug that's warm and soft and fits well. I cry bitterly hurt tears into his shirt, and his hug tightens. "I'm such a bonehead."

"No, you're not!" I get mad about that too. "This is an awfully hard situation and I know it's not easy for you. But if you're a bonehead then *I'm* a bonehead and I don't want to be a bonehead. We did this thing together. Both of us were there and there was nothing wrong with what we did!" My forehead is against his collarbone and I can feel him shiver either from my words or from the cold. "We just liked each other and had sex. Is that so bad?"

"No," he whispers. "It's not. I'm sorry. I'm so sorry."

"What are you sorry about?" I tip my head back.

"I shouldn't have said that. About taking care of the baby during the day. Not without . . ." He abruptly unhands me and falls to a crouch, balancing on the balls of his feet. He grips his hair. "I'm so scared, Eve. I'm so scared that I'll make a promise to you that I can't keep. What do I do if I can't keep it? What then? I just . . . I want to make everything all right for you. And I can't. I just can't. I'm so sorry."

For some reason, his hysteria calms mine. "Oh. You still don't *know* if you're going to be around." I name it for what it is. "I . . . guess that with you telling your family and giving me that painting, and us hanging out at Good Boy, and the appointment today, I kind of thought you were signaling that you had decided but hadn't bothered to even talk to me about it . . . but, okay. If you're still not sure . . ."

He doesn't say anything. I study him down there. Whatever is happening to him looks very hard. But him reassuring me that we'd figure this out together, that seemed very . . . easy.

"Ethan . . . why *did* you say that about taking care of the baby during the day?"

He's frozen for a second and then he shakes his head, staring down at the sidewalk. "It was stupid. It just . . . came out." Finally, he looks back up at me. "Eve, I don't know what I can reasonably promise you. Between the bar . . . Eleni . . ."

I eye him for a long moment and then decide that with our relationship as nebulous as it is, I really—sadly?—don't have very much to lose. "Ethan . . . don't think, just answer. Do you *want* to be involved?"

I ask the question so fast he doesn't have time to guard against it. It's a direct hit. His face opens plainly. It's Sunshine Ethan. The easy happiness and desire that emanates from somewhere deep and unimpressionable. The very light that drew me to him in the first place.

His phone starts buzzing in his pocket.

The clouds draw over the sun and he closes his eyes.

"Excuse me . . . Are you two coming back? Or . . . ?" The waiter is leaning out the front door of the restaurant. "Because you still have to pay for your food. And you left your, uh, pictures."

I blink down at Ethan, the pain etched across his face, and as strung out as I feel, I still want to make him feel better. "Ethan, dear. We forgot the baby in the restaurant."

He gives a watery laugh and stands up slowly, bringing his hands to his knees and then walking himself up straight. "Oh, boy."

We go back in and eat a very quiet meal. We have to get on different trains so we hug goodbye on the street. I can hear the crinkling of the photo folder where Ethan presses it against my back. It's a strange hug. There's something resigned about it. It's heavier and less tentative than his normal clinch. This feels like an *I'm sorry* hug. It makes me nervous and I don't like it nearly as much as his *Can-I?* hugs.

When we separate, he walks backward for a moment and waves at me with his free hand, the photos limp down by his hip. Then he turns his back. And he leaves.

Fifteen

It's a Saturday morning and I have tears in my eyes as I watch a woman with a beach ball under her shirt unroll a yoga mat and stretch into Warrior A.

She's the most pregnant person I've ever seen this close up. Her shirt has given up on life, curling up at the hemline and revealing pink stretch marks over her pale belly. She's sweating, her dark brown hair pulled into a neat bun. She exhales all of her air with her voice, a loud *haaaaaaa* that makes the others in the room turn towards her, but she doesn't give a flying fuck. She's got other things to think about. Like the fully grown person levitating between her ribs and pelvis right now.

I'm drawn to her like she's a celebrity and I roll my mat out next to hers.

"I hope this isn't rude," I say. "But you. Are. A *total badass*." It might be the cheesiest line I've ever fed to someone, but I mean it down to the marrow of my bones.

"Thanks," she says without smiling. "I'm River." She reaches out for a handshake.

Last night I sat at my counter eating my mandatory after-dinner bowl of cereal and looking at the new ultrasound photos I'd recently magneted to my fridge. That perfect tiny hand, a profile of a sweet little face. The person who, at some point, is going to be eating a bowl of cereal sitting right next to me. Words like *natural birth* and *sleep training* floated up out of the ether and taunted me. I mean, my God, I'm going to have to make sure this kid gets a Social Security number. How does one even go about that?

I whipped out my phone and the cursor blinked menacingly from Google's home page. *Go down the rabbit hole, Eve,* the internet beckoned. *Find out just how much you don't know. Attempt to panic-research yourself into a knowable future.* Ha.

But then a thought occurred to me. I think I might have been waiting (patiently? Yeah, no) this entire time for Ethan to make up his mind and provide me with a little stability. But . . . what if that stability came from me instead?

What if instead of panic-research, I found a way to prepare myself a little. Because no one else is going to be able to do it for me.

I don't have questions so much as, ya know, rabid fears. Questions require answers. But fears? They require *camaraderie.* So. I did google something. One simple phrase: *ways to meet other pregnant people in NYC.*

There are ten or so of us in this prenatal yoga class. Some are visibly pregnant—though none as much as River—and some who seem much earlier along. We arrange our mats and smile shyly and ultimately wait in silence.

A triangle chimes and a woman in extremely sexy yoga wear floats into the room. She's got an eyebrow piercing and an exposed midriff the approximate dimensions of a cereal box. I don't think I'm imagining the collective sigh from those of us in the room who are currently expanding at alarming rates.

"Welcome, welcome," she says. "I see some familiar faces and some new ones. How are you feeling, River?"

"Million bucks," River responds with a grunt. She's the only one of us who isn't sitting, and I have a feeling it's because once she goes down she doesn't come back up.

"My name is Melody," the teacher says. "And I'd like to

start things off with a share-out. We'll go around, say our names and pronouns and, if you're comfortable, say how far along you are. I'd also love to hear your intentions for this class, what you'd like to get out of it, so that I can help you get there. We'll start here."

We all go around one by one saying names and pronouns and numbers. Everyone is at different stages, but everyone seems pretty stoked about being pregnant. I get nervous when it's about to be my turn.

River goes before me. "I'm River. She/they. I'm a week past my due date and my intention for this class is to get my damn water to break."

There's some nervous laughter (from others) and some genuine laughter (from me). And then it's my turn.

"Hi, yes, hello everyone. My name is Eve. She/her." I cover my nerves with a joke. "I'm twenty-oneish weeks along and I feel like I could bench-press a car."

"Please don't attempt that," Melody says, and everyone laughs, including me. "I take it you've got that second-trimester energy?"

"Yes." I nod vigorously. "It's weird . . . I didn't think that I could possibly feel like *myself* while being pregnant, because pretty much as soon as I found out, I've felt like . . . not me. Exhausted and mood-swing-ish and, well, you all get it, you're pregnant too."

Ten heads pretty much nod in unison.

"But then over the last few weeks I've started to feel back in my body again . . . like someone who just happens to be pregnant, not like pregnancy is my entire identity. It's actually . . . kinda fun."

A few of them nod, a few look at me like I'm a complete turncoat, and River gives me a smile like I'm a sweet, naïve moonchild who's never seen the red mist of battle.

"And what are your intentions for this class?" Melody asks me.

"Oh. Ah . . . I'm not sure. I . . . this was a surprise," I say, pointing to my bump. I get a few chuckles and a few sympathetic nods. "And I'm still getting used to . . . being a pregnant person. I've never spent any time with other pregnants. So . . . here I am."

I'm here to claim my place among the other gestators. No more keep-it-to-myself pregnancy.

A secret is only a secret if no one knows about it. What's a secret that everyone knows but no one talks about? It's *shame.*

And isn't that exactly how I've been treating this? Too-big shirts that don't actually hide reality and not a word to my coworkers? Telling my family at the last possible moment, under pain of Christmas? I spent months not even thinking the word *baby.* I've asked Ethan for exactly nothing. I haven't sought out any other pregnant people or read anything pregnancy related other than the pamphlets from the OB-GYN. There's a reason why Nurse Louise is the only person I ever ask about pregnancy.

There's taking it slow, and then there's clinging to denial.

And *then* there's River on all fours. They've stripped their shirt entirely off. Their sports bra is begging for mercy. This person is all tits and belly and sweaty hair. They're breathing loud enough for it to echo and don't care if we stare.

Secrets cower at the feet of this badass.

I take myself through the class, pausing and sweating and groaning and smiling. I gulp water at the end of the class and sit with my legs akimbo. I wave to the others and watch out the front window as River waddles down the sidewalk (shirt back on).

I walk home slowly. It's one of those late January days that's a complete and utter gift. Warm sun for no reason. Birds, blue sky, the whole nine. I keep my jacket open and my belly out. I go home and wash up and then, finally, muster enough energy for an errand I've been putting off ad infinitum.

I take a train to MamaBump, a resale shop selling everything pregnancy. As I stand out in front of the shop—looking in at the maternity clothes and strollers and stretch mark creams and nursing pillows and teething rings—I can see all the little ways I've denied that this pregnancy was happening. Really happening. Culminating in a new person on earth.

No more pretending that I'm the same old Eve.

I'm Eve plus one.

It's time.

Time to show off the bump.

"Oh, finally," Christina groans when I walk in to work on Monday.

I'm wearing a tight-ish dress (designed with room for a baby bump) and have my jacket draped over my arm. There's nothing to distract from my shape.

She gestures to my belly. "Can we talk about this at last? I thought my head was going to explode from all the mouth-shutting I was doing."

"Oh, you knew?" I ask her.

She drops her chin and gives me the eyes. "Eve. *Please.*"

"Really? I thought the big mustache I slapped over it was a really good disguise."

She laughs and then kind of sobers. "Are you coming to those drinks tonight? Because Ryan is coming and she's sort of sensitive about pregnancy lately. I swear all of our friends are having kids."

I blink at her. I like Christina. I really do. But I'm suddenly struck with the urge to flick her on the forehead. I was expecting a simple *Congrats, Eve.* Now I feel like a pest for having the nerve to be pregnant in front of Ryan. "Oh. Er . . . okay? Not going to the drinks tonight" is all I can manage.

The elevator ding-a-lings and a group of chattering co-workers spill into the reception area. I turn and see seven people all staring at my midsection.

Jesus Christ.

"Yup," I say with a shrug. "Pregnant."

Half the people come towards me (the women); most of the others awkwardly sidle away (the men).

First up is Bevi. She looks cross. "You should have told me," she says with her hands on her hips. "I could have been juicing for you this whole time!"

"Oh. Right. Well, tomorrow's a new day." I feel scolded.

Next is Lorraine, who looks like Mrs. Claus if Mrs. Claus were thirty-five. "I didn't even know you were married," she says. The crucifix around her neck catches the light and nearly blinds me.

"I'm not."

"Oh. Congrats, then," she says, and it definitely sounds like she's telling me *Good luck in hell.*

Yeah. That's enough of that.

I turn towards the annex.

"Congrats, by the way!" Christina calls after me. I wave at her and keep going.

Micah and Xaria are already filled in on the news, thanks to Bevi, who scurried along in front of me. They both congratulate me, though Xaria is side-eyeing me in a calculating sort of way. Micah is pulling my chair out for me and . . . bowing? He may never have been this close to a pregnant woman before. He can barely make eye contact.

It's a long day of more awkward interactions with co-workers until four-fifty-five PM when the door of the annex swings open and in waddles Marla, our other pregnant coworker. She looks just about ready to pop. She's got one hand on her belly and the other carting a little wicker basket.

"Sweetie!" she says to me, a huge smile on her face. Her skin is positively glowing right now. Maybe it's the pregnancy hormones or maybe it's just Marla. She's always been a very sunny person. Her locs are twisted back from her face in a high bun and she's wearing a jumpsuit thingy that I badly want. She's perfect.

She crosses the annex to me in slow steps and then proudly presents me with the basket. "I went out on my lunch break. There's a great baby shop about two blocks from here. Do you know it? It's called Little Bears. Anyhow . . . these are the only pacifiers my babies have ever liked. This right here is truly the only swaddle you should ever buy. Let's see . . . I loved this book when I first got pregnant. There's a ton of good ones that I can recommend to you, but this one actually prepared me for birth. And these are just some goodies for you. Low-sugar chocolate, a shower bomb, and . . . what else? Anyhow. I'm so happy for you! You look beautiful!"

I'm not sure if Marla expected to get the crap hugged out of her, and frankly, I have to come in at a pretty extreme angle to accommodate for the two in-uteros between us, but here we are. I hug her as tight as I can, though we've never done anything like that before.

"Thank you so much," I tell her, from the bottom of my heart. And I mean it so much. "I really, really needed this," I whisper to her.

"Getting a lot of weird reactions?" she whispers back. "Yeah, that'll happen."

We break apart from our clinch and then we're both just standing there, grinning at each other. I look at her bump, she looks at mine.

"Boom," she says, and gently taps her belly against mine.

I burst out laughing. "That's a first for me."

"I just wanted the babies to say hi." She glances at her watch. "Hmm. Well, I need to get going but let's have lunch next week? I love talking pregnancy and babies and all that jazz. And besides, I've been through this before, so any questions you might have, I'm here."

"Marla, I love you." And I fully mean it. She's just turned my entire day around.

I'm thrilled. I'm filled with helium. I float all the way home.

Sixteen

If my life were a movie, this is when we'd get a montage. Shall I prepare one? Sure. Here we go.

The rest of January and most of February goes like this: I feel like a million bucks in my new pregnancy clothes. I'm cutely round and hungry a lot but mostly filled with energy. I get on the train and if my coat is open someone almost always gives me their seat. My co-workers are equal parts awkward, sweet, and ignoring of my state. I work on the newsletter for work with a raptorlike voracity, but I've started to avoid Xaria around the annex. Do I finally say farewell to my dream of being a policy analyst and join the dark side—ahem—the finance team? My rabid desire for job security is at war with my aversion to budget-slashing. Marla and I start having lunch twice a week and I can't believe we haven't been doing this all along. She's one of the most candidly upbeat people I've ever met. She shows me pictures of her children smiling, screaming, and snotting, and sleeping in the middle of the living room floor. I ask her, *Be honest, what does your house look like at the end of the day?* She texts me pictures of a toy-strewn hurricane-hit-it living room and I hyperventilate. Then twenty minutes later she sends another picture of her living room neat and tidy with a caption that says *One thing at a time.* For the first time I'm kind of *excited* about having a kid.

I'm seeing Willa and Isamu and Shep a lot at their house, but only together as a group. I don't sleep over again, because if I did, I'd probably accidentally ask Shep to put his hands under my clothes again. Every ten seconds of every day my mind wanders to his too-long hair, his brown-gold eyes, the scent of the inside of his coat. Every twelve seconds of every day I mentally Taser myself.

I go back to prenatal yoga and laugh with the other almost-moms at how hard it is to even unroll the yoga mat these days. Dustin mails me a gigantic cardboard box covered over in crooked tape. It's a little bassinet that connects to my bed so that I won't have to get up when the baby needs me at night. I take a selfie smiling next to the box and send it to him.

Rock on, mama, he texts back. It's a gold-star compliment and I wear it in my smile for days.

But the thing about montages? They omit a lot.

Here's an alternate montage. Here's me checking my phone as soon as I come aboveground from the train. Here's me checking and double-checking my email every seven minutes even though I know for a fact I have my notifications on. Here's me refusing to go out on the weekends anymore, especially not to Good Boy. If Willa wants to do something with me, we walk in the park or watch movies at her house. Here's me avoiding the eyes of the nurses at my next doctor's appointment. Only Nurse Louise is the recipient of one sad smile.

Because, yes, pregnancy is the biggest thing that's happening in my life right now. The second-biggest thing? I haven't heard from Ethan *once* since he walked away with half of our ultrasound images.

Yep. You heard it here first, folks. I'm knocked up and ghosted.

Well, maybe *ghosted* isn't fair because I haven't reached out to him either. But every time I think about texting or calling him, I think about his phone lighting up on his kitchen counter and Eleni seeing it.

I spend a lot of time thinking about Ethan crouching down on the sidewalk outside the restaurant. I think of him offering to be with the baby during the days. I think of the fact that he hasn't contacted me once since. I'm glad I've started to search for stability elsewhere. Because there's no fruit on that tree, my friends.

I'm in my apartment on a sunny Saturday most of the way through February, looking at the internet and doing some light crying, when the buzzer to my apartment does its fuzzy zappy ding.

I cross over to it. "Hello?"

"Hey, it's Shep. I have some stuff for you. Can I come up?"

I scrub at my face and buzz him up, take a deep breath, and let it out all at once, pasting a smile on. But the second I swing open my apartment door, his face falls. "What's wrong?"

I sniff and try to keep my face from crumpling down. "I'm fine!"

"He still hasn't reached out?"

"Nope. And I was just torturing myself by researching birthing classes and imagining attending them alone."

"Eve, I could . . ." I see the rest of the sentence gathering in his mouth. His generous mouth. His soft-looking perfect mouth with that tongue I've been daydreaming about.

Absolutely not.

"Don't," I tell him with a very bossy finger. "Don't offer or I might say yes."

He has a grocery bag in his hands that he shifts from one arm to the other as he struggles out of his coat and kicks his boots off. "Why can't I offer?"

"*Shep,*" I say, both hands on my hips. Shep absolutely cannot, *cannot,* attend birthing classes with me. The only thing more painful than attending them alone might be attending them with a man who is happy when you're happy. Who will turn his life upside down to help others, but my silly little pregnant heart will want it to mean something that it probably doesn't. Shep is not the father of my baby. And I absolutely cannot pretend, in any way, shape, or form, that he is. Nothing good will come from that.

"But—"

"Ix-nay, arling-day."

That is apparently enough of an answer for him because his argue face turns to his *don't aggravate Eve* face. "All right, all right," he grumbles, and heads towards the kitchen, where he starts unpacking the bag.

"What is all this?" I ask him. He's up to his shoulders in my fridge, rearranging and fitting things inside.

"Groceries," he says, his voice muffled behind the enormous head of cauliflower he's jimmying into the produce drawer.

"Well, duh. Why did you bring them?"

"Because I went shopping and thought of you."

I nearly swallow my proverbial gum. "Oh. Wow. Thanks." I look around. "Where are all *your* groceries?"

He pokes his head out of the fridge. "I couldn't carry it all so I just got yours. I'll go back for myself later."

"You . . . went shopping for yourself, thought of me, scrapped the plan, and just bought me a bunch of produce?"

He closes the fridge and dusts off his hands. "Is that a problem?"

A problem? Yeah. It's a huge one.

You ready for that third montage?

Okay, there I am, defiling my detachable shower head on a regular basis. You know how much porn I've watched in the last month? More than in the rest of my life combined. My erotica stash has never seen so much action. My ebook reader slams a Gatorade when it sees me coming.

Remember that innocuous little word Nurse Louise said to me once? I believe it was *overdrive*? Well, yeah, apparently that was code for the absolutely unreal sex drive that some women get later on in pregnancy. I swear to God I should invest in a mechanical bull with a dildo strapped on. I'm being crude, I know, but being so horny you watch professional sports just to see man-sweat will do that to you.

Lately I'm finding myself siding with judgy Lorraine from work. You *should* be married when you have a baby. Her reasons are religious. Mine are that I believe every pregnant person deserves to be within arm's reach of something readily humpable at any given moment.

And he asks if it's a problem that he's grocery shopping for me in *that* T-shirt that's showing me the exact shape of his wide shoulders? And then he bosses around my produce with those clumsy-big fingers of his? And then he washes his hands and puts his weight on his elbows and leans towards me, head cocked to the side? A wash of stubble on his face? Brown eyes and messy hair and his *Shep* face that I just wanna sit on?

Yeah. It's a problem.

"Nope!" I squeak. "Thanks, by the way. I was thinking of doing an early dinner anyhow."

"I'll make it," he says. "Were you hoping for anything in particular?"

I've reached my limit. If he does one more nice thing for me right now I'm going to absolutely destroy our friendship. With my teeth.

"Just—You—Sit." I'm steering him by his shoulders over to the barstools that line my kitchen counter. He's goes willingly but at the last second resists.

"Are you sure?"

I do a quick experiment and try pushing, with all my

strength, on his shoulders. He doesn't budge. Honestly, he barely looks like he notices.

I take a step back and survey him. "Sit," I say again.

He does.

I'm all skeptical eyes and scuttling sideways like if I don't keep him in my eye line, I'll turn around and he'll somehow be ten times hotter.

"Where'd you get that T-shirt?" I ask him testily as I slap fixings for double-decker fried egg sandwiches and fruit salad on the counter. What I'm really asking is where he got all the muscles underneath it, but that's neither here nor there.

"Some store. At least let me dice the fruit." He's leaning across the counter, fingertips on the cutting board, sliding it towards himself, and that's the story of how I realized that even sitting on the stool, Shep's body is almost the same length as my kitchen.

I flip the eggs and then rummage around for a big bowl for the fruit salad. Shep scoops handfuls of melon into it. Each piece has been chopped messily into a different shape and size. It's so cute I'd like to personally kiss each and every piece.

I quickly turn my back and start assembling the sandwiches. They are a very private recipe that is delicious to me and only me. A smorgasbord of cheese and random junk from jars in my fridge door and, yes, pickles, and vegetarian deli "meat" straight from the fridge. They are likely disgusting and I would serve them to zero people on this earth who aren't Shep. But for some reason, I have this hunch that he's going to like it.

"That's . . . horrific," he says after his first bite.

Okay, so maybe he won't like it.

"Well, give it back, then!" I say, trying to slide his plate away from him.

"No! No. It's horrific in a satisfying way." He reclaims the plate and takes another gigantic bite. "It's the bad boy of sandwiches. I'm not supposed to want it, but I do."

"Definitely the sandwich from the other side of the tracks."

"I don't think I'm going to be able to look at myself in the mirror after this." He's already halfway through his sandwich and I'm satisfied with his reaction.

We finish our sandwiches and Shep quickly cleans up the kitchen while I scoop out fruit salad for both of us. By tacit agreement we move to the couch and put our feet up on the coffee table and stab the melon chunks one by one, savoring them like they're bites of ice cream.

"Nothing like a good honeydew."

I pat the top of his head. "Oh, sweet innocent Shep. The honeydew is only there to better illustrate how far superior cantaloupe is."

Instead of batting my hand away, he leans into it and sets his clean bowl on the credenza behind the couch.

If anyone needed proof that I'm lost in the weeds for this man, it's the fact that I don't jump up to find a coaster.

After a moment, he reaches up to loop his fingers around my wrist, puppeteering my still hand against his hair, making me pet him.

Do friends lean against each other and pet each other's hair?

I can't think about that right now. I can't think at all. This is wonderful.

I set my bowl aside too and give in. His hair is the blond-brown of a lion's mane and just a bit too shaggy to be an actual style. I'd like to take a swim in it. A lazy summer's backstroke, with the sun so bright you're forced to close your eyes.

I'm transported back to familiar summer afternoons, floating on my back and getting lightly roasted in the sunshine.

"When was the last time you made it to Setter's Pond?" I ask him.

His eyes pop open. From this close, they're a far lighter brown than I'd thought they were. Almost yellow. Almost gold. Late-afternoon sun. That buxom orange right before it gives up and fades to twilight.

"A couple of years ago. I brought Heather. I wanted to show her where we spent our summers. But it wasn't the same."

"What do you mean?"

"Someone added a boat launch so there were a lot of boaters and you could tell the part with the rope swing had become kind of a party spot. There were beer cans and stuff all around. It wasn't like when we were kids." His eyes are on me.

I can't watch my fingers get lost in his hair or else I'm going to do something very silly, so I watch my own feet instead. "It used to be so quiet when we would go."

He nods. "I'm sure it's more idealized in my head but I remember it as you, me, and Willa. Nobody else around."

"Peanut butter sandwiches and bags of potato chips."

"Raspberry lemonade," he says, and I feel a thrill that he remembers it the same way I do.

"Remember that big beach towel your mom would pack for us? The queen-sized one?" I ask.

"Of course I do. I used to claim it and lay on one tiny corner of it, hoping that you'd take the other half."

I laugh, but my blood has suddenly turned to electricity.

"Really?" I ask.

"Sure," he says. "Nobody wants to share a towel with their sister in a two-piece."

I laugh again, but this time my blood is fizzling back to normal. Maybe he didn't quite mean what I thought he might mean.

"I miss naps at Setter's Pond," he says. "That was the best sleep of my life."

"You always were a very proficient sleeper," I remember with a nod.

"Not since Mom died."

I catch his eye. "Wait. Really?"

He scrubs a hand over his hair and our fingers brush. "Yeah. I mean, it's gotten a lot better than it was, but for a long time I was barely sleeping. Hey, what's wrong with your feet?" he asks, squinting down at them. I've been slowly kneading them against the edge of the coffee table, the way kittens do against their mother's bellies.

"Nothing. Just pregnant."

"They're sore?" he asks, and before I can even answer, he's reaching for them, gathering them up and swinging them into his lap. I'm rotated ninety degrees so that my back is against the arm of the couch and he sits up straight in the center, slightly crowding me.

"You always have the best socks," he says.

These ones are so fuzzy they literally do not fit inside shoes, so they're my house socks, my weekend socks, my cry-and-look-at-birthing-classes socks.

But right now they're my try-not-to-moan-like-I'm-orgasming socks and I can see this is going to be a challenge.

Shep's fingers are bossy-firm and for a man who chops melon with reckless abandon, he is methodically, carefully, taking care of every inch of my foot.

His fingers freeze and I feel his eyes on my face even though I've got two hands covering it. "Are you all right?" he asks.

"Jesus *fuck* don't stop," I groan, and he resumes. I feel him shift, hear a throat clear, and I do believe that my response has punted us soundly out of friends-definitely-do-this territory.

There are things I don't know about Shep. And they are things that I cannot, *cannot* ask about right now sitting on this couch. They are sweaty things. Hem-of-his-T-shirt-caught-between-his-teeth-so-it-doesn't-get-in-the-way things. They are things that require a warm washcloth immediately after and his body as a pillow for falling into exhausted, sated sleep. Not even if I were drunk right now could I ask him about that.

"Should we watch something?" I ask, pulling my feet off his lap and straightening up.

"Oh." He looks at the place my feet just were. "Sure."

He leans over and grabs the remote and hands it to me. I channel surf and land on *Thor*, the funny one. "Ooh! Yes. We're just in time."

"In time for what?" Shep asks.

"The big haircut."

"Huh? I haven't seen this movie before."

"Oh. Everything is going down the shitter for Thor and blah blah blah, he gets his hair chopped off. It's my favorite part."

"And that's your favorite part . . . why?"

"You'll see."

He narrows his eyes and studies the screen with such concentration I want to just scream. He's so cute I can't stand it. The big moment happens and he still looks confused. He turns and sees my face and then understanding descends. "Ah. You like it because you think he gets even hotter after his haircut."

"Duh."

"Really? Haircuts?" Shep cocks his head to one side. "I always think men look so stupid right after they get a haircut. You can see all their tan lines. It's very . . . back to school, you know?"

"You're entitled to your opinion," I tell him graciously. "You're wrong, but you're entitled to it."

He laughs and now that the haircut scene is over, I channel surf again. We land on a commercial for some kind of drug and one of the side effects that the fast-talking honey-voiced lady announcer lists is sleeplessness. I mute the commercial.

"Shep . . . back then. When you weren't sleeping. When you were struggling after your mom died . . ."

"I know," he says quickly.

But I have to say it all. I can't let him assume. "I would have been on the train in half a second. There's nothing I wouldn't have—"

"I know," he repeats.

"Do . . . do you do that a lot?" I ask quietly. Willa said that he's always felt like a sidekick. When do sidekicks get the spotlight? "Not tell people when you're hurting?"

"I'm trying to get better at it." He looks at his hands, which spread down over his knees. He leans forwards and laces his fingers, drops his head. "Honestly, I'm trying to learn from you. You're so good at saying how you feel. At *feeling* how you feel."

"Only with you. With everybody else I only say about one-tenth of what I'm feeling." Even with Willa these days. "Besides, I'm the hot mess express. It would be really grand to have nice, tame emotions that are best relayed on pink stationery with loopy handwriting and a lovely little stamp with an angel on it. *That's* how I'd like to start telling people how I feel."

He shakes his head. "I've seen your handwriting. All spiky and tilted. Total serial killer handwriting. Anyone who got a letter like that would think for sure you were threatening them."

I laugh. He laughs. He's still leaned forwards, his elbows on his knees, looking back over his shoulder at me. I tuck my feet to one side and play with the fuzzy socks. "Shep . . . I'd like to be a person you can tell how you're feeling. Even if you aren't proud of the feeling, you can tell me and it won't change how

I think of you. Especially if you're having a hard time. I want to know. I know that Heather took care of you, but I would have . . ."

I trail off because how the hell to finish that sentence? I would have what? Taken the train up to Heather's apartment and tucked him into bed? Made him hot cocoa? Listened to him talk for hours on the phone and made sure he had at least one square meal a day?

Yes, yes, yes, yes and yes. Yes to all. Of course I would have done those things for Shep. Just like I did those things for Willa.

He knows everything I don't say. "And *that's* why I didn't tell you . . ." he says as he points at the expression on my face. "At that point, my main priority was making sure Willa was all right. She had it harder than I did, I think. And I knew that you and Isamu had to be there, with her. If I'd told you I was roadkill on the shower floor, you would've shown up with a spatula. But Willa couldn't make it through without you. So I just . . . did my thing and let Heather take care of me and, honestly, it worked. That was the hardest time in my life, but I got to the other side."

"Is . . . is that why you didn't move out even though you broke up? Because relocating was just too much to handle?"

"Yeah. It was actually Heather's idea for me to stay, bless her. I broke up with her before my mom died. But she said I should take things one step at a time. She put her whole life on hold for me. We knew we weren't going to get back together. But she just . . . put me up in her guest bedroom and let me cry on her shoulder for a year. She's a good person. She's such a good person."

I've never been wild about Heather—it's hard to like someone who looks at you like you smell bad—but at this particular moment, I feel a swell of gratitude for her. I couldn't be there for Shep, but she was. And thank goodness. If he really was crying on shower floors, I'm glad to know he wasn't doing it alone.

"If the arrangement was working, why'd you move out, then?"

"She met someone she was interested in. I was convalescing. I'd made it through the darkest parts of grief, I think." He sighs and scrapes a hand through his hair. "Generally, it was just time."

"She's dating?"

"Yup." He nods and sits back. "Rick. He's a really nice guy. They're moving in together next month."

"Wait." I shake the cobwebs out of my head. "You've *met* him?"

"Yeah. Like I said, they started dating while I was still living there. He used to come over."

"Oh, my God. *Shep!*" I punch him on the shoulder. "Don't you *ever* look out for number one?"

"Huh?" He rubs at his shoulder, so I bat his hand away and rub at it myself.

"Sorry. I didn't mean to punch that hard."

"You're punching me because I like Rick?"

"I'm punching you because you don't have a jealous bone in your body and it's *annoying*."

Maybe I'm punching him for Rick. But come on, it's clear I'm punching him for Ethan. Shep rubs my belly and eats my sandwiches and wanted me to share a towel when we were teenagers, but he also smiles at Ethan and shakes his hand and seems sad that he's ghosting me. It's confusing and frustrating and poor Heather must have spent a fair amount of time wanting to smack Shep in the face with a pillow.

He cocks his head to one side, his eyes searching mine, and I can tell that he's trying to parse out my meaning.

I unmute the TV, his eyes on the side of my face, and we settle into a documentary about coral reefs. I wake up an untold amount of time later to Shep pushing the hair out of my face. There are two Sheps and I'm confused. One of them is leaning over me and one of them is lying behind me, holding me. I'm warm and comfortable and could lie like this until morning.

"Eve," one of the Sheps says. "You should go to bed."

"Hmmm?" I ask.

"It's late," the Shep standing over me says.

"Oh."

I sit up and the dream Shep disappears.

I wobble when I stand and he grabs me by the elbow. I toddle towards my bedroom and then the sheets are being pulled back and I'm crawling in and the lamp is clicked off and look, there's dream Shep again. He's there on my side of the bed. I make room for him. My hair gets brushed out of my eyes again.

"Sleep well," he says. My bedroom door clicks closed, and he goes.

Third Trimester: How to Style a Beach Ball

Seventeen

I'm at work inventorying manila envelopes with my head in a closet when someone taps my shoulder.

I pop out of the dark closet and am practically hissing at all the sunlight the program staff get up here on the eighth floor. The admin annex is a flat-gray cave with mauve accents. We like it so dank in there you can hear the condensation plopping off the tips of the houseplants. Everybody else gets to live in the sunshine.

I blink the light away and find Xaria staring down at me. "You're a hard woman to track down these days," she says dryly.

Probably because I literally run when I hear her high heels a'tappin'.

"Just busy!" I chirp.

"Head back down to the annex with me?"

I nod and she falls into step beside me. We take the elevator downstairs together and I file after her into her office.

"So," she says bluntly, her eyes burning a hole through my soul. "Have you made a decision?"

I shift on my feet. "To be honest . . . I haven't had a lot of time to consider it. I've had . . . uh . . . a lot going on." My hand naturally curves around my belly but Xaria's eyes do not look down.

"I know a whole new job description might seem like a lot, but you'd slip into it fairly easy. You obviously know all the players already."

I have begun to have a suspicion. And it's not a nice one. I think Xaria is on the hunt for a lackey. If I were her, I, too, would be sick of being the bearer of bad news, of getting glared at during all-staff meetings. I, too, would want someone to start doing my dirty work.

But am I really gonna agree to be the one cutting budgets and telling the red pandas to take a hike?

"I know I'm pushing you, Eve. It's only because I think you'd be great at this job and I'd like to work with you in that capacity."

I defrost a little bit. Her genuinely wanting to work with me hadn't occurred to me yet. "I just . . . I really don't know."

Her eyes snap and I can see that I've tap-danced on her patience. "Eve, I can't pretend I'm not disappointed," she says. And then lifts her palms to me and shrugs. "I'd like to fill this position sooner than later and I figured you'd jump at the opportunity. I didn't expect you to leave me in limbo."

I bite back the fierce urge to apologize. "I . . . I know. I promise I will make my decision soon. Things are really shifting for me, personally, and . . . I just need a bit more . . . time."

She looks like she wants to say more, but then she just sighs and nods.

When I leave her office I see Bevi and Micah scrambling to look busy. Neither will look me directly in the eye. I don't like what Xaria has to say, but at least, *at least* she is actually talking to me. She's certainly not avoiding me.

And just like that, Ethan has entered the anxiety chat.

This has been happening to me lately. I feel a moment of frustration? Suddenly I'm thinking of Ethan. Someone jostles me on the train? I'm incensed thinking of Ethan's shoddy handling of this situation. I get a paper cut? I end up tearing up over Ethan. Xaria thinks I'm leaving *her* in limbo? She doesn't know the first thing about limbo. I can almost pretend I'm cool with being cut out of his life until something else, anything else, goes wrong and then all the injustice of it threatens to turn me into a dragon lady. A pregnant dragon lady.

If Ethan were here right now I'd incinerate him with all the frustration and embarrassment that's just been injected into me by Xaria. I pick up my phone. All it would take is one text. I could cut him down to size. The size of a baby carrot.

I want my ultrasounds back, you coward, I type out. My finger hovers over *send*. I imagine the text jumping out of his phone and face-planting him into his own terrible behavior. I imagine him spiraling into despair, so ashamed he can barely brush his teeth anymore.

My self-righteousness suddenly doesn't seem so victorious.

This is the kind of text that feels so ecstatically good for about ten minutes. And then you spend the next year trying to undo it. Even if he deserves it. Like it or not, he's the father of this baby under my dress, and if I rage-raze the relationship to the ground, it's not just me who potentially loses him. I delete it letter by letter and go back to not speaking to the person who is not speaking to me.

I spend the next two hours placing orders for office supplies and trying not to publicly cry. There should be a rule against your work life and private life both being in shambles. One shamble at a time, please!

I oscillate between frustration and anxiety for the rest of the workday and drag myself home at five on the dot, feeling all sorts of inadequate.

Well, if there's one place on earth where I rule the world, it's my own bathroom. In an attempt to lean into the happiest parts of my life, I'm headed out tonight to see a movie with Willa, Isamu, and Shep. Ethan and Xaria are still simmering in my gut, so I decide to make myself feel better by getting a little dolled up. I wash and dry my hair and decide to try a YouTube tutorial for this complicated braid thingy. I get halfway done and my arms start to ache so I inspect it with a hand mirror and decide it actually looks nice half-up/half-down like that.

Yesterday at lunch Marla took me to a pregnancy store in Grand Central and secretly used her loyalty points to buy me not one but two different jumpsuits. I slide myself into the black, long-sleeved one that's floaty around the ankles and send her a selfie just like she'd made me promise to do.

Inspecting myself in the mirror, I look very, very pregnant. Unmistakably pregnant.

I put on some makeup and feel comfortable and cute and . . . pretty. The dolling up is a success!

I'm headed to the place that Shep is going to be tonight and I can't tell if it's butterflies or the baby doing some sort of complicated wiggle-dance. Maybe both.

I take the train and even though it's evening, when I come aboveground at Union Square, it's almost fifty. I wonder if spring will come early this year.

The last time I was here, I didn't buy Christmas presents and ended up hiding inside Shep's jacket. I can't help but wish for the exact same outcome this time.

My steps quicken.

I stop at a crosswalk and bounce on my heels, a slow bubble of excitement in my stomach. I follow the river of people across the street, the movie theater up ahead.

It was raining earlier so everything is sparkly-reflective-colorful and the lights of the marquee are almost blinding. Wouldn't it be grand for the lights to clear and there would be Shep? I'd cross the sidewalk to him and tumble into his arms and the magic of a warm night in March would suck us away into another dimension where we could kiss and explore and flirt with zero concerns. *Okay, tap the brakes, Hatch.*

Unfortunately, when I blink the lights from my eyes, I find myself face-to-face with Jeff Burrows exiting the movie theater.

Figures.

Jeff Burrows went to our high school and, when we first moved to New York, was one of the only people that Willa and I actually knew here (besides Shep). Naturally, we reached out to him. We hung out just enough times to remember that we hadn't liked him much in school and we didn't like him much in adulthood either. He's good-looking in a sort of condescending way and has a knack for running into me in the city at the exact wrong time.

I hope he doesn't see me. I hope he doesn't see me. Maybe I can just scoot past—

"Eve Hatch," he says, stopping in my path.

"Oh. Hi, Jeff. How are you?"

His eyes skate down my body and nearly explode. "You're pregnant."

"What?" I shout. I look down at my belly and slap my hands over my mouth. "Holy shit!"

He rolls his eyes at my theatrics. "Congrats. Hey, it's so weird to also run into you because I just spotted Shep Balder in there." He points over his shoulder to the theater. A sly, knowing smile crosses his face. "Are you meeting up with him? Don't tell me he's the baby daddy."

I gape at him. What is it about a pregnant belly that makes someone think they're allowed to say something like that to you? I grind my teeth.

"It's not Shep, Jeff." I put my hands on my hips and give him my best don't-fuck-with-pregnant look.

He cows, but not enough. "Really?"

"You want it in writing?"

He laughs and I wish I hadn't made a joke out of it.

"You're married, then?" Jeff guesses.

"I'm not with the father."

Jeff makes a vaguely surprised noise, but then his face turns sly again. "This must be killing Shep, then." His eyes are on my belly.

"What?"

He smirks. "He was so protective. I personally saw him get his ass beat over you at least twice in high school."

"That can't be—"

"Man, this is *so* like him. Still following you around after all these years. Even when you're . . ." He gestures at the baby bump and laughs like this is all a joke. My life. And Shep's place in it.

Have you ever seen a pregnant woman drop-kick someone? Well, you're about to.

Unfortunately for Jeff, Xaria and Ethan have ignited a roiling fire in my gut today and yes, yes, let's point it at him. He's messed with the wrong pregnant dragon lady. I take a step into his space and he jolts backward to accommodate the belly.

"Who are *you* sleeping with these days, Jeff? Got any STDs? How about major life events? Been dumped lately? Thoughts on becoming a father one day? Worried about male pattern baldness? No? Well, you should be." My pointer finger's come out to play and it's about half an inch from Jeff Burrows's nose. "Hmm, let's see." I take a step back and exaggeratedly survey his body from head to toe. "Which parts of *your* physical appearance give me the right to opine on *your* personal life? Or, better yet, your sex life?"

His mouth has flopped open, but unfortunately it's not with chagrin. I see outrage burn in his eyes.

"Whoa, whoa. Calm down—" he splutters.

"Oh, baby. I'm just getting started." I draw breath.

"No." Suddenly a purple-leather-gloved hand is in between us, wagging a bossy finger in Jeff's face. "Nuh-uh. No way." I turn and see a tiny woman with a nest of gray hair pinned under a floppy hat. She's got enormous glasses on and a scowl so potent I expect Jeff to shrivel like dried fruit. "I *know* you are not shouting at a pregnant woman on the street, young man."

"I wasn't shouting," Jeff insists, looking back and forth between the two of us, trying to figure out if we know each other.

"By the looks of her," the lady continues, giving me the up-and-down. "She's, what? Eight and a half months along?"

She's way off, but she's my one-woman army right now so I nod vigorously. "Yeah!"

"So I don't care if you were shouting or not," she says to Jeff, eyes narrowed. "If you aren't bending over backward for her, then you're doing it wrong."

"I just . . . I wasn't . . . That's not . . ." Jeff mumbles, and oh, look, there's the chagrin I so badly wanted to see a few moments ago. He lifts two hands and shows me his palms. "I'll just go."

The lady makes a shooing motion and I watch Jeff just sort of back up and disappear into a crowd of tourists trundling past. I turn to my savior. "Wow. Thanks."

"Tell me he's not the father, sweetie."

I pull a gargoyle face. "Oh, God no."

"Good. Now, get inside out of this cold! It's not good for the baby. And get off your feet, you'll get varicose veins." Her eyes narrow. There's a litany of overbearing advice brewing on her tongue.

"Thank you!" I say brightly. And then scamper into the theater, safely out of her view. I breathe deeply and try to calm the adrenaline in my veins.

"Eve!" Willa waves at me from the other side of the lobby, then charges towards me.

"Hi. Where's Shep and Isamu?"

"Bathroom. Hey. What's that face?" she demands, surveying my expression.

"Oh. I just ran into Jeff Burrows and—" I open my mouth to explain but then realize that I can't actually explain unless I tell her what he said about Shep.

That it's killing him I'm pregnant with someone else's baby.

Shep getting his ass beat over me.

It can't be true. If Shep had gotten beat up in high school, there's no way I wouldn't have known. So there's not even any reason to bring it up to Willa.

"And what?" Willa asks, hands on her hips. "What did he say to you?"

"Just some stuff about my pregnancy. He was surprised I wasn't married."

She rolls up her sleeves and glares out at the sidewalk. Uh-oh. I grab her arm. "Don't worry about it. He's gone and it wasn't that big of a deal. I'm just . . . sensitive right now."

Her face falls. "Still haven't heard from Ethan?"

I make a puke face. "No. But I almost texted him today. I had a moment of unmitigated rage and I nearly took it upon myself to completely RIP his self-esteem."

"Why didn't you?"

"Father of my child, high road, better not to act impulsively, et cetera, et cetera."

"Well, you know what? None of that applies to *me*," Willa says, and winter blows through the lobby as her eyes darken and a crown of icicles bursts from her hairline. She's daydreaming about smite. "That's it. You won't let me hunt down Jeff? Fine. Ethan will do. I'm gonna head down to Good Boy and *smoke* this motherfucker."

But I don't even have time to grab the back of her sweater before she pauses, sags, and turns back to me. "Ugh, I can't ruin *my* relationship with him either," she grumbles. "If he ends up a part of your life then he's gonna end up a part of *my* life, and if we're on bad terms, then that'll just make things awkward for *you*." She points to the *you* in my belly. Her hands find their way to her hips. "Loving your kid is really inconvenient, you know."

"I know. It means you have to be a better person. What a burden."

She laughs but then, on the tail of the laugh, her eyes get glossy. Her expression freezes and she turns around, dashing her tears away. I've had that happen to me before, when one emotion skates in on the heels of another. *Loving your kid is really inconvenient, you know.* I wonder if she accidentally meant that in more than one way.

"Okay, so tell me what you said to Jeff." She signals at me to finish the story.

I give her a quick rundown of my male-pattern-baldness speech and she laughs and crows and gasps in all the right places.

"Can you even believe I said that?" I ask her.

"Of course, I can believe it. You've finally unleashed your strongest, baddest, bitchest, bad bitch to ever bad-bitch her way—"

"Are these even compliments?" asks Shep from behind us.

"Of course," Willa asserts. "She ran into Jeff Burrows and had to bad-bitch him out."

"Wait, really?" Shep turns towards me in alarm. "What happened?"

"And she won't let me hunt him down and make him cry," Willa gripes.

"He's here?" Shep straightens and swings around, his expression gone icy.

"You think we could make it into the theater without you

two opening a can of whoop-ass on someone?" Isamu says dryly. "We're going to miss the previews."

"Yes, let's go." I put a hand on each of the Balders and push forwards.

"Wait! Wait!" Willa throws her hands up. "Popcorn."

"Yes. Good call," I say. "Let's get an absurd amount. Enough to drown in. I'm starving."

"You got it." She surveys the semicrowded lobby. "You two go get seats. Isamu and I will meet you there."

Shep and I head up the escalator towards our theater.

"What did Jeff say?" Shep prods.

"Oh, it was no big deal. I mean, he's a total dick, but we've all known that for a very long time. He was surprised I was pregnant and even more surprised to find out that the baby wasn't y—" I clear my throat. "That I'm not with the father."

We step off the escalator and I realize that Shep hasn't kept walking. I look back and he's staring at me, a look in his eyes I can't quite interpret. He catches up to me, his eyes burning into me. "So, what did you say?"

"It's not worth repeating." I have to get off this topic or else I'm going to do something reckless, like ask Shep if it's killing him that I'm pregnant with Ethan's baby.

The ticket kid scans our phones and we head into the theater. It's not crazy crowded, but in another few minutes it'll probably be tricky to get seats all together. The first preview has just started.

Shep and I slip down an aisle and sit down. There are a few free seats on either side of us.

I busy myself with taking off my coat and pink hat and arranging my bag at my feet and when I look up, I almost scream.

Because Shep has also taken off his coat. And his hat. And he's sitting next to me, eyes on the screen, with a brand-new haircut.

And I mean, this thing is a h.a.i.r.c.u.t.

A tiny bit shaggy on top, but really, very short, faded on the sides, and look, there are the cords in his neck and who knew that foreheads were, like, so hot? Sleepy Shep is nowhere to be found.

I immediately face forwards because I physically cannot look at him and keep my tongue in my mouth at the same time. I feel his eyes on the side of my face so I quickly glance at him.

"Everything okay?" he leans in and whispers.

I *feel* his words in my ear and it's all I can do to nod.

Popcorn. I need copious amounts of popcorn. I'll stuff it into my mouth in handfuls and de-sex-ify this moment.

Right now, all I can do is pretend I'm super into this preview (which features a bunch of cartoon hamsters performing some sort of heist). But on the inside my mind is whirring. His hair *had* been getting awfully long. So maybe he just needed one. Maybe it had already been scheduled. He went at his regular time to his regular guy and just happened to get a really dramatic haircut. Or maybe this is how short he always gets it cut and I just happened to have never seen him in the immediate aftermath.

Or.

Or maybe I told him that men with fresh haircuts were absurdly hot to me and he went out and got one. And now he's sitting there in a button-down shirt that I've never seen before, with the sleeves rolled up, forearms out, and he's watching me watch this dumbass preview.

How does one get to the bottom of such a haircut?

Does your haircut mean you love me?

I may or may not be experiencing some difficulty with playing it cool.

A last-minute crowd of people surge up the aisles and they

all seem to know one another, they're talking up and down the stairs, shining their phone flashlights to keep from tripping and scanning the theater for open seats.

Willa and Isamu are there too, logjammed behind a group. Willa is holding an enormous vat of popcorn over her head and trying to poke her way around them.

But she can't. They flood into the seats and almost instantaneously both the seats on either side of Shep and me are taken.

"Oh, I was saving those," I say to the teenage girl who has just sat next to me. Her face falls and she glances to her side. There is a very cute boy sitting there. Her eyes immediately go puppy-pitiful.

"Please," she whispers.

I turn to Willa, who's watching from the aisle, and she shrugs and leans across some people to hand over the popcorn.

"Don't worry about it. We'll sit down there."

She points where there are a few empty seats still and then, would ya look at that, Shep and I are alone in a crowded room.

I spend the first twenty minutes of the movie attempting not to hyperventilate as I consume a Thanksgiving turkey's quantity of popcorn. He gets up and slides out of the aisle and comes back four minutes later with a bottled water. I gratefully take it and drink half in two gigantic gulps.

There's no chance he's finding any of this attractive, and that's *good.* That's the way it's *supposed* to be.

I finally lower the trough of popcorn to the floor and as I'm screwing the water bottle into the cupholder between us, Shep catches at my hand.

My heart stops.

He lifts my hand towards his face and inspects the Daffy Duck Band-Aid on my thumb.

"What happened?" he asks, his breath in my ear and my hand cradled in his.

I turn, he presents me with his ear, and I would like very much to trace that line of freshly trimmed hair. "Stapler," I manage.

He frowns and lifts his head, his fingers gently pressing at the edges of the Band-Aid.

"Was it bad?"

I shake my head.

We've pretty much covered all the Band-Aid ground that one can cover, so I fully expect him to rescind my hand to me. Instead, he turns it over, palm down, and starts fiddling with the two rings I wear on my pointer finger.

They're simple. Thin gold bands with one tiny stone apiece. They nest neatly together. He toggles them against each other, making the gems kiss.

I'm holding my breath as he lifts my hand closer to his face to inspect them.

"Are these new?" he leans in and whispers.

I blink at him. It's an interesting question. One that implies that he regularly notices my jewelry. "Yes."

"Did you buy them for yourself?" We'd be disturbing the people around us if he weren't whispering so quietly. He's gently placing each word into my ear. His warm breath making me shiver, his nose touching the shell of my ear.

I nod and point at the first one. "First trimester." I point at the second one. "Second trimester."

His face lights up, and he studies them with renewed interest. I haven't told anyone else that I've bought myself good-job jewelry. Two little milestones. But then again, no one else notices enough about me to ask.

He curls my fingers under and inspects the rings, and then he flattens my fingers straight, palm against palm. "You're tense," he whispers. And then proceeds to torture me. He massages the big muscle at the base of my thumb and slides up each finger. He wiggles the knuckles and gently kneads and prods and opens and closes my hand.

Wordlessly, I reach across myself and present him with my other hand and I swear he swallows down a smile. When I get tired of leaning, I pull away with a little smile and he automatically picks up my first hand again. He twiddles the rings again and does a tiny bit more massaging. It isn't long until that's dissolved into him drawing designs against my palm. He's not even pretending to watch the movie.

My eyes close and my whole world spirals down into focus. The only thing I care about is whatever the hell he's drawing on my palm.

A square with a triangle on top and then a few small stars atop that. Maybe a house with a night sky.

He runs his fingers over my palm and I get the idea he's wiping his canvas clean. Next comes waves and a palm tree. A desert island, clearly. I think he might add two stick figures. There's a pause and then something small that I can't decipher.

Next are two circles, one big and one little. Next comes . . . a dog maybe? A cat? Then, finally, as the credits roll, one last shape. An arrow. And it's pointing up my arm, straight towards me and—I fear—straight towards my heart.

Eighteen

After the movie the four of us tumble out onto the sidewalk and the air is muggy and slightly chilled. A distant roll of thunder surprises me.

"Should we walk somewhere for a drink?" Willa asks.

"I think I'm gonna pack it in," I tell her. My heart has nearly beaten itself out over the last two hours and I desperately need a soft bed and a dark room.

"Should we get you a cab?" Shep asks.

"Oh, I'll just take the train."

"There's one!" Willa says, jumping forwards to flag it down. I guess the Balders have spoken. I'll be going home in a cab.

The cab has stopped half a block down, so I head in that direction when there's another crack of thunder, this one much closer than the last. A few raindrops pancake themselves on the top of the cab as Shep holds the door open for me.

"It's raining, you guys," I tell them. "Why don't we all take the cab. I can drop you somewhere on the way home."

It starts to really rain, and a balmy fifty-degree night in March is very different from a rainy fifty-degree night in March. Isamu jumps into the front seat and Willa pushes me gently into the cab. The Balders sandwich me into the middle seat.

Willa gives the cabdriver my address and off we go.

Manhattan slides past and we speed across the bridge

back to our borough. Every time the cab sways I find myself pressed more and more into Shep's warmth. This has been an entire night of sitting next to Shep, only this time there's no movie theater armrest between us. If I closed my eyes I could probably count his ribs against my arm. One, two, three, four . . .

"Oh, Isamu, look!" Willa bursts out as we stop at a red light in a familiar neighborhood. She lunges forwards and grabs the back of his headrest. "It's that bar . . . do you remember?"

We're at a stoplight and he's squinting through the rain. "Is that . . ."

"Sure is."

He turns around and gives her a very transparent smile. "Should we . . ."

"For old times' sake," she agrees before she gives me a quick kiss on the cheek. "Text me when you get home, sweetie."

And then the two of them are slamming out of the cab and running through the rain, hands over their hair, and into the bar.

"Wow."

"Wow."

"So . . ." I say. "*That* was pretty obvious. You think they—"

"Banged in the bathroom of that bar at some point? Yeah." He shivers. "Oh, Christ. I'm definitely wearing my noise-canceling headphones tonight."

We both laugh and I tip my head back. I can't help but notice that at some point during the scuffle of Willa jumping out of the cab, Shep's arm has ended up along the back of the seat. It would make a lot of sense for me to unbuckle and slide into the seat that Willa vacated. It would make sense, but I don't do it. Instead, I stay exactly where I am, partially crowding Shep into his door while he partially crowds me with his arm along the back of the seat and there's a lot of crowding and none of it makes sense and everybody seems pretty okay with it, okay?

The streets melt past and the night melts around the cab and inside the cab I'm melting against Shep. I close my eyes and let the car rock me into him. Everything's an excuse to be close to him.

"We're here," he says quietly, bringing his mouth down to my ear. He pays the driver and slides me out onto the street.

"You're not—" I point at the cab that's pulling away.

He shakes his head. "I'll make sure you get upstairs okay. You seem beat."

I *am* a little dead on my feet. My bedtime has seemed to get earlier and earlier over the past few weeks.

And then we're in my apartment. Alone together again. The rain is sparkling against the windowpane, but everything is dry and warm and close in here.

We take our coats off and then our shoes, and he walks a slow circle around me. My heart beats hard and heavy in my chest. The baby kicks in response. He comes to stand in front of me, looking down at me. Neither of us has turned on any lights. I think my apartment is in on the secret.

He takes a deep breath and so do I.

He was so protective over you.

There's a buzzing energy in my toes. They want me to tip up, give me three extra inches. They want my arms around his neck, my fingers in the buzzed hair at the back of his neck. They want his stubble against my cheek. They want *irrevocable* and they want it now.

"You never wear your hair like that," he says in a low voice, his eyes on my complicated braid, and then on my face.

"I wanted to look pretty," I whisper. *For you,* I don't whisper.

I've said too much and I can't bear to hear what he'll say

next. "There are too many pins, though," I say in a rush. I'm just talking to say anything because if we keep staring at each other like this I'm as good as naked, as good as breathing his air, as good as in love and gasping for more.

I reach up and fumble with the pins in my hair, my fingers clumsy with nerves.

"Let me help you," he says, continuing his circle around me. His hands are in my hair.

I spent so much time this afternoon getting that braid right. Lacing myself up for him. And there he is, his heat at my back, slowly, gently, taking me apart. Each piece he frees comes to settle at my shoulders and I shiver with the brush of it. It might as well be his fingertips.

"There you go," he murmurs.

I turn around and am face-to-face with his sternum. "I'll, um, just be a second. There's lemonade in the fridge if you want."

I scuttle to my bedroom, choose my most comfortable pajamas. I quickly scrub my makeup off in the bathroom and I'm shiny and pink when I get out, but I'm also warm and clean and this man has already seen me without makeup too many times to count. So I get to not care. I get to just wear these soft pajamas (jogger-style pregnancy pants with white and blue triangles and a matching tank top) and go out there and let him be utterly delighted with me.

And he is. His smile is genuine and shy and a little exasperated as he watches me walk out into the living room. "You're so cute."

I'm not convinced he meant to say that out loud.

I'm so glad he did.

He's happy when I'm happy.

"How're you feeling?" he asks. I plunk down on the couch beside him and he instantly reaches for my socked feet.

"You don't have to do that, you know," I say, but it ends on a pleased little groan, completely negating my point.

"Here." I try to right myself. "Let's tradesies." I pat my lap.

He blinks. "Huh?"

"Gimme your feet."

"You're going to rub my feet?"

"Sure. You're rubbing mine."

"Eve. Yours are so cute and little. Look." He holds one of my feet on the palm of his hand. "My feet are the size of your femur."

"Cough 'em up." I reach down and tug at his pant leg. His leg does not move an inch. I spy a smattering of blondish leg hair that makes me feel suddenly very shy.

"No chance. Man feet are . . . not on the table tonight."

"Well." I'm stymied. "Come on, I don't want to be in debt to you."

He finds a tender spot and I involuntarily hum and go boneless. "This is not a hardship," he says with heavily lidded eyes. "But if you're worried about it, you can play with my hair later."

My eyes flick to his haircut and the shyness increases.

Haircuts and massages, he's really got his brand down.

"I should go soon," he says low. "If I want to be safely ensconced in my bedroom before Isamu and Willa get home. Or else I might witness something I can never unsee." He groans. "I really need my own place." His eyes slice over to mine. "Any interest in coming to look at places with me tomorrow? I have some appointments set up."

"Definitely!"

"Good. They're, uh, mostly in this neighborhood so it shouldn't be too tiring. The first one's at ten."

"Shep . . ." I can't believe I'm going to say this. "If . . . if you're going to be coming back here in the morning and, um, you'd rather not sleep at Willa's tonight, you could always just crash here."

His hands stutter on my feet and his eyes are burning into me, but I can't look up from the loose thread at my knee. I physically can't.

"Okay," he says.

"I think I have an extra toothbrush, hold on."

I'm up and trembling and skittering into the bathroom. I have an entire organized basket of extra toiletries and I very well know it. I grab one and walk it out to the living room to him. He takes it.

He goes into the bathroom and I'm left to stare at the couch he just vacated. It's far too small for him to sleep the night. I could blow up the air mattress I keep for guests but . . . but . . . but . . .

"Shep?" I'm talking through the door.

"Mm-hmm?"

"I doubt you'll be comfortable on the couch, so you can sleep in my bed . . . with me. We can watch a movie and then just . . . fall asleep whenever?"

I don't give him any room to argue. If he wants to leave, he can. If he wants to insist on the couch, he can. If he wants to sleep in my bed with me . . .

He appears in my bedroom doorway and I stop breathing.

I'm already in bed cross-legged, my laptop open, sitting on the covers.

His eyes are dark and searching me, his short hair mussed. He's wearing his jeans and an undershirt. And then he does the thing. The one thing that's hotter than a fresh haircut. He rests his elbow on the doorframe over his head and lets his wrist hang down around forehead level. I can see armpit hair and the scaffolding of his rib cage.

Hello, sir, you look like you've come to absolutely destroy me.

He doesn't say anything. Just comes into the room, eyes on mine, and walks around to the empty side of the bed. He sits, his back to me, and gives me his profile. "I don't have any sleep pants."

"That's all right. I'd give you some but I don't think they'd make it past your knees."

He laughs, stands, and takes his pants off in front of me.

I should look away, but instead I stare. Navy blue, in case anyone was wondering. Perfect ass, for the record. Shadows at his lower back. I cover my eyes with my hands because I am completely perving on him. He laughs again when he turns around and sees me in that pose. I feel the covers shift, the bed dip, time stop. "All clear," he says.

I look at him and now I know what color my cheeks are, because his are the same highlighter pink. He's tucked in and on his side, already having slid one big hand underneath one of my pillows. My bed will never be the same after this.

"Movie?" I gulp. And for the second time that night we watch some crap we don't care about nor will ever remember.

But alas, not even the tension of lying in the same bed as Shep can keep me awake when I'm this pregnant. I wake up as the credits are rolling. I carefully get out of bed to pee, trying not to wake Shep.

When I come back, the movie is completely over and I quietly close the laptop and set it on the nightstand. When I click off the light, he stirs and rolls to his back.

"All right?" he asks in a gravelly voice.

"Mm-hmm." And then we fall back to sleep together.

I wake up in the morning two feet from Shep, both of us facing each other, curled like swans. I think of the arrow he drew on my hand. I can still feel it burning into my skin. It's in bed with us right now.

He stirs, his eyes moving behind the lids, and then his lashes dip-dip-swoop and we're staring at each other. It's a dozy perusal; nothing quite feels like the real world yet. The light from the window is grainy and it sounds like the rain is still coming down. His eyes are sleepy and happy. Our worries are not invited into this moment.

He slides his face to the inner edge of his pillow and I do the same. Two feet becomes six inches just like that.

"Good morning," he whispers, and then reaches forwards and pulls an eyelash off my cheek.

I say nothing, because I can't say anything. Every word is trapped, along with all my air, in my lungs. His hand floats back to my cheek; he touches the eyelash spot again and then slides to the back of my head. He pulls us together, our foreheads touching. We're point-blank and all I can see is the blurry summer brown of his eyes. His eyelashes go fingertip to fingertip with mine. Our noses slide, greet each other. His fingers slip through my hair, all the way down to my scalp.

I can't speak and I can't stay still. I'd crawl inside him if I could. My entire body is spelling out the word *yes exclamation point.* I scoot another inch towards him, but my belly precedes me and presses firmly against his belly.

"Oh!" he says, and lifts his head to look down at the bump. He pulls the sheets back. "Good morning to you too."

I'm blinking up at him. We, in fact, did not just kiss. But the reason he pulled away was in order to say hello to my baby bump, so . . . I'm confused. But not hurt? Disappointed but . . . elated? He's up on an elbow, smiling at my baby bump and then turning back to me. He blinks down at me, a slow expression, filled with a depth that only decades of knowing someone can give you. This here is a man who knows me. And I *feel* known. His palm is warm against my cheek, and then he's tucking my hair behind my ear.

"I'll make you breakfast," he says. And gets out of bed.

Nineteen

Shep makes breakfast while I take a good old-fashioned panic shower. Because Shep got a haircut for me. Shep held my hand in a movie theater. Shep slept over and pressed his forehead to mine in my bed. My life is suddenly very, very different than it was a month ago.

Ethan may have gotten my uterus pregnant a while back, but I'm pretty sure Shep got my heart pregnant. In the back of a movie theater, using nothing but his fingers.

That was gross. Sorry.

I am no longer confident this thing with him is ignorable. I . . . ? Think . . . ? I . . . ? Might . . . ? Love . . . ? Him . . . ?

A little?

Just a skosh, I swear.

But here's the thing about having the father of your baby start ignoring you: you become sort of allergic to the idea of losing anyone else.

I'm not delusional. I know that starting a relationship with someone while pregnant with someone else's baby takes some varsity-level dating skills that I likely do not have. But when the person you'd like to date is someone you've loved dearly since your childhood and the idea of losing him makes you want to roly-poly yourself into a forever-hole. Well . . . yeah, *it's not a good idea, Eve!*

Not to mention the fact that what used to be my saving

grace has now become the thing that lances through my mind when I'm falling asleep. A white-hot *no!* that makes me sweat.

It's this: everything's a pregnancy symptom. It used to give me comfort. *These feelings for Shep don't mean anything! Just wait until you're not pregnant anymore and they'll go away.*

But now I can't stop thinking *Jesus Christ, what if they go away when I'm not pregnant anymore?* Could I stand it? Could he?

I think I love him and I'm not sure there's anything to do about it. Anything that would be fair to him. Anything that wouldn't potentially destroy a decades-long relationship with someone who has made it pretty clear that he's a lifer. If I had to make a list right now of people who will almost definitely be there for me after the baby is born, it's him. He's the list.

And I refuse to throw away the list just because I'd like to kiss his kiss. On top of him, naked.

Besides, the truth is, I'm not sure how he even feels. He's never given me a hand massage in a movie theater before, but I've never been this pregnant and this alone before either. Shep loves me, duh, he loves me. But does he looOooOoo Ooove me? Because there's a pretty big distance between the two and I'd rather not trip and face-plant in the middle.

Shep's happy if you're happy. Willa confirmed what I've always suspected. What a wonderful character trait. What a terrible character trait. Sure, Shep is flirting with me. But I'm also flirting with him. Exactly how far does this happy-if-you're-happy thing go?

These are the thoughts I torture myself with.

In the middle of blow-drying my hair, a thought occurs. What if I pulled a little switcheroo on Shep? What if I decided to be happy when *he* was happy. Instead of the other way around? What if I helped him move out of Willa's and get settled in a new spot that he loved? What if I used my spice rack superpowers and feng-shui-ed the crap out of an apartment and made a home for him?

He's so sweet, so warm, that he makes everything blurry. But my determination to treat him well sharpens my understanding of him: Lovely Shep. Perfect Shep. Lonely, transient Shep.

Well, no more!

I shall find this man an apartment of his own if it kills me.

My new battle plan must be written on my face because he physically jolts when I emerge from the bathroom. I inhale breakfast and then clap my hands together.

"Let's do this," I say menacingly.

"Um. Okay," he agrees hesitantly.

Unfortunately, the listings in my neighborhood are mostly underwhelming. There's one nice one but it's unbelievably expensive. My apartment is seeming more and more like a diamond in the rough.

We've utterly and completely confounded each of the different realtors we've met with today. Shep and a pregnant woman are vehemently looking for a one-bedroom or studio. I can see them grappling to understand our relationship, wondering if we're planning for this baby to sleep with us in our room forever.

I ignore them by carefully inspecting each and every unit with jolly curiosity. Everything is interesting to me. The laundry rooms in the basements. The elevators with their sticky gates that have to be pulled closed before they'll go. The one apartment that has a mysterious door that won't open.

Shep is having less fun. I can see him getting more and more discouraged when his dream apartment doesn't magically turn up.

I check the list on Shep's phone. "There's one more apartment to see," I tell him. "It'll be perfect, I swear."

He laughs at my completely uninformed confidence. "They didn't even add photos to the listing. I'm not optimistic."

"We persevere!" I demand.

It's not until we get off the train and approach the address that Shep and I realize what would have been totally obvious if we'd looked at the map a little bit harder: this new apartment is on the same block as Good Boy.

"Oh."

Shep dips at the knee and catches my eye. "Eve, let's go. There will be more apartments in better locations."

"Are you here to see the apartment upstairs?" a woman calls to us from the doorway. "I'm the owner, if you want to come up."

The owner is a short, older lady with dark brown skin and white glasses. She's wearing a somehow stylish conductor's cap, overalls, and Converse. She's wiping what smells like furniture polish off her hands and when she's done, she shoves the rag into her back pocket.

I glance at Good Boy but turn back to her with resolve in my heart. We need to at least see the apartment first. Shep is my number one priority right now. Ethan can go take a hike.

"Nice to meet you," I say, striding towards her with my hand out.

She shakes our hands and then directs us to the stairs and when I wobble a bit on the last landing, she clamps a hand to my elbow. "Careful, kid," she says.

Then she swings the third-floor apartment door open and good, sweet lord it's the *perfect* apartment. Sunny. An original wood mantel with terra-cotta tile work covering up where the fireplace once was. There are gigantic windows with wide windowsills, perfect for potted plants. The kitchen has clearly been updated recently and has enough room for an honest-to-God dinner table. The living room leads into a bathroom (with a window!) and the other door leads to a bedroom.

I turn to the owner. "What—why—*how does an apartment this good exist?*" (*At this price* is my implied incredulity.)

She laughs at my flabbergasted awe. "My husband and I have lived here for almost thirty years. We started renovations a few years ago and decided to rent out the top unit. We haven't liked the last few tenants, so we decided to drop the price on the unit this time around."

"You thought you'd get a different clientele with a lower rent?" Shep asks in confusion.

She nods. "When it was higher, we were getting a lot of young people on Mom and Dad's allowance. They'd blow in and out at all hours, not particularly concerned about their neighbors or their neighborhood. No, we're looking for someone who wants to live *here,* you know? Not just anywhere nice." She glances at my belly. "A family looking to put down roots would be perfect."

My heart gallops, the baby kicks, Good Boy leers from down the block, Shep smooths out a wrinkle in the shoulder of my sweater.

"Can we see the rest of the apartment?" he asks.

"Of course. The only weird thing about this unit is that you have to walk through one bedroom to get to the other," she says, and shows us just that.

"Huh," Shep says, his brow lowered.

"Oh, but that wouldn't matter for you, Shep," I insist. "One of them would just be your home office and you wouldn't have to worry about walking through it. It wouldn't matter."

I say "home office" and the owner's eyes immediately go to my belly again, but she doesn't say anything.

She gives us a little space and as soon as she's gone, I turn to him. "You have to get this apartment," I tell him. "We'll get you a sectional that'll go here. And bookshelves. A dinner table, Shep, *a dinner table.* Your bed will be in the back bedroom where it'll be insulated from street noise and have a view of the backyard. Just picture it in the summertime! All those green leaves through the window and your old green quilt at the foot of the bed? It'll be perfect! I *promise* I'll make it perfect for you!"

He laughs and puts his hands in his pockets and looks around a little more. "You really like it that much?"

"I *love* it."

"And you swear you wouldn't feel weird about coming over, given the location?"

"I . . . honestly, I might. But I'll still come over no matter what. Once you're inside, it's heaven."

"Are you *sure*?" he asks again. He walks over to me and picks up my hand. He twiddles my two rings and then sets my hand back by my side and puts his hands back in his pockets. "Because you being comfortable in my house is pretty much the only criteria I'm currently using for picking a place."

I nearly gasp for breath, because as far as I'm concerned, he's just attempted murder. But instead, I put my hands on my hips and glare at him. "Well, *my* main criteria is finding you a lovely place to live where you feel utterly at home."

He blinks at me, nonplussed. "It doesn't have to be that serious, Eve. I just need somewhere to land for a little—"

I press a finger to his lips. "Yeah, yeah. I'm making a home for you, just try and stop me."

He's staring at me from behind my hand and I know that look. That's the look a man gives you right before he leans forwards and blows your life into a million pieces—but the owner comes back through the front door and we step away from each other.

I let them talk specifics for a minute as I keep wandering the apartment. From the front window, you can actually see a sliver of Good Boy. It's weirdly close. Serendipitously close. My heart does a hollow little cough. I've got two hands on my baby bump, painting a long line from rump to head.

Shep and I leave and immediately walk in the other direction from Good Boy and turn the corner. We keep our brisk pace all the way to the train.

I'm quiet.

"You all right?" he asks before we go underground.

"Yeah. Just . . . I need a nap, I think."

He plays with my rings again. "Will you text me when you get home?"

I nod.

"Thanks for coming with me today," he says.

I nod again.

"Are you breathing?" he asks.

I shake my head.

He laughs. "Breathe, Eve. It's very important."

I do what he says and we head down the stairs together. His train arrives first, but he lets it pass. My train arrives second and he waits while I board and find a seat. He ducks down, catches my eye through the window and waves. The train pulls away and it feels wrong. I'm not supposed to be speeding away from Shep.

But I'm also intensely relieved. The idea of running into Ethan was a lot worse than I thought it might be. I get off the train and feel so glad to be in my safe little neighborhood. There's the Jewish bakery. There's the bodega where they sell hot dogs on a stick. There's the orthopedic shoe store and the dentist that has a huge plaster tooth over the door. I'm so glad to be safe. Where I live. Where there's nothing to run from—

I freeze halfway up my block.

Because there's a man sitting on my stoop. He's sweaty and breathing hard and wearing running gear.

He's got copper-red hair and tears on his cheeks.

Twenty

"Ethan."

He springs up to his feet. He's sitting on the top step of my stoop and I'm standing at the bottom. He bounds down to be on the same level as me, wiping his cheeks.

"Eve."

"Um. Hi?" I say. Because what else do you say to the father of your baby who has more or less ignored you for weeks?

"Hi. Sorry. I just . . . was out for a run and . . ."

He ran to my house.

I should probably invite him up to my apartment but . . . last night there were raindrops on the windowpane and Shep in my bed and I just . . . don't want Ethan in there right now.

"Wanna go for a walk?" I offer hesitantly.

"Yes!" He's clearly deeply enthusiastic about the fact that I haven't tossed a (non-existent) martini in his face. "A walk sounds great."

A bus is trundling up the block as we speak, so we take the six-minute bus ride to Prospect Park in relative quiet. We walk along the bike path and the clouds part. Big puddles of drippy sunlight dapple the blacktop as we wind our way through the park. Last night's rain washed the winter away. There are a few tentative buds on the trees, and their mild green is accented by the gray clouds that are rolling off towards the ocean. Joggers bop past and a biker tugging a wagon full of helmeted children questions his life choices as he heaves one pedal and then the next.

"So," Ethan says, his voice gravelly. "Can I explain?"

"Your radio silence?"

He nods and looks slightly ill.

"Sure, I guess."

He puts his hands on his hips and his chin almost down to his chest as he walks. "Eleni found the twenty-week ultrasound images and . . . it was too much for her to handle. She, ah, doesn't want me to contact you. And she . . . tends to check my phone and email and stuff."

Oh, boy. That's not great.

I thought he went on a contemplative run and just wound up at my house. But it's sounding an awful lot like he *escaped* and came to my house.

"Dude," I say. "Are you okay?"

He grimaces. "Yeah?"

"Um. All right. I'm trying to understand . . ."

He blows out a breath. "She's having a very, very tough time with all this and . . . I don't think it actually occurred to her that you and I might be friends."

"Can I see a photo of her?" I blurt out.

"Of Eleni?" He blinks at me.

"Yeah."

It would be so much easier to just decide Eleni is the bad guy and everyone else gets to be the good guy. But, of course, Eleni is a person, with complex feelings of her own, just like mine. And so is Ethan. They're not stick figures holding up labels for what kind of person they are.

He's looking at me like this is a test and he's almost positive he's about to fail it, but I actually want to see what she looks like. I need a real face or else I'm going to trick myself into believing that she's the root of all my problems.

He digs his phone out of his joggers and finds a photo and hands it over to me.

Was anyone else expecting a six-foot-tall model type? I-will-eat-your-soul hot and wearing, like, leather pants and a mesh bra or something? Because that's apparently who I've been picturing this entire time.

But no. Eleni is a normal-looking woman in a red blouse with a blue flower embroidered on the front. She's got very tan skin and curly hair in a ponytail. One of her front teeth is crooked. She's pretty. And smiling at the camera like she's absolutely bonkers for the person taking the photo.

I hand the phone back to him. "Where'd you meet her?"

He gives the ground a sad smile. "Greece. I was there traveling on my own and she was visiting her dad. She was born there but moved here with her mom when she was little."

"And you've been together ever since?"

He clears his throat. "Off and on."

Mind your own business, Eve! "And . . . she checks your phone and email to make sure you're not contacting me?"

"She's not a bad person," he says defensively.

I'm really not sure there's a way to positively spin *surveilling all forms of communication in order to make sure you're not interacting at all with the woman you're having a baby with,* but if Ethan doesn't already know that, I'm probably not the one to tell him.

We walk in silence for fifty feet or so and a group of pregnant power-walkers charges past.

"All right," I say eventually. "You're clearly in a hard spot here, Ethan. I get that. But you *totally disappeared.* Right after you sort of said you were going to help out? It hurt. And it was confusing. And I'm supposed to be peaceful right now, you know! Not wondering whether or not you're abandoning this kid without so much as a word!" I'm accidentally getting fired up, fueled by the disorientation, the rejection, the worry he's caused over the last month.

He hangs his head, the weight of my words borne on his back.

"Dealing with that . . . trying to understand you . . . trying to make the best decisions I can based on the very little I know . . . it's been a lot to wrap my head around. And now you're here and I'm just trying to figure out what all of this means for—"

"You?" he fills in weakly.

I shake my head. "The baby."

He stops walking and turns ninety degrees away from me.

"I . . . cannot believe I'm this guy. I hate this guy," he whispers.

"Oh, come on."

"It's true." He's resigned when he turns back to me. "I'm failing *everyone.* I consider it a miracle that you're even talking to me. The last month has been . . . and now I see you and you've gotten so much . . ." He doesn't say *bigger,* but he holds his hand away from his belly to show how the bump has grown. "And I just *missed* it. Like, you're the one who's making the baby. Literally the only thing that's required of me is to just be there, and I'm fucking missing it!"

Couldn't have said it better myself, actually. I'm not sure if it soothes me or annoys me that he gets it.

I hesitate, because if I'm wrong about what I'm about to say, it'll be the smackdown of the century and I'm really, really not sure I'll come back from it. "Ethan, I've gotta be honest here . . . you act like someone who *wishes* he could be active in this kid's life."

He looks utterly wretched, in sweaty running clothes, half his face in bright sun and the other in shadow. His hands are on his hips and he's staring at me in the way people do when they're really seeing something else. For his sake I wish the heavens would open and dump buckets of cold rain over him. Really pound the misery out of him. He looks like all he wants is for the punishment to just giddy-up and *arrive* already.

"I think she just . . ." he starts, and I poke at his elbow to nudge him back into walking. Once again, I've asked him if he wants the baby, and we end up talking about how Eleni feels about it. We fall into pace alongside each other. "I think she just really needs me to say that you and I didn't have a connection at all." He glances at me. "That it was just a totally random thing and it was bad sex and I regret every single part of it. But the truth is . . ."

"We *did* have a connection. And it was really good sex."

"Right?" He gives me a *very* small smile.

"Yeah." I nod. "I mean, up against the wall, an orgasm apiece, and a quality snuggle afterward? That's like, varsity level, right there." I go up for the high five and he must take bro code very seriously because even in his wretched state he automatically high-fives me back.

He looks at his hand as if he doesn't know how it even got there. I laugh at the befuddled expression on his face and after a startled moment, he laughs a little too.

"Now that we're talking about that night," I start. "I think it bears mentioning . . . if I'm being honest . . . you were really different."

"Yeah, uh, that night was special." He glances at me.

"I'm not talking about our, ya know, *epic connection.*"

"Then what are you talking about?" he asks.

"Oh, I guess . . . I don't know you that well, but did you know that you have a sort of top gear?"

"Huh?"

"Yeah, it's like this unfiltered charm. A full-throttle smile."

He shakes his head in confusion so I continue on. "That

night I liked you so much and it was so easy, and that was because of *you*. You made everything really simple. I'm not . . ." I clear my throat. "One-night stands have historically been very rare for me. And never anything to write home about. So it takes a very . . . comfortable person to make that into a reality for me. And . . . you were that person. You were sweet and happy and yeah, like I said, you made everything easy."

He's gone a pleasant pink and he doesn't quite seem to know where to look. "Thank you." Some kids kicking a soccer ball back and forth come running in our direction and Ethan dives to the side and intercepts the ball before it goes into the ravine at our left. He bounces it on his foot once, twice, and then volleys it back to the kids. *Thanks, man!* He smiles after them but it fades as his brain brings him back to our conversation. "It's funny that you saw me in that way because I was actually in a kind of screwed-up state that night. Eleni and I had *just* split."

He's just unknowingly made the point that I'm trying to make. I steel myself because here come the tough cookies. "I know. I remember. But Ethan, what I'm trying to say is, as a third party who didn't know anything about your life at that point, that night, to me, you seemed . . . free."

Sometimes the good news hurts more than the bad.

As soon as the word *free* vibrates into life, it's wounding him. His shoulders crunch inward, and his eyebrows are two arrows, pointing down to his mouth that is also pointing down to his heart, which has one of his hands pressed over the top of it.

It's hurting him, what I've said, and maybe, maybe, it's hurting because he's recognizing it as the truth.

That night between Ethan and me, it felt electric with possibility on his end. He had this lightness about him. The kind of lightness that comes only after you've just shed something really heavy.

"Fuck," he whispers, and veers off the bike path into the woods. Call it a sixth sense but, yeah, I'm sensing that the fact that he's almost sprinting through waist-high brush into a dark, dank wood means he could use a minute of alone time. I think of him in his office asking me to close my eyes while he reacted however he needed to react for a minute. I wait for him on the bike path.

He emerges not too long after and immediately starts plucking leaves and burrs off his clothes. "You—you're telling me," he says. "That you think I was *relieved* to be broken up?"

It's not accusatory. It's a genuine question.

"All I'm saying, Ethan, is that that was a really great night. There was real *joy*, real electricity in everything we did together. But I don't think that was because . . . of you and me. It wasn't because you and I are destined for some great love, or something, you know? So my guess is that there was something *else* fueling that."

I don't say the rest, because, after all, it's just a guess. But perhaps the amount that he was glorious that night was in direct proportion to how good it felt to him to be away from Eleni.

And still, he wanted her back.

Sometimes the bad feels better than the good.

For better or worse, being pregnant can lend you a bit of gravitas. Look at me, the wise old pregnant, doling out relationship advice like I know what the hell I'm talking about. But obviously there's a limit to how much you can talk out of your ass about someone else's relationship, and I am nearing mine.

"It wasn't just me who was like that, Eve," he says quietly, after two hundred feet of silent plodding. "You were different too."

"Really?"

He nods. "I think that's why I was so drawn to you. You had a very . . . new-chapter vibe going on."

"Huh."

Unlike me, he keeps his thoughts to himself, and I'm glad he does because there may or may not be something to excavate there and I really don't want to do that out loud right now. I shiver.

"Let's get out of the cold," Ethan says. And I know he doesn't mean together. He means let's part ways and go warm up in our separate homes with our separate lives. And that, that's okay because it has to be okay.

Twenty-One

Yet Ethan's words keep circling in my mind.

I suppose it's time to go back in time:

It's a hot September Saturday and I'm sweating my tits off on my front stoop. My A/C unit needs to be replaced but the hot weather is, like, days away from wrapping up for the season and I just can't justify the cost. Instead, I sit on the stoop and watch the cars go by and once an hour on the hour I trade the bodega man two quarters for a bright purple Popsicle.

I might have to use an ice pack to be able to fall asleep tonight.

My cellphone rings and even before I can get it to my ear, Willa is already shouting. "Put on your sluttiest bar wear because we're going out!"

"What are we celebrating?" I hold my Popsicle sideways to avoid a drip and it starts to slide off the stick. I catch the whole thing in my mouth at once and have no choice but to chew through the cold.

"Shep's moving to Brooklyn! He finally moved out. He and Heather are done. He packed a bag and he's headed to stay at my place. Come celebrate with us!"

I'm struggling through an iceberg-level ice cream headache, so it takes an extra few seconds for those words to really circle the toilet bowl of my brain and make it down the drain.

"Wait, *what*? He and Heather broke up?"

"Meet us at Bar Twelve at seven, okay? They have killer tacos."

I run back inside, shower and change into **not** my sluttiest bar wear, and have just enough time to take the train over to them.

When I see them sitting there on opposite sides of their booth, plates of tacos already strewn around between them, I feel such a swamping love for the Balders I nearly choke.

Our night goes something like this: tacos and drinks, drinks and dancing, bodily removing Willa from a karaoke bar, more dancing, more drinks.

It's one of those nights that's a blurry downhill slalom of shouting people and sweat-hot sidewalk and arms around one another's necks. Shep . . . really doesn't seem very sad to have broken up. In fact, at one bar, a George Michael song plays and he one-mans an entire dance floor for twenty of the most ecstatic seconds of my life before Willa and I join him.

It's not as drunken as it might seem. We're intoxicated with the euphoria of being together.

When's the last time we had this much time just the three of us? It's been years. Years.

We grew up and Willa got Isamu and Shep got Heather and I've had the occasional Derek every once in a while. But there has almost *always* been a fourth. An observer. A person who witnesses the dynamic but doesn't participate in it. And even when it's Isamu, who I adore, it changes the mood.

But tonight, we're the only three people in our world.

We've been unintentionally bar-and-food-truck-crawling our way south. At eleven we get one giant falafel sandwich and eat it on the swings at a playground, passing it back and forth. By midnight we've made it down south of the park and there's one last place Willa wants to go.

It's a local dive and, as usual, the crowd parts for Willa and we follow in her wake. She gets three mystery drinks from the bar and crowds us into a corner booth that smells like forty-year-old cigarettes and B.O. The drinks are lemonades with shots of vodka on the side.

Shep laughs when he realizes what she's ordered for us. "Just like that one night, right?"

Willa and I experimented a bit with alcohol in high school, mostly just the two of us. But one time Shep joined us. He had been going through a skateboarding phase and had taken a tumble that had earned him a black eye and a split lip. Willa, Shep, and I hung out in their basement and Willa disappeared upstairs only to reappear with this exact combination of drinks. Vodka and lemonade chaser. "To Shep," she'd toasted. "Who failed pretty hard at something really cool."

On this night, she lifts her shot glass and we do the same. "To Shep," she toasts. "Who did something really hard. Because he's brave. And is deciding not to be afraid of failure."

And I recognize it for what it is, it's the lost half of Willa's original toast. It's her celebration of courage and failure and letting life beat you up because you decide to really try.

The vodka goes down and then the lemonade and there go the three of us. Laughing and then melancholy and then laughing again. There goes our childhood, so much time spent living on top of one another. There we go into adulthood, inviting in others, asking some of them to stay, asking some of them to leave. Here we are, together again. Together again.

After the shots we decide to pack it in. In a perfect moment of meant-to-be, two cabs play tag down the street outside the pub. Willa chases them down and Shep and I are left standing on the curb.

"Well," he says, tugging a hand through his shaggy hair. "See you tomorrow? Now that I live in the same borough as you?"

"Sure!" It's been a literal decade since *see you tomorrow* was a possibility with Shep.

He and Willa get into their cab and I'm about to get into mine, when I realize I desperately have to pee. I apologize to the driver, get out, and scan the block for restroom options. I could go back into the pub, but without Willa, it seems a touch seedier.

And there, four storefronts down, is a bar with red siding and . . . a dachshund leading an owner right inside. Curiosity gets the best of me and I go in.

I quickly use the facilities and am about to leave but . . . something about the champagne fizz of this evening is just not fading. I feel alive and hopeful and filled to the brim with *see you tomorrow.* I don't want it to end. I just . . . want to sit and savor it a little longer. I order a seltzer with lime at the bar. My brain takes me over and over the night I just had. Every wonderful blurry moment of it. I have one, desperately clear thought: *I wish I could keep this night forever.*

I look up, and that's when I realize the bartender is a beautiful man, and he's watching me smile into my drink.

He crosses over to me, leans his elbows on the bar, and the rest, my friends, is history.

Twenty-Two

You know in movies when someone swears and instead of bleeping it out, they just make the person say it in suuuuuuuuuper slow motion? Well, that's kind of what the rest of the afternoon is like for me.

Ethan was right. I *was* different that night.

It might sound ridiculous to say that apparently I was so happy Shep was finally single that I slept with a stranger but . . .

If Ethan is telling the truth and I really did have a "new-chapter vibe going on," you know what the title of that chapter was? *See You Tomorrow.*

Ethan was so subconsciously happy to be free from Eleni, and I was so subconsciously happy to have Shep around again, that we (un)subconsciously smashed our bits together (literally).

I don't know why this realization throws me for such a loop but . . .

I call Willa, invite her for dinner, and she heads right over.

By the time she arrives I have Thai food takeout and black cherry seltzer ready for her.

"It's weird to see you without Shep hanging around," she says as she scoops food onto our plates. "If he hadn't already been out of the house, I was considering putting on my catsuit and rappelling down the side of the building so that he wouldn't follow me here."

"He had plans tonight?" I try not to sound too curious.

"Yeah. He took the train up to the Bronx to buy a new bike he found on Craigslist. Seems pretty far to go to get a bike but anyways, enough about him. Spill, please." She thinks we're here to talk about Ethan. I told her that he showed up on my stoop, but I haven't told her the details yet. So I do.

At first she makes a face like he's a rotten egg, but she softens a bit when I explain how miserable and confused he was. At the end of our conversation about him, we've come to the same conclusion I've already come to: I need to just get on with things. Either Ethan will get his shit together and figure out how to fit the baby into his life, or he won't. And I can't control that.

"Thank Gawd you're not in love with him," Willa says, clearing our plates away.

When I don't respond she freezes and then turns around slowly.

"Hold on . . ." she says. "You're *not* in love with him, right?"

I laugh and shake my head. "No. Definitely not."

It's the perfect opening. My stomach flips. Am I really gonna bring this up? Once Willa knows, there's no going back. But if anyone has seen it, Willa has. She'll tell me if it's real.

She heads into the bathroom and pees with the door open. I make myself comfortable on the couch and call through the open door. "Hey, can I ask you something?"

"Sure."

"It's about something Jeff Burrows said to me the other night."

She groans. "Ugh, that asshole," she calls.

I can't quite decide how much to tell her. "He said that me being pregnant . . . must be hard on Shep."

Silence. More silence. The toilet flushes, the sink runs.

"Willa?"

"Mm-hmm?"

"Did you hear me?"

"Yeah."

"Do you know what he could have meant by that?"

She comes back in fanning her hands to air-dry them. "I wouldn't give it too much thought."

"Right. Okay."

"Unless . . ." She flops back onto the couch and nudges my leg with her foot. "Unless you've already given it a lot of thought and decided that you think *you* know what it means."

I turn my face towards the window but it's too late, she's already seen the expression I can't wipe away.

"No! No. *No*," she growls, crawling towards me.

"Hey! HEY!" She's taken one of my wrists and pinned it over my head. "You're accosting a pregnant right now!"

"Eve Daisy Eileen Marlene Sharona DooLittle Hatch," she says, and now I know she means business because she's hit me with the made-up names. "Do you currently have a *crush* on my *brother*?"

"No! He's . . . the worst! He's unattractive and rude and he's never there when you need him. He smells bad and is thoughtless and he never tries to feed me or surprise me or make me happy."

"Oh, God," she says, and rolls away from me. "This is worse than I thought!"

I'm torn between my instinct to deny everything and my instinct to spill my guts to my best friend.

"I'm *confused*," I finally say. "This is *Shep* we're talking about here. And then, on the other hand, it's *Shep*. You know what I mean? How could I—What if I—Besides, Nurse Louise once said that everything's a pregnancy symptom."

Willa makes a face. "Even feelings for someone? Doubts."

I give myself a hug around the middle, rub the baby's back, head to rump, and don't look at Willa.

"Are you . . . gonna tell him?" she asks.

I hate to give my fears the whole stage, but they've already put their Elvis wigs on and squeezed themselves into white sparkly jumpsuits. "I want to. Honestly, I think he probably already knows. Being around him has just been . . . But what if . . . what if as soon as I give birth my feelings just zap away back to friendship?" Willa scoffs, but I soldier on. "And beyond that he's actually really hard to read, you know! He's happy when you're happy. You said it yourself. So if he's just mirroring me, then how am I supposed to know how he really feels!"

"Eve," she sighs, looking pained. "You cannot wreck my brother. You do not have permission to wreck my brother."

"I . . . I don't want to wreck anybody."

She gives me her toughest expression. "Of course you don't. But you're going to if you do that thing."

"What thing?"

"Your I-don't-know-what-I-want thing."

"Hey!" Well, *that's* irritating. And maybe true. "Is that . . . that's really a thing?"

"Of course! You live this bouncy, cloudy existence where everything is both magical and confusing and you never get what you want because you don't *know* what you want. You've never known what you want."

"Ouch! Jesus. Slow down a little."

"I'm sorry, but if it's Shep's heart on the line I can't let him be collateral damage."

I do a quick and painful inventory. My position at work? All I do is avoid Xaria and resent the program staff. The baby? The words *keep being pregnant* come to mind. I couldn't even say I wanted the baby. And now Shep? I think I want him, but I have no idea for how long in either direction that feeling exists. How long have I wanted him? How long will I in the future?

"How sure is anyone about anything?" I demand of Willa.

"I am literally one hundred percent sure of what I want at almost all times. I don't always get it. But at least I know I wanted it."

I wilt. "Is it a crime to not know everything immediately?" I ask.

"No." She's wilting too. "You're allowed to move as slowly as you need, Eve. Just . . . be honest with *yourself*, please."

"Okay." I'm even more confused than when this conversation started, but . . . also weirdly relieved? "Man, nobody slaps me out of pregnant hysteria like you."

"You really think this is pregnant hysteria?"

I purse my lips at her. "Didn't we just go over the fact that I know nothing, ever, and I'm going to work on it?"

She laughs and raises her hands. "All right, all right."

She got this direct delivery of information from Corinne. Her mother was good at not letting people hide in their shells. Corinne had a few more naturally derived spoonfuls of sugar than Willa has but that's part of Willa's charm.

And this is what I need. Someone who loves me who will tell me the truth. Push me. Protect me. Something I've been considering slowly rises to the surface. Now is the moment.

"Willa?"

"Hm?"

"You can say no to this. And that would be totally fine. But I thought I'd ask . . . Would you want to be my partner for birthing classes?"

It's like she's one of those rubber pugs that you squeeze around the middle and their eyes pop out. Only, when her eyes pop out, she also bursts into tears. I can't tell which of us is more shocked by this reaction. She needs both hands and a tissue for these tears. These are the kind of tears that make you thirsty. I deliver a fresh glass of seltzer and she inhales it down to the bottom. And then there are more tears.

"I. Thought. You. Weren't. Going. To. Ask. Me," she sobs. "Shep told me you were stressed about going alone. And I thought I'd already ruined everything."

"Willa . . ." I'm speechless.

"I'm *so* sorry, Eve. I know I've been so *weird* about all this. Your pregnancy. God, when I think about how I first reacted when you told me you were pregnant I just want to *slap* myself. And I've been trying to get back to normal, trying to find ways to help you, but that's only making me even *more* weird. And—" *HONK*, she blows her nose. "I really, really want to go to the classes with you. But I didn't think I had the right to ask. I can't believe you still want me to."

Willa, who always asks for what she wants, was afraid to ask for something. That's how difficult this was for her. "Willa . . . I can't even begin to imagine how tricky and painful this has been for you. Me being pregnant, when you've been trying for so long. I . . . really wanted you to be happy for me. And at first, I was hurt that you weren't. But I *know* you. You've been my best friend since we were preverbal. And I realized something recently." Very recently. Like literally this second. I take a deep breath. "If you could have been happy for me, you would have been. The fact that you couldn't . . . that just shows me how much pain you were in. And that means that you've been doing a lot of work to get comfortable for me. And . . . I love you."

She collapses forwards, elbows to her knees, and her face in her hands. She looks small again, the way she did the day I told her I was pregnant. "We weren't 'just trying.' "

My stomach fish-flops. "What?"

She takes a deep breath and drags her hands down from

her face. Her eyes are swollen and her skin is blotchy. "I lost a pregnancy last year."

"Oh, *Willa.*" I scoot across the couch and slip my hand into hers. She lets me and I'm so grateful for that. "Oh, Willa. Oh, Willa." What to say? "I'm so sorry. I had no idea."

"I know. I kept you in the dark about it . . . Honestly, even when I first got pregnant . . . I didn't even tell Isamu for two weeks."

"When . . . did it happen?"

"About two months after Mom died. I was eleven weeks along." More tears spring up, but these are silent ones.

She looks up after a long moment, unlacing our hands to mess around with her tissue. "I got to tell her, you know. Right before she passed, I got to tell her that I was going to be a mom. She was so happy." Those last words are a strangled whisper that dissolves away into silent pain.

"When I lost the pregnancy . . . I couldn't . . ." There weren't words then and there aren't words now. She doesn't go on for a long time. "Isamu knew, obviously, and he told Shep, one night, because he needed someone to talk to about it. But *I* just couldn't tell anyone. I didn't have it in me. I'm sorry. I'm so sorry."

I think of Shep during that time. *Willa had a harder time of it, I think.* But he didn't think. He knew.

"Willa. You don't have to apologize."

"I feel like I do."

"Okay. Well. Thank you for telling me. Thank you for helping me understand and letting me in."

Now she turns to me and we're hugging. "Please don't hate me for all the weirdness. The secrets," she whispers.

"I could *never,*" I say vehemently. I didn't hate her when I was having trouble understanding her and I certainly don't hate her now.

"I'm a mess," she whispers.

What an honest thing to say. My friend who hates being anything less than her best.

"Me too. I'm such a mess. I'm sorry I didn't see your pain. I just thought . . . your mom's passing . . . I didn't see the rest. What a horribly difficult thing you went through."

She nods yes but then crumbles and shakes her head no. "But I've always been able to be there for you. It's one of the things I like the best about myself. And Eve, the way you were after my mom died. You saved my life. I just hate that I haven't been able to repay you. You've needed me and I've just been . . . *weak*."

"No, no, NO." I'm hugging her again. Have you ever wanted to hug all the bad feeling out of someone? Like water from a sponge? I want nothing more than to wring her free of it all. "Willa, you know how we're best friends?"

She laughs and sniffs. "It rings a bell."

"Well, maybe we've been concentrating too hard on the *best* part, but really the key word in there is *friend*. It's friend, not wife or partner. When we were kids we were each other's only, you know? No other friend or boyfriend came close. I was your number one and you were mine. But after you met Isamu . . . I'll never forget how many times you called and texted while you were on your honeymoon. Wasn't that, like, so annoying for you?"

She gives me an affronted look. "I didn't want you to feel left out!"

"Of *your* honeymoon? Don't you think it would be weirder for me to feel included?"

We laugh and she gives me a little *maybe so* shrug.

"I'm just saying," I continue. "We'll always be Willa and Eve, Eve and Willa. But it's okay that Isamu is your number one now. It's okay to have things that only he knows. It's okay for us to go through things on our own or to feel some distance because that particular phase of life is making it that way."

Her eyes are glossy. "I don't ever want to grow apart from you."

"God, me either. But if we hold on with an iron grip and not ever let anything change, we're gonna crack. I mean . . ." I almost don't say it. "I've been scared to talk about the baby because I thought it would exacerbate the weirdness between us."

Her face crumbles for a moment and then burns with resolve. "You have to talk to me about it, Eve. Even if it's hard for me, you have to. For God's sake, you're having a baby! You can't *not* talk about it."

"I know. I'm starting to realize that. Luckily I've had . . ."

"Shep," she whispers, and wipes at her eyes. "Pretty soon the baby will be your number one."

We're quiet for a long moment. "Willa? No pressure, but if you ever wanted to talk about it . . ."

She sniffs, nods, and gives me a gift. She tells me everything.

Twenty-Three

Willa, Ethan, and Shep battle-royale one another in my brain.

Shep's fingers in my hair, our foreheads together.

Ethan charging into the woods at the word *free.* His face half lit by sunlight, his desires clearly torn in two.

And most of all, Willa. Willa and her pain that was a million times bigger than I even knew. And her warning: *Please don't wreck my brother.*

I'm a loopy, dazed mess until Monday after work when I head to Lower East Side Partners in Obstetrics and Gynecology to get updated on my vaccinations. I'm absurdly disappointed when it's a nurse I've never met before who administers the shots. I'm holding the cotton ball on my arm when I ask her, "Is Nurse Louise working today?"

"Yeah. If she hasn't gone home yet."

"Is there any chance I could see her?"

"Oh." The nurse gives me a slightly annoyed look but nods. "Let me check."

A few minutes later there's a tap-tap on the door of the exam room and Nurse Louise is poking her gray-brown head inside. "Ms. Hatch."

"Nurse Louise!" I swear, one of the first things I'm gonna do when I'm postpartum and back on my feet is jump straight into Nurse Louise's arms.

She steps into the room and I see she's got her purse and coat over one arm.

"Were you just leaving? I'm sorry."

She sets her things down and puts her hands on her hips. "What's wrong?"

"Nothing. Nothing. I just . . ." I don't know where to start.

Instead of answering, she opens a drawer and pulls out a plain Band-Aid for my shot. But she reconsiders and trades it out for a Sesame Street Band-Aid and hands it over to me. She clearly gets me. "How about we get a cup of coffee?"

She guides us to a little twenty-four-hour diner half a block down from the clinic and we slide into a booth.

She orders black coffee for herself and gives a little smile when I order a tall glass of grapefruit juice. "Are you craving a lot of citrus right now?" she asks.

"Yeah. For a long time, I couldn't have any because of heartburn. But right now, it's all I want."

"I remember that part."

It's the exact segue I need. "Can I ask a question about when you were pregnant?"

She leans back in the booth, a friendly frown on her face. "Sure."

"When you told people you were pregnant, what were their reactions like?"

She purses her lips and studies me. "Mixed, I suppose. Some people have a lot of baggage around it."

"Hm."

She thanks the waiter when he brings us our drinks and then, to my complete surprise, dumps about four packets of Sweet'N Low into her coffee. "I take it you had some lackluster responses to the happy news?" she asks, eyebrows raised over the brim of her cup as she takes a long draw.

"Yeah. A lot of the people I told . . . most of them, actually, their immediate reaction to the news was basically *What does your pregnancy mean for me?*"

She nods, like that's expected.

"Even my best friend," I say.

"Well," she says with a little shrug. "No best friend is perfect."

"Of course, of course. Including me. Because I totally missed this huge thing . . . At first I thought the news was hard for her because she's had a lot of fertility struggles and she really wants to be pregnant. It's just that . . . when I first found out . . . I really, really needed help and it threw me off when she went all cold on me. But then I come to find out that, well . . . basically there was a lot going on for her that I didn't know about and me being pregnant . . . I think in some ways it prevented me from seeing her pain. I was only thinking about myself. Because . . . I think I felt like the only one who really *was* thinking about me? If that makes any sense? So, if I didn't put me first, then no one would?"

I think for a minute about all the people I've told, and Nurse Louise waits patiently. "I had one friend at work who was genuinely happy for me. She ran out and bought me a pregnancy basket of goodies that very afternoon. But for most other people at work it was so *awkward*. My family was a bit of a mixed bag. The father of the baby . . . he's required a lot of . . . spoon-feeding. I just got so many not-exactly-happy reactions!"

It feels awkward to say all this out loud. Oh, poor, poor Eve. She needs more people to tuck her feelings into bed at night. But also it's *true*.

"I think it's okay that you didn't see your friend's pain right away," she says eventually. She takes a deep breath and looks out the window at the street. "You were in your first trimester. It's only right to think about yourself first in your first trimester." She turns back to me. "It's the way it works. It's all about you at the beginning because, for everyone else, your life changes once the baby is born. But for the mother, your life changes as soon as you find out you're pregnant. And for a while, you're the only one who really gets it. Because it's happening to *you.* So yeah, don't be too hard on yourself for putting yourself over your friend at the beginning . . . Besides. That all changes, doesn't it? Putting yourself first? I'm just gonna take a guess and say that somewhere in the second trimester, the baby started wiggling around and kicking and you stopped thinking so much about yourself and a lot more about the people around you?"

I blink at her. "How the heck did you . . . ?"

She shrugs. "I've been there. Three times, in fact. Pregnancy is a bell curve. You think about yourself at the beginning a ton. Then you think about the baby and other people for most of the rest. And then right at the end, when birth is looming, you start thinking about yourself again. I don't know if it's like that for everyone, but most of the moms I've talked to have felt that way. Must be biological or something. Pregnancy hormones are the strongest force on earth as far as I'm concerned."

Nurse Louise is studying me, her eyes narrowed and her lips pursed. "So. Have you? Gotten any help from anyone?"

"Oh. Well. Yes, I have. My best friend has really tried, even though it must have been so hard for her. And that's more meaningful than I can even realize, I think. And I've gotten some help from one of my brothers. And then a *lot* of help from this one other person in particular."

"Your inopportune crush," she guesses immediately.

"How'd you guess?"

She looks at her own reflection in the bottom of her coffee cup. "Him? Her?"

"Him. Shep."

She gives a little smile at whatever I do with my face when I say his name. "What's he like?"

"Um. He's tall and kind of floppy. I've known him forever. But recently . . . Let's see. He cares about if I have food in the fridge. And gives me foot rubs I don't ask for. When I told him I was pregnant, he was *happy* for me. He . . . wants me to be okay. Sadly, I don't think he has a selfish bone in his body. If he did I wouldn't be so worried about him putting me first every time."

"There's a theory I've had for a long time. You want to hear it?"

"Of course."

"Well," she says, twisting her coffee mug one direction and then the next. "Most people are self-centered. And I'm not talking about selfishness. I mean it literally. Their center is their own self. Like yours was in your first trimester. They understand the world only through their own experiences. Whatever happens around them, they ask, *What does that mean for me?* But then there are a select few who are *other*-centered. And when things happen around them, they ask themselves, *What does this mean for everybody?* And that sounds like Shep. It doesn't surprise me that you've come to have a crush on someone who considers you."

I feel dizzy.

"Can I ask something?" she asks after a beat.

I clear my throat. "Shoot."

"That woman at work, the one who was happy for you, who brought you the pregnancy basket. Is she a mother?"

"Oh. Yeah. She is."

"I figured."

"You figured she'd be happy for me because she'd been through it all before?"

"No. Because of my self-centered versus other-centered theory . . . It's not just the pregnancy bell curve. It's a lot of what *motherhood* is too. Moving from being self-centered to being other-centered. A huge chunk of motherhood is realizing that your children are little bits of your own self out there eating cereal straight from the box and learning to pay their own taxes and wondering whether or not now is the right time to adopt a cat."

I laugh at her examples and wonder exactly how old her children are.

"You're saying that as a mother you think of your kids before you think of yourself?"

She pauses. "Not a hundred percent of the time. But yeah, part of becoming a mother, for me, was coming to terms with the center of my world being something that wasn't my own self. It's harder than you might think."

"Sounds terrible."

She laughs. "Can I tell you a story?"

I nod vigorously.

"Snow Boot Day," she says. "Was an annual holiday in my household. Sometime in the fall, I'd drag my kids up to the outlets in the Bronx and I'd buy each of them one perfect pair of winter boots for the year. And we'd make it a whole event. Coke slushies and soft pretzels and a matinee action movie before we came home. It was . . ." she reflects, "a hemorrhage of money."

I smile. She's gone soft talking about the past. About her children.

"The kids loved it, of course. All that sugar and a movie in the theater. But do you know why *I* loved that day so much?"

I shake my head.

"Because I worked full time for that money all year long. And then I got to buy these perfect warm boots that would keep them comfortable all season. There was nothing better." She's smiling into the past, her fingers wrapped around her mug.

I smile too. "I've heard parents talk about that before. That your children are like your heart walking around outside your body."

"For me, at least, it wasn't just my children. Motherhood changed my view on the entire world. At first it was just other children, the kids who'd play with my oldest at the playground. You see the grown-ups who push them on the swings and you realize that each kid is someone's whole entire heart. Soon it was the middle schoolers. And then it was the high schoolers. And then, eventually, it was the middle-aged people and the older people too. Once I started seeing the web, I couldn't *stop* seeing it, all the people who love all the people."

And here I thought Nurse Louise was sandpapery when really she's all unexpected Sweet'N Low.

"So . . ." I think about what she's just told me. "That's what it means to be other-centered? To see the web? To treat everyone like they're somebody's favorite person on earth?"

"In part."

"Oh, *God*." I groan. "That makes so much sense. I think I've really been an ass. You know how much time I've spent thinking about myself all my life?" I cover my eyes for a moment. "I've got such a long way to go."

She lifts her hand and requests the check. "It hurts to realize that the world is so much bigger and more complicated than you thought it was. It'll always hurt." She sighs and pushes my grapefruit juice towards me, wanting me to finish it. She points dead center at my belly. "And all you can really do is *be* there. And wipe your kid's face. And try. And learn from your mistakes. And once a year, there's an absolutely perfect day, where you get to buy them boots that you know, *you know* will keep all ten of their perfect toes warm and dry. And that's the good stuff. It truly doesn't get better than that."

The phone rings. I know he won't answer. But I have never left a voicemail for him before and I figure now is likely the right time.

"Ethan, hi, it's Eve. I hope you get this. I just . . . I want you to know that it's okay to be confused. I'm confused too. All the time. So, I get it. I really do. And . . . just because this has all been a lot for me doesn't mean that I don't have sympathy for you. I know this is a lot for you too . . . Look, I want to say this at least once. And I hope you can believe me. But I'm actually gonna be okay. I am so unbelievably lucky. I've got a family who is mostly stoked about this. I've got friends, I've got . . . I am just really, really not alone. So, you don't have to worry that I am. This isn't . . . all on you. If you can't be here. You can't be here. And I'll be all right. Just, be well, okay? I wish you all the best. I really do."

I hang up the phone and the tears I'm expecting don't come. In fact, I feel relieved. I actually have no expectations for Ethan. Which means that he is not currently disappointing me.

I barely know him, if I'm being honest. And I can't say whether involvement or not in the baby's life is a good idea. All I know is that I'm lucky enough not to have to depend on him.

I am not the girl he loves so much he cried on the sidewalk. And that's . . . okay.

I'm not the center of Ethan's world. And, actually, I'm not the center of my own world either. It's an oddly *light* feeling.

It's like I've been focusing on a tiny script for years, the words all repeating *me, myself, I, me, myself, I, me, myself, I,* but now I'm sitting back and letting my eyes relax and luxuriating as I sink down into the blissful blur. This isn't all about me. It isn't all about Ethan, or Willa, or Shep, or even the baby. It's a web and—God, what a perfect system because—each of us is somebody's favorite.

Twenty-Four

Monday, Tuesday, and Wednesday are all in the high fifties and sunny, and when I wake up on Thursday to birds chirping and a forecast of highs in the sixties, I take a rare personal day from work. There's been an odd galloping inside me since I met with Nurse Louise, and I think I need to exercise it out.

Around lunchtime, at peak sun, I take the bus up to the park and I do the exact same walk I did with Ethan just days before. Only this time there are buds unfurling on almost every branch of every tree I pass. Everything is tulip-stem green and waxy with fresh growth and it smells so good out here, I'd like two bottles of it, please.

People are jogging and biking and sprinting full speed out of winter and into spring.

I'm walking up the long, slow hill on the east side of the park (though I guess it might be a long, fast hill for those who are not prepartum) and there's a crowd of people spilling into the bike lane. They cheer and cheer. There's a girl with a stick and a blindfold taking wild jabs at a piñata shaped like the Red Sox logo. She lands a solid blow and everybody screams. She gets one more good one in and a firework of contents explodes onto the grass and blacktop. The kids all cheer and converge and then squawk in disappointment when the haul turns out to be little cellophane-wrapped sandwiches and baggies of baby carrots. The adults howl with laughter at the children's outrage.

I'm laughing, one hand on my belly, and suddenly, so badly, I wish the baby could see what I just saw. Meaning: for one bright moment, I wish the baby were ex-utero. Terrestrial. Here with me in a stroller. There are two hearts in my body right now and in a few months, I'm going to set one of them free into the world.

The galloping is back full force.

Oh, my God. Clear as a bell. That's what this is.

"I *want* you. I'm excited to meet you. *I'm excited to be a mom.*"

I'm halfway up a hill while the season charges forth and my heart charges along with it. No more passive acceptance of my situation. This is my life, on purpose. I didn't choose the way this pregnancy started. But I can choose the way I bring this kid into the world.

With joy and full desire: "I want you."

It's racing at me, I can picture all of it, right here on this very spot. A baby in a terribly knit cap slung across my chest while I huff up the hill, laughing and chatting with Shep. A toddler in overalls, hands spread wide and tripping from foot to foot while Shep and I dash after, arms outstretched. An elementary schooler, standing up on a bike while the wind billows their T-shirt, Shep and me clapping from the sidelines.

Wanting means I get to look ecstatically forward to the future. Wanting means I get to fling open the doors to my life and say *come in.*

I stop walking, two hands on my belly—booty and head as usual—and the little rump roast must *feel* that something is happening to its mama because there it goes. I feel the head rotate; I feel the baby moving. There's a stretch, a strain, I breathe through it, and then the baby has settled into a new position.

The leaves are green, the people are laughing, the wind

turns everything alive. I'm here and I'm not alone. There is someone here with me and they are, currently, part of my body.

All those months ago, sitting on a stoop with Shep and crying into his shirt. "Your body will take care of you," he'd told me. Did he know? Did he know that what was once just my body would become this person, right here under my hands? Who needs me, needs me but has already done so much for me in return?

I sat on that stoop and couldn't imagine being anything but scared of whoever this person was going to be. They weren't even a person to me yet, they were bad news I'd had to tell Ethan. Nausea and fatigue and a whole lotta what-the-hell-am-I-gonna-do.

But here, under the green, in the swollen, hopeful park, right this very second, I am accompanied by someone who loves me, I can just *feel* it. My body, the baby's body, connected where it matters most. I am, at this very second, doing perhaps the most intimate thing one person can ever do with another: giving life with your very own body.

"Is this what he meant?" I ask the baby, not caring if anyone watches me talk to the bump. "When he told me that my body would take care of me, he already knew I'd love you like this, didn't he? He already knew . . ."

That I wasn't going to be doing this alone.

Because the baby would be there.

And he'd be there too.

He was telling me, all those months ago, that he wanted me. Infinitely kind words in a dark moment. *I'll never leave you* whispered in a secret code that he was content for me to never solve.

That's what wanting without taking looks like.

Other-centered as he is, maybe he's been waiting for *me* to do the taking.

I've been thinking that Shep is hard to read, thinking that he's just been mirroring my own emotions back to me. But what if . . . what if he's exceptionally *easy* to read. Maybe the only thing hard about Shep is accepting that the sweetness we've created between us could possibly be real.

Would I offer up *my* T-shirt as a snot rag? Would I buy groceries and fill up *his* fridge? Has Shep been teaching me how to want little by little?

Shep running to catch up with me in front of Good Boy. Shep's coat surrounding me on the train. Shep giving up his bed. Shep's only requirement for a new apartment is me being comfortable there.

He is not deciding whether or not he's gonna be involved.

He is never gonna leave us.

And there on the bike path, with the baby shifting and children screaming about the injustice of health food, I finally understand my own heart.

Please be closer.

Please, more.

Please eat food out of my fridge and let me pet your hair.

Please just stay still and let me make your apartment perfect for you.

Please be closer.

I have an answer for Willa. But infinitely more importantly, I have an answer for myself.

I'm tears and laughter and adrenaline. "You feel that?" I ask the baby. "This is the exact chemical cocktail that happens when you realize you're flat-out in love with someone, no caveats. Take notes. Maybe you'll be a little quicker on the uptake than I was."

I'm still laugh-crying, standing in the bike path, when I see him. Up the hill. Walking towards me. There he is. Out of nowhere. Shep. Right when I need him. How does he do this? He must be *magic*—

Oh. Wait. No. That's not Shep. That's just some tall dude talking on his cellphone. As he comes closer to me the differences become even more stark and I shake my head at myself.

I think this might be what "got it bad" looks like. If you look it up in the dictionary there's a very pregnant woman in overalls and Crocs with socks and a fuzzy fleece coat. She's got her hair in a braid that she's praying some tall, lovely man will carefully undo with big, clumsy fingers.

When you finally admit you want someone, the main perk is that you get to ask to have them.

Why deny it? I want to see him, see him, see him. Now.

Mr. Eyelashes. Mr. Movie Theater. Mr. Old Friend in a New Light.

Shep answers on the first ring.

"Hey!"

"Hi." I feel suddenly shy. Was his voice always this deep? "Um. Have you had your lunch break yet?"

"I'm a freelancer," he says. "My entire day could be a lunch break."

"I took off work today and I really, really wanna see you. Like right now."

"Yes. Done. I'm there."

Is there any compliment higher than someone dropping everything for you?

"You have the time?" I ask.

"I don't care. I'll quit. Where are you?"

I'm laughing and sending him my location pin in the park.

"Shoot," he says. "It'll take me a half an hour to walk there, I think. Can you hold on to this exact feeling for that long?"

"What about your bike? Willa mentioned the other day that you got a new one?"

"Oh." There's a long, awkward pause. "I guess I could . . . but . . ."

"Great! Just come meet me."

"Yeah. Yeah, all right. See you soon."

I realize that I can't keep walking now that I've sent him my pin, but there's a handy bench not too far from the carrots-and-sandwiches Red Sox haters, so I figure I'll have enough entertainment to last me.

About twelve minutes later I'm just walking my granola bar wrapper to a trash can when there's a blur of movement.

It's Shep, on a bike, riding in circles around me.

"Hi!"

"Hi." He comes to a stop, one foot on the ground, one of his pant legs rolled up so it won't get caught in the gears, and that's when I notice it. His bike. His new bike—the one he took the train up to the Bronx to buy and then rode all the way home—has a baby seat fastened onto it.

He sees whatever my face is doing and goes immediately sheepish. "I—it's not a big deal—I needed a new bike anyhow—and I saw this one and thought—just in case—it might just be a good thing to have."

I face-plant into a new reality. One where taking a single step towards Shep means taking *every* step towards Shep. I want him. I want to tell him. And the possibility of failure suddenly burns white-hot in my gut.

He's looked at approximately every inch of the park that isn't me. When he finally does glance at me, either the sun is suddenly ten times too bright or he's so embarrassed about this he has to squint.

"Say something," he mutters.

I take two steps towards him and grab him by the zipper of his hoodie. It's Shep warm, sun warm, everything is lion brown and lemonade tart and tears are pinching my eyes.

"What if we fool around like crazy for like three weeks and then it just falls flat?" I ask him on a whisper.

"Huh?"

"What if we break up in a year?" The tears crack their shells and roll down my cheeks. "Does the baby still get to ride on your bike?"

"Eve."

"What if we try this thing for a while but then you meet your soulmate on a plane. In Paris. And she can pull off all-black outfits and smokes cigarettes with no regard for the future. What then?"

"Eve."

"Dirty diapers." I start a list. "No sleep. I'll look like shit a million percent of the time. I'm already a mess. What'll happen when there's a whole other person's mess added into it? Package deal? Package deal mess?"

He's alarmed now. "Hold on. Slow down." His hands squeeze my shoulders and they firmly glide down to elbows to wrists to fingertips. "Is this all because of the bike seat? It doesn't have to mean all that."

I cannot be consoled. "You've met the Dereks, Shep. They were *weird.* What if I'm absolutely *terrible* at this? And I ruin everything?"

His face softens. "Instead of panicking about possible endings . . . I wonder if . . . maybe we should . . ." He stops and looks around. We're definitely drawing a bit of attention. Pregnant woman sobs and accosts a man's sweatshirt while he's still wearing it. I'd watch that.

He takes me by the hand and wheels his bike off the path towards the woods. He uses a wizened old tree as his bike's kickstand and then leads me around the other side of it. We're shielded from view.

"Slow down," he says, finishing his sentence from before. There's gravel in his voice and an easy determination in his eyes. Instead of racing to an end, he wants to go honey-slow with me. He wants to experience every single second, especially this one.

His hands squeeze my shoulders again; my back is against the tree. And then he finds the *one* thing that's hotter than a fresh haircut or doorway elbow-leaning. He plants one of his hands on the tree over my head and leans in.

He's inches away.

"We can't have a first kiss!" I blurt.

He pauses, leans back. "Why?"

"Because then we'll *have kissed.*" I've got two hands on my cheeks and I think my eyes must be the size of lightbulbs.

He laughs and gently removes my hands from my cheeks. "Yes." He takes one of my hands and puts it on the back of his neck. He guides the other around to meet with the first. I'm slow-dance-style hugging him and he made it that way.

He's leaning in again. He's all eyes and eyelashes and breath. The first day of spring swells around us, crowding us towards each other. "Do you really not want to?" he asks. "Or are you scared of change?"

"I'm scared of *everything,*" I tell him, and for some reason that makes him smile.

"Okay. I'll help."

I close my eyes and then there's his forehead, pressing warmly against mine. I blink my eyes open and he's point-blank with me again, the way we were in bed. "Here," he says. "We've been here before. Not so scary, right?"

"Not scary," I manage. "Well, a little scary."

He laughs and his eyes change shape and please, please, *please* can I have this moment forever? He was right. Slow is good. I want it in such slow motion it becomes the rest of my life.

Our eyelashes flirt, our noses slide.

"I'm right here," he tells me.

If it's scary, he means. *He won't leave me,* he means. *This isn't something I'll be doing on my own,* he means. He'll be here with me. As always, Shep is here with me.

And it's *that* that has me tipping my face up to his.

The first touch of his mouth is light, warm, ends in a smile and a rush of breath. My eyes are squeezed so tight it takes stages to open them. When I do, there he is, brown eyes and waiting. I move an infinitesimal amount towards him and his lips are back. The second kiss is a press, even warmer, a nip of his lips against mine. The third is a slide. His hand finds the hinge at the bottom of my skull and my head tips back, my mouth opens. He makes a sound. It's a delicious, private sound that is for me and only me.

Hi, it's me, his tongue says to mine, and now I'm the one making a noise. His free hand goes from my hair to my cheek down my neck and rests for a moment, palm over clavicle. My arms tighten around his neck and bring him even closer. We start to tip to one side, losing our balance, but, of course, he catches us, one hand against the tree and all my weight in his arms.

The sun is in my eyes and everything is opening, blooming, starting new, my heart is growing petals. His fingers are touching my scalp, sliding down my spine. He's got a forearm locked at my lower back. He's everywhere. It's not enough yet. He tries to end the kiss but I chase him back and open his mouth with mine. He grunts. And then we're slow tongue and a pinch from my teeth. His hands close into fists and then open back into warm palms. There's a thumb painting an arc against my cheek, his breath is inside me. And then his forehead is against mine, our eyelashes kiss, my eyes follow his.

He pulls away and presses his forehead into his forearm, which is on the tree over my head.

I make a valiant effort at getting my bearings. I've somehow started gripping my own elbows around his neck. He's basically wearing me as a turtleneck.

He reaches back and loosens my grip, turning his head and kissing the inside of my elbow through my fuzzy fleece. He kisses the middle of my forearm, yanks my sleeve back, and kisses the inside of my wrist. He opens my fingers against his cheek, kisses my palm, and then arranges my hand at my side. My other arm gets symmetrical treatment.

"I can feel the earth turning right now," I whisper.

He laughs and then starts the arduous process of straightening himself back to his full height. It takes a while. There's a lot of him.

"Hold on," I say, pausing him. "Have you been standing like that the entire time?"

His legs are making him into an upside-down Y, his feet about four feet apart from each other.

"There's quite a height difference here." He waves his hand between us. "Among other geometrical obstacles." He's grinning at my belly. Which he then greets with a sweep of his hand. "Hi."

He's back to his full height, flattening his hair with one hand.

"Hey," I say, with a poke to his chest. "We kissed."

He gently takes my elbow and leads me back around the tree. He grabs his bike by the handlebars and we start walking.

The adults from the piñata party have apparently taken an interest in us. There are a lot of eyeballs and side-whispers and absent baby carrot munching as we walk past them.

"Hey," I say again to Shep, who seems to be staring into the abyss. "We *kissed*."

We've automatically started walking down the hill instead of up, and even though our steps are slow, the world seems to zoom past, a moderately paced free fall.

"Yes," he agrees, and then glances at me. "And how are you feeling about that?"

"How long is your lunch break? Can we go to my house? I didn't even get to touch your shoulders yet. Let's go eat plain donuts and Popsicles at my house. And . . . maybe Greek food?"

He laughs. "Taking it well, I see."

I eye him. He's looking a little dizzy up there. "And you?"

"I'm good," he assures me. "Just suffering through, you know, acute euphoria. So you're back on plain donuts, huh?"

"And Popsicles and Greek food." I give him a sly look. "And you, if we're talking about things I want in my—"

He puts two fingers over my lips. "You will literally kill me if you finish that sentence."

I shrug a shoulder. "You're gonna have to get used to it."

He blushes and we keep walking.

"Up against a tree," I muse. "That's not quite how I pictured it."

"You've pictured kissing me." It's not a question. More of a statement. One he seems to need to say aloud in order to believe.

"I've spent an awful lot of energy trying to *stop* picturing kissing you over the last few months."

His eyes are on the side of my face as we make it to the park's southeast entrance.

"Ooh! Bus!" I shout.

"You go get on and I'll just lock up my bike and be there in a second."

I do the pregnant lady *I'm a'comin'* waddle and the bus driver opens the side doors to holler, "Don't run, honey! I won't leave you!"

I'm a gasping mess when I get on the bus and I fumble for my MetroCard. But then Shep is behind me, his forearm clamping over my collarbones, and swiping us both through.

He doesn't unhand me and we duck-walk to a free area. People are smiling at us, glancing at my belly and then smiling more.

"Here! Sit!" a teenage girl says, halfway standing up from her seat.

"That's okay!" I wave her back down. "I'm happy right here."

"We can see that," a middle-aged woman says as she peers at me over knitting needles.

The bus kicks into motion, Shep grabs the overhead bar, and I grab him around the middle, pressing my smile into his sternum. We have to stand a little funny to accommodate for the belly but it works. I press my ear to his chest and isn't it so wild that you can go forever knowing someone and never really listen to their actual heartbeat until they kiss you behind a tree?

The bus stops and starts, stops and starts. When we finally get off at my stop it's been a little lifetime. He points with one thumb to the bodega. "Do we have everything we need, or should I stop and pick up some stuff?"

He must see the word *condoms?* written across my forehead because he laughs and blushes and scrubs a hand down his face.

"I meant, like, *seltzer* or *Popsicles* or *potato chips* or something," he insists.

"Oh. Seltzer, yes. But I have to pee. I'll leave the doors unlocked for you!"

He nods and watches as I safely cross the street and then I'm racing upstairs. I pee for nine years and it's a blank, mind-buzzing heaven. I wash up and blink at myself in the mirror.

I look ecstatic. Red cheeks and wide eyes and kissed lips. My hair is frizzy and my fleece is zipped all the way to the collar. This is how I looked when he kissed me. And then he suffered acute euphoria.

I take my hair down and go to my bedroom, hanging up my fleece in the closet. It's hard to say what's sexy right now, but all I can think about is comfort, so I quickly shuck off my overalls and T-shirt and change into a long-sleeved dress I haven't worn yet. It's loose and blue and soft.

I hear him come through the door, whistling—there go his shoes *thump-thump*—and head straight for the kitchen. Ice cubes, seltzer. I meet him in the living room. He's got two drinks in his hands and a look on his face I can't interpret.

"You changed clothes."

"I looked like a dork."

"You looked perfect."

He sits on the couch, puts the drinks on coasters. As I approach, I wonder if this'll be awkward. How to sit next to someone you just kissed for the first time? I should have googled that while he was in the bodega.

But instead of awkward, I go on autopilot and fix the problem by sitting down almost on top of him and putting my mouth on his.

"Mmmmph," he says, half in surprise, half in pleasure. I think for a moment he might try to slow us down, but then his fingers are in my hair and he's dragging me onto his lap. I'm sitting sideways, my feet off to the side, and he's leaning me back, kissing me silly. This might just be the deepest kiss of my life and we've barely started.

I'm the best thing he's ever tasted. I know because he whispers that in between kisses, his eyes on my mouth and his hand reflexively tightening in my hair. I can't hold this leaned-back position forever but he doesn't seem to mind when I switch to straddle him. At all. He's got one hand pressed into the small of my back and one hand touching and touching at the clasp of my bra. He's still over the top of my dress, but even so, he wants that bra undone and he's forcing himself to go slow.

When my legs start to cramp from that position, I push us over onto our sides. My back is to the back of the couch and he's twisted, his top facing me, but one leg on the floor to keep himself from falling off the narrow cushion.

Our mouths go from demanding/pushing to soft/asking and back again. My fingers hurt from death-gripping his T-shirt. All the ice in our drinks has melted.

"Okay, wow," he says, an untold amount of time later. He stares at my ceiling and seems to be having some trouble breathing. He turns his head to look at me. "We haven't fed you yet."

"Food is for losers. More kissing." I reach for him and he obliges for all of three seconds.

"Let me feed you," he says against my lips.

I growl in frustration but also because it hurts to have your heart squeezed like that. "Oh, fine."

He's up off the couch and poking around my kitchen. "Were you serious about wanting Greek food? If not, I can make something. Stir-fry? Baked potatoes?"

"Tofu bibimbap," I decide, and he laughs.

He quickly puts in an order at the Korean restaurant a few blocks away and comes back to sit with me on the couch. He puts my drink in one hand.

I set it aside and give one of his hands a thorough inspection. Wide fingers. The kind of thumb that has an obtuse angle where it connects to the base of his palm. None of the lines on his palm touch one another. It's a wide-open field, nothing but possibilities. There's not a single closed door on this man right here. Except that he's gone quiet. His cheeks are pink and he's lost, staring impenetrably at our nestled hands. I cannot think of a worse time for someone to be gathering their thoughts.

"Shep?"

"Hm?"

"You all right?"

He sandwiches my hand between his and glances up at me. "I was just thinking . . . kissing you . . . I've been waiting twenty-five years for that."

The words go cardboard flat and flop to the ground. I'm aghast. "Twenty-five *years*?" I ask. Surely he means days. He must mean days.

He gives a little laugh at my expression and strokes my jaw, gently closing my wide-open trap. "Give or take."

"Since you were *six*?" I ask.

His gaze is back on our tangled hands and it takes a moment for him to bring his eyes to mine. "Eve, for as long as I can remember I have always wanted to be as close as possible to you."

"Oh, for fuck's sake!" I fling his hand back to him and haul myself off the couch. I'm holding my heart with two hands and seeing fireworks. "You can't just *say* stuff like that!"

He has two hands on my shoulders and he's lowering me back on the couch. Somehow the glass ends up in my hand again. I drink it to the bottom just so he'll stop handing it to me.

"You . . . don't like hearing it?" he asks.

"It makes me so happy I might pass out," I tell him. "And I mean that literally. I feel faint."

"Okay. Hold on." He's back a moment later with a string cheese and an apple. I can see the wisdom here so I make quick work of both. He disposes of the wrapper and the core and comes back, picking my feet up and starting in with his thumbs. "Better?"

"Yes. No. I'm overwhelmed."

"One step at a time, Eve. I know we just kissed for the first time. And I just told you how long I've . . . But one foot in front of the other, yeah?"

I pull my feet back from him and hook my fingers in the collar of his shirt. I don't have much of a lap right now, but there's room enough for his head. He looks confused until he realizes I'm reimbursing him for the foot rubs. His eyes flutter closed when I give his hair a friendly tug.

"We haven't seen each other since Sunday," I say, and his eyes open.

"Mm-hmm."

"And we only texted a few times."

"Right?"

Well, he's wanted to be close to me for twenty-five years, so maybe he can handle a little clinginess. "What if I told you that I didn't like waiting that long? And that I want to see you tomorrow. And every day. And, oh, lord, pregnant and off my rocker might not be the best time to start dating me."

"It's the perfect time to start dating you."

I don't think he's lying because he's looking awfully happy down there.

"It's not just a clingy thing that I want to see you every day. But every time something happens with the baby and no one else is there to observe . . . I just get so bummed. I mean look. *Look.*" I grab my phone and toggle through some pictures. "This was my belly on Sunday and this was my belly this morning. That much growth in half a week! And no one was here to see it but me."

He looks at the pictures for a ridiculously long time. Long enough I start to get self-conscious. "Okay, give it back now."

He holds it out of my reach. "Gimme a break, these are my first topless pics of you."

"I'm not topless! I'm wearing a *bra.*"

"Still, there's your belly. I almost never get to see your belly."

I frown for a second. "I wish you could've seen my belly

pre-pregnancy. It was pretty hot. Who knows what it'll look like after this. I'm guessing melted butter."

"I did see your belly pre-pregnancy. Many times."

"Oh, right. Swimming at the pond. But you never got to touch it. What a shame."

"I did too!" he insists. He's looking up at me from my lap, my fingers lost in his hair, and my dizzy feeling comes back. His brow furrows. "You don't remember?"

"You touching my stomach? No."

"It was at Kevin Zemeckis's pool party. His parents came home unexpectedly and we all had to run. Remember?"

"Vaguely."

"We piled with a bunch of other kids into a van and you either had to sit on Zach Cartwright's lap or mine."

This part I remember a little better. "Easy choice. Zach Cartwright was a total dipshit."

"Well, either way, I felt like I'd won the lottery. We couldn't get the seatbelt to buckle over both of us, so you told me to hold on tight to you. And I did."

"I remember that part. I was cold because I was wet from the pool, but you were dry and warm."

He nods. "I didn't swim. And when you got off me, there was a big wet stripe down my front from the pool water." He lets out a long breath. "Eve. If you want to see me every day, you want someone to measure your belly, I'm clearly game."

Before I can answer, my buzzer does its fuzzy ding and Shep dislodges from my lap. "We've gotta get your super to look at that bell. I swear it even *sounds* like a hazard."

He slips his shoes on, jogs downstairs, and comes back up with our food in hand. We eat side by side. At the end of the meal, he leans in and gives me a soft kiss that makes my stomach tumble dry low. He pulls back suddenly.

"Holy shit, how much hot sauce did you put on your food?" he demands.

"Not a lot!" I insist, and reach over for the bottle.

He inspects the label. "This is like . . . ulcer with a cap on it."

He gulps water and eyes me, so I cover my mouth with my hand. "No more kissing, I promise."

"Well, that's a terrible promise." He tugs me forwards, kisses me deeply, and then pulls away again. "Yeah, no, can't do it. Sorry. You ate fire."

He grabs the plates and runs into the kitchen, and I can hear him quickly filling up a glass of water two, three times to wash down the spice. Then I hear him move on to washing the dishes. He's just in the next room, but I feel a little at loose ends without his mouth here to show me that everything is okay.

But then the baby stretches and pokes and jams upward towards my ribs and I laugh. "I wasn't ignoring you, I swear!"

I put my feet up.

"What do *you* think about all this?" I whisper to the baby. "Oh, who am I kidding. He's the first person you ever kicked for. You clearly like him as much as I do." I stroke a hand over my belly.

I close my eyes and listen to the sounds of Shep puttering around in the kitchen, and the baby and I sit together and the baby stretches and I can barely remember what it felt like to worry I was going to do this alone.

Twenty-Five

"Oh, Jesus."

Shep is standing in my bedroom doorway and he looks to be in physical pain.

After lunch, I took a nap, woke up, and still Shep stayed. The sun dipped low, he fed me a peanut butter and jelly sandwich while we sat side by side on the floor (why? I don't know. When you've gone full Tweety Bird for somebody, when they sit on the floor, you sit next to them). And still Shep stayed. I jumped into the shower after that and *still* Shep stayed. Now I'm standing in my bedroom in a short robe with a rope of wet hair over my shoulder and this . . . is apparently working for him.

He takes one step into the bedroom, then pauses.

"Come sit on my bed while I decide which pajamas to wear."

"You're changing out of that?" he asks dimly, sitting down on the bed.

"You really like the robe that much?"

"Yes. It, uh, shows all your shadows."

"My shadows—Oh." I look down and see that the robe is gaping slightly open and yes, there is a pretty interesting shadow down the middle of my chest. "One thing about pregnancy is definitely tits."

"Definitely," he agrees.

I hold up two different pajama sets to see which one he likes better. "This one or this one?"

"Lemme see closer."

I walk over and hold them up but he snakes an arm around my back and now I'm standing in between his spread legs and his nose is drawing a line up the side of my throat.

"Very smooth," I say, but I don't think he's listening.

And then I'm not listening either because those are his lips walking their way under my chin to the other side of my throat. The shoulder of my robe gets pushed an inch, two inches to the side and then he's pretty much making out with my shoulder and I haven't breathed in forty-five seconds.

My knees buckle and he tightens his grip around me. "Whoa."

I have two hands on his shoulders. "You've just *literally* made me weak in the knees!"

"Sorry?" He slides the fabric back into place in apology.

I promptly climb up onto the bed and lean back on my pillows, yanking the fabric back off my shoulder. He's already rearranging, one knee between my legs and a fist planted on either side of me. These are lengthy, deep kisses that only end when I twist my face to one side and he goes back to my neck.

I'm being tasted, bitten, soothed. He's drawing patterns into my skin and if I were a little more clearheaded, I might try to decipher what they were. As it is, it's all I can do to dig my fingers into his shoulders and endure.

I push at his shoulders and he immediately surfaces, his eyes bleary and charged. "Okay?" he asks.

I push again and he flops heavily onto his back. His weight shifts the bed and it knocks my nightstand lamp to the floor.

He winces. "Sorry."

"Why do I find that so cute?" I demand, crawling on top of him.

"I don't know but I'm very glad you do." He pushes himself up onto his elbows and meets my mouth halfway. My robe is off both shoulders, held up by the slope of my breasts and, I don't know, the single last thread of my clarity?

Am I about to fuck Shep on the same day as our first kiss? Is that a good idea? Is it rushing things? I legitimately can't tell.

"All these fucking hormones," I say.

"I—huh?" He pulls back and in order to push myself off a cliff, I reach for the hem of his T-shirt and wow. That's a very nice treasure trail.

"Nice," I tell him.

He laughs and turns his head away for a moment but lets me continue pawing him. "What about hormones?"

I've just found his hip bone so it takes me a minute. "Huh?"

I think he's still listening but he's given up on eye contact. He tongues the line of my robe up over each breast and spends a very special amount of time in between. His hands walk themselves down my spine and keep on going. He's got two handfuls of ass and looks like he might not make it through.

"Horniness. Extreme horniness," I gasp when he fully sits up, me on his lap still, and drags his hands up to the sides of my breasts. The heels of his hands wander into some very interesting territory. "Many women experience it during pregnancy. Because of all the hormones."

He lifts his face and catches my eye. I'm not ready for the fact that touching my ass apparently makes his voice quite deep. "Are you one of those women?"

My entire body nods. "Shep, I truly can't take it. I want to use you like a cat scratch pole." I bury my face in his neck and groan when his stubble is the stabby-good kind that'll definitely leave marks on my skin. "And you smell so *good*."

"Better than a train car?" he asks, the ghost of his smile on his lips, his pupils almost completely blown out.

"I could *live* inside your puffy coat. Seriously. Can I have it? I want it as a sex dungeon."

He laughs but abruptly stops when I bite his pulse point. "Eve."

"Hmm?" My hips have started moving against him of their own accord. His hands are back on my ass and I think for a moment he might still me, but instead he helps me, his hands encouraging my movements.

"I can help with the horniness issue."

"Great. Get naked, please."

He laughs. "Right now?"

"Completely naked is preferable, but from the waist down is all I really need."

He's laughing more. "You're saying that you wanna fuck *right* now?"

"Yes. Immediately. Yesterday, if possible." I'm glorying in the fact that Shep just said *fuck* and he meant it as a verb. A verb that we should do to each other. Delicious.

"Wow," he says, reaching back and tearing his shirt off. His hair is messy from the shirt and he's got a hairier chest than I would have thought and muscles and an inch of softness over that. I immediately resolve to buy a video camera and make some homemade porn with this gorgeous individual.

"What?" he says.

Whoops. Seems I said that last part out loud. "Nothing."

He's laughing again. "Can we table the porn thing?"

"Porn table. Yes. Got it. Our relationship is off to a great start."

I scramble for his belt buckle, give up, and just go for the knot on my robe. I slide it off and throw it to the ground. And here I am on top of Shep buck-ass naked.

"Fu-uuu-uuuu-uuuuckkkkk." He covers his eyes and flops onto his back. When his hands slide down and reveal his eyes again, they are completely black and attempting to memorize every inch of me.

Some men are graceful as jungle cats, according to Nora Roberts. Shep is not one of them. He sits up and face-plants himself into my cleavage. He puts two hands on either side of my breasts, and I think he might be punishing himself for loving me.

"Don't asphyxiate in there, please," I say to the top of his head.

"What a way to go." I can barely hear him through the muffle.

He kisses his way out of my cleavage and his warm mouth closes over one of my nipples.

"Sensitive!" I hiss, dropping my head back and digging my fingertips into his shoulders. He grunts acknowledgment and changes pressure, his eyes on my face and, yeah, wow.

He shifts us and I'm on my back and he's kneeling between my legs. He sits back on his heels. "This view . . ." He trails off. "Are you comfortable?" he observes.

"It's just a lot of weight." I gesture to the belly.

"Is your side better?"

"Definitely."

He rolls me to my side and takes a minute to skate a hand up from my ankle to my hip. He looks like he's going to say something but thinks better of it and just uses his teeth on the same path. When he presses his teeth into my hip bone I shiver.

"I don't think we're gonna be able to do it face-to-face," I say, gasping for breath. "I think it's gonna have to be from the back."

His head pops up, his eyes still black. "That's, ah, not a problem."

He's crawling in front of me now, lying on his side too, and reaching for his belt buckle. He gets the tricky part open and then slowly moves his hand away, his eyes on me. He wants me to do the rest.

My hand touches the leather of his belt and he inhales on a hiss. He rolls onto his back and up onto his elbows again, watching me. I yank on the belt and he lifts his hips, it comes free, and I toss it onto the floor. Next is his jeans button and it's a butter-smooth release. His breaths are barrel deep and washing over me. When my fingers grip the zipper pull of his fly, he groans.

I look up at him.

"Top five personal fantasy," he explains, his eyes on my hand. "You unzipping my jeans."

That is just, really, really the kind of thing somebody likes to hear.

So I do it. I pull the zipper down and reveal a perfect section of heaven-blue underwear that is pulling very hard to one side.

"This is so wonderful," I tell him, and he grins. Happy and turned on all at once. His hands come to my face and mine to his chest. I balance over him to kiss and his hands trace a twisting line from breasts to ass and back. He's taking reverent handfuls and attempting to suck all the oxygen out of the room.

Buzz.

It's a very familiar fuzzy buzzing.

We pull back and stare into each other's eyes and try to remember the English language.

Buzzzzzz.

"The door," I eventually say.

He blinks and looks at my bedside clock. "It's past eleven."

Buzzzz. Buzzzz. Buzzzz.

I sit up on my heels. Whoever is ringing my doorbell is not disappearing into thin air, like I wish they would.

He sits up too and fishes around for his shirt. To my dismay he's tucking and zipping and smoothing himself back into place.

"Nooooooo," I whisper in despair.

He smiles at my reaction. "I promise I'm not taking it away for good."

I get out of bed too and pull on some underwear and a bra from my drawer.

"Noooooo," he says, his eyes wide with alarm.

"See?" I say with a finger point. "It's terrible to watch someone put on their clothes."

I'm tugging on one of the pajama sets too.

"You can stay in bed," he says. "I'll just be right back."

BangBANGbang.

Someone is using their fist against my front door. I barely have time to register that Shep has stepped in front of me, one hand behind himself, on my hip. "How'd they get upstairs?" he asks.

"The door doesn't always automatically latch downstairs. Sometimes it's open."

He grumbles something else about my super and then squeezes my hip. "Stay here, please."

There's one more bang from the front door and then some softened tapping. "Sorry," a voice says from the hallway. "Didn't mean to knock so loud."

I recognize that voice and I hurry forwards to grab Shep's elbow before he swings open the door. "It's Ethan."

"He sounds drunk," Shep says, holding my eyes. "Do you want to talk to him? Or do you want me to send him away?"

I melt and press my cheek to his heart. "Oh, it's so nice to have a Shep." When I look up at him, I see a touch of relief there. "Let's make sure he's okay."

Shep nods and heads to the door, unlocking it and pulling it open.

Ethan has yet to gain his sea legs. He's sagging and stumbling just standing there. "Eve?" He blinks around Shep and finds me standing in the middle of the living room in my pajamas.

"Hi, Ethan."

"Sorry," he says, stumbling forwards and starting to kick off his shoes. "Sorry for being so loud."

He is one of those immaculate people whose clothes can remain perfectly buttoned and neat even when nearly falldown drunk. Everything except his face, which seems to have gone slack and tight at the same time. He overbalances and Shep catches him by the elbow. It's only then that Ethan seems to register his presence.

He squints and tries to focus. "Shep?"

"Hi."

Ethan pulls his arm away. "This fuckin' guy."

"Hey!" I say, stepping forwards.

"You know you're always around, right?" Ethan says to Shep. "Where do you even *live*? You're always here."

I guess it's true that the two times Ethan has come into my house, Shep has either been here or arrived shortly thereafter.

"And what are you doing here at—" There's about twenty seconds of fumbling his phone out of his pocket, exiting out of some messages and then squinting at the time, holding his phone close and then far in order to see it. "Eleven fifteen on a Thursday night."

"Ethan," I say in exasperation. "That's not exactly your—"

"Oh, fuck," he says, and wobbles to the chair he's sat in before. He's looking back and forth between me and Shep. "You're *together*, aren't you."

He doesn't wait for confirmation, probably because he doesn't need it.

He puts his head in his hands and pulls his own hair. "Fuck!"

"Ethan!" I'm alarmed and walking towards him, but Shep is slightly angling his body in between me and Ethan.

"How about a glass of water for him," he whispers.

I nod and head into the kitchen. I'm halfway back when Ethan speaks again.

"I left her, you know."

Water slops over the rim of the cup as I abruptly stop walking. "Eleni?"

At the sound of her name, his eyes turn red and he scrubs the heels of his hands into them. "Yeah. Just a few hours ago."

"Oh, Ethan."

Shep has sat down on the coffee table kitty-corner to Ethan, his hands in his pockets and sympathy in his eyes. "I'm sorry, man."

"She wanted—and I just couldn't do it." Ethan says. He's really crying now, tears that don't even make it to his cheeks before he pushes them away with his fingers.

"She wanted you to never see me or the baby again," I guess.

"And you wanna know the worst part?" Ethan says. "When she realized I was leaving her . . . she told me she'd just been bluffing. That I could see the baby if I wanted but not you."

He folds over himself then, his forehead on his knees. Shep looks up at me and I immediately cross to him, reaching for his hand as we both watch Ethan quake.

"Bluffing," Ethan says into his knees. "Who *bluffs* to someone they love?"

Self-centered people, but I don't say it out loud. Probably not the time.

"And now you're together." He's sitting back up and there's tangible frustration in his face. He went soft and despairing when talking about Eleni, but if Shep's back on the table, so is his ire.

"I think we should talk about this when you're not drunk," I tell him. "I'll make you a bed on the couch. Or an air mattress?"

"While you sleep in there with him? Ha!"

He's slipping forwards off the chair and Shep lunges, catching him by the shoulder. Ethan's body does a familiar gagging heave.

"Oh, shit," he says. Shep has him up and is pointing him towards the bathroom and I watch in horror as they stumble together. Ethan is through the bathroom door, I hear the toilet lid open, and then wince when I hear the unmistakable splat of puke on the tile floor.

Shep stands in the doorway of the bathroom, resignation on his face but a remarkable lack of anything else. He looks over at me. "Could we have some paper towels and a plastic bag? Maybe some disinfectant?"

I gather up the cleaning supplies and am trying to step around Shep to get into the bathroom when he just gently takes them from my hands and kisses me on the forehead. "It's late," he whispers. "I'll take care of this. Why don't you sleep? Or at least lie down?"

He doesn't wait for my answer. Instead he steps into the bathroom and closes the door behind him.

I toddle to the couch and sit down. I hear Ethan puking again. Then they're talking and I can hear that too.

"No, don't. Stop cleaning my puke. Jesus."

"It's fine. Just make sure you get it in the toilet next time."

There's more retching. A toilet flush. The sink runs.

"You're such a good guy, Shep. God, you're so nice. Fuck you, Shep. You're such a fucking *good guy*."

I'd like to march in there and slap the red off Ethan's head for talking to Shep like that, but Shep speaks before I can even get off the couch.

"Don't say 'fuck you' to me, all right?"

"Why? Because it's not *nice?*"

"Because it *means* something to be that rude to someone. And you need to be better than that."

"God. It just had to be *you,* didn't it." Ethan sneers. "Everywhere I turn and there you are. Almost every time I see her, you're there or she's talking about you. I should have known. You're *everywhere.*"

"Well, I've known her a lot longer than you have."

Ethan barrels on. "You know how disorienting these last few months have been for me and every time I almost get my bearings I turn around and there you are again. And now . . . and now you're *with* her. And it's so clear . . . You're like the nicest, most generous, lovable guy on the planet and you're *with* the mother of my child. Do you have any idea how insufferable that is?"

Shep laughs and it's the first sound he's made that's not exceedingly kind. "Ethan, are you *kidding* me?"

"What?"

"*Of course* I know how you feel. You're a handsome, successful guy who is usually very nice, and *you got the love of my life pregnant.* You wanna talk about insufferable?"

My mouth is open in shock. My heart is leading a marching band.

"Oh," Ethan says. "Shit. Do you hate me, Shep? Please just tell me you hate me."

"No. I don't hate you. Sorry to disappoint. I actually think you're a really worthwhile person. You've made Eve cry before. I don't like that. But despite everything that's happened . . . my hunch tells me that you're going to be there for Eve and the baby. And that means something to me. I'm . . . grateful for that. You being a good guy is a good thing for Eve. So it's a good thing for me. Hating you would be a waste of energy."

The sink is running again. "Besides," Ethan grumbles. "We can't hate each other if we're going to see each other all the time." There's a pause. "It's obvious you're endgame for her. I knew it when you came into the bar that one time. The look on her face . . . she got so excited it made the baby kick. *My baby*. Kicking for Shep fucking what's-his-name. Jesus Christ."

"Ooooohhhhkay." I'm swinging open the bathroom door because hell if I'm going to let Ethan tell Shep how I feel before *I* officially tell Shep how I feel. "Ethan, now that you're done redecorating my bathroom floor, do you want a cab or a floor bed?"

If he notices that he's been abruptly downgraded from couch/air mattress, he doesn't comment. "Just gimme a blanket," he mumbles.

I do just that, handing him a blanket from the closet and digging out a toothbrush for him. By the time I'm done peeing and Shep is done taking the puke trash out and washing up, Ethan is already asleep.

We go to my bedroom and close the door. The bed is mussed from our previous activities and I love that Shep knows me well enough to take time to straighten the covers before he pulls them back for us to get in. We slide in on either side, Shep clicks off the nightstand lamp that's just resumed its place on the nightstand, and we meet in the middle of the bed. I sandwich his knees with mine.

"Not exactly how I pictured our first night together," I whisper, our noses touching.

He smiles and gives me a soft kiss. "You know, this actually *is* how I was picturing it. Not the Ethan part. But the snuggling part."

We kiss again and the words *love of my life* float up to the surface. "Shep . . ."

He gives me two more kisses and I recognize them as tiny little stop signs.

"Could we wait?" he requests. "To talk about everything. Until it's actually just the two of us?" He pauses. "Well, three of us." One of his palms finds my belly. "But four is a little bit of a crowd."

I nod and sigh and roll over and Shep is there, snuggled up behind me, his breath in my hair and his hand on my side.

Twenty-Six

I'm on my lunch break the next day, sitting on a bench in a (very) small, grassy courtyard on 44th Street, eating a taco salad when I get a text from Ethan.

It simply reads: *Hate me?*

I can't tell if it's a question or a request.

How's your stomach? I text back.

Hangovers are instant karma. He texts again. *Not that that's all I deserve for last night!* And again: *Even after everything I said Shep made me an omelet with a side of breakfast potatoes this morning.*

I laugh to myself. Oh, Shep. *He's a better person than me,* I text.

And me too, Ethan replies. *I'll find a way to make this up to you, Eve. To you and to Shep.*

I blink at the text. It's the first real promise Ethan has ever made to me. I wonder if he realizes that. *Okay,* I say simply. *You know where to find me.*

I quickly send Shep a text. *Did you make Ethan breakfast this morning, you absolute prince?*

I immediately receive a gif of a cartoon princess curtsying.

You can stop wooing me now, I text him. *We've already kissed. Now you can watch TV with your pants undone and scratch your nutsack and stuff.*

You certainly have a very vivid style of flirting, he texts back. And then: *But my nutsack appreciates the green light.*

And on that lovely note, I finish lunch and head back towards the office.

My feet take me towards the side entrance and there, behind an eight-foot-tall window, are about ten toddlers crawling and shouting. It's the daycare that WFA partners with.

"Whaddaya think?" I ask my bump.

The kids look happy enough. Half are at tables that are covered over in newsprint, coloring with crayons the size of deli pickles. The other half are crawling around in an area with foam flooring while a teacher tries to get them to watch a puppet show. But, oh, look, there's one kid in the corner. They've got long curly hair and fat tears rolling down their face. Oh no. Someone help! I don't like this at all. I could never leave my rump roast at a place where—Oh. And here comes a teacher in a smock and a long red ponytail. She's on one knee in front of the child and talking. They head together to the far side of the room, where I assume a bathroom is. Well, that's not so bad. I sigh and head back to work.

As I take the elevator upstairs to the admin annex my brain automatically zooms me to Shep. *His legs in a Y while he kissed me in the park:* my stomach flips. *His forehead post-haircut:* I put two hands over my face. *Making out like high schoolers on the couch and then making out like grown-ups, naked on my bed:* euphoria rockets through me and a squeak of joy erupts from my mouth.

The elevator dings, I step off, and as the door closes behind me, unbidden, Willa's words float up out of the ether. *Everything is both magical and confusing and you never get what you want because you don't* know *what you want. You've never known what you want.*

But . . . that's not true for me anymore. For the first time in my life I know exactly what I want.

I want the baby and I want Shep, obviously. And . . . I flex the feeling a little bit. It's got power, breadth.

I realize, with a racing heart, that I could extend this feeling out to other parts of my life if I choose to.

A great thing about knowing what you want is that you can start racing towards it.

I stride with purpose through the annex.

Micah fumbles papers as he takes in the expression on my face. Bevi overflows a houseplant when I march to Xaria's door and plant my feet.

I take a deep breath and knock on her door.

"Come in."

Xaria, hip-deep in paperwork, is wearing cat-eye glasses and a zebra-print dress. Her hair is freshly blown out and as shiny as the grand-prize car on a game show. She brings herself to the surface as her eyes focus on me.

"Eve. What can I do for you? Take a seat."

I take another deep breath and try to calm the flipping in my stomach. I take a seat and keep my back ramrod straight.

"I want to talk to you about the finance assistant position."

"Great," she says. "I was hoping you would."

I'd start talking, but she's turned her attention to her computer. She clicks around for a moment and then turns her screen and I'm greeted with a website for accounting classes.

I blink.

"The org would foot the bill for the classes. And for leadership training as well."

"Accounting and leadership . . ." I sum up and trail off. Neither of those things is required for a finance assistant position. "That's . . . that's . . ."

"My position?" She smiles and maybe for the first time, it's warm. "I realized something recently, Eve. All this talk about lateral moves. I was never very clear about the fact that I've been eyeing you to eventually replace me."

"*What?*" And here I thought she'd been lackey recruiting.

Her eyes are narrowed again. "I didn't think you'd be *this* shocked. Why do you think I've been so adamant about moving you to the finance side of the team?"

"I . . . Sorry. I'm a little scrambled. Let me get this straight. You want to set me up to become the head of the finance department?"

She raises one hand to slow me down. "Well, like I said, we'd transfer you over to the finance department and continue your training for a few years. And then someday . . . well, that's the track I'd like you to be on."

"Why *me?*" The question just pops right out.

"You're one of the most versatile employees here. You have your hands in every single department. HR, finance, facilities, the website, proofreading for projects. You understand the way the org works, you see the holes that need to be plugged, you're well liked. I think you're an obvious candidate."

I rub my belly and try not to seem *so* gobsmacked that she's seen this potential in me. "You . . . you got all of that just from me writing the newsletter?"

Her face quirks a little. "The newsletter is what made me realize that you feel the way I do about the org's future. No one who doesn't actually care about the integrity of WFA would spend so many hours a month on something like that."

Okay. Now's the time for what I stormed into this office to say. Now or never, Eve. "Xaria . . . all of that isn't just out of the goodness of my heart. It was kind of *a plan.* I thought that if I continually showed my understanding, my analysis . . . well, you should know . . ." I take a deep breath and then the plunge. "I want to be a policy analyst someday."

She blinks. Eyes me from toes to nose. Blinks again. "A policy analyst."

"Yes. I know it would be a big transition from the admin team to the program staff. And I know it's not . . . Look, it's why I originally applied to work here. Working in conservation has been a lifelong dream and I knew I wasn't qualified for the PA position, so I applied to the admin team and hoped I could acquire experience and knowledge and when there was an opening they might hire from within."

I guess I pictured her tossing me out on my arse. Traitor to the admin team and all. But as she studies me, her expression changes from discerning to almost curious. "What was your undergrad degree in?"

I grimace. "Bachelor of science. Ecology."

She narrows her eyes, nods. "It's a good start, but I'm sure you know that almost no one gets hired in one of those positions without at least a master's. In a more relevant field."

"I know. I just . . . I have so much hands-on knowledge. I guess I just keep thinking . . ."

"Why not go back to school, then? If you want it so badly?"

I'm barely keeping from gaping at her. This is absolutely not how I pictured this conversation going. She's being weirdly . . . cool.

"I don't know, it just . . . seemed like such a big risk. All that school, and what if I *still* didn't get the job?" I tell her, my eyes cast down. I gesture at my belly. "And I guess school is kind of off the table now."

"Why?" She raises an eyebrow.

I gesture again at my belly and take a risk with a joke. "There's a kid in here, you know."

"You think you'd be the only new mom attending classes?" She's so wholly unimpressed with my assessment that I'm immediately, laughingly, humbled.

"I know that you did that when you were pregnant," I concede. "But I'm not sure . . . every option just seems so hard. For me, but also for the baby."

"Everything's hard, Eve. All of life. For everybody. You can't spare your child that."

Parenting advice from Xaria? Jeez, when did everybody get so multifaceted?

"You're right," I say slowly, gathering my thoughts. "But . . . working full time, school at least half time, when would I get to be with the baby? And how would I ever pay for that much childcare?"

She sighs and rotates a little in her chair. "I really hate these sorts of questions."

"Sorry?"

She fishes under her desk and comes up with a spray bottle, making her way around to her plants as she talks to me. *Spritz, spritz.* "I hate those questions because it keeps women who are clever and levelheaded in low-level positions in order to be able to see their kids." *Spritz, spritz, spritz.* "It eliminates so many qualified people from jobs they deserve to have. That's why I do not want to leave the finance department to a man."

"Not even Micah?"

"Micah's a doll," she says by way of reply. "But Eve, I cleaned the toilets here. I served coffee to the boss's secretary's secretary for years. I worked twelve hours a day for decades. School and more school. I was patient. I didn't quit when others got promoted before me. And I've watched you over the years slowly expand your job description so that you have your hand in almost every department. I've seen how comprehensively you understand the way we work around here. You know every employee, every project, every partner. Everything from the muffins at the all-staff to the newsletter you write. And you get it all done within your work hours. You've never even applied for any overtime. You know how much work ethic that takes? It's not every administrative assistant who decides it's their personal job to keep the roof on the place. That takes ambition and I like that."

I have never in my life heard myself described in this way. I've always thought the fact that I was still an administrative assistant indicated a distinct *lack* of ambition. I feel energized and dizzy. I'd like to run a lap around the building and simultaneously lie down for a quick nap.

"I want to retire," Xaria continues. "But I want a *woman* in this position. The person who takes this job has to have fought tooth and nail on behalf of their integrity."

My heart is leaping. She's got a spray bottle in one hand and the other hand on her hip. She is a warrior goddess and if I weren't afraid it would lead to an *I've fallen and I can't get up* situation, I'd bow down. "I'm so grateful you've considered me for this, Xaria. It's one of the greatest compliments of my life. And you're right. I want to stay here. I want to make this org more effective. But . . . I want to do that by becoming a policy analyst." I clear my throat. "And if that takes going back to school . . . then I want to find a way to do that."

It's a hollow pounding in my chest. This saying-what-I-want thing is hard on the old cardiovascular system. How many times have I told myself that school was going to be impossible and that if I just kept going as is, someday they might realize that all my admin experience makes me a perfect candidate? And how many times did I already know that was unrealistic and unlikely?

Exactly how much fooling have I been doing?

And better question: why?

She sighs and stows her spray bottle away, sitting in her chair. "Well, I can't say I didn't wish you had this particular fire for accounting."

"I'm sorry."

She looks away from me for a long while, her eyes upward on the tiny window at the top of her wall. She turns back and there's resignation in her eyes, but something else too. "When you get back from your maternity leave, we'll have a meeting. You, me, and HR. We'll figure out a way for you to juggle work and school. It might mean a cut to your hours, but I'll bet we can keep you on the insurance."

I resist the urge to demand she repeat herself, to get it in triplicate. Because she has just casually offered to eliminate one of the biggest obstacles to me going back to school.

She purses her lips and sighs, her attention drifting back to her computer screen, like she hasn't just completely changed what is possible for my future. "We'll talk when you're back."

I drift back to my desk and keep waiting for the stupidity to rush in. I've officially told Xaria to stop considering me for the highest-paying job I could possibly get with my level of education. I've officially said out loud that I want to go back to school. I've officially said out loud that I want . . . anything.

This feeling is terrifying and satisfying in equal parts.

First I told the baby. And then Xaria. Now there's one more person I have to lay it all out for: the man who put all this into motion. He doesn't have any idea how much I want him. But he's about to.

Twenty-Seven

As soon as I get off the train back in my neighborhood I call Shep.

"Hi." His voice is hot chocolate.

"Any chance you're still at my house?"

"Ummmm."

"I'm taking that as a yes."

"I like it here! I went home and grabbed my laptop and a change of clothes this morning. Are you almost home?"

"Just walking up the block. I'll see you in a sec."

It's strange for someone to be home when I get there. My apartment feels in motion. There are Shep's gigantic shoes haphazardly welcoming me home. A timer is beeping in the kitchen and one of the windows is propped open, letting a breeze cycle through the apartment.

And the most important detail? Shep taking bread out of the oven. He taps the seeded dome of the loaf and listens to the specific sound it makes. Then he sets it on top of the stove and turns to me, pulling oven mitts off.

"Hello," he says.

I cross to the kitchen and wash my hands, looking around my apartment. There are apples in my fruit bowl that I didn't put there. Water droplets sparkle on the leaves of my spider plant. The ultrasound that I keep magneted to the fridge has been straightened.

There, in my mind, is the daycare under WFA, and wooden

blocks and teachers kneeling down and all the tears my kid will cry that I might not be there to see. Just imagine all the Shep-made bread that this kid might eat after school while I'm still tapping out emails at work. I dry my hands and turn to look at Shep, who is currently looking at me.

"Shep . . ." I start, and then immediately lose courage. But I think of the bicycle seat and I have to ask. "When you picture this . . ." My hands gesture vaguely around the kitchen, and then between him and the baby bump. "Are you picturing . . . co-parenting?"

His face changes and I'm suddenly feeling a little faint.

My hands are in his and he's leading me to the couch. We sit almost on top of each other. Either his hands are shaking or mine are. I can't tell.

"There's a long answer and there's a short answer," Shep says, enveloping my hands in his hands. "Which do you want first?"

"Short. Then long."

"Okay." He lets out a long breath. "The short answer is that for a long time when I first found out you were having a baby, I mostly just thought about all the ways I could help you. But since I felt the baby kick, I've kind of . . . sort of . . . started to get excited about *knowing* the baby. I mean . . . it's your kid, so you know it's gonna be awesome. But . . . I'm not assuming anything. Sometimes hope can feel like pressure, you know? So I'll be Uncle Shep or friend Shep or just Shep or whatever. I don't need . . . a title. I just want to be here. For as much as I'm invited to be here for."

"Okay," I say after a long pause. *Hope,* he said just now. *This baby isn't bad news,* he said to me all those months ago. "What's the long answer?"

He paints a line down my arm, from my elbow to my wrist, his eyes stuck to his fingers, and I get the odd feeling like maybe he won't answer me. "I know the last few days must have been a lot for you. First with me and then Ethan . . ."

I dip my head to catch his eye and there's an expression there that he tries to wipe away but can't.

"Eve . . ." he says slowly, his eyes still stuck to the path he's tracking up and down my arm. "If things between you and me . . . if they feel different . . . now that Ethan is single . . ."

"What?" I'm on my feet, both hands on my hips, and he's gaping up at me. I think I jumped up so fast I caught a little air. "Shep—"

"Can I say something?" He's sitting, looking up at me, his knees on either side of mine, holding both my hands.

"Of course."

He drops his forehead to my fingers and just holds, holds, holds there for the span of two or three breaths. When he looks up at me, he's a changed man. His eyes wide, mouth slightly open, breathing hard. This is a man with something to say.

"Eve . . . there is no explaining what the last few months have meant to me. Every little moment. You with your mouth so full of food you can't talk. You texting me random crap. Being able to just drop by and you opening the door, happy to see me. But the big stuff too. That night . . ."

I don't even need him to go on. I know exactly which night he's talking about. "That night," I agree with a nod.

His eyes are distant; he's back there in the lavender room with his hand under my shirt.

"Sharing that with you," he says. "Falling asleep with you like that, it's the closest I've ever felt to someone. And it was a door, that moment. Don't you think? We opened that door and then all the other moments cascaded in. Eating dinner at your house, just the two of us. Flirting at the movie theater. Falling asleep in your bed. Unbraiding your hair. Apartment shopping. And then, and then, and then . . . the park. All of that was possible because this little person, right here"—he smooths a hand over my belly—"chose *that* exact moment to kick. It was the most special moment of my life."

He lets out a shaky breath. His eyes are lion bright—summer sunshine bright—and I'm captured. Unmoving. Pinned to the dartboard. "If you can't tell . . ." he says. "If it's not totally obvious . . . I'll say it because I've really, really needed to say it for a long time . . . but, Eve, I love you more deeply than I've ever loved anyone else. I'm bananas for you. So in love I . . ."

He cuts off and drops his forehead to my fingers again. I want to scream with relief, with joy. I've gone hot and cold and everything in between. His hands open and close over mine, his head still tipped down. I have the feeling he's really going through it down there. He's gripping and pressing and grabbing at the shoreline with nothing but his fingertips. I squeeze his hands back because I feel like if I don't, he might just blow away, out to sea.

"I need you to know," he says. "I needed to tell you so that you were never confused. Or had to wonder. And I needed to say it out loud for myself."

My heart picks up like a wagon gaining speed downhill. Why is this weirdly starting to sound like a goodbye? "Shep—"

"But like I said, if things feel different because Ethan is single now, I honestly am not expecting anything from you. I just wanted to tell you, at least once."

I let out a fierce, barking laugh that's about ninety percent shock. Because the only man I think I've ever truly loved has just informed me that he loves me more deeply than he's ever loved anyone else and then encouraged me to explore a future with another man. "*Shep,* you can't possibly think—"

But couldn't he? Ethan is the father of my child. He's kind and successful and he and I had enough of a connection and attraction to sleep together. I sobbed when I found out he had a girlfriend and—most importantly—*I haven't told Shep how I feel yet.*

"Hold on." I'm holding two hands up and taking a deep breath. "I'm not about to let you let me down gently in the name of"—I gesticulate at the general moment—"whatever this is. Hell no. No. Ethan interrupted sex last night but he is not going to interrupt the moment you tell me that you're so in love with me dot dot dot. I wanna know the dot dot dot, all right? So, no. No to that. You know what? I'm going to take us back in time by a few minutes, okay? Yeah, that's what we're gonna do. I just got home and walked through the door and you were sitting on the couch waiting for me. Okay?"

"Uh." Shep is looking at me like he can't quite focus on me, his eyes blown, and his breaths still shaky. But what's he gonna say? No? "Okay."

I clap my hands once and then turn a circle. It doesn't seem like enough so I turn another circle.

"Um," he says. "What are you doing?"

"I'm obviously taking us back in time."

"Oh. Is that how that works?"

"Duh." I'm still slowly revolving. "Time travel is super easy. I don't know why more people don't use it."

I stop turning and face him. "Hi. I'm home from work," I say.

"Hello," he says. Still nervous, still willing to play my ridiculous game.

I step forwards and laboriously climb onto his lap. "This was smoother in my imagination," I say as I scooch and scrape my legs up either side of his thighs, inch by inch. His hands automatically clasp behind my back. "Anyhow," I say, eye level with him, my fingers curled under the collar of his T-shirt, the backs of my knuckles pressing into his skin. "I love you too and I was really hoping you'd be my boyfriend."

He's gone solid. A block of ice doesn't have shit on Shep. I grant him a few shocked seconds and then I give his collar a yank. "Shep."

Life comes to his eyelids and they start butterflying. "I'm sorry," he says on choppy air. "I'm sorry, would you say that again?"

"Is it really that much of a surprise?"

"Eve. Say it again."

"Boyfriend and girlfriend. You and me. Sitting in a tree, et cetera, et cetera. Did I leave anything out?"

"Yes."

"Oh, right. I love you."

His hands come unclamped behind my back and travel up my spine, one trailing the other. Over my shoulders, up the sides of my throat, and then my jaw is being cupped. It's a firm touch. The touch of someone who's just been told he's loved. His kiss is soft, softer, softest. Our mouths open against each other and Shep is everywhere. Everything. I'm so warm, tingling down to my fingertips, aching where I press against his belt buckle.

"Shep," I gasp when he moves to kiss the hinge of my jaw. My head lolls to one side and everything is just blurry colors and a strong arm bracing me behind my back. He comes back to my mouth and I have never been kissed like this. My mouth is a flower and he is gently, thoroughly trying to get at the nectar in the center. His stubble leaves a delicious scrape in its wake when he moves back to my throat. I'm tipping back and he's holding me as he walks his mouth down to my collarbone. He takes a soft bite, kisses it better, noses my collar to one side. It's not enough skin for him, so he grabs my sleeve at the elbow and gives it a firm tug. He kisses my bra strap and follows it down to my armpit. He huffs my scent and groans.

"I can't believe you just said that," he says into my skin.

"Yup. Oh, boy." I'm clinging to his shoulders as he tips me back and nuzzles my chest through my shirt. One of his hands has slid up my side and lingers, a perfect L shape, under my breast. I wiggle, wanting so badly for him to put me out of my misery already.

Oh no. What if Shep wants to go slow? What if he wants to woo me little by little? What if he's seconds away from straightening my shirt and respectfully tucking me into bed?

"Can I see you naked again?" he asks, his voice almost too low to hear, dragged over concrete, up a mountain, across the ocean, twenty-five years of waiting in that voice. "I mean, can I get you naked? Bath? Shower? Bed? Floor? Couch? I don't care. I just . . ."

He's trailed off, his eyelids falling lower and lower after each suggestion until by the end, I can barely see any of his lion brown.

"Yes. Bed? I know it's not the most risqué locale, but—"

He's set me on my feet, stood up, and then started leading me by the hand towards the bedroom. He pauses, turns, and starts kissing me again. I'm a human magnet. He's fully bent down to reach me and we scramble together, making out and side-stepping and *bam* apparently smacking Shep's elbow into the doorframe.

"Are you okay?" I ask, breaking free from the kiss.

"Huh? What?" And then we're kissing and stumbling again. He's never cared less about his elbows. He sets me up on the edge of the bed and plants a fist on either side of my hips. This kiss twists us, makes us dizzy. I pull away for a moment and attempt to get some oxygen to my brain.

"All right?" he asks, gruff and low, doing that thing where

his eyes dip and chase mine just to keep looking at me. He's all shoulders and short hair and leaning into my space.

"I don't think I've ever wanted someone more," I whisper. My trembling fingers attempt to untuck his shirt. "Clothes are terrible. Oh no. I'm nervous. Let's do this. Fast."

He's laughing, pressing his nose along mine, staring at me from a centimeter's distance. "Eve," he says.

"What's that?"

"The first person I ever wanted to sleep with was you. You pretty much *are* sex to me. So if you don't mind . . . If it's not too much trouble, maybe I'll just enjoy myself a little, and if you need me to go faster, you can just tell me, okay?"

Well, who am I to argue?

"Oh, okay," is my brilliant response.

He's laughing again and I'm being divested of my clothes. Everything is unbuckled and sliding and tossed away. I'm sat up and laid down and lifted and rolled. It takes long minutes because he has to stop in each place to kiss and press and nuzzle. I'm down to my bra and underwear, on my knees, facing away from him on the bed and he seems to have a particular affection for the dimples above my ass. He's on a day trip up my back, each rung of my ribs is making his acquaintance. I'm wiggling, heated, melting, making little noises. I feel his teeth at the clasp of my bra. He scrapes it against my skin and I make another noise. Maybe he's a genius because he correctly interprets it as a different kind of pleasure. He lifts the clasp away from my skin and gives me a very comprehensive back scratch. I'm a cat, arching and purring and he's laughing.

I look over my shoulder. "Speed up," I demand.

He nods and immediately obliges, unclasping my bra. I toss it away and his hands slide around my front, taking two warm handfuls of my breasts and we both groan. He kisses at the spot where my throat meets my shoulder and kneads and pets me and I swear, my underwear have never been more useless. I can feel my own heat, wet between my legs and I'm starting to actually ache for him.

I turn around and thank God my bed is high enough to put me almost at eye level with him this way. I yank again at his shirt and he lifts his arms, letting me tear it off over his head. He makes to move towards me again but I stop him with one palm in the air. His eyes are pinned to my chest, his mouth half open, his rib cage expanding with deep breaths.

I can finally understand why he wanted to go slow. Because look at all this body before me. I test his strength under my palms. He's sturdy, unmoving. Chest hair and hot skin. He didn't wear a belt today (how obliging), so I unbuckle his jeans and push them down, sending them to hell for all I care. And he's there in green boxer briefs that bulge to one side, straining away from his leg. He toes off his socks and chases me with his eyes. I reach forwards and guide his arms open, making him stand in a T, and lean forwards to bite his biceps. I kiss my way up his arm, over the rounded muscle of his shoulder and into his neck.

And then he's hugging me and kissing me and I'm hugging him and kissing him and it's so much heat, so much skin. We're slipping and dragging against each other. And holding and lacing fingers. He's stepping back and looping his fingers in the band of my underwear.

"Yeah?" he asks.

"Yeah. Yes. Full disclosure, grooming down there is a lot harder when I can't see over the bump," I tell him. "It's not the neatest it's ever been. Maybe just think of it as . . . artsy?"

He laughs and takes a shaky breath and drags my underwear away, inch by inch, down my legs.

He surveys me down there and groans into two hands he's pushing into his face. Then his fists are on either side of my hips and he's kissing my mouth. "Hi," he says against my lips. "Can I go down on you?"

I'm one big head nod.

His knees hit the floor and there's stubble against the inside of my knee. He's all lips up my thigh and placing my knees over his shoulders. I squeeze him. What a wonderful way to hug someone. He seems to agree, his fingers hugging me back where he grips me at my ass. I'm leaning back on my hands and the bump precludes my view, which is a shame, but it means I get to just close my eyes and feel, which is not a shame.

He opens me with his thumbs and kisses me hello. I hiss and jump and he immediately gentles. "*Very* sensitive," I whisper, and he rewards my honesty with a soft circle of his tongue. He wants to be everywhere at once and his tongue and lips begin a luxurious tour. I wish I could say that I got to enjoy that for an extended period of time, but after approximately twenty seconds of soft, exploratory circles and one preliminary suck, I'm a stiff rush of color, gasping his name and digging my heels into his back. I drop my head back and make an anguished noise because it feels so good I'm a melted candle now, it feels so good the world is pixelated, it feels so good all I can say is his name and internally beg God for oxygen.

He lifts his head, breathing hard and staring up at me. "Did you just come? Already?" He's blinking.

"I'm just a *very* horny mess right now," I tell him, gasping.

He's scratching at the back of his head. "I—wow. That's like, a superpower or something."

"Yes. I'm magic. Put a condom on, please."

He's on his feet and disappearing out of my bedroom and into the bathroom. I hear the crinkle of a plastic bag and then he's striding back in, tearing open a box of condoms and ripping one open.

The second, the very second, he's close enough to the bed,

I slip my fingers in the band of his underwear and tug him towards me. He's strong and warm and he's got these hip bones that just end me. Whoever designed Shep was like, *How about we make him so sturdy that some lucky lady can pin her entire life to him?* We push his underwear down together, him standing in front of me and my legs open on either side of his knees.

It might not be a surprise, but I've never seen him naked before. And you never know what to really expect from a man during the *big reveal* but this is just *perfection*. His hands flex at his sides while I take a minute to get acquainted. Smooth skin, piping hot and sliding, I press my cheek into him, turn my head and steal a kiss. His fingers find my hair that's fallen in front of my eyes and he tucks it back behind my ear. I bump the tip with closed lips, lift my eyes to him, and push him through the barrier of my closed mouth, keep pressure, take as much of him as I can. He makes a wounded sound and cradles the back of my neck. It's all so lovely, I do it again and this time he can't seem to help but push forwards, one knee on the bed and his hand at the back of my head.

"Eve," he whispers, thrusting just a tiny bit before he pulls out of my mouth and fumbles with the condom. He positions it and we both slide it down into place. I scramble back on the bed and turn over onto all fours. I look back over my shoulder to see him staring at me.

His eyes are burning so bright I have to look away, plant my forehead on the bed, and just breathe. The bed dips with his weight and then he's over the top of me, a complete shelter, his elbows on either side of mine, his chest to my back and his chin nestling in to the crook of my neck.

"I love you so much," he whispers. He kisses my cheek, smells my hair, gently squeezes me down into a full-body hug. I can feel him hot and hard against my ass, but by all accounts this embrace is strictly affectionate. I turn my head and twist so our mouths can meet. "I'll never love anyone the way I love you," he says, his tongue a warm, tasting press against mine. "Being with you is the only thing I've ever really wanted."

I tear away from the kiss and push up from my elbows onto my hands. Either I've just gained superhuman strength or he gets the memo, because he pushes up too. I feel him behind me, his hands smoothing over my hips. He finds me with his fingers first. A soft trace. I melt and push back.

"Please," I say over my shoulder.

"You want me?" he asks, his eyelids low, his body so goddamn big, his fingers stroking me like all he wants is to give me everything.

"Please-yes-now," I say. "Please-I-want-you. Please-sex." Not eloquent but he's a quick study.

He's a slow, edgeless press, blunt and overwhelming. I'm so wet, so achy, so ready, but still, he meets resistance. He pulls back, dips his hips, and presses again. I wiggle against him. The first angle is always the trickiest and it's been a really long time since I've had sex. I bring my hand to where we meet and massage myself open for him. His fingers are there too, slipping against mine, and together we liquefy me. Centimeter by centimeter he pushes in and then we're there, ass to pelvis, he's fully inside and I can't help but grin over my shoulder at him.

We did it! I think triumphantly, happily. But then I see the look on his face.

He thinks *I'm* sex? Nah. That look, right there, *that's* sex. That's a man who is willing to destroy himself over lust. His fingers grip my hips and he pushes forwards, his head dropping back to suck at air. He bumps me forwards, I push him back. We find our rhythm and it's slower than I might have thought, neither of us wanting to pull very far away.

I've always felt vulnerable, vaguely porny, in this position before. But right now? Right now it is so . . . comforting. He's got me. He's just *got* me. His hands are hugging me everywhere, warming me, greeting me, reveling in me. Everything about him is asking to be close and then closer to me. There are his hands sliding sweetly over my back, his fingers gripping my shoulders. There's my hair, brushed out of my face, his legs firm and strong behind mine. There he is, nudging me so deep I bite the blanket. And then he folds forwards and there is his breath in my ear. He carefully keeps his weight off me but his voice is desperate for me, his rhythm picking up. Our fingers thread, his tongue in my mouth. He says my name into my skin and I feel every letter.

Things intensify, heat and friction, but my body can't hold this position forever.

"On our sides?" I say to him. And he immediately sits up and pulls out. I want to yowl at the loss but I'm quickly appeased when he arranges me on my side, my head down by the foot of the bed, and spoons me from behind. This time when he pushes inside, we fit perfectly, like I was waiting for him, and we both curse and tighten and gasp. He's got both arms around me, my hair must be in his face, but he doesn't seem to care. He picks up the same grinding rhythm and I see every air molecule. I take his hand from my breast and guide it between my legs. Our fingers tangle, slip and slide and I'm tightening, winding up, close to letting go.

"More. Friction. Please," I gasp.

He plants one big foot on my wall over my pillows, bracing us, and damn that is just so wonderful. I stare at that foot. The grip of his toes, the tendons straining. His hairy leg, his big hand gripping my breast, his other hand between my legs, his breath in my ear. And then he's saying my name and swearing and *yes, fuck, so good, fuuuuuuuuu* and he loses it. He pump-pump holds. Pump-pump holds. Shaking and gripping me and his ecstasy is inside me and I'm high off it.

He falls still but I'm so, so close, so I tell him so, and he immediately animates again. He's still inside me, still pretty hard, his fingers working, his hips moving slightly, and then I'm there too. It's an aching, dizzying orgasm that originates from the deepest place he's hitting me. It spirals out, straightening my entire body, pointing my toes, digging my fingernails into his hip.

When I collapse down, my muscles unwinding, there are kisses against my shoulder, firm fingers between my legs, and then him holding the condom while he pulls away.

"Mrhghehgoaroahdohfigls," I say, making perfect sense.

"Mm-hmm," he agrees, and rolls out of the bed.

I lie on my side and count threads in the blanket. Time passes. Seconds? Minutes? Shep is back.

"I need a shower," I groan.

"Sure," he says easily. "But first . . ." There's a glass of ice water and I drink deeply. Then there's a heavily buttered slice of fresh bread, still warm. I'm licking butter from my fingers when a raspberry is pressed into my mouth.

"Where'd you get these?" I ask. The taste is tart and sweet and I'm honestly not sure my body can handle any more carnal pleasures.

He shrugs. "I know you like them."

I scowl at him. "One of these days I'm going to wake you up with a blowjob and feed you honeydew off toothpicks and give you foot rubs and make you ravioli for lunch with raspberry lemonade and totally and completely befuddle and spoil *you* and see how *you* like it."

He laughs. "Yes. Karma's a bitch."

Twenty-Eight

We're on our sides, facing each other, our heads on the pillows and the blankets up to our necks. Our legs are tangled and his hand lies against my hip, his fingers resting over the crack of my ass.

"So." He clears his throat. "How is everybody feeling?"

I smile at his nervousness, so grateful to get to see this side of him. Every side of him. "Good? Loopy? I've never had sex with someone who loved me before."

He frowns. "That can't be true."

"Definitely true," I say with a nod. "I've had very nice sex before, very enjoyable, but you . . . you really love me, huh?"

My hand happens to be over his heart and it kicks against my palm. "What gave me away?"

"Well, the plain English certainly clarified things," I say with a smile. "But everything gave it away. The way you touch me. The look in your eyes."

A thought occurs to me and I prop my head up on my hand and put on a very stern face.

"Hey," I say, and trace my thumb over his lips. "You never agreed to being my boyfriend."

He kisses my thumb. "I kind of thought the"—he waggles his eyebrows and puts on a French accent—"*passionate love-making* was enough of a nonverbal agreement."

"No." I'm adamant. "I'm gonna need it in writing."

He takes a finger and places it over the bump. "Boyfriend,"

he spells out loud and with his finger, he finishes the word by drawing an arrow pointing at himself. "Girlfriend." He draws an arrow pointing towards my heart. "Rump roast." He draws an arrow pointing towards the baby.

I laugh. "You're always drawing arrows."

"Yeah. I've never been very stealthy about how I feel about you, I don't think."

But the thing is, he has been.

"Hey," I say with a firm finger to his chest. "No more Heathers, all right?"

"Deal." He agrees easily. "And how about we go ahead and say no more Dereks?"

"Easy peasy lemon squeezy." I pause. "Um. How are we feeling about Ethans?"

He kisses my palm. "You are entitled to exactly one Ethan."

I lay my head on the pillow so we're almost nose to nose. "You really have no issue with him at all?"

He takes a deep breath and some of the easy, jokey atmosphere tightens up. "Eve . . ." he says eventually. "Me being decent to the father of your child. It's not because I'm, like, so great. It's—it's a strategy." He blushes and scrubs a hand over his face. "That makes it sound nefarious and that's not how— Look, are you ready for the long answer that I didn't really give you before? Well, here it is: pretty much all the choices I make around you all serve one purpose. I . . . want to be part of your life forever. And Ethan? The father of your baby? He's likely not expendable. But me? Childhood friend who throws a fit over choices you made that have nothing to do with him? Probably expendable. So . . . yeah. You're not going to get any fits from me. I definitely don't want to make anything harder for you."

"Hey! You are not expendable. You're . . . I can't think. What's the word? In-spendable? I don't know. What's the word?"

"I don't know. 'Not expendable' works." He has a small smile on his face.

"And . . . it didn't *not* have something to do with you. The night I got pregnant."

"Huh?"

"I don't know if you want to know this or not, but I *might* have been feeling extra . . . frisky. Because you were suddenly single."

"So . . . you slept with someone else?" He's gone still.

"I mean . . . yeah? I don't think I even knew that I wanted to be sleeping with you. Hindsight's twenty-twenty."

He groans and tips his head back. "I knew I got in the wrong cab. As soon as I sat down, I thought to myself, *Why the fuck are you in a cab with your sister right now?* But . . . I didn't want to rush things."

"I don't think it was a mistake. Any of this. Even though my body knew how happy it was to have you really back in my life . . . Well, I'm not sure my *brain* quite knew yet. But even if I had known, what would I have done? Probably freaked out and avoided you for a while. I wouldn't have had any idea what to do with you that night, if you had gotten into my cab. I needed to meet you little by little. In this new way. You know?"

He's drawing arrows again, his eyes on his own fingers. "So, how you feel about me . . . it's, ah, new for you?"

"New? No. Not exactly."

"Can I ask . . . um. How long?"

I squint one eye and think. "I'm not totally sure. But . . . probably lemonade and vodka shots?"

"You're kidding," he says.

"What?"

"That night . . . I thought for sure you knew how I felt that night. I'd been hiding it for so long already, but then it was literally all over my face and—"

"Wait. What? What was all over your face?"

"The bruises."

I realize then that he's thinking of the lemonade and vodka shots that happened when we were teenagers. Jeff Burrows's voice comes back to me. *I personally saw him get his ass beat over you at least twice.*

"Those . . . those weren't from skateboarding?" I whisper.

He lets out a long breath as he shakes his head. "No. That was . . . I got beat up in the locker room because some guys . . . it doesn't matter now." He's reading my face. "You really didn't know."

To Shep. Who failed pretty hard at something really cool.

"Willa knew."

He nods, reads my expression, and his face falls with realization. "Oh. You meant the other lemonade and vodka shots, huh? The ones last year?"

To Shep, who did something really hard. Because he's brave. And is deciding not to be afraid of failure.

He laughs a little, it's self-deprecating. "Figures. If you'd loved me as long as I've loved you, we probably would have been having this conversation a long time ago."

"Full disclosure. I have no idea how long I've loved you. Maybe always." I draw a couple arrows myself. "Parts of how I feel about you have always been there. I'm still getting used to it. All of it. You say you were transparent, but I certainly didn't know you felt this way."

He takes a long, deep breath. A Shep breath. In for an eternity and out for even longer.

When he speaks, his voice is low. It's a secret. For my ears only. "It's weird, you know, loving you this long, it's something that's just always kinda been there for me. A companion, sort of. But it's also something I've really struggled with. Because . . . I clearly was not always very brave about it."

"Because you didn't tell me?"

He nods. "How can I explain it . . ." He pauses again for a long time. "I knew you were out of my league." I start to interrupt him. "No, don't argue. I had two left feet. I was a dorky, awkward loser. I knew you didn't . . . like me. So I just kept it to myself. I think that I thought it would make you uncomfortable to tell you. And I wanted to always be your friend no matter what."

I don't like the version of himself that lives in Shep's head, but he's already moving on with his story and all I can do is listen.

"I moved to New York and for the first time I was living . . . without you and Willa. And honestly? Parts of it were a huge relief. I wasn't constantly comparing myself to Willa, or feeling like the guy who'd never, ever get the girl. I missed you like crazy. But I also . . ."

"Bloomed," I finish for him, thinking of his years in undergrad. He became less shy, more sociable. He made friends playing pickup basketball and joined clubs at school. He went out drinking and called Willa in the middle of the night wasted, which always made us crack up.

"Yeah. And right while I was smack-dab in the middle of that relieved feeling, I met Heather. And I think I thought that my feelings for you must have been over? Because I was able to love her. But they never really went away. And then you moved here and they *really* didn't go away. That's when I told Heather."

"You told her?"

"Of course. I couldn't keep something like that from her. It was huge. I thought it would end our relationship."

"But it didn't."

"Nope. She didn't want to throw away what we had. I think she figured I'd grow out of it eventually."

"Aha. That explains why she always looked at me like I smelled bad."

"Well, she did her best. But yeah, that's kind of why we stayed in our borough and didn't hang out with you a lot. It made her very uncomfortable. With good reason."

"So . . . what changed? Things just stopped working with her?"

"No, actually, things between us were really good when we broke up. I think we could have continued on like that for a long time. Maybe not forever. But for a long time." He's drawing designs on my belly, gathering his thoughts. "It was Mom who changed me." My heart skips. "Right before she died, remember, I went and spent, like, five straight weeks with her in Michigan? Well, she wasn't able to do much more than chat. I'd push her around in a chair for an evening walk, but mostly, all we did was talk and talk and talk. She told me that she wanted me to work on being brave. She told me that love, if you keep it all closed up and try to stuff it down, it turns into resentment and anger. It turns sour. And that if I never, ever told you how I felt, eventually I wouldn't be able to be your friend anymore. She told me I'd lose you if I wasn't brave. If you didn't love me back, then I could let it go and eventually be your friend again. And if you felt it back then . . . yeah. But no matter what your answer was, I had to tell you."

A memory surfaces. "That day in Central Park. Right before your mom died. We held hands and cried . . ."

He nods quickly, knowing exactly what I'm talking about. "I'd *just* had that conversation with my mom. And I knew that telling you how I felt, honestly, hat in hand, well, that meant leaving Heather. Which I did, about two hours before I met up with you in the park. It was . . . sort of my step one to finally getting to you. But I still couldn't . . . find the words. Then, you know the rest. Mom died. Willa needed you more than I did,

Heather was willing to help me through. I just . . . stayed where I was for a year before it was time to get going on the whole bravery thing. And that's when I moved to Brooklyn."

"Exactly coinciding with me getting pregnant," I groan.

"You were right when you said it wasn't a mistake. Any of it. Think about what it took for us to be able to open up to what could be between us. For me, it took my mom passing. For you, it took a monumental change like pregnancy. But we got here."

"We're here now," I agree.

"Finally," he whispers. And I love that word.

Twenty-Nine

We get one blissful day—Saturday, in which we spend the morning in bed and then the park, followed by an afternoon traumatizing my couch—before Willa decides the jig is up, bringing Isamu along to bang on my apartment door around dinnertime, demanding to be let in.

Isamu gives me and Shep a *you asked for it* shrug and then plays on his phone on my armchair. Willa stands over Shep and me with her hands on her hips and scolds Shep roundly for disappearing for days at a time. When she finally points her finger at me, she says one thing and one thing only. "Do you love him?"

I breathe a sigh of relief. This question is a softball. "Yup."

She glowers at me. I glower back.

"All right, well," she says with a clap. "Now I guess you're 2getha 4 eva." She actually does the numeric gestures with her fingers. "So don't screw it up."

The next few weeks are filled with the kind of moments you hold in your heart for the rest of your life. The weather firmly rolls into the sixties. It's sunny one minute and rainy the next, and both are fun. Shep and I sleep at my house almost every night, and we spend every weekend together. We see year-old movies at the dollar theater next to the park and take long, slow walks around the lake.

April 1 is his move-in date at the apartment down the

street from Good Boy, and he starts paying rent, but he doesn't really move anything in.

Also? Every single day I wake up bigger. Noticeably bigger. I'm short, and there's not really anyplace for the baby to go but out, but still. By the time I'm thirty-three weeks and waddling to my first birthing class with Willa, I'm basically a perfect sphere. I can't believe there are seven more weeks to go. You'd think I'd be scared because that's not much time, but honestly, I'm more scared about seven more weeks of growing.

The birthing class is two three-hour classes a week. Apparently giving birth is a lot more complicated than *lie down and push.*

Willa and I get buzzed into the building. The classes are on the second floor of a brownstone. The front parlor room is like the lobby and a few other pregnants and their partners are milling around, giving us polite smiles and curiously eyeing the very anatomically accurate models positioned around the room. I turn and realize that the other half of the lobby is a bit of a shop. There are bassinets and bonnets and teddy bears and binkies and boppies and whoozits and whatsits and enough baby accoutrements to make you want to scream.

And from the look on Willa's face, it does make her want to scream. Not a good sign.

A woman named Briar comes around and checks all the couples in one by one, sending them back into another room for the class. When she gets to Willa and me, we're the very last people. I give the woman my information but by the time she turns to Willa, Willa's gone chalk white.

Briar looks back and forth between us. "Are you the birthing partner?" she asks Willa.

Willa pauses. "Uh, yes, yes, I'm here with her for the class."

"So you're planning to be there with mom when she gives birth?"

Willa frowns. I frown.

"Um. Sorry. Can we have a sec?" I ask Briar.

As soon as she makes herself scarce I turn to Willa. "How're you doing over there?"

Her bottom lip is trembling. "Eve—"

"That bad, huh?"

"It's just a lot more baby stuff than I pictured."

I nod and take her hand. "Am I silly for not totally understanding that you attending these birthing classes with me means you'd also . . . be the one in the room when the baby is born?"

"No," she says. "Or, if you are, then I am too. Because I don't think I'd quite put that together yet either." She squeezes my hands. "Do you want me to be the person in the room when you have the baby?"

I study her ashen face. "Not if it hurts you, Willa. And I don't mean that in a strictly altruistic way. If you're freaking out on the big day . . . well, I really think I'm going to need to be focused on myself."

She looks miserable. Her eyes are caught on a special baby carrier that lets you carry the baby on your back. "I don't know . . ." she says in a husky little voice I'm not sure I've ever heard her use before. "I don't know if I can do this."

My friend who knows exactly what she wants out of life and sprints towards it. Her heart has been broken and it's thrown her off in a million ways. I open my arms to her and she drops her head to my shoulder and we both cry for a while. I cry for her and for myself and she cries for me and for herself and that's the way it is. About ten minutes later, Briar comes back out to check me in for the class and Willa is gone. I go to the class alone.

. . .

Shep isn't saying anything about the boxes. Or the piles.

I've joined an email list for gently used baby crap, and boy did NYC show up. The problem is, I have no idea what I need so I start saying yes to everything. I've picked up everything from strollers to burp cloths to tiny little sun hats. As soon as I see it listed, I desperately assert to myself how badly I need it. But then, this magical thing happens the second I cross the threshold to my own apartment. I suddenly have no idea what to do with it. An entire corner of my perfect apartment is piled eight feet high with rubber-ducky-printed bouncy chairs and little pink breast milk heaters. Help.

I know that Shep notices. I see his eyes see it all. But he just goes about his Shep business. Cleaning up the kitchen after dinner. Handing down a cup of tea and a low-sugar cookie on sunny afternoons. Making me moan in bed. Tucking me in afterward.

But today, I've had enough. Shep is reading an article on his phone, lying lengthwise across my couch, when I slam my laptop closed.

"What the *fuck* is a sleep sack and why the *fuck* would someone ever need one!?" I scream my question to the universe.

And when I say *scream*, I mean scream, because Shep goes from reclined, ankles crossed, to full height, both feet on the ground, eyes wide. "What?" he shouts back. "What?"

I repeat my question, this time in a voice so low and menacing I swear his eyes dilate. "Um. It's a little sleeping bag for a baby. It reduces the risk of SIDS," he answers, his feet dancing him sideways into the kitchen.

"And how do you know this?" I ask him.

"I read a couple A-to-Z books. About pregnancy and baby care." He's back from the kitchen and handing me a glass of seltzer in one hand and a cheese stick in the other.

"Well, why didn't *I* read those books?" I demand, as if that's something he should have to answer for. "I'm thirty-four weeks, the general size of a yoga ball, this baby has both feet pressing directly on my ribs, and yet *I haven't read a single book*."

He takes it in stride but doesn't sit until I take a vicious bite of the cheese stick. "Some people learn how to do this from books, well in advance, and some people learn on the fly. I figured since you're one style I should be the other style."

I set down the cheese stick wrapper and the now-empty glass and glare at him. "You can't just shut me up with snacks, you know."

"I wouldn't dare," he replies solemnly, even though it's exactly what he's just done. He opens his mouth again, cautiously. "Do you want to talk about how to prepare for the baby?" His eyes flicker, momentarily, to the hell corner where Craigslist threw up.

"No!" I say, stalking to the kitchen and rifling around for the one measly piece of chocolate I'm allowed a day. "And if you ever bring it up again you can take a hike."

"Noted," he says from the living room.

A few quiet seconds pass.

"If," I start, peeking around from the kitchen. I can only see the back of his head, but I swear I can tell he's just started smiling. "*If* I did want to talk about it, a little bit, what would you say?"

"*If* you wanted to start talking about it, I'd help you organize things into what we might need to use right away and what we might need to use down the line, when the baby is older. It wouldn't be nearly as scary as it might seem. And . . ." He turns so he can see me, one arm along the back of the couch. "And I'd have to ask you one really hard question."

I glare at him as I reenter the living room. He is not cowed. "You know curiosity is my weak point."

I've sat on one end of the couch, a peace offering for how much of an ass I'm being right now, and he leans down and picks up one of my feet. Apparently this question requires acupressure in order to pass a vibe check.

"Is it possible," he starts, strong-thumbs my arch, and then keeps going. "That you haven't unpacked any of that baby stuff yet because you don't think this is the right place to unpack it?"

"What?" I screech, sitting up so fast my head spins. I look at the pile of crap. I look at my apartment. And then I burst into tears. "No! Never. I'm never leaving here."

Shep is kneeling next to me and I'm gathered into his arms.

"Everything is changing," I sob into his shoulder.

"Not everything. I promise not everything."

"What am I gonna do without my apartment? I love this apartment." I can't say it out loud, but he's right. My perfect apartment is not perfect for a baby. The walls are thin, the bathtub leaks, there's barely enough room for the infant bassinet in my room, let alone a full crib.

Shep's hands write a love letter on my back. "You could keep it. For a little while, at least until your lease is up."

"You know I can't afford two rents." My words are watery and trembling.

"Eve, I'm asking if you want to move into my new place."

I freeze. My heart is gone so fast it's already over the horizon. "Are you serious?"

"Yes. And I could either move in there too, or I could move in here and give you space over there. Whichever ends up working out the best. Or, we could break your lease, pay the fine, and be done with it and all three of us can just live in that apartment together. You know there's room."

"Shep," I say, my hands on either side of his jaw. "You want to live *full time* with me and the baby? *And* the baby?" I double-emphasize that part, just in case he didn't get it the first time.

He takes a deep breath and leans into one of my palms. "I want to do what's best for us, Eve. I want to help as much as possible, especially in those first few months when you and the baby are still figuring everything out. And if that means sleeping over all the time and changing diapers and feeding you and taking the baby on walks while you nap, then great. If that means holding down the fort over here while you and the baby figure each other out over there, then great."

I have absolutely no idea what to say to that and he must sense it because he just pulls me into another long hug.

Days go by before I realize why it is I can't answer Shep's big question. Because I'm not the only one who needs to answer it.

I have just enough time after work to squeeze in a quick visit to Good Boy before my last birthing class. It only occurs to me after I walk in unannounced that maybe I should have texted Ethan to let him know I'm coming by. We've seen each other a few times since his messy drop-in at my place. Full-hearted apologies over French toast with Argy looking suspicious. A few walks in the park.

The waitress who used to flirt with Shep gives me a huge wave and wades through a small gang of golden retrievers to get to me. "Hey, mama! How are you? How are you feeling? Wow, you're humongo! Hey! You never told me you were preggers with boss's baby." She ticks her finger at me. "He only told me a couple weeks ago. Anyhow. Congrats. Ethan's the best. He's gonna be a really good dad. And by the way, heard what happened with Eleni. Good riddance. That girl is a piece of work."

She leans in, gives me a quick shoulder hug, and then

points me back towards Ethan's office. "Boss is in the back," she says.

I float away from her. I'm not sure a single conversation (if you can even call it that, considering I didn't say a single word) has ever made me feel better or worse. It's the first time anyone has insinuated to me that Ethan might be good at this. And yeah, I do not want credit for Eleni not being around. That one is all on Ethan.

I knock on his door and he opens it absentmindedly, his eyes on a sheaf of paper in one hand. "What's up—Eve! Hi!"

He's dancing back and pulling out a chair for me. "Sit! Sit!"

Bones is resurrecting herself from the bed in the corner to come push her nose into my hand, and I consider it the highest of honors.

"Thanks. I thought I'd stop by on the way to my birthing class tonight."

"Oh. Where are you taking them?" he asks. "I've been going to Baby Breath in Cobble Hill," he says almost offhandedly.

"Wait. What? You're attending *birthing classes?*"

"Yes." He's having trouble making eye contact. "I wanted to be . . . ready . . . just in case . . . you know."

"Man, what's it like being a single dad in the class? Being a single mom is weird enough."

He blinks at me. "Shep isn't there with you?"

"No." I shake my head. "It didn't work out that way. Shep is my boyfriend. My *person.* But . . . we weren't together when I was signing up for them and at the time I thought Willa would go with me." I shrug. "I guess I've just . . . taken it as a sign that the classes are something I should do on my own. It hasn't been so bad to go alone. It's me-time, I guess."

Ethan's quiet, looking at the floor for a while before he

clears his throat. "Yeah, uh . . . it's weird. I have to practice all the techniques with the instructor. Which is . . . well, it is what it is. But like I said. I just wanted to be prepared in case. But there's no . . . no pressure. I don't have to be there if you don't want me there."

"Ethan, I didn't even know you *wanted* to be there. In the room."

"I do," he says simply.

Two of the teeniest tiniest words in the English language but when you smash 'em together . . .

"You . . . do?"

He takes a deep breath. "Yes."

His answer is firm. Calm. Decidedly lacking in Eleni.

I have no idea where to put it. For now, my only choice is to set it aside and inspect it later lest I start shaking him by the shoulders and demanding to know the exact number of diapers he'll be changing.

"So, was there something you wanted to talk about?" he asks gently, his butt parked on his desk and his long legs stretched out next to his chair. Bones is leaning against him, tongue askew, one leg kicked out. He absentmindedly pats her head.

"Oh. Yes. Now I'm the one saying 'no pressure,' but I was wondering what you'd think about me and the baby moving into an apartment down the block from here?"

Ethan stands up straight, his hands immediately going to his pockets. "Wait. Really? Are you serious?"

"I *think* so. What do you think?"

"I . . . yes. That would be incredible. I live just around the corner. Well, right. You know that already. You've been there. When we . . ." He clears his throat. "But that would be amazing! I'm pretty much either at my apartment or here so I could come over on a moment's notice whenever you needed."

"Shep might live there too," I tell him gently. "We haven't decided yet."

"Oh." Ethan's hand is on the back of his neck. "Shep is going to live with the baby. Wow. Um. Okay. Wow."

"Probably," I tell him honestly. And then I take the biggest leap I've ever taken with Ethan. Bigger than telling him I was pregnant. Bigger than telling him that he seemed free when he was away from Eleni. "You know . . . *you* could live with the baby too. Sometimes. If you wanted to have a couple nights a week or every other week. Or take the baby up to see your family every now and then. Or whatever. We . . . haven't talked about custody at all."

It's a huge word. Terrifying in both scope and ramifications and I can see that it turns both of us cold.

"I'd want to put a formal arrangement in place," I continue. "But I just want you to know that if you want to be involved . . . I want that too. Okay?"

The guy's a leaky faucet and I really like that about him. He rubs tears away with the shoulder of his button-down. "Thanks, Eve," he whispers. "Thank you."

Thirty

"Eve, park it! Now!"

"Eve, for the love of . . ."

Willa shouts at me from one room and Ethan shouts from another. Isamu is unpacking glasses in the kitchen and Shep is gently removing a giant picture frame from my hands and guiding me back to the lawn chair they set up for me.

"Everyone is touching my things," I moan.

"I know," Shep says, bending down and kissing my forehead. "But you need to rest. Just tell everybody what to do, okay?"

Yep. I'm thirty-seven weeks along and moving apartments like a total glutton for punishment. I hate not being able to get everything exactly where I want it. I couldn't even pack the way I wanted to. Everything got moved over here in great gobs and I'm going to lose my mind watching everything get dispersed to random locations. But I also really, really, really needed all hands on deck to get my new apartment unpacked and set up immediately.

"I can't believe you kept this," Ethan calls, walking his mother's painting to where I can see it. "If I were you I'd have trashed it when I started being a dick."

Willa laughs involuntarily. She fully intends to give Ethan a hard time from now into infinity, but he's actually been quite likable over the last few weeks. He's been super helpful in the move, and he and I have worked out a plan for the first few weeks that the baby is home. He's making an effort and it shows. It's impossible to hate him. Even for Willa.

"I want it to go in the baby's room," I tell him, and his eyes go a little soft as he brings the painting to the baby's room and he and Willa argue over which wall to put it up on.

A glass of water is pressed into my hand and I look up to see Isamu. "You're, um, leaking." He goes bright red.

I lean down and sure enough, there is a small puddle of water underneath my lawn chair.

"Well," I whisper to him. "That might be because I'm in labor."

Yep. An hour ago my water broke while I was leaning over the sink fixing my hair. I thought it would be like somebody upturned a bucket all of a sudden. But it was more of a *pop!* and a dribble of water. I've started getting awfully crampy and with each wave of cramping, a little more water rushes out. If I don't get out of this lawn chair and start marching around and doing things, I'm going to tell everyone. And I don't want to tell everyone. Yet. I want to wait as long as I can until they make me go to the hospital.

His eyes grow wide, he purses his lips, and he glances at the room where Willa is currently unpacking my sock drawer. "Okay. Should you call someone?"

"I'm supposed to call my OB-GYN."

He's nodding his head. "Yes. Um. Will you? Do that? Please?"

I pat his shoulder. "Sure."

He helps me stand and I dig my phone out of my pocket. I'm sure there's a big wet spot on the back of my dress/shirt thing, so I sidestep out to the hallway so no one besides Isamu sees.

Lower East Side Partners in Obstetrics and Gynecology answers on the first ring. I get buzzed through to Dr. Bridget

Muscles, who officially advises me to go to the hospital immediately because my water has broken. But from my birthing class I know that most women wait until contractions are four minutes apart. Then she tells me she's not on call tonight so she likely won't be the one delivering the baby.

I thank her. Hang up. And then immediately call another number.

She answers on the fifth ring.

"Nurse Louise? Oh, thank God you answered."

"Who's this?"

"It's Eve Hatch. You gave me your personal number when we had coffee."

"Oh. You're lucky I answered. I thought you were a political call."

"Well, I'm glad you answered too because my water just broke."

She goes into nursing mode and asks me all the same questions Dr. Bridget Muscles asked me. And then she also tells me she's not working tonight.

My stomach plummets. "You won't be there?"

It's not until this exact second that I realize that every single time I've pictured this over the last nine months, Nurse Louise has been there in my imagination.

"You can do this," she tells me. "You've been through the birthing classes. You've got your support system. And at the end, you'll hold the love of your life in your arms. Trust me. You can do this."

"Okay," I say on a deep breath.

And with that, I go back into the apartment where no one but Isamu knows. And then I wait three hours without telling anyone.

. . .

"**Folks! Folks!" The** security guard is shouting at us. "You don't have to wait in the security line if she's in labor. Just come on through."

I'm a grateful, waddling mess as I circumvent the security line with Shep and Ethan in my wake. I pause midstep, a contraction hits, and I do my quick little pacing-breathing-hand-flapping thing that has started happening sometime in the last half hour and seems to sort of work.

I've had nightmares about the moment I check in to the hospital. I've pictured some judgmental nurse in scrubs loudly pointing to Ethan and Shep and demanding that I choose which one will stay by my side while the other one goes and waits outside by the garbage cans. To my relief, the nurse is actually pretty bored by it all and doesn't let either of them back until I've had my first exam. I really don't want to leave them, but the nurse is so official, so I wave goodbye and am escorted through double sliding doors and into a sort of laboring-woman weigh station. Each little paddock is separated from the others by a thin curtain and I can hear at least three other women hoo-hoo-ha-ha-ing their way towards motherhood. I'm told to lie down on this little table thingy, but another contraction hits and the physician's assistant finds me pacing, breathing, and hand-flapping.

When the contraction has subsided, she helps me onto the table and gives me a physical exam. It's a lovely and intimate moment defined by the snap of rubber gloves and blunt pressure on my cervix. Delish.

"You're five centimeters," she tells me, and I'm so relieved. I'd been worried they'd tell me I wasn't far enough along and that I should go home. In fact, I think on the cab ride here I may have broken Shep's fingers and screamed the words "If these turn out to just be Braxton-Hicks I want a fucking *refund!*"

She leads me to my room and another nurse joins us. She tries to talk to me but a contraction hits and I'm so over this laboring-alone bullshit. "Get. My. Boyfriend," I pant to the nurse once the contraction is over.

Moments later, Shep is there. I'm in a gown, standing in water (that is still leaking and seems to be in endless supply), and then I'm falling into his arms. "Don't leave again," I sob into his shirt. "Stay here."

"I won't," he swears. "I promise. I'll stay here for all of it. I promise."

There's another contraction and this one is so much worse than the last. It's like someone has turned the volume up to one hundred. I'm screaming into Shep's chest and going down to my knees and breathing? What's breathing. I'm so tired I'd like to be at the bottom of the ocean. Maybe I am at the bottom of the ocean. Maybe that's why there's only endless pressure.

The nurse is back and she's saying something to Shep.

He relays it to me in simple terms and I fall in love with him all over again. "Ethan or no Ethan," he asks.

"I don't. give. a fuck," I tell Shep between gasping breaths. And I really don't. I thought I'd have strong opinions on this issue, but now that I'm in survival mode, as long as Shep is here, I don't really care what else happens.

A few minutes later Ethan is there. I'm screaming into Shep's chest and maybe I'll puke and it's endless it's endless it's endless. Then there's a lot of Ethan's voice. I don't listen or don't understand but Shep is shifting me, getting me into a seated position and then sitting behind me. I think Ethan is showing him what to do with his hands. The next contraction hits and then another on top of that, there's no break between the two of them. I'm sweating and Shep is holding me up.

Someone is feeding me broth and wiping my forehead. And I dimly register that it's pitch-black outside. How long have we even been here?

I'm examined twice more? Thrice more? I can see on Shep's face that the nurse thinks I haven't progressed much. Why did the beginning go so fucking fast and now everything has stalled?

I'm comatose between contractions. I think it's sleep? But really, it's just a dark place where nothing can touch me and nothing exists. As soon as another contraction starts I'm on hands and knees and crawling across the floor. Shep holds ice packs on the back of my neck and inches along with me. Someone fans me for literal hours on end. Maybe Ethan? I don't know.

I'm in the black space. I can smell Shep-sweat under my face and someone is stroking my hair. "I can't do it," I say. "I can't do it. I can't do it."

I'm rolled forwards, my arms placed over something bouncy and my cheek pressed against cold plastic. It's a yoga ball and there are new hands on me. "Shep? Shep?"

"I'm here," he says, kneeling in front of me now, holding a cloth against my forehead. The new set of hands is an unfamiliar touch, firm and intense, and it stays with me all the way until the next contraction takes me. Sheets are placed under my knees and I labor like this, leaning on the ball and squeezed and prodded in the right places.

There's more veggie broth and some temperature taking. I'm placed on an IV and put in a bed. I roll to one side and then the other and this time when I get an exam, it's good news.

Someone says something to me, but I don't hear. They say it again.

The third time, cool hands have me by the jawbone. "Hun. If you feel the need to push, you have to tell us. It's just about time."

I blink at the face that's close to mine. "Nurse Louise," I gasp. "You're here."

"I brought the yoga ball," she tells me. "Do you have to push yet? Can you tell?"

"I don't know," I gasp.

She nods. "Then it's not quite time. Just keep going. You're doing well, kid."

I can't explain what it does, but it does something. Nurse Louise is here. For a moment, she feels like Corinne. She is nothing like Corinne, really, but for a moment, she ushers her in here, into this room.

The next hour or so is a complete blur. The contractions are one on top of the next and I'm somewhere back and forth between the black space and suffocating under the weight of contractions, convinced I cannot do this.

But then, something happens. It's an odd change. There's strength down to my fingers again.

"Pushing!" I shout to whoever is standing behind me, thumbs in my lower back. It's Nurse Louise. Then it must be Shep's lap that my head collapses into. Ethan shouts down the hallway and the medical staff is back.

Someone checks me. It's go time.

I don't recognize the doctor but I don't care. Shep is here. Nurse Louise is here. Ethan is here somewhere.

Nurse Louise teaches me how to push through a contraction. When to breathe, when to rest. There is no more black space. Only pressure pain, not enough oxygen, and the vivid relief of pushing. Shep is urgently requesting more oxygen and I don't know what he could possibly be talking about until an oxygen mask is pressed over my face between contractions. It helps immensely.

Time blurs. I'm being held on every side. I look down and Ethan is helping hold one of my legs up.

"The baby is crowning," the doctor says. "It could be anytime in the next few pushes."

"You're doing it, Eve," Shep says in my ear.

Ethan looks back at me. "Thank you," he says, his voice steady and his eyes piercing mine. "Thank you."

That *thank you* is what does it. Because at the core of it . . . Yes. This is for someone else. There is only one reason that anyone would ever endure something like this and it's for the person who has yet to make an entrance. The person I'm about to meet. If I can just find the strength. If I can just keep pushing.

I'm breathing and screaming and Nurse Louise is counting the push seconds in my ear. There's tight, bursting pressure and then suddenly, an instant, dizzying relief. Someone hot pink and squirming is in the doctor's hands. I collapse sideways, onto Shep. There are tears everywhere between us. His face is soaking wet. "You did it," he sobs into my hair. "You did it."

I can't take my eyes off the squirming baby.

"Give me" is all I can say, digging for the strength to lift my arms. "Please."

They put the baby, wriggly and wet, onto my chest, and it's the sort of weight that completes you. This perfect cap of wet-matted hair is all I can see, but this person is everythingeverythingeverything.

"Hi," I say through tears. "Hi, I'm your mom."

There's a face right next to mine and it's Ethan's. He has one hand on the baby's head, his eyes bloodshot and glittering.

"She. Has. Red. Hair," he says before dissolving down into sobs. His forehead is pressing my arm, his hand still on the baby. "Thank you. Thank you," he's chanting. "I love you. Thank you."

I don't know if he's talking to me or the baby, but it doesn't really matter. Because right now, in this moment, me and the baby are one thing for Ethan. We're his family. We made it. All the way here. A nine-month journey. And it's just beginning.

Thirty-One

A while later, after a million more things happen, we're shuffled out of labor and delivery and into an inpatient room for the night. Nurse Louise follows us there and gets us all set up. I still can't believe she came.

"You came," I say for the hundredth, weepy time.

"You did so well," she assures me.

She stays just long enough to help me to the bathroom and to make sure I eat something. She leaves with a pat to my cheek and heads home.

"When did she . . . why? How?" I ask after she's gone.

"Shep called her," Ethan says from the chair next to the bed where he's currently holding our little girl. He can't tear his eyes away. "He got her number from your phone and asked her to come."

Shep is lying in the bed next to me, completely asleep. The man who didn't leave me. Wouldn't leave me.

Later, a nurse comes in, sees him sleeping there and Ethan in the chair, and informs me that I'm only allowed one overnight guest. Shep, hearing her voice, rouses and starts climbing out of the bed.

"Wait!" Ethan says, looking extremely startled. "You can't leave, Shep."

"She says I have to." He points at the nurse.

"No." Ethan shakes his head. "Shep. No. You gotta stay."

He turns to the nurse. "Please, can't you bend the rules? I won't sleep or take up space. How about that? I'll just be a completely silent overnight guest. Eve will sleep so much better if he's here. I'll hold the baby and let them sleep, come on, it's better for everybody."

He's turned on the full wattage of his smile and it's clearly almost working on the nurse.

He holds up the sleeping baby and goes for the kill stroke. "Don't make me leave my baby girl behind."

The nurse is no match for that. She throws up her hands and leaves.

"Thanks," I tell Ethan. "Didn't know you felt so passionate about Shep sticking around."

"We're attached to each other now," Shep says from somewhere near my armpit, his eyes closed again.

"When did that happen?" I ask them.

Shep lifts his head, makes eye contact with Ethan, and the two of them burst into private laughter.

"When you were laboring," Ethan answers, "I was the brains and Shep was the brawn."

"He had to tell me everything to do," Shep says groggily. "I definitely should have taken a birthing class."

"No," Ethan says with a shake of his head. "Then there wouldn't have been anything for me to do."

The baby starts fussing and I immediately take her and try my best at breastfeeding. It is all going to take a lot of getting used to. I hold her for a long while after she's fallen back asleep. All I want to do is look at her. With her perfect translucent skin, her eyes closed so tight, the red fringe of her eyelashes.

"Sleep," Ethan eventually whispers. "I'll hold her."

And he does. And he doesn't sleep a wink.

. . .

The next day we fill out the birth certificate paperwork.

"Why Miriam?" Shep asks.

"Apparently it means 'wished for.' And above all, I want her to feel wanted," I tell him.

On the other side of me, Ethan's eyes are lasered to the end of the pen as I curve around the final *h* in my last name. I lift the pen and I can hear his breath catch. I press it to the paper and time stops. I draw a hyphen and he lets out all of his breath at once, collapsing down, tears in his voice. "Thank you," he cries again. "Thank you, thank you." He's been saying that a lot.

A few hours later we are successfully discharged and we leave the hospital with Miriam Hatch-Rise. We get a cab and both boys spend an absurd amount of time checking and re-checking the car seat. Ethan gets irritated with Shep, and Shep just patiently perseveres. Even when they're bickering there's something endearing about it.

It isn't until the cab gets off the highway one exit too early that I remember we're going to my new apartment, not my old one.

I'm internally panicking at the mess we've left behind. Boxes and boxes yet to be unpacked and none of the baby stuff set up. It's going to be such a long night. But when we finally make it up all those stairs, Shep swings the door open and everything is . . . beautiful.

"What the . . ." I sag against the doorframe and just stare at the photographs on the wall. The gigantic flowers in the vase. The bowl of fruit. "It's *perfect*."

Both Shep and Ethan are grinning at me.

"Willa called Dal immediately," Shep tells me. "And he got on the next plane up here to set everything up. I'm pretty sure he just finished. He's at an Airbnb down the block."

"Dal flew here," I say dimly.

"Dustin and Mal came too, actually. He told them he needed help. They're all together."

I blink at Shep. "Even Mal?"

He laughs at the face I'm making and takes me by the elbow. "You should sit."

And he is not wrong. Giving birth is no joke.

"Bed or couch?" he asks.

"Bed, but first I want to see Miriam's room," I mutter, shuffling to the far side of the apartment. The pile of crap has turned into a perfect little nursery. Ethan's mother's sunrise painting hanging over a crib Miriam won't use until I move her out of the bedside bassinet. I love it. In a perfect world, I would have been the one to place every lamp and measure the distance of the crib to the door. But good thing it's not a perfect world, because instead of doing it on my own, this apartment just became a love letter from my brothers. From Willa and Isamu.

Shep helps me into pajamas and I crawl into bed, collapsing in a pile.

He opens the bedroom door and calls out to Ethan. "You need sleep too."

I'm pretty sure Shep is the only one who actually got any real shut-eye last night.

Ethan comes into the bedroom with Miriam in his arms. She's in a teal cap and a red blanket and I already know that putting her in colors that clash with her hair is going to be my new favorite thing. "She's fussing a little."

"She's probably hungry." I reach for her and Ethan hands her to me, his hands going to his pockets.

"I'm hungry too," he says with a huge yawn.

"I'll make food for everyone," Shep says from the doorway.

Ethan sits on the foot of the bed, slightly on top of my feet.

"It sounds trite, but when people call babies 'bundles of joy,'" I muse, "they mean it completely literally, don't they?"

"Mm-hmm." Ethan has melted backward in stages. His feet hang off the bed and he's lying perpendicular. His head tips to one side and he is *gone.* Miriam nurses to sleep and I hold her and watch her and time melts away.

"You're a love letter too," I whisper to her. "Without Ethan, you wouldn't exist, and without Shep, you wouldn't have made it into this world. That's because they love us so much. You're here because we all love you so much." I'm rambling and maybe it makes sense, but sometimes the truth doesn't make sense and that's all right.

A savory, warm scent precedes Shep into the room. He gives a small smile when he sees Ethan passed out on the end of the bed. There's a bowl of something warm in one of Shep's hands and a tall glass of water in the other. Will I ever get tired of seeing him look at me like that? How could I? Does anyone ever get tired of being wanted? Does anyone ever get tired of wanting in return?

He sets the food on the nightstand and reaches for Miriam. "You should eat if you can," he whispers. "I'll hold her."

I eat pasta and nestle back into the pillows and watch the long arcing path that Shep is taking back and forth around the bed. Miriam is cradled in his arms, barely the length of his forearm. "Hmmmm-hmmmm," he hums to her over and over.

I feel as new as Miriam. The person I was nine months ago is gone. Tears are leaking out of my eyes and into my hair. Because I miss my old apartment. I miss being Willa's backup dancer. I miss the girl who bounced through life and had a grand old time never quite getting what she wanted and not knowing why. But I don't think I'll miss her for long.

I'm just a little raw. And who wouldn't be? I've been blinked into existence, grown and protected by those who love me, and then that little nugget Miriam cracked open my shell and brought me here, to my new life.

Later, my brothers will come. Later, Willa and Isamu will come.

Later, Miriam and I will get in a giant tin can and we'll fly across the country to visit Corinne and my parents with flowers in our hands.

But for today, I'll let my eyes get heavy while I watch Shep hum my girl in circles. Today, I'll let Ethan sleep on my feet.

Today, we'll all be brand-new together.

Acknowledgments

It's so wonderful to genuinely swell with so much gratitude and then get a chance to set it down on paper. What follows is a list of people who helped make this book into a book. But more important, it's also a list of people who have helped make me into *me*. I would say that *thank you* doesn't feel like enough, but then again, when you really mean it, *thank you* is one of the most powerful phrases we can ever use. So!

Thank you, endlessly, to my agent, Tara Gelsomino, without whom I simply would not have a career. A big professional misfortune brought us together, but that ended up being my good luck. You have truly become my compass. You were the first person to read any iteration of this manuscript, and getting your thoughts on the first draft was one of the highlights of my professional life.

Thank you to Whitney Frick for bringing me into this wonderful home at Dial. Thank you to Madison Dettlinger, Brianna Kusilek, Deb Aroff, Michelle Jasmine, Maria Braeckel, Avideh Bashirrad, Regina Flath, Donna Cheng, Cindy Berman, Elizabeth Rendfleisch, and Ana Jaren for the countless ways you've all made this manuscript into a book.

This brings me to Emma Caruso, my editor. I am in awe of your brain. Your ability to see both macro and micro at the same time . . . thank you for combing this book until it was silk. This story needed a corset and I would never have had the hutzpah to yank those strings if it weren't for you. Your thoughtful ideas, attentive listening, and creative solutions made editing this book *possible*. Something that I didn't think was, well, possible before I met you. Thank you, most sincerely, for reading my manuscript and feeling the feelings and calling me on that phone call that dropped like fifty times. I was maybe six weeks postpartum and a mess and so hopeful, and I hung up the phone and cried because someone had read my book and understood what I was going for. I will never stop being grateful for your persistent understanding. To write a novel requires so much attention, and to edit it with someone who has held on to every single detail is gratifying on a level I can never explain. Thank you.

Thank you to Ruby Lang, Hannah Sloane, Georgia Clark, Camille Kellogg, Claudia Cravens, Justine Champine, and Samara Breger.

To Allison Carroll, you are my ace. It's been a long time since I was able to include you in an acknowledgment, and I'm thrilled to be able to do so now. I've never had someone believe in me the way that you do. I learn from you every time we talk. Both the breadth and depth of your expertise just wows me. You are both a thorough and creative thinker, and it makes my writing so much better. I want to do this forever with you.

To Noah Choi, my friend who always shows up, thank you for helping make this book a positive force in the world.

To my Sands fam, thank you for your curiosity and genuine delight at every development in my career. You make me feel cool, and sometimes I really, really need that. I love you guys.

To my Ambro fam, thank you for being there alongside me on my motherhood journey. Thank you for loving my kids the way that you do. Mom and Dad, your encouragement and unlimited pride in me have made me who I am. I'm a writer because you piled my room with books, cared about the stories I made up as a kid, and then believed I could make this career work as an adult. This is my best life and you planted those seeds. Thank you from the bottom of my heart.

To Jon, you're impossible to ever capture in your entirety, but the best part of every male lead I have ever written has been inspired by you in some way. The parts I love most about both Shep and Ethan, they're you. The patience, self-discovery, gentle love that comes from a well with no bottom . . . Emma asked me once how I can write male characters that are so genuinely decent. It was my immense privilege to be able to burst out laughing at that question. Because that's when I realized that whenever I write something from a male character and I'm not sure about it, I just ask myself, would Jon do that? And if you wouldn't, it doesn't make it into the book. Also, one last thing: it's unhinged to write a book right before you have a baby and then also immediately after you find out you're pregnant with another baby, but you were always so confident that this book would make it all the way from my heart to the world. That belief buoyed me immensely. I love you.

Finally, and most fervently, I want to acknowledge my kids. Frank and Sonny, you took turns co-piloting while I was writing this book. I was growing you as I was growing this story. And (of course) you were growing me as well. This book only exists because you do. I love you to infinity.

Ready or Not

CARA BASTONE

Dial Delights

Love Stories
for the
Open-Hearted

Behind the Book

When I was nine months pregnant with my first, I was so swollen that I could wear my husband's wedding ring without it falling off. This was fitting, because I could no longer wear my own! (If I wanted to keep my ring finger.)

This also felt fitting, because wearing someone else's wedding ring feels akin to walking a mile in their shoes and, there at the eleventh hour of pregnancy, I was getting all kinds of new perspectives on love.

Even though I was bloated (achy, grumpy, sleepless) and exhausted (picky, teary, restless), the end of my pregnancy was still one of the most romantic times in my entire life. First of all, I was juiced with hormones. Every single one of my daily experiences was being seen through the prism of my emotions. Everything was colorful and miraculous and fleeting. I was ripe-to-bursting with feeling. A bite of perfectly chilled watermelon? Tears. Clean socks? Tears. A single balloon floating away into the clouds, getting smaller and smaller? Forget about it.

But more than just my five senses informing me that every single moment was the most sensorily romantic moment of my life, it was also the first time in existence that I got out of my own way and accepted all the help I ever needed. My husband would *get out of bed to get me a glass of water!* Can we all just reflect on the mental fortitude, the devotion, the selflessness that is required of that act? I got foot rubs. Dinner delivered to the living room couch.

It wasn't just my husband who was caring for me so righteously. Casual friends became close friends as they called just to check in and dropped by with stretch-mark cream. My elderly neighbor rang my doorbell and demanded I walk laps around the block with her, convinced it would make labor easier. I was asking my mom questions I'd never thought to ask before, suddenly feeling the urge to cram for motherhood. I showed the world a new and different side of myself, and in return I saw a new and different side of the world.

Strangers were running to open doors for me. Grinning at me in the grocery store. Insisting I cut the line at the bank. I'd foregone makeup, was sweating buckets, publicly groaning. And, still, the world seemed to think I was lovely.

I was exhausted, elated, and mystified. I'd longed to feel lovely my entire life, and there, swollen and grouchy and very oddly shaped, I'd somehow embodied it.

It was in those moments that the idea for this story first came to me. That the most meaningful romance doesn't wait to arrive once you feel ready. It doesn't wait for your bangs to grow out or your skin to clear up. Romance doesn't love you more because you are (almost) perfect. Romance loves you because you are (charmingly) imperfect. Romance sees you trying your hardest at a very difficult point in your life and thinks, *you know what, I think she could probably use a sandwich right now.*

It was filled with this particular helium, on the cusp of the biggest adventure of my life, and bursting with ideas, that I found myself completely unable to sleep. Also, I had an eight-pound baby attempting to stand up straight in my womb, but let's just say it was the creative energy that was getting me out of bed in the middle of the night to write.

I'd hit my due date and thought, I better get started on this new novel before the baby comes. So, in the middle of every night for two weeks, the beginnings of this novel were born. (My baby was born in the middle of the night at the end of those two weeks.) I loved what I'd written. I was electrified by the story, and I treasured the creative record I felt I'd kept of so much of what pregnancy was like for me.

I didn't touch the novel again for (surprise, surprise) almost two years. At that point, I had just found out I was pregnant with my second. This time I thought, well, I better finish this novel before the morning sickness kicks in. Which I did! I will forever cherish this novel about pregnancy that I started while pregnant with my first and finished while pregnant with my second. The words, story, humor, heart: it all flowed easily and *quickly*. I was up against an urgent and inexorable timeline, and I pushed myself like an athlete. The end result is Eve's story (with my story hidden within and peeking out from between the flowers) and my two beloved children.

This book is deeply important to me because baked into it are lessons I want to keep with me for the rest of my life: Even when I feel ugly, let the love in. Let someone care for me, tenderly, because they love me, not because I can't do it myself. Feel creativity with an urgency and thrill that literally gets me out of bed. Put half-baked ideas down on paper and work hard to round them out and rejoice when it works. Remember that change, opportunity, a new day; it's always growing inside me, and the best thing I can ever do is let it out into the world.

Discussion Questions

1. How do you think Eve's perception of herself as a surprise baby or "a check without a box" impacted her relationship with her family? How do you think it has impacted her perspective on parenthood before she was pregnant? How does having her own unexpected pregnancy affect her perception of her childhood in retrospect?

2. Eve works at Wildlife Fund of America, but in what she calls a "dream-adjacent" job as "an administrative catch-all, plugging holes in every single department." Discuss your feelings about Eve's approach to her work. How does her relationship to her job change throughout the book? How does her experience shed light on the realities of working in the nonprofit world?

3. Eve opines that there are three types of "child-havers": those who were born to be mothers, those who have kids because it's what you do at a certain stage of life, and those who might start thinking of having kids when they meet the right person. What do you think of this philosophy? How do you think it fits into Eve's decision to keep the baby? Where do you think you fall in these types?

4. Willa is Eve's ride-or-die best friend, someone with whom Eve has navigated a lot of "not easy." But Willa struggles

with Eve's surprising news. How did you feel about Willa's initial reaction towards the pregnancy? What about how she deals with it over the course of the novel? What did you think of the portrayal of Willa's own experiences with fertility and motherhood, and how it impacts their friendship?

5. Eve and Willa eventually realize that their perception of their friendship has to be flexible to make accommodations for their life-changes. Does this hold true with your experience? Do friendships always change as we age and grow? How do we make room in our lives for new people while still holding on to the old?

6. What did you think of Ethan, the father of Eve's child? What about his own relationship struggles? How did his and Eve's relationship develop over the course of the novel? Did you imagine another outcome for them?

7. Eve describes herself as someone who holds herself in "perpetual audition for a feature in *Better Homes & Gardens,*" someone who loves her apartment and helps others find their homes. How do you think this element of her personality fits into her character as a whole?

8. Eve describes Shep as a "dork and everyone loves him." But she begins to see him differently over the course of her pregnancy. What did you think of Shep as a character? How did you feel about the development of his and Eve's romance?

9. Shep's gentle nature causes him to take a backseat for a lot of his life until he realizes he has to step up for Eve in her

time of need. What are the subtle ways he tries to be brave throughout the story? In your opinion, would he have been able to take the leap with her if she hadn't gotten pregnant?

10. Eve talks with Nurse Louise about how she's gotten so many "not-exactly-great" reactions from people when revealing that she's pregnant. Discuss some of these reactions. Why do you think pregnancy can be so fraught? Why do you think so many people react with, as Eve says, "what does this pregnancy mean for me?" Do you have any experiences in navigating this? If so, how does this relate to your own experiences?

11. How did this novel shift your perceptions or thoughts about unplanned pregnancy, motherhood, and romance? Compared to other portrayals of pregnancies in other books and media, how was this story similar or different?

12. Willa inspires a revelation in Eve about herself on how she struggles to know what she wants: "My position at work? All I do is avoid Xaria and resent the program staff. The baby? The words *keep being pregnant* come to mind. I couldn't even say I wanted the baby. And now Shep? I think I want him, but I have no idea for how long in either direction that feeling exists." How does this align with your perception of Eve? How does this change over the course of the book? How does pregnancy affect Eve's relationship to both honesty and bravery?

13. Discuss the theme of family in the novel. What does this story have to say about the families we are born into versus the ones we find? How is the concept of family represented

in this story? In what ways did this book support or challenge your definitions of family and friendship?

14. Nurse Louise tells Eve that motherhood changed her entire view of the world, enabling her to see the web of "all the people who love all the people." How do you think this relates to Eve's journey to motherhood? If you are also a mother, how else has motherhood shifted your view of the world around you and how people relate to one another?

PHOTO COURTESY OF AUTUMN LAYNE PHOTOGRAPHY

CARA BASTONE is a full-time writer who lives and writes in Brooklyn with her husband, her sons, and an almost-goldendoodle. Her goal with her work is to find the swoon in ordinary love stories. She's been a fan of the romance genre since she found a grocery bag filled with her grandmother's old Harlequin romances when she was in high school. She's a fangirl of pretzel sticks, long walks through Prospect Park, and love stories featuring men who aren't hobbled by their own masculinity.

carabastone.com
Instagram: @carabastone

About the Type

This book was set in Goudy Old Style, a typeface designed by Frederic William Goudy (1865–1947). Goudy began his career as a bookkeeper, but devoted the rest of his life to the pursuit of "recognized quality" in a printing type.

Goudy Old Style was produced in 1914 and was an instant bestseller for the foundry. It has generous curves and smooth, even color. It is regarded as one of Goudy's finest achievements.